Innocent Blood

Also by Iris Collier
Spring Tide
Requiem

Innocent Blood

Iris Collier

PIATKUS

To Catherine

Chapter 1

Chief Inspector Douglas McBride took a gulp of champagne and thought longingly of the row of fine malt whiskies on the shelf in his study back home. He wondered where Ian McKenzie kept his store. Surely he, of all people wouldn't mind if . . . how many times had Douglas heard him say that he too couldn't abide champagne? All the same, it seemed a bit rude. Then he thought; for pity's sake, they'd been out all day shooting McKenzie's birds. The least he could do was to offer his friends a wee dram. Leave the fizzy frozen stuff to the ladies.

Douglas would be mighty glad when tonight was over and he could get to his bed. Not much chance of that yet, though it was gone midnight. Dinner might be finished with, but judging by the noise coming from the room next door – a squawking of bagpipes and stamping of feet – the rest of the guests were settling in nicely to the swing of the eightsome reel. He'd been lucky to have escaped so far. McKenzie's study, with its log fire and comfortable armchairs, was a welcome haven, but for how long? At any moment the door might open – and he was trapped. An enviable trap, admittedly – McKenzie lived in great style, Douglas thought, as he looked with admiration at the heavy antique desk, the bookcases full of leather-bound books, and the elegant Victorian fireplace with its famous inset mosaic panels depicting scantily clad women with too much hair. Yes, McKenzie certainly had style. Reivers Hall must cost a bomb to keep up, though. And he was still buying things: pictures; a collection of carriages, locked away in a barn; a state-of-the-art master bathroom with a sunken bath big enough for a football team; and landscaped gardens. He'd even diverted the local river to flow through the grounds of Reivers Hall. Everywhere you looked there were waterfalls and ponds and ornamental footbridges where guests could linger and gaze at the views. Vistas, they were called; Douglas savoured the word. Patricia had used it when she'd taken him round the grounds before dinner. They'd tamed nature, she'd said; not that he thought the landscape needed taming. This part of Northumbria was renowned for its wild and spectacular scenery. It was amazing how wealthy men were always throwing their money away. And good luck to them, he thought, as he took a gulp of champagne. McKenzie lived in a magnificent house; he'd got a beautiful wife; he enjoyed an enviable lifestyle. What more could any man want?

At that moment, what Douglas wanted was his bed. His legs ached from walking over rough ground all day. His dress shirt and bow tie felt like a strait-jacket. Never again was he going to accept an invitation to a day's shooting which involved staying the night and playing the part of the perfect guest . . .

Just then the door opened and Mary Cameron came in. He felt his heart turn a somersault: a strange feeling which he'd experienced for the first time in his life that morning as the company assembled for the shoot. It had happened again at dinner, when he'd been seated next to Mary Cameron: not only had his heart turned several somersaults, but his tongue had seized up and he'd been reduced to a stammering teenager. All because Mary Cameron was wearing a low-cut dress which revealed voluptuous breasts and had a face that glowed with health and vitality and a mass of hair the colour of autumn leaves. All she'd done was smile at him, but he'd been so overcome that he'd had to lower his eyes and pretend to scrutinise his plateful of roast duck, which suddenly seemed unappetising. Ridiculous! Usually, there was nothing he liked better than a beautifully cooked duck after a day out on the moors . . .

Now it was happening again. And this time she was going to pounce; there was no escape. She marched across the room and took his arm.

'So here you are, Chief Inspector! I can call you Douglas, can't I? After all, you're not about to arrest me! Put that glass down. You're going to dance with me. Ian's disappeared and we need you to make up the numbers.'

Panic seized him. It was years since he'd danced.

'Mary, I can't. Now be a good girl and leave me out of this. I'd be the laughing stock of the whole room if you let me loose in an eightsome.'

She laughed, and his heart lurched again. It was a lovely laugh – a rich chuckle. Like gravy, he thought: brown, succulent, smooth.

'We'll be finished with the eightsome in a minute. "Dashing White Sergeant" next. That surely must appeal to you. Isn't your sidekick a Sergeant someone or other?'

'Venerables might be a white sergeant, but he's far from dashing. Now run along with you, lassie, and find Ian.'

'But a dance will do you good, Douglas. Not that you need good doing to you,' she added hastily. 'You're a fine figure of a man. In your prime,' she said in her seductively soft Highland brogue.

'And you're a great flatterer, Mary. But I'm willing to believe you, though you'll still not get me involved with any dashing white sergeants. I'll go and look for Ian, tell him he's needed urgently on the dance floor.'

'I expect he's taking a wee nap somewhere. He always does that on big occasions. What with all the shooting and that huge dinner, he's no doubt worn out.'

Lucky old Ian, Douglas thought enviously. Why should he get all the sympathy? He risked a glance at Mary; she was particularly animated tonight, her face alight with mischief. God, what a tragedy for her husband to die when he did! Charles Cameron hadn't lived to see Mary in her full glorious maturity. Why did men do these foolhardy things? Taking a yacht out in a Force Seven gale off the West Coast of Scotland when a woman like this was waiting at home for him . . . it was incomprehensible.

'Come on, Douglas. Dance first, then you can escape.' And Mary seized his arm and dragged him into the room next door. A blast of hot, stale air, smelling of sweat and brandy overlaid with expensive perfume, greeted him as they went in. He felt slightly sick. Much to his consternation, everyone turned to look at them and he was briskly propelled into line by several pairs of hands. He saw Willy Graham, his old friend from Coldstream, wave to him from the top of the line. Patricia McKenzie, his hostess, beamed at him with just a hint of mockery. She was another fine woman, a few years older than her sister Mary who was only just nudging forty. Patricia was closer to fifty but her dress revealed a firm figure – the same creamy breasts as her sister. Her long auburn hair was gathered in a smooth knot at the back of her head. A fine-looking family, he thought. From north of the Border, of course. McDonalds. The real McCoy: McDonalds from Skye. Pure Highland stock. Not like the McKenzies, who'd been Border reivers back in the Middle Ages. Cattle thieves, robbers, murderers.

He looked round the room, less embarrassed now. All the big-wigs of the County were there. The Grahams, the Selbys, the Milburns; all the Border reiver families, representing solid wealth acquired over the centuries from mining, heavy industry and shipbuilding. Their ancestors had been Victorian entrepreneurs. Now their descendants were enjoying the fruits of all that energy and enterprise. Douglas felt an outsider. He had nothing behind him except his house in Berwick, which his uncle had left him, and a modest sum in the building society. No use trying to save a fortune on a policeman's salary. He felt a pang of regret for all the things he'd missed out on – a wife to show off to his friends, children to carry on his name . . .

But this was not the time for introspection. Mary yanked him into place in the line, and with a tortured yelp from the bagpipes they were off. Somehow, due largely to Mary's prodding, he didn't make too much of a fool of himself. But when the music died away with an anguished shriek, he extricated himself from her grasp.

'Once is more than enough. It's time I followed Ian's example and found myself a wee nook to hide in. I've work to do tomorrow, you know. *Today*, I mean.'

'On a Sunday? Surely not. Besides, we've only just started.'

Douglas groaned inwardly. Were all women like Mary Cameron? Didn't they ever give up?

'Get away with you, lass. Find yourself a younger man; or come with me to find a whisky.'

'Douglas McBride, you're an old stick-in-the-mud. Isn't he, Pat?' she said to Patricia McKenzie who'd come over to join them.

'No more than Ian. They're two of a kind. Why don't you go and find him, Douglas, and tell him I want him? He'll no doubt offer you a dram. You come with me, Mary, and meet someone who's been admiring you all evening.'

Women, thought Douglas, as he watched Patricia drag Mary over to some enthusiastic young man. *First they butter you up, then they drop you like a hot brick when something better appears on the horizon.*

He wandered off, unnoticed. He walked along softly carpeted corridors, stopping to admire gilt-framed oil paintings of the Cheviots and the coast near Dunstanburgh. Then up the wide staircase to the first floor. Pictures everywhere: the sort Douglas understood and liked. Nothing modern. Hunting scenes. Old sailing ships. Piles of dead pheasants and decanters of port.

He stopped to examine cabinets stuffed with delicate Chinese vases and porcelain figures of oriental gentlemen with long beards dressed in long overcoats. He didn't know much about antiques, but anyone could see that these things represented thousands of pounds. He thought of the security problem. He'd begged Ian to install a more up-to-date alarm system, but it hadn't happened yet. He remembered all those mullioned bay windows with their flat roofs, and the convenient drainpipes down the side of the house. Reivers Hall would be a doddle to break into, unless Ian invested in a pack of rottweilers and a sophisticated electronic alarm system, complete with security cameras.

He tore himself away from the Chinese figurines and opened the first bedroom door, knocking gently before he entered. It was a large room. On the double bed pyjamas were laid out neatly, with a nightdress on the other pillow. The next bedroom was similar. At the far end of the corridor he knew he'd find Patricia and Ian's bedroom; it had been pointed out to him when he arrived, and his own room was nearby. He hesitated, reluctant now to invade his host's privacy and disturb his nap. He'd take a quick peep, and if he was asleep, let him be. After that, he could slip away into his own room and nobody would miss him.

He opened the door. The corridor was gloomy at this end so he switched on the light. He peered in. It was a fine room with a four-poster bed, its curtains tied back. Most of the bedrooms had four-posters: they suited the style of the house with its imitation oak beams and its armorial bearings over the doors.

Douglas thought of his own warm four-poster and yawned. Where the hell was Ian? The bathroom was *en suite*, and the door was open. Might Ian have been taken ill as a result of too much champagne? Douglas walked across and looked in. Nothing. He noted the massive sunken bath with its gold-plated taps and marvelled at Ian's extravagance. Then he remembered the dressing room. He'd been most impressed by the idea of a dressing room: all the couples he knew simply shared a wardrobe. Maybe Ian had retreated there when he got bored with the party, hoping he'd be less easy to find.

He walked across the room and opened the door. The room felt cold, as if a window were open. He flicked on the light.

Ian was there all right. His six-foot frame was dangling from an overhead beam, his feet just a few inches from the floor. On the floor nearby, a footstool had been kicked aside. As Douglas looked, disbelieving, his stomach went into convulsions. For Ian was naked, except for a woman's skirt draped awkwardly over the lower part of his body. Ever the professional, Douglas automatically registered the colour and fabric of the skirt. Green. Green, shiny material. He counted ten and got back control of his body. Then he looked up at Ian's face. He was dead. No real doubt about that. But he had to make absolutely sure; and he had to get help. Mustn't touch that knot which had cut so deeply into Ian's neck. Forensic would never forgive him if he botched this one. He thought of those thirty guests dancing away downstairs. *You fool, you damn fool*, thought Douglas. *You had a beautiful wife who was devoted to you. You had everything to live for. Why, in God's name did you need a deadly erotic thrill?* Patricia, dancing away downstairs; how was he going to tell her?

Deeply shocked, but forcing himself into the usual routine, he took out his mobile and called Berwick. He needed an ambulance, a police surgeon, and the Forensic team. Quickly. Douglas was back in the saddle again. This time with a vengeance.

On Sunday morning, the fifteenth of September, Father Paul Dalrymple adjusted his stole in the sacristy of St Frida's Church in the village of Fridale, glanced across at the safe to check that it was safely shut and left the sacristy, locking the door behind him. It would be a while before the Little Sisters arrived.

Then he went to meet his parishioners, who were assembling by the lychgate. It was a quarter past nine and the choir had already formed into a group. The thurifer was frantically trying to control the censer, which was rather too enthusiastically puffing out clouds of aromatic smoke. The two acolytes were giggling together; Father Paul had to call them to order. Grumbling that the breeze had blown out their candles, they reluctantly positioned themselves at the head of the procession. The crucifer, Derek Fairbrother, was late, of course; he was always late, thought Father Paul with some irritation. Soon he'd be off to Durham to begin his degree course and then Father Paul would find someone else to carry the cross. Someone who could be trusted to arrive on time.

It was a great day for the villagers of Fridale. The patronal day of their patron saint, St Frida, happily coincided with Harvest Festival.

Father Paul would dearly have loved to arrange a proper procession, like the ones he'd seen in Spain and Italy, where his counterpart would wear a splendid chasuble and carry a gold monstrance so everyone could see and venerate the Blessed Sacrament. But he knew that although this corner of Northumberland, close to the great house of Reivers Hall, contained a tiny pocket of Anglo-Catholics, there was a limit to the number of 'Popish practices' he could inflict on his parishioners. He sighed deeply. A young man, full of religious enthusiasm, austere in his private life, he resented being continually reminded by his churchwardens that this was the North East of England, and not Rome.

He watched the crucifer arrive, riding his bicycle with a verve that drew admiring looks from the two acolytes. Father Paul frowned. Yes, it was certainly time Derek went off to university. He was beginning to have a disruptive influence on the acolytes, as well as other female members of the congregation. Now it was time to go. The acolytes had stopped giggling and the thurifer was getting even more anxious. And Derek had finally collected the cross from the churchwarden.

Seeing that all was in order at last, Father Paul signalled to the thurifer to lead the way to the village square. Thurifer first; then the acolytes, followed closely by Derek with his cross; then the choir. The congregation was left to straggle along as best as it could. Most of them were regulars, Father Paul noted as he took his place in the procession, although one or two tourists had come along to see what was going on. He also spotted one or two of the gentry who hadn't gone to the McKenzie party last night and therefore weren't contending with the subsequent hangovers. Alec Montgomery, for instance; a good friend of Sister Anne's. He waved to Father Paul and crossed the road to fall into step beside him.

'Nice day for the procession, Father,' Alec said briskly.

'A bit too much wind for the acolytes. They can't get the candles to stay alight.'

Alec laughed. 'They look fine to me. Are the Sisters going to join us?'

'No; they'll be in the church when we get back. They're not too fond of making an exhibition of themselves.'

As far as Father Paul was concerned, Alec was one of the best: a good friend of the Church and the Little Sisters. A big man with a big stride, he was finding it difficult to match his pace to the state-liness of the others in the procession.

'Not up at the big house yesterday, Alec?' said Father Paul, hurrying to catch him up.

'Me? No, I'm a rotten shot. I haven't got the figure for all that tramping over moors.'

Father Paul glanced at his friend's solid frame. Perhaps he would not have enjoyed the enforced exercise, but he certainly would have done justice to the dinner. The McKenzies' hospitality was renowned.

Over the hedge he caught a glimpse of the white habits of the Little Sisters as they made their way to the church. 'We can relax now, Alex. The Sisters are on their way.'

'That's good. If you ask me, it's just plain madness to leave the church unlocked on a day like this, with so many strangers about. I've nagged and nagged Sister Anne to let the Treasury of Durham Cathedral have the Gospel. It's ridiculous that a priceless national treasure should remain virtually unprotected in a parish church; but she's as stubborn as a mule. She won't let it go.'

'I do sympathise with her, Alec. St Frida brought it here from Lindisfarne in AD 658 and it's been with us all that time. I know it's tempting providence to keep it in the church, but the safe is pretty sophisticated and no one knows the combination except Sister Anne.'

'And mighty careless she is, Father. I once found the safe wide open after she'd shown the Gospel to someone. Sean O'Neill, it was. He could easily have hit her over the head and walked off with it.'

Father Paul liked the young Irishman: A quiet academic from Trinity College, Dublin, he wasn't likely to bash an elderly nun over the head. But he was passionate about St Frida's Gospel according to St John; and he wanted it returned to its native Ireland. After all, St Frida herself had been Irish. She'd come over with St Aidan, after he'd befriended her following a dreadful attack she'd endured from a robber. She'd worked alongside him in Lindisfarne, and after he'd died she'd come South, clutching the Gospel to save it from the raids of the Vikings. Yes, the young man had a good reason for trying to persuade Sister Anne to let him return the Gospel to Ireland. And it would certainly be safe in Trinity College. But Sister Anne was adamant. Frida had brought it to Fridale; and here it was going to stay.

8

'I don't think Sean would resort to violence,' he said equably. 'But I agree. The Gospel ought not to be in that church, however sophisticated the safe.'

They were approaching the village square now, past the petrol station, the village shop, and round the ancient pump which still stood in the centre of the square. Then they would return the way they'd come, back up Church Lane and into the church, where they'd celebrate Mass. Just showing the flag, thought Father Paul. Just reminding the people of Fridale that they had a church, a very ancient one; so why not come along and join in an act of worship?

There was a holiday atmosphere about that morning. The square was full of onlookers, many of whom he'd never seen before. Children were running about; impatient dogs tugged at leads; parents tried to keep order; old people stood quietly, showing respect. Alec walked on to exchange a few words with Derek Fairbrother. Father Paul waved to the owner of the village shop: a good sort, but a thorough heathen. He spotted Sean O'Neill, quietly watching from outside his cottage. They were approaching the new estate now. There was a path between the houses leading to garages at the back, with an archway over the path. Father Paul caught a glimpse of a man standing under the arch. Not the ideal place from which to watch the procession, he thought. But perhaps, on second thoughts, he was just waiting for someone. He looked overdressed for the pleasant September weather. The collar of his anorak was pulled up round his face, almost meeting the brim of his woolly hat. Father Paul turned to see that the procession was moving in an orderly fashion; and then the shot rang out. And Derek Fairbrother dropped the great silver cross he was carrying, and fell face down on the road.

No one moved. A dog barked; someone screamed. Father Paul ran to Derek. He bent down, looked at his face, at the neat hole in the side of his head. He felt for a pulse. Dazed with horror, he looked up.

'I can't feel anything. Pray God he's not dead. I can't believe it! Someone must call an ambulance. Quickly. Oh, Derek, Derek, stay with us. *Please*.'

He stood up, and looked around. He thought of what he must do. But was there time? Could he get to the church and back again before the ambulance arrived?

'Stay with him,' he said to Alec Montgomery, who was standing by his side. 'I must get the holy oil. Just in case,' he added, conscious that Alec was looking at him in amazement. 'Perhaps you could . . .'

'Call an ambulance,' shouted Alec, seeing what was needed and taking charge of the situation. 'Derek's been shot. And get the police too. Stand back, everyone. Don't touch anything until the police get here.'

Numb with shock, Father Paul managed to collect himself sufficiently to run back to the church. Dashing past the Little Sisters of Saint Frida, who had already taken their seats in the front row of the pews, he collected the bag containing all that was necessary for the administration of the Last Rites. 'It's Derek Fairbrother,' he shouted. 'He's been badly hurt.' He couldn't wait to explain further.

Then he ran back to the square where Alec Montgomery was heroically trying to keep order. 'No one must leave the square,' he was saying firmly when Father Paul arrived. 'The ambulance is on its way. And the police. They'll want to talk to everyone. Stay where you are, and keep away from Derek.'

Thanking God for people like Alec Montgomery, Father Paul knelt beside his crucifer. Derek looked very pale. Very still. Father Paul feared the worst. Sadly, he made the sign of the cross and began the first prayer.

When he'd finished, he whispered, 'Why, Lord? Why Derek? He'd never even harm a fly.'

Chapter 2

'You're quite sure about this, McBride?' said Superintendent Blackburn, irritated by the abrupt termination of his customary Sunday morning lie-in. 'Ian McKenzie didn't die by his own hand?'

Douglas, exhausted from his sleepless night, nodded wearily. 'There's no doubt, thank God. We've got a case of homicide on our hands.'

'*Thank God,* McBride? I don't understand. Homicide's hardly something to give thanks about.'

'It's better than the alternative, sir. For the family, I mean. Think how they must feel.'

'I am, McBride, I am. The family's my main concern. The McKenzies of Reivers Hall are scarcely nonentities. With the exception of the Grahams of Coldstream they're one of the leading County families.'

Douglas sighed. The one thing he disliked about his superior was his unabashed snobbery where the victims of crime were concerned. 'Whether someone's a member of the blue-blooded aristocracy, or a fisherman from Craster, murder is murder.'

'All right, all right, McBride. I've no time for one of your sermons. Let's start again. You've been up at the Hall all night, I take it?'

'I have that. And I'd be grateful for some coffee if it's not too much to ask. Do you want me to run through the sequence of events?'

'If you please. And take a seat, man; don't stand there dithering. Coffee coming up.'

Blackburn spoke into the intercom. Almost immediately a young

11

constable came in carrying a tray with two mugs on it and a jug of freshly brewed coffee.

'I take it you'll want it black. You look as if you need waking up.'

'An hour's sleep would put that right.'

'Later, man. If you're lucky. Now get on with it. This is a major incident, remember. Time's of the essence.'

No need to tell me that, thought Douglas, as he sat down and took the mug from Blackburn. 'Dinner went on a bit, sir. Lots of courses. Ended around quarter to eleven. Then the dancing started, and the socialising. I retreated to McKenzie's study. Then Mary came in and dragged me off to the other room; she thought I was being a bit of a wallflower.'

Blackburn's eyebrows shot up. 'Mary? Who's Mary?'

'Patricia McKenzie's sister. A widow – husband died in a yachting accident three years' ago. The sisters are McDonalds; the McDonalds of Skye. Another ancient and noble family,' said Douglas, avoiding Blackburn's scowl. He went on.

'Ian wasn't dancing. No one had seen him since dinner. So I went to find him. Good opportunity to get away from the dancing, I thought. And there he was strung up on a beam, stool kicked over, dressed in one of his wife's skirts. I thought it was a classic case of auto-erotic asphyxiation.'

'Not Ian McKenzie, surely! He's one of the best shots in the County. And his family have strong connections with the Northumberland Fusiliers.'

'Everyone's got their weaknesses, sir.'

'Not Ian McKenzie. He's real gentry.'

'Especially the gentry. They've got more time on their hands. Anyway, the pathologist was adamant. Couldn't say too much at this stage – you know what they're like – but they said he'd been dead for an hour or so and there were two marks round his throat, not the single mark you'd expect if it had been self-inflicted. One was a deep indentation with scratch marks round it, presumably where he'd tried to claw at his attacker. His features were purple and congested; protruding tongue; lots of haemorrhaging capillary blood vessels round the eyes. All indicators of strangulation. Then they – we think there must have been two attackers – undressed him, draped one of his wife's skirts round him and hoisted him up. It would take two people to do that; McKenzie was a big man. This gives us the second mark where the rope which they used to string him up bit into his neck. Not the same as the first mark, and not at the same angle.

'Entry was gained through the dressing-room window. It's a bay window – Reivers Hall has lots of mullioned bay windows with drainpipes running up beside them, an invitation to all the thieves in the country if you ask me. The intruders were careful. No finger-prints, so they must have worn gloves. A couple of scuff marks on the drainpipe, from their shoes I suppose. The ground is hard at the moment, so there are no clear footprints, but the men are doing a detailed search as we speak. The window was forced open. That wouldn't have been difficult – there are no locks on the upstairs win-dows. Only downstairs. It's surprising how careless millionaires can be.'

Douglas pushed his mug towards Blackburn who refilled it auto-matically.

'What time did you find him?'

'Half past twelve.'

'And he left his guests soon after dinner? Time of death was between eleven and twelve. What was everyone else doing then?'

'Drinking. Cavorting around in the drawing room. Thirty people having a good time – they wouldn't have noticed anything. We're still taking statements. But there are no particular problems so far. Except for Ian, everyone can vouch for one another during the period when McKenzie was killed.'

'Why wasn't he missed?'

'He was, but we all thought he'd gone off for a wee zizz. He was no spring chicken and we'd walked miles that day. Combined with lots of food and wine . . .'

'Any staff around?'

'The butler, Arthur Bloodworthy, was on duty. No joy there. He's been with the family thirty years and is devoted to the McKenzies. Besides, he hasn't the imagination or the sophistication to dress up the corpse in women's clothes. Mrs Bloodworthy cooked the dinner, helped by her daughter Irene and the daughter's friend, Janice Hudson.'

'What about waiters?'

'Two. Both well-known to Bloodworthy. Apparently, they always help out on these occasions. One's a ghillie – assists at McKenzie's shoots. Fraser's his name. Pete Fraser. Young chap, seems pleasant enough. Apparently happy in his work. The second waiter was Tom Emmerson. Local lad.'

'So after dinner was over, three people looked after thirty guests?

13

Two of these three can be described as faithful family retainers. That leaves Emmerson. What's his alibi?'

'Difficult to pin him down. The two waiters were on the go all the time. The guests say they were serving drinks pretty much constantly, but one of them could have drifted off for a few minutes. There must have been the occasional lull in the drinking – when the next dance started, for instance. But I doubt Emmerson had anything to do with this. He certainly couldn't have done it on his own. Not strong enough. He's a poor physical specimen. And if he'd been gone for more than five minutes, he'd been missed. Same for Pete Fraser. It would have taken longer than that to murder McKenzie, dress him in women's clothing, string him up . . . One thing's for sure, someone had it in for McKenzie. Someone hated him; hated him enough not only to kill him but to humiliate him after death. Someone wanted to blacken McKenzie's name for all time. Patricia's devastated. Can't take it in. Mary Cameron will be a great blessing to her sister at this time. How can people be so cruel? To desecrate a corpse . . .'

'Revenge, McBride. That's what I think. And a terrible way to deliver it. The killers not only wanted McKenzie dead, but shamed. Revenge and hatred – a powerful brew . . . You know what you've got to do?'

'Get back to the Hall.'

'Check all the statements. Guests, staff, wife, wife's sister. We could have a domestic on our hands here.'

'You think so? Surely no one in that house would want to kill McKenzie? He always seemed so popular.'

'Things are not always what they seem. Now, we know the attackers came in through the window. Someone in the house could have tipped them off. After all, how else did they know McKenzie would be in his dressing room at that precise moment?'

'Maybe they came in for burglary. After all, Reivers Hall is jam-packed with antiques.'

'Burglars don't hang about to string up their victims and dress them in women's clothes.'

'They might have strangled him because they had no alternative. They broke in through that window and found Ian having a nap in his armchair, say. Once they'd killed him, one of them could have suggested they make it look like he'd been having a kinky sex session that went wrong. Who knows, it might have appealed to their sense of humour.'

'I do admire you, McBride. Your creative prowess after a sleepless night is truly amazing. But I really don't think your reconstruction of the murder holds water. In fact, I think it's downright farcical. Burglars aren't known for their wit and ingenuity. What they want is to get in and get out again as quickly as possible. No, I reckon Ian McKenzie had enemies. This was a deliberate and calculated act. Your job, McBride, is to find out who these enemies are. Find out who hated him and why. A nice bit of old-fashioned sleuthing for you, Douglas my boy,' said Blackburn jovially. 'Sherlock Holmes territory. Get the statements back here as quickly as possible and we'll see what the computer makes of them. Incidentally, have the press got wind of this yet?'

'We've not released any information. But the news will leak out sooner rather than later.'

'Then just say there's been a death. Don't go into details.'

'Of course not. We don't want the press to have a field day. Think of Patricia – and Mary.'

'Mary's made an impression on you, McBride, that's for sure.' Blackburn sounded suspicious.

'We've only chatted over dinner, sir. She's a mature lady. A good-looker, though, I must admit.'

'She gave you the glad eye, I suppose.'

Douglas looked pained. 'She's pleasant company, that's all.'

'Keep away from the lassies, Chief Inspector. They're trouble – especially for a man of your age. Away with you now, man. Back to that house of yours and collect your pyjamas.'

'Sir?'

'You'll have to stay at the Hall for the time being. The only way you'll get to the bottom of this crime is by Trojan horse tactics.'

'Infiltrate the enemy camp, you mean?'

'That's what Trojan horses usually do, isn't it? Set up an incident room and get yourself a bed. You're a lucky devil, aren't you?'

'There's no joy in a homicide investigation.'

'You've not got a butler in your own house.'

'No, but my housekeeper Mrs Fairweather's good enough for me. I'll have to tell her I'll be away for a few days.' However, despite his protestations, the prospect of staying at the Hall – and getting to know Mary Cameron better – cheered Douglas up considerably.

The phone rang; Blackburn answered it. He listened intently, glancing at Douglas with growing anxiety. Douglas, sensing trouble, paused by the door of Blackburn's office, and waited.

'It never rains but it pours down in bloody torrents,' said Blackburn as he put down the receiver. 'Someone's been shot in Fridale. In a religious procession of all things! Hell's teeth, don't say we're having another outbreak of homicide. Not now, just when we're short of senior officers. We'll have to get reinforcements, damn it. Turner's still in hospital after that bypass operation. Jackson's in Spain somewhere, on annual leave . . . You'll have to start on this, McBride, until we sort things out. Get Sergeant Venerables out of his bed and down to Fridale.'

'What goes on in Fridale?'

'Usually not much. There's a religious community there. They own a famous manuscript – St Frida's Gospel, I think it's called. I wonder if they're mixed up in all this? Sounds unlikely, but then you never know . . . McBride, get moving! Let's clear this little lot up quickly. I don't want the Yard Snapping at our heels.'

'What's first, sir? Reivers, or Fridale?'

'Both man, both! It's not as if they're miles apart. You've got a team to do the spade work. There might just possibly be a connection between the two murders. I'm not a great believer in coincidence. Anyway, that's for you to find out. Get on with the detective work, man! It's what you're good at. And get us some results soon. There could be promotion for you out of this.'

'Really? Do we need two Superintendents in Berwick?'

'I don't mean Berwick. There's a vacancy coming up in Durham.'

'Durham? I wouldn't be seen dead in Durham!'

And, knowing an exit line when he heard one, Douglas left. He walked to his house overlooking the Elizabethan ramparts of Berwick. He went in, packed a bag and left a note for Mrs Fairweather. Then he called Venerables.

Frank Venerables was awake when the phone rang. But he was still in bed. Looking fondly at the sleeping face of WPC Polly Stride. What a night they'd had, he thought. Polly – blonde, curvaceous, delectable – was the woman of his dreams. Old Douglas might have been living it up with the gentry, but he'd wined and dined common-or-garden Polly Stride and got his reward. Polly was just what the doctor ordered: a policewoman with no inhibitions. She understood his needs, all right. And the phone didn't wake her up: sensible girl, he thought, as he picked up the receiver. At the sound of his boss's voice he was immediately alert.

'Fridale? Now? But it's Sunday . . .'

Venerables' half-hearted protests tailed off as he listened. Polly, sensing trouble, opened one eye and shut it again.

'Two possible homicides, you say? Why aye, man, things are hotting up at last! You'll come and pick me up?'

Venerables put the receiver down and looked at Polly. 'I've got to go, lass. You know how it is.'

'I ought to. I'm in the police force too, aren't I?'

He bent over and kissed her. 'You're a good lass. I'll be back as soon as I can.'

'Don't make it too long, or I might get fed up waiting.'

'You stay right where you are, pet. I fancy you like mad – you know that, don't you?'

'You're not bad yourself, Frank.'

'If it weren't for the fact that old Douglas will be here at any moment, I'd—'

'Get away with you, man,' said Polly, burrowing down under the duvet. 'You've had your ration for the time being.'

Trying not to feel too hard done by, Venerables got dressed and went down to meet Douglas.

Chapter 3

'Derek died in the ambulance on his way to hospital, Chief Inspector,' said Father Paul, turning to face Douglas and Venerables, his eyes full of sadness. They were in the Rectory, a spacious Victorian red-brick building designed to accommodate a large clerical family and unsuitable now for a single man. Father Paul was clearly deeply distressed. He paced up and down his study, pausing occasionally to look out of the window towards the church, as if he were expecting the Angel of Death to appear at any moment.

'There was nothing I could do except to give him the Last Rites. The doctors tell me he would probably have heard me. At least I was able to comfort him as he went on his way. But I feel so sorry. So guilty. The procession – it was all my idea. The parish didn't really approve, they would have been quite happy to stay in church and have the usual Sunday service. But I wanted to show the world who we were, what we do. There are a lot of tourists in the area at this time of year, and I wanted them to see that we are a Christian community as well as a tourist attraction. I told myself I was doing it for the Lord – but no. It was vanity, pure vanity. I was doing it for myself, to show what a splendid priest I am. Derek didn't really want to come along today. Well, he was a teenager, he had other things to do. But I insisted; and now I have to live with the guilt. How can I comfort Derek's parents, knowing that I sent him to his death?'

'Don't blame yourself, sir,' said Douglas, feeling desperately sorry for the young priest who looked as if he'd just left theological college. 'The procession was an excellent idea. After all, today is your Feast Day; your patronal festival, I think you call it. Although we might not be into processions round here, I know they can draw a community together. Anyway, you have a right to practise your

19

religion as you choose. But have you met much opposition to your high-church practices from the parish, sir? No graffiti, windows broken, that sort of thing?'

Father Paul stopped his prowling. His young, candid face was white and tense, his hands tightly clenched. He stared blankly at Douglas.

'Good gracious, no, Chief Inspector. This is a very peaceful village. You make the people of Fridale sound like the Roundheads. We're very tolerant. Everyone's very supportive of the Church and the Little Sisters, proud of our association with St Frida. There's never been any opposition. Never. Now, Chief Inspector, I know you must ask questions, but I too have work to do. The village is deeply shocked and I must see Mr and Mrs Fairbrother again. My duty is with my parishioners.'

'I understand. You've got your job to do, and I've got mine. I won't keep you any longer than is necessary. But I must ask you to think back to the procession. We're trying to build up a picture. My men are interviewing everyone who was in the square and obviously they've marked the spot where Derek fell. Forensic have already indicated the direction from which the shot came; it hit Derek on the left side of the head, so the attacker must have been standing somewhere on the left side of the square. Did you notice anything unusual? Anything that might have struck you as being a bit odd, out of place? Think back, sir, if you can.'

'Please, don't call me "sir". I've no right to that title.'

'What shall I call you?'

'Most people call me "Father". Father Paul. Yes, I'm trying to remember . . .'

Suddenly, his strength seemed to desert him and he sat down heavily in the chair behind the desk. He ran his hands through his short, prematurely greying hair, cut close to his head like a monk's tonsure.

'There were lots of people around. Children, families. People like processions.'

'Were you leading the procession, er – Father?' said Douglas, hesitating over the unfamiliar form of address. He felt ill-at-ease in the exotic atmosphere of Anglo-Catholicism. For a moment he thought of his own father, a Scottish Presbyterian minister, and the austere Edinburgh manse which had been his home when he was a boy.

'No. I never lead in church either, when we move up the aisle.

20

Bobby leads – he's the incense bearer – followed by the two acolytes. They like carrying the candles, it makes them feel important, and it's good to get the young involved in our worship. Then Derek comes with the cross . . . *came*, I should say – Oh, God. I'm so sorry. So sorry.'

He slumped forward on the desk and Douglas saw that his thin body was racked with sobs. Venerables cleared his throat.

'And after the crucifer, Father?' he said.

'The choir, of course. Six of them. Then me.' He tried to get a grip on himself, wiping his eyes roughly with the back of his hand.

'Did anyone walk with you? Any other – ecclesiastical gentlemen?' said Douglas, valiantly grappling with the unaccustomed vocabulary.

'No, my churchwarden was off sick and we haven't got a deacon. I'm on my own.'

'Did you speak to anyone as you walked along? Any parishioners?'

Father Paul brightened. 'Yes, Alec Montgomery joined me for a minute or two. I think he found our pace a bit too slow. He spoke to Derek too.'

'What did you talk about?'

'Oh, parish matters. The Little Sisters, the Frida Gospel – you've heard of it?'

Douglas, remembering Blackburn's reference to a famous manuscript, nodded. 'You can tell me more about it later on. Now, sir . . . Father. I want you to go over this again . . .'

'Chief Inspector, I really must go. The Sisters are distraught . . .'

'I'm sorry, but if we're to catch Derek's assailant, then we must be quite clear what happened. It might be simpler if we draw a sketch. Not a work of art, just a rough map,' said Douglas, noting the look of horror on Father Paul's face. 'Like this.'

Douglas picked up a sheet of paper from a pile on the desk. With a biro he drew a cross in one corner.

'Now, here's the church, and here's the road. Up here's the village square. There's the pump in the middle, then there's the petrol station and the shop. What's over here?'

Concentrating hard, Father Paul drew a passable sketch of the new houses, and the archway.

'Good. Now mark where the procession'd got to at the time of the shot. Start with the chap with the incense – Bobby, you called him . . .'

Father Paul marked down the people in the procession using appropriate symbols – smoke for the thurifer, candle flames for the acolytes, a cross for the crucifer. Then he added circles for the six members of the choir and a bigger circle for himself.

'Where was Alec Montgomery?'

'He was never in one place for long. But when Derek fell, he was here. Near Derek.'

'Then put him in. Anyone else you can remember?'

'Sean was over here, watching from outside his cottage.' He drew another circle, near the shop.

'And who is Sean?'

'Sean O'Neill – a clever young man from Dublin. He's a friend of the Little Sisters, in Britain to study religious manuscripts. We all love him, Chief Inspector.'

'And the shot must have come from over here. Where you've drawn these houses. Did you see anyone standing over there?'

'Yes, there *was* someone,' said Father Paul, looking relieved. 'Of course! I should have remembered. How clever of you, Chief Inspector, to make me reconstruct the procession. A man was standing under the archway. I remember thinking it odd that he wasn't mixing with the rest of the crowd. And he seemed to be overdressed for the time of year. Most people were in jeans and cotton shirts, but this man was wearing a heavy padded jacket, with a woollen hat pulled well down over his face.'

'Was he tall? Short?'

'Average, I think. I didn't take much notice of him. And I'm afraid I couldn't see his face.'

'Did you see him make any sort of movement?'

'No, he was just standing there, quite still.'

'He would have been level with Derek Fairbrother when Derek was shot,' said Venerables, who had been studying the artwork intently.

'Right! We've got something to work on. Venerables, circulate Father Paul's description and start the house-to-house enquiries. Someone else might have seen him.' Venerables left the room. 'Father Paul, think carefully. After Derek fell, did you see the man again?'

'I was fully occupied. I couldn't let Derek die unattended. At that moment, his soul was my priority.'

'Who called the ambulance? And the police?'

22

'Alec saw to all that. He was marvellous. A real tower of strength. I had to get the holy oil from the church, you see.'

A pity you didn't look to your left just before you set off for the church, Douglas thought. 'I shall have to speak to everyone who took part in the procession, Father. Someone else might have spotted that man. Just one more thing – please bear with me,' he added, noting the look of impatience on the priest's face. 'I know you have lots to do. But can you tell me whether, to your knowledge, Derek Fairbrother had any enemies?'

'Chief Inspector, it is inconceivable that anyone would want to shoot Derek. He was popular at school, good at sport, expected to do well in his examinations. He was looking forward to taking up a place at Durham University. He had loving and supportive parents. He was loyal to the church – after he was confirmed he carried the cross for us. He had everything going for him. He was seventeen years old, Inspector. He had no enemies.'

'Then why was he targeted?'

'Sometimes the Devil singles out the innocent to be his victims.'

'Aye, it looks like it. But somehow I think there's a human agent responsible for Derek Fairbrother's death.'

Suddenly there was a loud knock on the study door. Without waiting for an invitation to enter, an elderly nun burst in. She was tiny, fluttery, like a small bird, dressed in a white habit, her hair covered by a neat head-dress. Clearly in a state of extreme agitation, she ran across to Father Paul, ignoring Douglas entirely.

'Father, come quickly! Something quite dreadful has happened. Mr Montgomery asked us to check the safe in the sacristy, because he was worried about the Gospel. He thought the shooting might perhaps have been a device to distract our attention away from the church. And he was right! Someone has taken St Frida's Gospel. It's gone. The safe's empty. Oh Father, what are we going to do? After all these centuries . . . we've let her down. Our beloved Frida! She entrusted the Gospel to us, and we've let her down.' And the nun began to weep helplessly, like a child.

Father Paul went across to her, put his arms round her thin shoulders. 'Are you sure, Sister Anne? Quite sure?'

She nodded emphatically. 'Yes, Father. There's no doubt. Oh, forgive me, Father. I have been a negligent steward. I'm so sorry.'

'Hush. Don't blame yourself. It's not your fault. We are struggling against an evil force, Sister . . . More Devil's work, Chief Inspector,' the priest said, looking at Douglas. 'He's singled out this little community, maybe because we're more godly than some – and he's determined to destroy us.'

'You won't be destroyed, Father,' Douglas said firmly. 'Now let's get over to the church. Maybe someone removed the Gospel temporarily – to examine it, perhaps – and intended to put it back before it was missed.'

'How could anyone do that? It's impossible to open the safe without knowing the combination. And I'm the only one who knows it, apart from Father Paul.'

'The safe didn't open itself, ma'am. Unless the Devil's equipped himself with a degree in modern electronics, I don't think he's behind this. It sounds to me like a case of good old-fashioned burglary. Now, let's away to the sacristy.'

Feeling like the proverbial camel needing only one more straw to break its back, Douglas followed the others out of the vicarage to the church. It seemed unbelievable that in less than twelve hours he had stumbled upon his friend's corpse, been summoned to the Scene of Crime of a second murder, and was now apparently plunged into the investigation of a major art theft. And all this was nothing compared to the emotional upheaval he'd experienced ever since he'd set eyes on Mary Cameron. Now the strain was beginning to tell, and it required a major effort on his part to focus on the scene which greeted him when he arrived at the sacristy.

The tiny room smelt of candle grease and incense, with overtones of damp and furniture polish. Built in the fifteenth century, long after the rest of the church which dated from the time of St Frida's arrival in the area during the seventh century, it had a narrow lancet window, with Victorian stained glass depicting the Madonna and Child. There was an open fireplace. But the focal point of the room that morning was the heavy wooden cupboard under the window, the door of which was swinging on its hinges. Inside he caught a glimpse of a steel safe; its door was also open.

'We don't keep any money in here, Alec,' a sturdy middle-aged nun was saying. 'It's only used for St Frida's Gospel. We keep our petty cash in another safe, in the convent itself. The thief hasn't touched that.'

'He wasn't interested in money, Sister Agatha,' Alec Montgomery answered. 'He had bigger fish to fry. I don't want to appear self-righteous, but Father Paul and I did warn you that you were courting trouble, keeping St Frida's Gospel on church premises. They simply aren't secure. It's a real tragedy – a terrible, terrible tragedy. Let's hope the thieves aren't already out of the country.'

Just then, he spotted Douglas going over to examine the safe; he looked at Father Paul enquiringly.

'Alec, meet Chief Inspector Douglas McBride,' said Father Paul. 'He's leading the investigation into Derek's death.'

'And now he's got another crime on his hands,' said Alec Montgomery. 'Not to mention the death up at Reivers Hall last night. News of that seems to be spreading round the village. Not another homicide, I hope, Chief Inspector?'

'Too early to say, sir,' said Douglas automatically. He looked keenly at Alec Montgomery, trying to take his measure. He saw a middle-aged, solidly built man with a pleasant round face which, in other circumstances, could be described as beatific. Flushed, healthy cheeks, and a smooth complexion. A man who kept himself fit, yet he was no countryman. His suit looked expensive, his hair well-tended, and his hands were pink and soft with clean, manicured nails. Wealthy, that was for sure. His pale blue tie looked expensive; his leather shoes were highly polished and showed no signs of wear. He looked like a man of independent means, looking forward to a comfortable early retirement. His voice was soft and melodious, with a faint London twang. A charmer, Douglas decided. He'd twist the likes of Sisters Anne and Agatha round his little finger. But his eyes were clear and honest. 'You can always judge a man by his eyes,' he remembered his mother telling him. Alec Montgomery's were grey and full of concern. He took Douglas's scrutiny in his stride, and met his gaze unflinchingly.

Douglas didn't want to discuss McKenzie's death. He got straight down to business. 'Why did you decide to open the safe this morning?'

'It was because of the shooting,' said Sister Anne, bobbing forward nervously. 'Alec – that is, Mr Montgomery – suggested we check the safe. He said Derek's death could have been meant to cause a diversion, enabling thieves to raid the sacristy while our backs were turned. So I did what he suggested and opened it.'

'And found the manuscript gone?'

'Yes. A dreadful moment! And Alec's quite right – he'd always tried to persuade us to move the Gospel to Durham, but we've looked after it for so long that we regard it as a sacred trust.'

'How long has the Gospel been in your Order's hands, ma'am?'

'Since 1867, when the Order was founded.'

'And before that?'

'The parish priest looked after it. Then it moved here, to the sacristy. Ten years ago we had the safe built – it was the best we could afford – and two years ago we had a new combination lock fitted. It seemed so safe! The church is always locked at night, and most of the day, except when we come over for our services. The sacristy is always kept locked. And we check the safe every day, to make sure all is well. Three barriers – but still someone got in.'

'It doesn't take too much ingenuity to unlock doors, unfortunately. Impressions of keys can be taken very quickly and new keys cut from those impressions . . . And if I'm right, this safe hasn't been forced. Someone who knew the combination opened it and locked it again afterward. You say only you and Father Paul knew the safe's combination, ma'am?'

'That's all. And I only told Father Paul in case I died suddenly, or lost my reason.'

'Are you quite sure of that, Sister?' said Douglas, looking at her keenly.

'No one else could know.' Sister Anne looked down, her face troubled.

'And you, sir,' Douglas went on, turning to Alec Montgomery, 'why are you so interested in this manuscript? You obviously feel deeply about it if it was the first thing you thought about after the shooting in the square.'

'Chief Inspector, do you realise that this church held one of the finest examples of the work of the seventh-century Lindisfarne monks? A Gospel of St John, written on vellum, and bound in leather, with the eagle of St John encrusted on the front cover in precious stones. It was most beautifully preserved, considering its age – written a century before the Book of Durrow. It's probably in such a good state because the verdigris pigment used has done little damage to the vellum. In fact, the Book of Durrow was strongly influenced by St Frida's Gospel. In Durrow, the gospel was according to Mark, and his beast was the lion. Both the lion of Durrow and the eagle of St Frida were drawn in the same stylised manner. The marginal

26

decorations are similar too; many of the drawings of animals are almost identical. But the ornamentation of Frida's Gospel is much more lavish. All those colours – rich browns, deep blacks, a wonderful flaming vermilion, all those yellows and greens – they shone like jewels. It's quite priceless, Chief Inspector. It could never be sold on the open market. Some private collector, probably overseas, will snap it up. A sad day for the village of Fridale. And a sad day for England if we don't recover it.'

'You sound like a connoisseur, sir.'

'I'd prefer to describe myself as an enthusiastic collector of beautiful things. I do know a bit about manuscripts. When I came to live here about five years ago, I'd already heard of the Frida Gospel and Sister Anne was kind enough to show it to me soon after I arrived. I must be one of the few people who have actually seen it twice. Sean O'Neill received permission to look at it back in August and Sister Anne kindly asked me to be there also when they opened the safe for him. Sean's from Trinity College, Dublin, Chief Inspector. Studying mediaeval manuscripts is his life's work. The College already has the Durrow Gospel and are anxious to get the Frida Gospel to add to their collection. The Lindisfarne monks were strongly influenced by the Irish monks, of course; many of them came over to this country with St Aidan, the Irishman, who founded the monastery on Holy Island. He brought St Frida over with him, so I suppose the Irish case for claiming a right to her Gospel is strong. What Sean's going to say when he hears about the theft, I can't imagine. He'll doubtless accuse us of gross incompetence, and with some justification. We're never going to live it down. Naturally, I believe it is ours. Not Ireland's. We've had it for twelve hundred years, so we must have a right to it.'

He paused. 'But we don't have it any longer, do we? My God, I still can't take it in. We must find it, Chief Inspector. It's so fragile. Of *course* it was the first thing I thought about after the disturbance in the square. Not a day passes when I don't think about the Gospel.'

'It was hardly a "disturbance", sir. A young lad was shot in the head – brutally murdered.'

'I know. I'm sorry, Chief Inspector. Believe me, I do find all of this very upsetting. It was instinct, really, that made me think of the manuscript at that moment. The world suddenly goes mad, and I can think of only one thing – the Gospel. I know it's selfish of me. But I can't bear to think of it being hawked round the world by a gang of thuggish criminals.'

27

'You say you saw it last month? Did anyone else see it after that, Sister Anne?'

'Only me, on my daily rounds. We only open the safe apart from that when someone specially asks to see the Gospel. Usually that's only art experts – like Mr Montgomery – or scholars like Mr O'Neill. We don't show it to tourists.'

At that moment, Venerables came in and Douglas went across to speak to him, leaving the others gazing into the empty safe as if willing the Gospel to materialise.

'How goes it, Venerables?'

'House-to-house going ahead, sir. No news about Father Paul's stranger under the archway. At the far end of the passage there's a new housing estate; it's fenced off, but it wouldn't be too difficult for someone to shin over the fence and make his way to the main road. If there was a car waiting for him, he'd be away before most people had collected their thoughts after the shock of the killing.'

'Someone might have seen him climbing over the fence.'

'Not this morning. It's a fine day. Plenty going on in the square, to put it mildly. But what's going on here?'

'More bad news. A theft. A bloody major theft. A mediaeval manuscript. Like the Book of Durrow. You've heard of the Book of Durrow, of course, Venerables?'

'Can't say that I have, sir.'

'Then I'll illuminate you later on. But get hold of Forensic. We'll need the whole place checked for fingerprints – not that there's much hope of finding any. Even an amateur would have worn gloves. Did you ever get the manuscript valued, ma'am?' he said, turning back to the group round the safe. 'For insurance purposes, perhaps?'

'No one would insure it, Chief Inspector,' said Sister Anne. 'It's beyond price. And no insurance company would cover it here, in a safe in a parish church. They would insist on it going to Durham Cathedral, or more likely to the British Museum. And that would be wrong. The blessed saint intended it to stay here in Northumberland.'

Biting back the obvious rejoinder, Douglas continued. 'We'll need a full description of the manuscript, ma'am. Photographs would help. I'll have all ports and airports alerted. And Interpol.'

'And let's hope whoever's got it is treating it with the respect it deserves,' said Alec.

'Indeed, sir. Meanwhile, I'd like you and I to have a further talk, if you don't mind. Will you be at home later today?'

'I shall go home as soon as your men have finished in here, and the Sisters are back in their house. This is very traumatic for them, Chief Inspector. They rarely come into contact with – shall we call it, worldly wickedness?'

'I realise that. It's good of you to be so concerned, sir. Now, if you can give me your address . . .'

'Certainly.' He produced a gold-edged card which Douglas put in his pocket.

'We shall have to see Mr O'Neill too, of course.'

Leaving Father Paul and Alec Montgomery to comfort the two nuns, Douglas went to join Venerables and instigate the necessary procedure following a break-in of this type. But he knew there was little chance of recovering the manuscript. Such a portable item wouldn't be difficult to smuggle out of the country. A sad loss for the Little Sisters; and a sad loss for England, as Alec Montgomery had so rightly said.

'There's a small caff just up the road, sir, and I could do with a bacon butty. I didn't have any breakfast. I can always think better with some food inside me,' said Venerables as they walked over to Douglas's car.

'I think better when I'm not dog-tired,' grumbled Douglas, clambering into the driver's seat. 'But if I can't have any sleep, then a bacon sandwich might just do the trick.'

They drove off to the little café just outside Fridale. It was a warm, friendly place which served hot food at all hours. They gave their order, and started straight away on mugs of strong tea, gulping the scalding liquid down gratefully.

'We've got a right hornet's nest, here, sir. A nasty business up at the Hall last night, I understand.'

'You can say that again. Someone had it in for McKenzie in a big way. I've got to go back there, laddie,' said Douglas decisively. 'The team are taking statements from all the guests, but I must have another word with the staff. Someone tipped off the killers – that's Blackburn's theory. Outside job planned with the benefit of inside information.'

'Do you think there could possibly be a link between the two deaths, sir?' said Venerables, checking his sandwich to see if Worcester sauce had been added as requested.

'Grown men always have the odd enemy, even if they don't realise it themselves. But I can't think of anyone who'd want to kill a decent young lad like Derek Fairbrother.' Douglas took a big bite of his succulent bacon sandwich, paused, then added mustard from the pot on the table.

'Maybe someone wanted to create a sort of diversion while they broke into the safe. If that manuscript's really valuable, they'd go to any lengths.'

'That's what Alec Montgomery – the big chap in the sacristy – thinks. Trouble is, it could have been stolen any time between Sister Anne checking the safe last night and this morning. Montgomery just assumed there must be some connection between the killing of Derek and the theft of the manuscript. Instinct, he said. That's why he suggested that Sister Anne should check the safe. Too late. The horse had bolted. I don't think there has to be a link. All eyes were on the procession in any case – no one would have been at the church.'

Venerables looked up from his sandwich, which needed his full concentration; the café had been generous with its bacon. 'Did anyone in particular have designs on the Gospel?'

'Sean O'Neill – but he was watching the procession. He wants the manuscript pretty badly. But he'd never steal it, surely? He's an academic. Academics don't go round nicking things; they get their kicks writing about them.'

'Father Paul seems to trust O'Neill. So do the nuns.'

'By the way, you seemed remarkably at home with Father Paul's High Church terminology, Sergeant. I wouldn't have expected it from you.'

'I don't know about High or Low Church,' said Venerables, licking his fingers appreciatively. 'I was brought up a Roman Catholic, me. We always called the priests Fathers.'

'And there I was, assuming you were a heathen! There's a lot I don't know about you, Venerables. You're a bit of a dark horse.'

'It's the best horse to be. Anyway, I'm sure Father Paul for one didn't have anything to do with the theft, or the killing. And we can rule out the nuns. Unless they're plotting an insurance fraud.'

'The manuscript wasn't insured. No one would take the risk on. No, I think we must concentrate on Sean O'Neill and Alec

Montgomery if we're looking locally for possible suspects. They're the only two people we know of with a serious interest in the Gospel. O'Neill wanted to take the Gospel back to Ireland, where he thought it belonged. And Montgomery is a self-confessed collector of beautiful things.'

'But he'd not be so stupid as to think he could put a priceless manuscript on his bookshelf and get away with it.'

'And neither could Sean O'Neill hope to slip back to Ireland unnoticed with the Gospel hidden in his luggage. Anyway, when you've finished your breakfast, you get off to O'Neill. Give him a thorough going-over. Check police records; ours and Ireland's. I doubt he's got previous, but . . . I'll go and see Montgomery later. You stay down here in Fridale. I have to get back to the Hall.'

'We're not going to manage this alone, sir. We'll need extra men.'

'We're a bit thin on the ground at the moment, but Blackburn's said he'll do his best for us.'

'Then can I have Polly Stride?'

Douglas finished his tea, and got up. 'You'll not need her down here, laddie. Actually I could do with her up at the Hall. There's two very sad ladies up there who could do with a bit of female comfort.'

'But sir . . .'

'No, sergeant. Never mix business and pleasure.'

Venerables looked the picture of innocence. 'As if I would.'

'Oh, you would if you had the chance. I've seen it happen before. And rumour has it that there's plenty going on between you and Polly Stride. No, we'll have her up at the Hall where's she's safe. As for you, just keep your mind on your job.'

Chapter 4

Now for the servants, thought Douglas, bracing himself for a long haul. *Always start at the top.* But in this case he didn't think the butler had done it. He told Arthur Bloodworthy to come in and indicated a chair in the makeshift interview booth which had been set up in McKenzie's study. Venerables would have said that a morning spent interviewing the Hall's staff was a waste of time; he loathed the meticulous checking of every statement, every fact. But Douglas knew that time wasted in interviews was time gained later on. It took time to gain people's confidence, time and tact; eventually, they might talk freely, or, as they became less guarded, make a mistake.

However, Arthur Bloodworthy gave every appearance of being a waste of time – and a pretty lugubrious one at that. Staring glumly at Douglas, he looked like an ageing bloodhound in urgent need of exercise, with his heavilylined face, brown eyes steeped in melancholy, and hanks of greying hair hanging down on either side of his face like flea-bitten ears. His speech was as slow as his demeanour, but he answered each question thoughtfully and carefully, even though they were exactly the same questions he'd answered the night before. Yes, he'd been on duty all night, and as it happened he, too, hadn't been able to get to bed either.

'Dinner finished around ten forty-five?' said Douglas patiently.

'That's right. Rose left with the two girls at about eleven. Left us – Pete, Tom and me – to clear up. Not much now as the new dishwasher saves us a lot of work.'

'And then you served champagne to the dancers?'

'Aye. After the first round the boys took over. Every one was mighty thirsty and the dancing made them even thirstier. The boys had to move a bit smartish.'

'And you, sir, what did you do while the boys looked after the guests?' Douglas saw Bloodworthy's face take on a darker shade of red. Clearly he'd resent the slightest hint that he might have betrayed his employer.

'I told you last night, didn't I? I stayed in the kitchen and pantry, clearing up. I was still doing that when you came charging downstairs.'

'And you didn't go outside during this time?'

'No. Why should I?'

'Not even to put the rubbish out? Or to take a breath of air?'

'Rubbish? Leftovers are always put down the waste disposal. Anything else is put in plastic sacks and kept in the cellar until the following day.'

'And so you didn't get to bed at all?'

'No sir, I didn't. None of us did. I don't expect you did either.'

'A long night, I agree. And a sad one. Thank you very much for your help, Mr Bloodworthy. Would you send in your wife now, please? Just to check her statement. It won't take long. And stay around, won't you, sir? It's possible we might need you again.'

Arthur walked ponderously to the door, his body sagging with weariness. Not much help from Bloodworthy, thought Douglas as he polished off yet another cup of black coffee. The epitome of the loyal retainer. Devastated by last night's events. Never done anything dishonest in his life – apart from, perhaps, the occasional nip from McKenzie's whisky decanter.

Rose Bloodworthy came in next. A stout woman, in her early fifties, Douglas guessed, with a pleasant round face and neat brown hair dusted with grey and gathered into a bun at the back of her head. She looked anxious, declining Douglas's invitation to sit down. She stood awkwardly in front of him, nervously folding the front of her apron into neat pleats.

'I won't keep you long, Mrs Bloodworthy. This must be a very great shock to you. However, I'd like to get one or two things straight. Perhaps if you could just take me through the evening. Dinner finished about what time?'

'You were there, sir. You ought to know.'

'I'm afraid I didn't look at my watch.' *No*, thought Douglas, *I was too busy looking at Mary Cameron*. 'I'd just like you to tell me everything in your own words.'

'Well, it ended around quarter to eleven. We'd arranged for the piper to start the dancing at eleven. That's when me and the girls left.

34

We gave Arthur a bit of a hand loading the dishwasher – he always makes a mess of that – and left him and the boys to sort out the rest. Janice, my daugher Irene's friend, went off to her disco, and Irene and I went to bed. There we stayed until we were woken up at that god-forsaken hour this morning.'

'I'm sorry about that. We had no alternative, under the circumstances. Now, you say you left around eleven. Did you see Mr McKenzie before you left?'

'We saw him get up from the dinner table. He talked to one or two of his friends, drank some brandy – he can't abide champagne – and that's the last we saw of him. Poor man. Look what he walked into! And all he wanted was his wee nap. He would have joined in the dancing later on, he always did, after he'd recharged his batteries. He enjoyed a lively eightsome.'

The nervous fiddling with her apron intensified, and her eyes filled with tears. Impatiently, she wiped her face vigorously on her sleeve.

'How did you get home, Mrs Bloodworthy?'

'We drove. Well, I don't much like walking through the dark, see, and we had to drop Janice off at her disco in Swarfdale. Then we went back to Rose Cottage. Arthur stayed on here, of course, to look after the guests. He goes to and from the Hall on his bike, so we didn't have to hang around and wait for him.'

'What time did you drop Janice off, Mrs Bloodworthy?'

'About ten past eleven, I should think. Doesn't take much longer than ten minutes to get to Swarfdale from here, not at that time of the night with no hold-ups.'

'And you actually saw Janice arrive at the disco?'

Mrs Bloodworthy looked indignant. 'Of course I did. I dropped her right outside. You get some funny types hanging around those places and I wouldn't let a young girl wander around on her own. Not that Janice isn't capable of taking care of herself.'

'And you saw nothing? No car, no motorbike, no vehicle parked anywhere? No one out taking a stroll? Walking the dog?'

'This is a quiet place, sir. Most people are tucked up in bed by half past ten, even at the weekend.'

'You saw no one in the grounds as you drove down to the gate?'

'Of course not. The guests were starting the dancing.'

Douglas sighed. It was always the same at the beginning of an investigation. No one had seen anything; no one had heard anything out of the ordinary. All the same, someone who shouldn't have been there had been at Reivers Hall last night. Someone who knew exactly when and where to find McKenzie at his most vulnerable.

He dismissed Rose Bloodworthy and asked her to send in the two waiters. No need to see the girls yet. Clearly they hadn't been at Reivers Hall when McKenzie died.

Pete Fraser came in first: an attractive young man, in his late twenties, sturdily built, with the sort of dark good looks which women admired. Wavy dark hair, worn on the long side; muscular legs; the shoulders of a body-builder. Even after a sleepless night, he still looked relatively fresh. He was wearing his uniform – white shirt, dark trousers and a tartan bow tie – as he had been in the middle of serving lunch to the few remaining guests who had stayed to give moral support to Patricia McKenzie and her sister. But despite Pete Fraser's natty uniform, he still looked the countryman. Then Douglas remembered: Bloodworthy'd told him that when Fraser wasn't a waiter he served as McKenzie's ghillie.

'A busy day for you yesterday,' said Douglas, indicating the chair.

'You can say that again. Out all day with the guns and handing round the bubbly in the evening.'

'Not a bad life, though. They look after you well? The family, I mean?'

'They're the best. Real County. A crying shame about Ian. I hope you catch the bastard.'

'That's what we're here for. Now, let's concentrate on you, sir. Do you come from round here?'

'A bit further south. Durham.'

'And how did you come to meet Ian McKenzie?'

'He advertised for help in the local paper a couple of years ago, and me and Tom got the job. Not that Tom's much good – it would have been better if he'd taken on Kevin – but for some reason he wanted Tom. I suppose he's good at waiting on folk – got the right smarmy manner – while I'm better out on the shoot. A pity, really. Kevin and I would've made a good pair.'

'And who's Kevin?'

'My brother. Younger brother, that is.'

'And what does he do?'

'Whatever needs doing round about – painting, decorating. He works up here sometimes. General handyman. He's building a garage at the moment.'

'Does he live near here?'

'We share a place. One of the cottages on the estate. Lake Cottage. Ian lets Kevin stay with me. He's good like that . . . Oh, bugger it!'

Douglas waited until the young man collected himself. 'Do you look after yourselves? Do your own cooking, that sort of thing?'

'Irene – Rose and Arthur's daughter – sees we're well fed.'

'I see. Nice girl, Irene?'

'We get along all right.'

'How has Mr McKenzie's death altered your circumstances?'

'Pat says the job's mine for as long as I want it.'

'Pat?'

'Mrs McKenzie doesn't stand on ceremony. Always asks us to call her Pat.' Suddenly Fraser got to his feet, taking it upon himself to terminate the interview. 'If you'll excuse me, sir, there's eight people having lunch in the dining room. We might have had a murder here last night, but people still have to eat.'

'I understand. I'm sorry to drag you away from your duties. Oh, before you go, could you tell me whether you went outside at all last night? For a bit of a breather, maybe?'

Pete turned and stared at Douglas. 'That's a damn silly question, if I might say so, sir. Thirty guests guzzling bubbly like water – now would I have time to go outside for a breather?'

'Don't worry, sir. There is a method in my madness. Could you send in Emmerson, Mr Fraser? I'd like to have a word with him.'

As Pete strode out of the room, Douglas gazed thoughtfully at the portrait of a McKenzie ancestor dressed in full Highland regalia, his heavily whiskered face staring down at him stonily. *It's all right for you, mate*, thought Douglas. *You're well out of this.*

The door opened and Tom Emmerson came in. If Pete Fraser oozed masculine rude health, Tom was his shadow. Tall, pale-skinned as if he'd been living in a cupboard for most of his life, his long face was fringed by dull and thinning fair hair. Cautious grey eyes examined Douglas warily. Hesitating before he sat down, he then perched awkwardly on the edge of the chair, wiping his hands frequently on his black waiter's trousers, as if they were sweating.

'I won't keep you long, sir,' said Douglas briskly. 'Local lad, is that right?'

'Yes sir. I live in the village.'

'On your own?'

'With my mum and dad. We've got one of the Council houses down in Fridale. Dad's the postman round these parts.'

'What brought you up here to the Hall?'

'Janice. Irene's friend. My girlfriend. Well, she was until she met Kevin – Pete's brother, that is. She dumped me pretty sharpish after that. Anyway, she showed me this advertisement in the local paper. Introduced me to McKenzie. They wanted a local bloke, you see, and I was able to get good references. I know how to wait at table. I used to be a waiter at Hunters Lodge – the big hotel outside Rothbury.'

'What made you leave Hunters? McKenzie pay better?'

'Yes. And I wanted to be near Janice. Not that that came to anything – she'd met Kevin by then. Pete got the other job, you see.'

'But you like it here?'

'It's a good position. I'll always be able to get another job, if I want to move on, with a McKenzie reference.'

'Got yourself another girlfriend?'

'Not yet.' He swallowed nervously, suddenly self-conscious. 'Not many girls look at me twice.'

'What about Irene? Arthur and Rose's daughter?'

'*Irene?* You must be joking. She's after Pete. Who'd look at me when Pete's going begging? Mind you, I never understand why they stay with him. He's always two-timing them. Dropped all the girls like hot bricks when McKenzie looked in his direction.'

'Really?' said Douglas evenly, fighting down a flicker of excitement. *Careful now. Don't frighten the man.* 'What exactly do you mean?'

Tom looked uneasy. 'Nothing. Just . . . Pete sometimes did jobs for him. Mr McKenzie expected a lot from his staff.'

'Do I take it then that you weren't all that keen on Mr McKenzie?'

'I'm not employed to be *keen* on him. I only did what he wanted me to do. He was demanding. I don't know why Pete put up with him. Nor Pat.'

'Pat?'

Tom was immediately defensive. 'She told us to call her Pat. She likes Pete too. She's always giving him the glad eye.'

'Does she ever give you the "glad eye"?'

'Me? Not on your life. As I said, girls don't take much notice of me. Not even old girls like Pat. She does like young blokes though. Toy boys. She wanted Kevin on the staff, but the old man put his foot down and took me on instead. Probably thought I was more reliable than Kevin.'

'And what about Mary Cameron?' said Douglas quietly, thinking that if he were going to open a can of worms he might as well tip the contents out. 'Does she like the lads too?'

'Mrs Cameron? She's a real lady. She'd never look at Pete, or Kevin. Mrs Cameron likes to keep herself to herself. She's classy. One day, someone'll come along and cheer her up, but not one of us. He'd have to be a real gentleman.'

Douglas felt his spirits lift. Tom Emmerson was proving to be very useful. It was always the resentful ones, he reflected, who were the biggest help. They just couldn't contain their envy. Pete Fraser, he was as slippery as an eel; it wasn't going to be easy to catch him out. But Tom was different. Nerves had made him talkative, and jealousy had made him indiscreet. On the surface, his statement looked perfectly straightforward: he'd been a loyal employee of Ian McKenzie. But Douglas could read behind the lines. Tom had a chip on his shoulder. Tom was an underdog; but an observant one.

This young man, thought Douglas, had potential. Treat him appropriately, and he'd sell his grandmother if the price was right. As for the others – Arthur, Rose, Pete – well, no joy there yet. But someone had watched Ian slip away to his dressing room. If Blackburn was correct, someone had given the green light to the attackers.

He was brought out of his reverie when Tom Emmerson, assuming Douglas's silence meant that the interview was over, stood up.

'Yes, you can go now, Mr Emmerson,' said Douglas. 'One last question – did either you, or Pete Fraser, or Mr Bloodworthy, go outside last night after dinner was over?'

'No, none of us did. We were too busy. Oh, Pete went out for a few minutes. But only to put out the crate of dead men.'

'Dead men?'

'Empty bottles from dinner. They clutter up the place. Pete put the crate outside the kitchen door. I expect it's still there.'

'What time was that?'

Tom shrugged his shoulders dismissively. 'I didn't notice. About the same time as the dancing started, I think.'

'After Mr McKenzie'd left the company?'

'I suppose so. He went off as soon as dinner had ended.'

'Thanks, Tom. You've been very helpful. I'll just take a look at that crate, if I may.'

Following Tom into the kitchen where Arthur and Rose were eating their lunch, Douglas went across and opened the kitchen door.

He peered out. There sat the crate of bottles. Looking along the side of the house, he saw the line of bay windows which represented the bedrooms. One of them, he felt sure, was Ian McKenzie's dressing room.

Back in the study, he called in PC Wilkes. 'None of the staff are to leave the building until I come back. And I shall need a plan of the house – a detailed one, showing all the bedrooms where each of the guests stayed. I've got to get down to Fridale, but I'll be back this evening and I'll need that plan then. Oh, and Wilkes . . .'

'Sir?'

'Keep your eyes and ears open. Listen to gossip. I want to know what goes on round here.'

Outside, Douglas called Venerables on his carphone. 'How goes it, Sergeant?'

'I'm with Mr O'Neill. He's being very hospitable.'

'Forget the tea and biscuits and get up here to the Hall by half past six at the latest. I'll need your young mind.'

'Nice of you to say so, sir.'

'Don't mention it. Now I'm off to have a wee chat with Alec Montgomery.'

Wishing that he had just a modicum of Venerables' young mind at his disposal, Douglas drove down to Montgomery Hall, a Georgian, grey-stone house, with a neat slate roof, a classical porch and three rows of neat sash windows. *Here's someone else who does himself proud*, he thought, as he turned in through the open wrought-iron gates, and sailed up the curving gravel drive to the front door. Compared to Reivers Hall, however, it was a modest home: in an earlier age, Douglas thought, it could have been the rectory, at a time when the squire and the parson worked together to keep the parishioners in order.

He parked his car and rang the doorbell; Alec Montgomery, as if he'd been waiting in the hall, opened it straight away. He led Douglas into an elegant entrance lobby with a black-and-white tiled floor, and then into the study. Montgomery's furnishings spoke volumes about his wealth. Even the study held a fine collection of oriental china – blue and white Chinese plates and bowls, all neatly housed in elegant wooden display cabinets. Douglas was invited to sit down in a sumptuous armchair, softly upholstered in deep blue velvet. Alec chose the sofa and settled himself down gracefully. Douglas took in the heavy damask curtains neatly tied back with silken tasselled ties. The view from the window was attractive. A smoothly manicured lawn curved down to a shrubbery, well stocked with exotic shrubs. Douglas thought of his own shabby oak furniture, inherited from a variety of relatives, his worn carpet, his threadbare curtains, and felt a pang of envy. An unusual emotion for him. *One day*, he thought, *I'll get rid of all that old stuff. Not that I could afford anything like this, but I could at least replace the carpet. Maybe I could buy a nice bit of Axminster . . .*

'Tea, Chief Inspector?' said Alec pleasantly. 'You've had a busy day.'

'You could say that, sir. Tea would be just what the doctor ordered.'

Alec rose from the sofa and went across to a table which held a tea tray all ready for the occasion. He brought a small kettle quickly back to boil and then made tea in an exquisite Chinese teapot. Douglas, watching these preparations, inwardly groaned: the last thing he wanted to drink at this moment was weak China tea. All very well in its place, but at times like this he needed strong tea, hot and dark, the sort he'd get in a roadside café. When it came, however, the tea was Indian, served with milk and sugar, and very refreshing.

Douglas took a sip and launched straight in. He didn't want this to turn into a tea party. 'I understand that you actually witnessed the shooting of Derek Fairbrother this morning. Father Paul tells me you were in the procession close by.'

'*Witnessed* is hardly the word, Chief Inspector. I was there, walking with the others. I'd spoken to Derek a minute or so earlier, just to say hello. When he fell, I went to him, naturally. I didn't immediately look round in an attempt to discover who shot him. I regret now that I didn't have more presence of mind.'

Was that sarcasm that Douglas detected? 'It's easy to see with hindsight what one should have done. Can you remember what happened next, sir? Immediately after Derek fell? Take your time. Every piece of information helps, no matter how small.'

'I'll do my best, but it's all rather confused. Father Paul was distraught. I asked someone with a mobile phone to call the ambulance – and yourselves, of course. I stayed with Derek and kept the crowds back. But it was obvious there was no hope.'

'Can you remember how long you had to wait before the emergency services arrived?'

'Not long. Five, six minutes at the most. Father Paul dashed off to get the holy oils and then the ambulance arrived, followed by the police. They took over. I wasn't sorry, believe me – I was shaking like a leaf.'

'And what did you do after Derek had been taken away? I know you must have been in a state of shock, but where did you go?'

'I suddenly thought of the Little Sisters and the Gospel. But your men detained us all, asking questions, and I stayed in the square until they told me I could go. You might think I was heartless to think of the Gospel at such a time, but I've always worried about the vulnerability of such a priceless work of art, kept unguarded in a church safe. The Sisters are so unworldly. They look upon the St Frida Gospel as a sacred trust, but times have changed since the seventh century. Thieves nowadays look upon religious works of art as no more than juicy commercial propositions. When Father Paul came back from the hospital with his tragic news, I told him I was going to the church to ask Sister Anne to check on the safe. The rest you know.'

'I understand. A sudden emotional trauma like the one you experienced can make us focus on the things we most value. But why assume there was a link between Derek's killing and the theft of the manuscript? I understand the safe was firmly locked when you got there, and the Little Sisters were sitting in the church waiting for the procession to return so Father Paul could begin the service of Holy Communion. Did you think that they'd sat there and watched the thieves dash past them to the sacristy?'

'The safe was last checked yesterday evening – Sister Anne makes a point of it before going to bed. The Little Sisters didn't arrive at the church this morning until the procession was well underway. I saw no reason why a clever thief, working with an accomplice, shouldn't have caused a rumpus in the square to distract attention from the church. I admit the timing would have been tight, but . . . I suppose I wasn't thinking clearly.'

Douglas leaned back. Montgomery hadn't told him anything new.

'If there's any more of that excellent tea, I'd be grateful for a refill. Then why don't you tell me a bit about yourself? You've got a nice place here, that's for sure.'

'Thank you, Chief Inspector,' Alec said, as he filled up Douglas's cup. 'I bought it five years ago when I decided to move up North.'

'Then you didn't come from these parts originally?'

'My ancestors did. They actually lived in this house – that's why it's called Montgomery Hall. It isn't me simply having delusions of grandeur. One of my ancestors was the parson here.' So Douglas's suspicions had been correct. 'The Montgomerys were Northumberland people through and through,' he went on. 'Border reivers in the Middle Ages, squires and parsons later on when times were less desperate and the reivers became law-abiding citizens. Later, after King James united the two countries, my branch went South. I was brought up in South London, Chislehurst. Very salubrious. When I started working, I lived at home and commuted to London each day. Then my mother died – six years ago now – and I decided to sell up and come here. I feel I've come home.'

'You worked in London, sir?'

'In the City. One of those big international insurance firms, dealing mostly with Marine Insurance. Very dull.'

'But very rewarding. Or so I'm told.'

'There were certain financial inducements, yes. Otherwise I could never have endured it. But when this house came on the market – well, it seemed like fate. It wasn't even that expensive. Property's much cheaper up North. And when my mother died, I inherited everything. I was an only child. Her house fetched half a million and she had invested wisely. I've been fortunate, Chief Inspector; I've more than enough for a comfortable retirement.'

'You said you were a bit of a collector, sir. I've been admiring your Chinese porcelain.'

'Then you show good taste. It's my little hobby – I love fine china. Especially oriental porcelain. Most of these I inherited from my mother. She was an avid collector too.'

'Now that's something I should like to do when I retire. Not that I will be able to afford to buy much; just one of those plates would cost three months' worth of my retirement pension, I expect. But I can still admire them from a distance. Visit museums, stately homes and the like.'

'Of course. It's always interesting to make a study of things of beauty. Ian and I became quite knowledgeable. We went to auctions and sales together. We were both enthusiasts. He too was worried about the Frida Gospel. But then, it was exquisite, Chief Inspector. Part of our heritage. Had Ian been alive, he would have been shattered by the theft.'

'Did you know Mr McKenzie well?'

'We were friends. I'm fond of Patricia, too. I visit the Hall regularly.'

'But you didn't go there last night?'

'No. I don't shoot, and dancing's not my scene.'

'But you could have joined us for dinner.'

'Chief Inspector, how could I possibly come to dinner and decline to participate in any of the other activities? It would have been very rude. Not to say greedy.'

'Yes, I suppose it would.' He took another sip of his tea, and looked searchingly at Montgomery. 'You must have been very upset by the news of Mr McKenzie's death.'

'Devastated, Chief Inspector. Absolutely devastated. Tomorrow I must go and see Patricia. Today I'm sure she wants to be alone, to start coming to terms with what has happened.'

'Indeed, sir. And now, sir, you won't be taking any trips to London or elsewhere in the near future, will you? I'd appreciate it if you stayed here for the time being. We most probably will have to see you again. Our men have already taken your statement, I think?'

'Yes. Along with all the other statements. And they're still at it, I understand.'

'We've a great many people to interview. But we'll get there in the end.'

'Chief Inspector – if you don't mind me asking – what action have you taken to find the Gospel?'

'Don't worry, sir. Just leave it to us. It's all in hand. Although, to be frank, it could be out of the country already.'

'The thieves won't be able to sell it on the open market.'

'And that makes our job that much more difficult. Chances are it's headed for someone's private collection; someone with a lot of money and not much interest in where his treasures come from. And you were one of the few outsiders who actually saw the manuscript, Mr Montgomery?'

'Yes. Most recently with Sean O'Neill.'

'And when exactly was that, sir?'

Alec paused. 'Middle of August, I think. Sean came here in July, at the end of his academic term, and it took him a while to get settled in, so . . . I know it was a Saturday. I have a feeling it was the twelfth. The Glorious Twelfth – a big day in these parts. And a red-letter day for me – getting another sight of something so precious.'

'Thank you for your help, sir. And thank you for the tea; most refreshing.'

'A pleasure. Back to Berwick for you now, I suppose, Chief Inspector?'

'Not yet. Mrs McKenzie's been kind enough to offer me accommodation up at the Hall. There's a murder investigation going on up there as well as down here, of course. We've set up an incident room on site.'

'Let's hope you make an arrest soon. On both counts.'

'Amen to that, sir. I'll leave you in peace.'

Smiling amiably, Alec Montgomery showed Douglas out. Douglas's head felt as if it were stuffed with cotton wool; he'd eaten nothing since last night's meal, except the bacon sandwich he'd had with Venerables, and he'd drunk too much black coffee and strong tea. He glanced at his watch: half past five. Time for a quick snack. He drove back to the roadside café and ordered a ham sandwich which he ate hurriedly. The he trudged back to his Volvo and drove up to Reivers Hall.

Venerables was waiting. He looked surprisingly cheerful for a man at the beginning of a double murder investigation, but his smile changed to a look of concern when he saw Douglas's face.

'You look all in, sir.'

'I'll survive. How was Mr O'Neill?'

'Mr O'Neill's a very nice man, sir.'

'So is Mr Montgomery. Cups of tea and polite conversation all round.'

'Always the same at this stage of the game.'

'You can say that again. Come on, let's get inside. We've a bit of catching-up to do. I shall be staying here tonight, so I've nowhere to rush off to.'

'I'm joining you.'

'Who says?' said Douglas indignantly.

'Blackburn's orders. Polly's here too.' Venerables looked triumphant.

'How cosy. I don't suppose she's staying the night?'

'Unfortunately not.'

'Thank God for that. She can get back to Berwick. I don't want her distracting you. Besides, I want all the information she can get on Alec Montgomery.'

'You're a rotten spoilsport, sir.'

'Your love life's not a priority right now,' Douglas said drily. 'But Polly has her uses. She's a dab hand with computers, that's for sure.'

'One of her many talents, sir.'

Arthur Bloodworthy greeted them as they went inside. He looked even more melancholy than he had earlier; he scowled quite menacingly at Venerables.

'If you'd like to go to your room, sir, I'll send you up some supper on a tray,' he said to Douglas. 'And you'll be eating with us in the kitchen – Sergeant.'

'Look, Bloodworthy, we've already discussed this. The Chief Inspector and I always take our meals together . . .'

'Not tonight, Venerables,' said Douglas wearily. 'Tonight I eat on my own. You do whatever suits the staff. They're facing enough disruption as it is.'

'Thank you, sir,' said Arthur, looking smug. 'I was only thinking of your comfort. By the way, the ladies aren't coming down to dinner. Mrs McKenzie sent down orders that she doesn't want to see anyone tonight, and Mrs Cameron's staying with her.'

'That's very understandable,' said Douglas, nevertheless feeling a twinge of disappointment. 'I'll be off upstairs, then. Some supper would be very welcome, Mr Bloodworthy.'

Once in his room, Douglas fell on the bed. *Just shut my eyes for a few minutes*, he thought; *then I'll go and see Venerables . . .*

He closed his eyes and was asleep instantly. He didn't hear Arthur Bloodworthy come in with a tray of cold pie and salad. He didn't feel the butler remove his shoes, loosen his tie and place the duvet over him. He slept soundly and refreshingly. It had been quite a day, all things considered.

Chapter 5

Douglas woke up just as the milky light of dawn dispersed the shadows of night. He glanced at the clock on the bedside table: the illuminated hands said five o'clock. In the *morning*, he realised with horror. With a disgusted exclamation, he swung his feet out of bed and stood up. He saw the supper tray on the table; however hungry he might be, he couldn't face cold pie and salad, not at that time of the day. He picked up the bedside electric kettle, meaning to fill it with water from the bathroom. Then he heard it. Not much of a sound, but his instincts were on the alert. He put the kettle carefully back on the table, and listened. The tiny click of a door closing. Someone was being mighty careful. He waited. Then he heard the muffled sound of bare feet padding down the corridor, past his room, towards the stairs. When he judged the feet were well past his room, he opened his bedroom door. Cautiously he looked out into the corridor. In the pale light he could just make out the shape of a man disappearing down the stairs. He instantly recognised the dark hair, the broad shoulders. Pete Fraser, on the prowl. Douglas hadn't heard him go past his room earlier in the night, but then he'd been out for the count. A herd of elephants stampeding down the corridor wouldn't have disturbed him. But whose bed had he shared last night, Douglas wondered? If he had shared a bed. Maybe someone had just wanted room service. Doubtful – Reivers Hall wasn't an hotel.

Back in his room, he took a quick shower, dressed, and went off to speak to Venerables and PC Wilkes. He knew they were dossing down in the incident room. There, on the sofa in McKenzie's study, he found the supine body of PC Wilkes. Next to him on a camp bed was Sergeant Venerables, curled up in a sleeping bag, snug as a bug in a rug.

47

He went over and shook Venerables roughly by the shoulder. 'Get up, man,' he said. 'There's work to do.'

Venerables opened one eye, saw Douglas, and promptly shut it again. 'For God's sake, sir. It's not even daylight.'

'The sun's been up an hour or more. Get yourself out of that bag, and I'll wake up Wilkes.'

But PC Wilkes was already awake and groping for his trousers. 'I'll see if there's any coffee, sir,' he said with a desperate attempt at brightness.

'Good idea. I'll come with you. We'll leave the sergeant to get up on his own. Here, lad – you'll be needing these.' And Douglas threw Venerables' neatly folded trousers over his face.

Wilkes and Douglas made their way to the kitchen, where Pete Fraser, dressed casually in jeans and a loose-fitting shirt, was already waiting for a kettle to boil.

'Three coffees while you're at it,' said Douglas. Pete grunted and reached for three more mugs.

'Up early, aren't you?' said Douglas sociably. 'Didn't you go home last night?'

'No, I was wanted here last night, so I stayed on. They've given me a hole to crawl into when it's too late to go home. They call it a "basement bedroom", but it's a cellar, really. No window. Still, at least I can get my head down, so I mustn't grumble. Breakfast won't be ready yet, sir, I'm afraid. Rose doesn't come in until half past seven.'

'Coffee will do fine. What time do you start work?'

'Any time I like. Officially when Rose comes in. There's not much to do this morning – most of the guests left last night. Still, there's the likes of you to look after, and I daresay the place will soon be swarming with reinforcements. Isn't that right?'

'Quite likely, sir. I hope we won't get in your way.'

'The sooner you come, the sooner you'll leave us all in peace.'

'That's right. Will you be seeing your brother today?'

'Kevin? I don't expect so. He's no reason to come here.'

'I'll need to speak to him soon. Any idea what time would be convenient for him?'

'He'll most likely be home now. He won't leave for work till seven or thereabouts.'

'Then we'll have our coffee, nip down to your cottage, and be back for one of Arthur's splendid breakfasts. Thank you, sir. Take

Sergeant Venerables his coffee, Wilkes, and tell him I want him to be ready in five minutes. And while I've got you on your own,' he said to Pete, who was sullenly stirring sugar into his coffee, 'can I just set something straight? When I saw you yesterday, you said you didn't go outside at all on Saturday night. Now, when I talked to Tom Emmerson, he said you went out just after dinner. To put a crate of empty bottles outside the kitchen door.'

'So what?'

'So why didn't you tell me that?'

'I didn't remember when you asked me. It didn't seem important.'

'Everything's important, sir, where murder's concerned. That's all for now. Thank you, sir.'

Picking up his mug of coffee, he joined the other two in the study. Venerables was dressed, Wilkes was drawing back the curtains, the bed was folded away.

'Comfortable night, Sergeant?' said Douglas innocently.

'Like hell it was! Wilkes got the sofa, and I had to put up with the put-you-up. I suppose you had the perfect night in your palatial apartment?'

'I did all right. Calm down – you'll not have to put up with this for long. I hope. Let's get to work. Wilkes, have you got that plan of the house?'

Briskly, Wilkes went over to the interview table, and picked up a large sheet of paper. On it was a very clear drawing of the house, with all the rooms neatly labelled, and the garages and outhouses marked clearly.

'Well done, Wilkes. You've done a first-rate job. I didn't know you were an expert in computer graphics.'

'Polly helped him,' said Venerables, disgruntled. 'The two of them were at it all night.'

'I knew that lass would come in useful! But let me have a look at this. Kitchen here. Terrace outside. Runs along the back of the house. Bedroom up here. And I know that's the McKenzie suite.'

'That's right, sir. Not far from your bedroom. But Mrs McKenzie moved out last night. Said she couldn't sleep in there ever again.'

'So where did she sleep last night?'

'Here, sir. Two rooms along from you.'

Douglas felt the old familiar tingle of excitement. So that was where Pete had spent the night! *The plot thickens*, he thought.

'So anyone standing outside the kitchen door,' he said to Wilkes, 'could signal to someone hiding – in this shrubbery seems the obvious place – once he knew McKenzie had gone up to his dressing room?'

'Easy as anything.'

'Right! We're getting somewhere. Now what were you doing last night, laddie, when Wilkes here was shut up with Polly?'

'Talking to bloody Arthur. And the lassies. Polly'd better watch out. Irene's all bum and tits, if you know what I mean – but quiet like. And mad about Pete. As for Janice, she's a real goer. Ready for anything – except she's supposed to be going out with Kevin Fraser. Incidentally, did you know that Pete's having it off with Mrs McKenzie when she feels so inclined?'

'I did have my suspicions. But I didn't know it was household knowledge. I heard him leaving her room this morning and caught a glimpse of the back of his head going downstairs.'

Venerables whistled. 'What a carry-on, sir! Her old man's not been dead two days.'

'She most likely needs a bit of comfort.'

'Still, it's not right, sir. Pete's heading for trouble, if you ask me.'

'Do you think Mrs McKenzie and Pete plotted to kill off the old man?' Wilkes chipped in. 'After all, they've got a good reason to get him out of the way. Wouldn't be in her interests to get divorced.'

Douglas looked at Wilkes severely. 'Don't be ridiculous, Constable. The Mrs McKenzies of this world don't bump off their old men for the likes of Pete Fraser. They've too much to lose. And by the sound of it, Pete wasn't averse to keeping the old man amused as well.'

Venerables whistled again. 'You mean Pete was McKenzie's bum boy?'

'I wouldn't go that far, laddie. Don't let your imagination run away with you. But I think Emmerson hinted that McKenzie might have fancied a bit of the other occasionally.'

'I find that hard to believe, sir.'

'No one's asking you to believe anything at this stage. Just keep an open mind. But if McKenzie was keen on the lads, then that would explain why Mrs McKenzie gets a bit restless.'

'It's a funny old world, sir.'

'You can say that again. And we don't know the half of it yet.

Now, we've just got time to see the other Fraser brother before he leaves for work – and still be back for breakfast.'

They drove down to the Frasers' cottage past glades of golden conifers gleaming in the morning sunlight. The road ran steeply down to the lake: a magnificent expanse of water which McKenzie's father had sculpted out of the landscape. As they drove along the shore a fish jumped, its scales winking in the bright light. A punt was moored under the willows; Venerables looked at it longingly.

'Just look at that. Me and Polly could have a grand day's fishing.'

'You'll have to wait till we've got a result, laddie. No time to catch tiddlers today.'

At the far end of the lake, nestling in a glade of rowan trees – their berries shining in the sunshine like drops of blood – stood Lake Cottage. It was a neat, stone building with a slate roof and a wooden door. Next to the cottage stood a barn. As Douglas drove up, a mean-looking dog came bounding out, barking in a paroxysm of rage. The door of the cottage opened and a man rushed over to the dog, hitting it sharply – unnecessarily sharply – on the face. The dog whined and skulked back into the barn.

'Kevin Fraser?' said Douglas accusingly as he got out of the car. He couldn't abide cruelty to dumb animals.

'What do you want?'

'A wee chat, sir. I'm Chief Inspector McBride and this is Sergeant Venerables.' They produced their identity cards.

'You'd better come inside.'

Ducking their heads to avoid the low lintel over the front door, they went into the main room of the cottage. A bare stone floor; a table in the centre of the room littered with empty beer cans; an open fireplace full of cigarette ends and screwed-up packaging from take-aways. Clearly the brothers weren't enthusiastic housekeepers. Kevin, his dark hair tousled and uncombed, slumped down in a chair and glowered at Douglas and Venerables. He had the same brooding dark good looks of his brother, but he was shorter and stockier, with the beginnings of a beer belly pushing up his stained and worn T-shirt. His jeans fitted a little too tightly over his muscular thighs, and his trainers were filthy.

'Sorry to get you out of bed, sir,' began Douglas.

'I was already up. I've got to get to work.'

51

'We won't take long. Nice little set-up you've got here, sir.'

'It suits us.'

'Needs the feminine touch, though – if you don't mind me saying. Bring any girls here?'

'Sometimes. Usually we go over to their places. Pete and I are both fixed up – we like a bit of privacy.'

'I hear you've got yourself a right little raver. Janice Hudson. Lucky man.'

'I told you – we're both fixed up. Anyway, what's it got to do with you who I see?'

'Nothing at all. Except I was talking to Rose Bloodworthy yesterday and she mentioned that after she and the two girls left the Hall at eleven o'clock on Saturday night, you and Janice went to a disco. She dropped Janice off outside. Is that right?'

Kevin yawned and scratched his head. 'That's right. I met Janice there – she turned up a bit after eleven. Over in Swarfdale, at Dave's place. He owns the Swarfdale Arms. Loads of people saw me there from half past ten onwards, before you ask. After it closed, it went on, unofficial-like, upstairs in his flat.'

'And you stayed there all night?'

'We left about three.'

'And then?'

'Went back to Janice's place.'

'And stayed there for the rest of the night?'

'Aye.' Kevin guffawed lewdly. 'We kept each other busy – get the picture? Next day was Sunday, so we had a lie-in. The kid was at his granny's.'

'Got a kid, has she? Yours?'

Kevin laughed. 'God, no, man! What'd I do with a kid? It's Jock's. She lived with him for four years before he upped and left. Janice held on to his house down in Fridale. Pays Jock rent. She takes in kids during the day. Calls herself a child-minder. Bloody nightmare. I keep well clear in the daytime. She knows what's what after dark, though.' And he sniggered again.

'Mind if we have a chat with Janice? Just to confirm your story?'

Kevin looked keenly at Douglas. 'Go ahead. Ask her anything you like. But I hope you don't think I had anything to do with the old man's murder. Or with the kid's, for that matter. I was tucked up in bed with Janice on Sunday morning, and she won't tell you any different.'

'I'm glad to hear it. Just point me in the direction of Janice's house, sir.' Kevin looked reluctant, but he did what Douglas asked.

The semi-detached house on the new estate in the village of Fridale looked neglected and uninviting. All the curtains at the front of the house were drawn. No one answered when Venerables rang the bell. After several attempts he walked back to the car.

'Doesn't look like she's there, sir.'

'We'll get back to her later. Meanwhile, I want to keep a careful eye on Kevin Fraser. I don't trust him an inch.'

'Nor do I, sir. And I don't trust his brother either. The pair of them stink to high heaven.'

'Good – that's what I like to hear. Up till now, everyone's been far too squeaky-clean. And dung heaps are fertile ground.'

And they drove away. They didn't notice the slight movement at the bedroom window, as one of the curtains was flicked briefly aside.

Chapter 6

'Now for the ladies, Sergeant,' said Douglas in the kitchen of Reivers Hall, having demolished a plateful of bacon and eggs and a couple of slices of black pudding in double-quick time. He stood up, pushing his plate aside. 'I want you to be there with me. Unofficial, of course. And go easy on them. Mrs McKenzie's grieving, remember. She'll be very vulnerable.'

'Some grieving,' muttered Venerables.

Just then his mobile phone bleeped and he took the call. He glanced significantly at Douglas as the voice at the other end embarked upon a monologue. Then the voice ceased and Venerables put the mobile away.

'That was Blackburn. Reinforcements on their way, sir. They don't think we're competent to deal with this on our own. Big guns coming over from Newcastle. Be with us today.'

'It's always the same,' said Douglas, disgruntled. 'As soon as we start to get our teeth into a murder investigation, they stick their noses in, if they think there might be a bit of glory in it for them.'

'They're not coming for the homicides. The Arty Farties've got excited over the theft in Fridale. They think we need sorting out.'

'The specialist Squad! I can do without them mincing around. Who's in charge? Some posh chap with a Fine Arts degree who fancies himself as Sherlock Holmes?'

'Better than that. They're sending us a lassie.'

'A lassie? That's all we need. Has she got a name?'

'She's called Felicity Flight. At least, that's what I *think* Blackburn said.'

'Felicity Flight? What a damn silly name. Some daft lass with droopy skirts and beads in her hair, no doubt.'

'Flat boobs and short legs. Reckon we should call her Flic – I'll have you know, that's French for cop,' said Venerables, dredging up his schoolboy knowledge of languages.

Douglas snorted. 'When do we meet this – Flic?'

'She's on her way. Going straight to Fridale.'

'Well, she'd go straight home again if I had anything to do with it. Come on, laddie. There's still work for us to do. Let's concentrate on what we know how to do best. Leave Polly to deal with Flic.'

Patricia McKenzie was waiting for them in what Arthur Bloodworthy called her 'boudoir': a small, very feminine room, furnished with satinwood chairs upholstered in a Regency-striped fabric. Pale cream curtains, held back by matching satin tassels, draped the windows; pale green and pink Chinese rugs were scattered strategically over the soft fitted carpet. Patricia, dressed casually in fawn trousers and a dark blue shirt, got up to greet them as they went in.

It was thirty-six hours since Douglas had last seen her and he was expecting to find her drawn and haggard after the dreadful experience she'd been through. But she looked remarkably well. Her face was paler than he remembered, but that was only to be expected; however, she'd taken the trouble to arrange her rich auburn hair skilfully at the back of her head, and her deep blue eyes were surprisingly clear. Newly bereaved she might be, but she still looked tough, sexy and very much alive.

'Come and sit down, gentlemen. I hope you're being well looked after.'

'Thank you, ma'am. Your staff have been most kind. May we offer our condolences? Mr McKenzie will be much missed. We're only sorry that we have to intrude on your grief.'

'You're simply doing your job, Chief Inspector. I want whoever killed my husband arrested and put behind bars. More than anything, I want that. So please don't hesitate to ask me anything you think might be useful.'

Douglas sat down gingerly on one of the elegant chairs. He didn't feel at all at home in this pretty, delicate room.

'We believe your husband's death was no random killing. It seems unlikely that it was committed by thieves disturbed during a break-in. We think it was a carefully planned, premeditated crime. What I have to ask you is, did your husband have any enemies? Any business associates with whom he had quarelled, maybe? Have you any idea at all who'd want to kill him in such a wicked way? I'm sorry, ma'am,' he said, seeing her look of distress, 'but we have to be realistic. We can't pretend your husband's murder was committed on impulse.'

'I'm sorry, Chief Inspector,' she said, visibly controlling her emotion, 'I'm still trying to come to terms with the horror of it all. What can I say? Did Ian have any enemies? Of *course* not. He lived a quiet life. His army days had given him all the excitement he needed, and he was happy to spend his retirement with his friends. The people he went shooting with, danced with. You met most of them on Saturday night. Ian had no enemies. He led the life of a retired country gentleman. Who could possibly want to kill him?'

'How about his artistic acquaintances?'

'You mean his collecting? All very small-scale. He liked going to auctions with Alec. Unfortunately he couldn't often afford everything he wanted to buy. Oriental art was his passion. He adored Chinese porcelain.'

'And Mr Montgomery always went with him to these auctions?'

'Sometimes.'

'Is Mr Montgomery an old friend, ma'am?'

'Oh, yes. Ian and Alec met at a mutual friend's house party in London around the time when Alec decided to leave the City. I think it was Ian who told him that Montgomery Hall was on the market. Alec's coming here later this morning to help me sort myself out. I don't even know about Ian's will yet. I haven't been able to find it, and the solicitor doesn't have it. I need some help. I'm hopeless about financial matters.'

'But Mr Montgomery didn't come here on Saturday night?'

'We didn't even invite him. He's not into shooting or dancing, and he can come to dinner any time. Besides, we knew he'd want to be up early to watch the Fridale procession on Sunday morning. He's very fond of that church – of anything to do with St Frida. She doesn't seem to have brought much luck to that poor boy, does she? A terrible thing to happen. Two murders in twenty-four hours. And in such a quiet place. Nothing much ever happens here. Maybe a bit of rowdiness when the pub shuts, but that's all.'

'You've heard all about that?'

'Alec phoned last night. He's distraught. He was passionately devoted to that Gospel – and to the Little Sisters.'

'Mr O'Neill is pretty cut up by all accounts too.'

Patricia went over to the window and stood gazing out at the avenue of copper beeches.

'Yes, well . . . the least said about him, the better.'

'I take it you don't approve of Mr O'Neill, ma'am?'

'Alec told me how much he wanted the manuscript. He badgered the Sisters endlessly to let him take it to Ireland.'

'But surely you don't think he would go to the length of stealing it?'

'Mr O'Neill is a distinguished academic gentleman,' Venerables put in stiffly. 'And a good Catholic to boot. He'd not stoop to crime.'

'But he could have got someone else to steal it,' said Patricia forcibly. She turned to face them, and Douglas was struck by the intensity of her gaze.

'It's not likely, is it? After all, give him time and he'd probably have persuaded the nuns to release the Gospel and send it over to Ireland. All above board, properly insured, properly transported. He told me – Sister Anne was already considering the idea of allowing the Gospel to be exhibited temporarily in Dublin.'

'We'll come back to Mr O'Neill later,' Douglas interrupted. Now – I must ask some personal questions about your life with Mr McKenzie, ma'am. All this must seem very intrusive, but your husband died in particularly distressing circumstances so we must find out everything we can.' He took a deep breath. 'Have you been married long?'

'Twenty years. That's long enough, isn't it?'

'And you were happy together?'

'What are you insinuating, Chief Inspector? We had a *perfect* marriage. We both loved this house. We had no children, you see. Somehow they never happened. This house was our child. Ian inherited it ten years ago when his father died. His grandfather built it. He made his money out of the Tyne shipbuilding yards and Ian's father extended and modernised it. He left everything to Ian, and when I die it will go to another branch of the McKenzie family. It has to remain in the family. It *belongs* to them. All that work that went into the building of it . . . Do you know that a whole hillside had to be flattened to build Reivers Hall? It was a labour of love. It's a tribute to the McKenzie energy and will-power. Nothing was impossible for those Victorian builders.'

'And now Mr Montgomery will take over the running of the place?'

'I never said that! Why do you always try to twist what people say? I know what you're hinting at – some sordid liaison, some secret affair. Well, let me tell you, Chief Inspector, that there's nothing like that between Alec and I. He was a close friend of my husband – and of mine. Very generously, he has offered to give me advice over practical matters such as the will, and the funeral – when the Coroner finally allows us to hold it. He is merely lifting the burden of responsibility from my shoulders. He never had anything to do with the running of my husband's estate – and he never will. Not as long as I'm alive.'

Suddenly the door opened and Mary Cameron came in. Douglas, seeing her again, felt his heart give the now-familiar lurch; she was even more beautiful than he remembered. Her hair was a gleaming, copper-coloured helmet; her eyes were the same deep blue as Patricia's. Like her sister she was dressed casually in emerald-green trousers that fitted snugly over her thighs, and a cream satin shirt that clung tightly to her generous breasts. There were shadows under her eyes which gave her a haunted look. It was the sister-in-law who looked bereaved, thought Douglas; not the wife.

He stood up as she came over and shook his hand. 'How nice to see you again, Douglas – if I may call you that,' she said in her soft voice which conjured up images of sun-dappled Scottish lochs.

'I should be honoured, Mrs Cameron,' said Douglas, his heart racing so fast now that he thought it might explode in his chest.

'And you must call me Mary. Is this Sergeant Venerables?' she said, offering her hand to Venerables, who gave it a perfunctory shake, and sat down again. 'And you, Pat – how are you?'

'Oh, I'm all right, I suppose. The Chief Inspector asks some probing questions.'

'I'm sorry, Mrs McKenzie – but we have to get to the truth about your husband's death.'

'The trouble is you don't believe me when I *tell* you the truth. Mary, please reassure the Chief Inspector that Ian and I were happily married and that I don't go round chasing every Tom, Dick and Harry that comes my way. Perhaps he'll take more notice of you.' And she rose abruptly and left the room.

Mary's eyes were the colour of the sky as she turned to look at Douglas in astonishment. 'Pat's not one to play around. She's always enjoyed the company of the young. She's always got on well with Pete, for instance. He's a real charmer – he treats her like a young girl. Perhaps she's a little vain – aren't we all, Chief Inspector? But I simply don't believe there's ever been anything more to it than a bit of flirtation and friendship. I know Pat like I know myself, and she wouldn't have been capable of betraying Ian. He and Pat were an *item . . .*'

'I'm sure they were. I do apologise for upsetting your sister. These are difficult times for her.'

'I know you have a job to do, but I think Pat's taken as much as she can at the moment, Douglas. Give her a little space. Alec's coming to see her later on; he's good for her. Why don't you come back this afternoon? She'll have gathered her strength by then.'

'That sounds like a good idea. Could you go and find Wilkes, Venerables? Tell him I want to see him in a few minutes.'

Venerables nodded; obviously relieved to escape from the scene of such emotional tension, he left the room hurriedly.

Douglas turned to Mary Cameron, avoiding her eyes; he found their brilliance too disconcerting. 'Could I have a word with you . . . Mary?' he said, hesitating over the unaccustomed familiarity.

'Of course you may. But not here. We both need a break. Why don't we meet up for lunch at the Watersmeet Hotel, on the main Rothbury road? It's a glorious day. We could have our little talk over a drink. Much more relaxing.'

Douglas thought of his schedule. But Mary Cameron could be an important witness and an interview was an interview, whether one held it in a makeshift incident room, or over lunch. And ladies of Mary's ilk deserved special treatment, didn't they? He hesitated no longer. 'Thank you. I'd be very pleased to meet you there.'

'Let's say twelve o'clock, then. I'll be out on the terrace.'

Douglas, his spirits lifting rapidly, went to join Wilkes and Venerables. He was conscious of Venerables' critical scrutiny as he went into the study.

'Not much joy from those two, sir,' his sergeant said evenly.

'Oh, I don't know. I think I ascertained that Mrs McKenzie was devoted to her husband.'

'You didn't mention our friend Pete Fraser then?'

'Venerables, she's only human. Bereavement hits us all in different ways. Anyway, her sister said she simply likes the company of the young, and there was nothing serious to it. Remember, her husband was quite a bit older than her.'

'I don't share your charitable sentiments, sir. I'm always suspicious of people who fall over backwards to tell you how much they love their husbands.'

'It doesn't pay to be too cynical, Sergeant.'

'Doesn't it? I thought that's what we were paid for – not to take anything at face value.'

Douglas was nettled. 'Evidence – that's what we want, Sergeant. Not personal prejudice against defenceless women. Wilkes, get yourself down to Janice Hudson's house, and check on Kevin Fraser's alibi. Sergeant Venerables here will give you the details. I'm off to Fridale. I want to take a look at Mr O'Neill.'

'You'll get nothing out of him, sir.' Venerables was defensive.

'We'll see. After all, he wanted that manuscript badly. And he's Irish.'

'Now who's prejudiced, sir?'

'It's just that we know nothing about him. That's all.'

Venerables realised he was getting nowhere – not with Douglas in his present mood, puffed up with sexual confidence.

'Perhaps we could have a lunchtime debriefing, sir. I'm off to see Polly now. She's chasing up Alec Montgomery on the police database. I shall have to report back.'

'Later, Sergeant.' Douglas had the decency to look embarrassed. 'I'm having lunch with Mrs Cameron. At the Watersmeet Hotel. To find out the background to the McKenzie set-up.'

'Why, you've always told *me* to keep away from the lassies.'

'She's no *lassie*, Sergeant. She's a mature widow.'

'They're the worst. More experience. Mark my words, sir – she's after you.'

'You've got a dirty mind, Sergeant. I merely want to talk to her over a drink and a sandwich. It's a little more civilised than squatting in her dead brother-in-law's study.'

'That's where it all starts. Over a pint and a butty.'

Douglas snorted with indignation. 'This is a *business* lunch, Venerables!'

'Then why not interview Mrs Cameron here? Like everyone else?'

'Because she wants some privacy.'

'That's what we all want. The next thing is you'll be getting your leg over. You'll need plenty of privacy for that.'

'That's enough. Just hold your tongue, Sergeant.'

Venerables sighed. 'I'm sorry, sir. Just take care.'

'When I need your advice, Sergeant, I'll ask for it.'

Sean O'Neill's holiday cottage was at the top end of Church Lane, a stone's throw from the village shop. It was an old Northumberland grey-stone cottage, one of a pair, where generations of farm labourers had lived until a canny developer had discovered that, with a bit of modernisation, these cottages made desirable and lucrative holiday homes.

Sean didn't seem a bit worried to see Douglas. 'My, my, I *am* going up in the world! First a Sergeant, now a Chief Inspector! I must be your prime suspect,' he said drily, as he led Douglas into the main living room. It was a pleasant room, simply furnished with pine chairs and a sofa-bed. A computer and printer stood on a table against the wall and paintings of the Cheviots and Northumbrian castles decorated the white-washed walls. Although the sun was shining, a log fire smouldered in the ingle-nook fireplace: a reminder that autumn was on its way.

Douglas studied Sean closely as he went across to the table to turn off the computer. He looked every inch what he claimed to be: an academic. In his thirties, he was tall with a scholarly stoop, a lean face prematurely lined, and untidy dark hair. He looked across at Douglas with mild blue eyes.

'Any leads yet, Chief Inspector?'

'Early days, sir. The trouble with police work is that if you don't want to make a mistake you have to pursue every conceivable line of enquiry. It's hard to imagine who could have wanted Derek Fairbrother dead.'

O'Neill looked apologetic. 'Actually, I was talking about the St Frida Gospel.'

Marvelling at the merciless single-mindedness of lovers of mediaeval manuscript Douglas looked at him severely. 'Aye – we're working on that too. I understand the last time you saw it was on the twelfth of August. A month ago.'

'About that, yes. Mr Montgomery was there too. And Sister Anne, of course. I was hoping to take another peep at it, but the Sisters are mighty possessive. They kept me in suspense. Too late now, of course. They should have done what I told them to do and allowed me to ship the Gospel over to Dublin without any further ado. We would have kept a close watch on it there.'

'I daresay you would have done. But people can be mighty stubborn when something's close to their hearts. By all accounts it was a very special manuscript.'

'*Special?* That's the understatement of the century. It was priceless, Chief Inspector. A jewel. A perfect example of the Lindisfarne school of illuminated manuscripts. It's a tragedy, so it is, to have lost it. The Sisters are paying for their stubbornness now. They think it's God's way of punishing them for their sins. But what sins that bunch of holy nuns commits beggars belief. It's human fallibility that's responsible.'

'You're an expert on manuscripts of this type, sir?'

'Expert is a big word. I know a bit about them. I'm making the subject of mediaeval manuscripts my life's work. Particularly manuscripts from this period. I'm working on the link between the Lindisfarne school and the Irish school. You know, of course, that the blessed St Aidan came over to Iona from Ireland, and then went on to found the community at Lindisfarne? Well, St Frida came with him. She had been raped in Ireland by brigands, and had had a child. Her own father threw her out, but St Aidan befriended her. They were devoted to one another. St Frida founded a community of nuns on the mainland near Bamburgh and there she stayed until St Aidan died and the Vikings came. Then she headed South. It would have been better for all of us if she'd gone back to where she came from. To Ireland.'

'And been rejected by her father once again?'

'He'd been dead a long while by then. Anyway, she came here; and for centuries the Gospel remained in this village, in the safe keeping of the priest, and, later, the Little Sisters. Until now . . . These are terrible times, Chief Inspector. As bad as the Border reivers. Worse, in fact. Even they stopped short at stealing St Frida's Gospel.'

Privately thinking that it was probably ignorance rather than aesthetic scruples that stopped the Border reivers from getting their hands on the manuscript, Douglas declined to comment.

'It takes a bit of skill to break open a modern safe, sir,' he said. 'If you're going to do it quickly and quietly, without leaving any traces, you've got to know the combination. I'd like to know who knew the combination code of that safe in the sacristy.'

O'Neill cleared his throat nervously. 'Sister Anne knew it, of course. And Father Paul. No one else, as far as I'm aware. Why don't you go and ask her yourself?'

Suddenly remembering the impending arrival of the Arty Farties personified by the feeble Felicity Flight, Douglas backed off. This was none of his business any more. 'May I check on one other thing? I know my sergeant went over all this with you – I've seen your statement – but can I ask you once again to cast your mind back to Sunday morning? To the time of the procession. What were you doing, exactly?'

'I just watched it go past. I was standing outside the cottage. I watched it go up to the square, past me, then round and back towards Church Lane.'

'And you were nowhere near Derek Fairbrother?'

'No. He walked past me, on his way to the square, but on the way back I was on the other side. What are you getting at, Inspector? That someone was aiming at me, and hit Derek by mistake? In that case, the killer must have been the worst shot north of Hadrian's Wall.'

Douglas was bemused. 'That never even occurred to me, sir.'

O'Neill hesitated. 'I just thought that maybe you . . . Look, I'd better tell you. If I don't come clean now and you find out later that I've been hiding something, I know exactly what you're going to say. I know what the British police are like if they get a whiff of anything connected with terrorism.' He took a deep breath.

'When I was still at school – I was sixteen, seventeen – I discovered that a good friend of mine in Cork was getting seriously involved with the Republican struggle. He'd relatives in Belfast and they were IRA sympathisers. One of them was actually a convicted terrorist, doing time in the Maze. Well, you know how it is when you're a teenager. You're impressionable, gullible – and you're easily persuaded. My friend gave me Republican books and pamphlets to read and I got idealistic about the whole thing. I think part of it was I was rebelling against my parents – they'd have died if they'd known what I was up to. Anyway, the year before I was due to go to university I went with my friend to Belfast. And I saw for the first time the suffering and destruction that terrorism inflicts. A great city, ruled by terror – it put the fear of God into me, I can tell you. I suddenly realised what an idiot I was being, pretending that violence and murder were ever justified, and I hitched a lift with the first driver I could find who was crossing the border back to the South. Left my friend behind in Belfast – I never saw or heard from him again. I read in the paper a few years ago that he'd got involved with the Provos and had been shot dead in a pub on the wrong side of town. Anyway, when I got back home I threw all my inflammatory literature straight into the dustbin and poured all my energies into my studies – as I should have done in the first place. I became a zealot about something a lot more worthy – mediaeval manuscripts. And if anyone suggests that the Provos have been waiting for all these years to get revenge on me for somehow betraying them, then I don't believe that for one minute. For one thing, I was never actually involved – it was a lot of talking and no action for me. I was just a silly kid. For another thing, if they'd wanted to punish me, they would have come after me in Ireland before now. So now you know the whole story. And I don't for one minute believe that Derek Fairbrother was shot in mistake for me. Believe me, the Provos don't make mistakes like that. If they wanted someone dead, they do the job properly.'

Douglas exhaled. He hadn't for a minute expected this. 'I see, sir. Well – thank you for being so frank. It's much appreciated. So – we have to assume that, for some reason, someone wanted Derek Fairbrother out of the way. God knows why. He was a popular lad by all accounts – lots of friends at school, a keen churchgoer. It's a dreadful business. His parents are devastated. I suppose there's one other possibility – that we've another Michael Ryan in our midst. But men like Ryan who suddenly go AWOL don't settle for just one shot – they spray bullets all over the place, try and take out as many people as possible. I think we have to go with the theory that Derek was singled out deliberately. Now, I must leave you to get on with your work, sir. And I do appreciate your being so helpful. I know how concerned you must be about the safety of the Gospel, but rest assured – we've got the cavalry coming over from Newcastle. The Arts and Antiques Squad – it's too important a manuscript to leave to us local boys. I'm sure they'll soon have it under lock and key. One thing's for certain, though – that Gospel'll be finding a new home, whether it's Durham, the British Museum – or even Dublin. It won't ever be coming back to the sacristy of St Frida's Church.'

* * *

Deep in thought, Douglas crossed over to the church and walked round the graveyard to the small Victorian red-brick house where the Sisters lived. An elderly nun let him in and showed him to the study where Sister Anne was talking earnestly to Father Paul. They both looked up expectantly when Douglas went in.

'No news, I'm afraid,' he said feeling desperately sorry to disappoint them. 'But it's early days yet. The search is on and the specialist squad have experience of these matters. It's an international matter now. Most countries are only too pleased to co-operate over a stolen work of art. But could I just check once again . . . the safe's combination. How many people could possibly have known it?'

'Just us, Chief Inspector,' said Father Paul, his young face deeply lined with worry. 'We were the only ones who had access to it. That makes it all the more distressing. I committed the numerical combination to memory, and Sister Anne wrote it down in a safe place, just in case anything happened to the pair of us. Not even the company which made the safe knows the combination. Unless we've taken to talking in our sleep . . . and even then, there's no one around to hear us. I can't think how the thieves came to get hold of it.'

'But someone did know. And that's what we have to find out. Perhaps if you do think of something – however insignificant it might appear to you – you could let us know. Everything's useful at this stage of the enquiry.'

'We shall certainly do that,' said Sister Anne, coming forward and looking at Douglas with such trust that his heart sank. Everyone was expecting so much of him! How could he let them down?

'Meanwhile,' she went on, 'we'll all be praying for you. St Frida's on your side. She'll show you the way.'

Thinking that he was going to need all the Divine assistance going, Douglas made for the door. As it shut behind him, Sister Anne gave a start. Silently, she and Father Paul walked together to the church as Douglas drove away.

Chapter 7

Douglas had ten minutes to change his mind. As he drove towards Rothbury he could have turned east at the crossroads and returned to Reivers Hall. That was what he should have done; that was the safest thing to do. He knew that. But he didn't want to play safe, not any more. All his life he'd backed away from the murky waters of personal relationships. Trouble, he'd called them. Not for the likes of him. But now the time had come to do what everyone else did – play with fire. Not so much fire, he thought ruefully – an ageing police officer having a drink with an attractive woman hardly constituted fire – more a puff of smoke. Even so, he could hear Venerables' voice warning him to keep away from the lassies. *Stop! Think what you're doing. That first wisp of smoke soon becomes a raging inferno . . .*

He could still change his mind. He could go back to Reivers Hall, call up the hotel, and leave a message for Mary Cameron saying he had unfortunately been detained and couldn't make their appointment. He could talk to Mary later on in the impersonal surroundings of the McKenzie study-cum-incident room with Venerables as chaperone. At the crossroads, he hesitated; then he crossed his Rubicon, and turned north. Why shouldn't he have a bit of fun for once?

Minutes later he saw the sign for the Watersmeet Hotel. He turned into the drive and saw, straight ahead, an elegant white building of indeterminate vintage, with a roof of weathered red tiles and large windows gracefully draped with net curtains. He parked his car and went in. He asked his way to the terrace and looked at his watch. Dead on twelve.

Mary had beaten him to it. She was sitting at a white circular table engrossed in the *Times*. Dressed in the same casual outfit she'd been wearing earlier in the day, she looked like an exotic tropical bird. Her beautiful hair gleamed in the strong sunlight; her skin glowed with health. A bottle of white wine stood already opened in a silver ice-bucket, with two glasses ready next to it. She folded away her paper, and smiled at Douglas. It was then that he knew, without any doubt, that he was in love with Mary Cameron.

Desperately trying to compose himself, he went over to her. The terrace seemed to be bathed in an unusually brilliant light. A row of scarlet geraniums, balanced along the edge of the terrace, gleamed brighter than he'd ever imagined flowers could do. The whole garden seemed to shine with a radiance that was quite unearthly. He felt like the prince in a fairy tale, coming to claim his bride. Life was wonderful. To hell with Venerables!

Minutes later, with a glass of Chardonnay in his hand, a simple but tasty lunch ordered – Mary's impeccable choice – and shielded from the bright sun by a splendid blue-and-white striped parasol tactfully erected by an attentive waiter, he settled down to interview Mary Cameron. She was so easy to talk to, so natural, so grateful for his attention, that he felt the luckiest man in the world.

'It's good of you to spare the time to speak to me personally,' she said in her warm Highland voice. 'I know that the rank of Chief Inspector carries with it a tremendous amount of responsibility.'

'It's really more of a co-ordinating job these days. The constables do the foot work. Then they all report back to me.'

Was this really himself speaking? It seemed as if someone else, someone incisive and confident, had taken him over, making him say things he'd never said before. Not even thought of.

'Even so, it must be very stressful. It must be a relief to go home and relax with your wife. I'm sure she looks after you very well. You look so young. It's difficult to believe you're really a Chief Inspector.'

For a moment he didn't realise what she was saying. Then light dawned.

'I'm not a married man, Mary. Marriage is something I never got round to. I've always been a worker. I've got a comfortable house which an uncle left me and I've got a good housekeeper. And that's it. Marriage was never a serious consideration. Perhaps I never met the right person. Not like my sergeant, now. He's already got through one wife; and still he chases the young lassies. He never learns. But I'm sorry your marriage ended in such a tragic way. You must have gone through hell.'

'So you already know something about me, Douglas? How efficient,' she said, as the waiter brought the platefuls of fresh prawns with their shells on, and sliced avocado. Douglas gallantly attacked one of the prawns and made a hash of it; fascinated, he watched Mary's delicate fingers move skilfully over her own plate. Then she passed her plate over to him, reached across and took his. 'Charles had trouble with prawns too,' she said, smiling across at him. 'But they're so delicious – they're worth the effort.'

How considerate she was, Douglas thought, as he speared a piece of avocado.

'I'd like to hear about your husband, if it's not too painful for you,' he said. 'I really know very little about you. Only that your husband died in an accident at sea.'

Mary sat back. 'Charles was a great seafarer. He loved his yacht – sometimes I thought he loved it more than me. He took it out in all weathers. I'm a fair-weather sailor and I used to worry about him when there was a storm, or a gale blowing. We had a house in Oban, you see; that's where we kept the yacht. Charles had a flat in Edinburgh. A gentleman's *pied-à-terre*. He was the head of a firm of solicitors – his father, Gordon Cameron, founded it and Charles took over. He was a good lawyer. I met him at a weekend house party. Ian and Pat were there too – they both knew Charles and liked him. They'd been married for five years then. They sort of pushed Charles and me together. Wanted us to be as happy as them, I suppose. We were married just three months after we met. It sounds extraordinary, I know, but we were very much in love.'

Douglas didn't think it at all extraordinary. He could see perfectly well how it had happened. 'So your husband and Ian McKenzie were good friends,' he said, trying to resume a professional manner. After all, this was supposed to be an interview.

'Oh, yes. Ian and Pat, Charles and I – we were a foursome. They often came sailing with us, in fact. Remember, Pat and I are both McDonalds – the McDonalds of Skye. We are a sea people. Charles shared Ian's enthusiasm for Chinese porcelain. They had a lot in common. That's why I can sympathise so strongly with Pat now. I know what it's like, to lose a man like that. I'm glad she's got Alec nearby. He'll be a great comfort to her.'

'Did Charles know Alec Montgomery?'

'Yes, of course. The three were great pals. We called them the Triumvirate. Alec didn't like sailing, of course – he doesn't like any sport. He's much too fond of his creature comforts.'

The waiter brought the next course – venison, cooked with shallots and mushrooms – and replenished the wine glasses. Douglas thought with a sudden pang of guilt and disgust of all the platefuls of pie and chips and bacon butties he'd eaten with Venerables. He vowed he'd never touch junk food again.

'Would you like to tell me about Charles's accident?' he said gently. 'You don't have to – it's not really relevant to the present case – but I want to know all there is to know about you,' he went on recklessly. He was rewarded by one of Mary's brilliant smiles.

'How charming you are, Douglas! I knew that we were going to get on as soon as I saw you. I said to myself – here's a kind and sensitive man. Handsome, too.'

Douglas's heart melted. 'I was thinking along the same lines. Here's a good-looking woman; and what's more, she's intelligent. I like intelligence in a woman. Keeps me on my toes.'

Basking in the luxury of mutual admiration, Douglas listened to Mary describing her life with Charles Cameron, his love for the sea, his addiction to sailing solo in rough weather, whilst the sun moved across to the West, and the level of the wine in the bottle went down.

'He must have been an experienced sailor,' said Douglas, sitting back, glass in hand. 'He must have heard the weather forecast, known about the strong currents off the West Coast of Scotland.'

'He always thought he knew better. Always out to challenge the elements. He thrived on danger. The weather forecast was only for a Force Seven and the ketch was designed to sail in all conditions. It wasn't one of those fibre-glass jobs – it was a traditional wooden boat, very stable, lovingly restored by Charles. We thought it almost impossible for it to capsize.'

'And he sank off Ardnamurchan Point, you said? Did they recover his body?'

'Yes, a week later. The tide brought it in on the other side of the Point. We never recovered the yacht; the water's very deep off that part of the coast. Too deep for ordinary divers to go down. Submarines patrol close to the shore there. Like Loch Ness – it's not far from Ardnamurchan – think how deep that is. After we recovered Charles's body there seemed no point in trying to raise the boat. So there it rests, three hundred metres down.'

'There was an inquest?'

'Of course. The verdict was accidental death by drowning. Oh

Douglas, it was quite dreadful. Charles and I were so close . . . But he was always reckless. I still miss him so.'

'A terrible thing. But you must allow me to help you – if I can. I'm not good with words, but my heart's in the right place. And I must say that I've enjoyed this meal very much indeed.'

He leant across the table and put his hand over hers. It was so soft and warm that he felt he wanted to hold on to it for ever. Much to his surprise, she didn't draw her hand away.

'Thank you, Douglas. You're very kind. Perhaps we can do this again. Why not dinner next time? There's so much to talk about. So much I want to know about you.'

'Me, Mary? There's nothing about me that would be of the slightest interest to you. I'm a bachelor, set in my ways; I've been a policeman since I was nineteen. That's all there is to know. One of these days I expect I'll be made Superintendent. Then they'll decide I'm too old for the job and retire me on a police pension, and I'll live out the rest of my days in Berwick. Not very glamorous, I'm afraid. No yachts – no Chinese porcelain.'

'But you're kind, steady, and loving. That's much more important.'

'You think so? I hope I don't disappoint you, Mary.'

'I'm sure you won't. My instincts are always right.'

Douglas looked at his watch, and nearly fainted. He jumped up. 'It's half past three. It's incredible how quickly time passes.'

'Must you go? It's a lovely afternoon. The garden is so beautiful at this time of the year, and there's a wonderful walk down to where the two rivers meet. That's why the hotel's called Watersmeet.'

Douglas thought of Venerables waiting impatiently for him up at the Hall. He thought of all the work he had to do; the reports to write up, the decisions to make . . .

'It's a crying shame, but I must go.'

'I understand. You must have so much to do. But we'll see each other again, won't we? And I don't just mean at Reivers Hall.'

She got up and came round to face him. Leaning forward so that he caught a glimpse of her creamy breasts swelling out of the open neck of her top, she kissed him on the cheek.

Speechless with emotion, he picked up the bill and walked to Reception.

* * *

71

'I'm sorry I'm a bit on the late side,' said Douglas briskly as he
entered the McKenzie study. 'I got – caught up. For God's sake, look
at the pair of you,' he exclaimed, his good humour instantly evapo-
rating. 'Haven't you any work to do?'

Venerables was lounging back in an armchair, his eyes closed;
Wilkes had his feet on the desk. 'Pull yourselves together! There's
work to be done.'

'You said it, sir,' said Venerables sardonically. 'Some of us haven't
been lucky enough to take a long lunch break.'

'Surely you've eaten?'

'Aye, Wilkes and me shared a chip butty.'

'I don't like your attitude, Sergeant. I'm late because the interview
went on longer than anticipated.'

'No, sir. You're late because a lassie's been giving you the glad
eye and priming you with booze. I can smell it from here.'

'That's a damned offensive thing to say. One bottle of white wine
between two people, that's all we had. No worse than a pint down the
pub. And don't start taking liberties with me, Sergeant. Show some
respect.'

'I'm not taking liberties. I'm worried about you.'

'Then stop being an old woman. Mary Cameron was very helpful.'

'Oh, yes? What did she have to say that was so riveting?'

'It appears that her husband – Charles Cameron – and Ian
McKenzie and Alec Montgomery were all good friends.'

'And she took three and a half hours to tell you that?'

'Venerables, I'm warning you . . .'

'All right, calm down. I know my place. But, just for your information, you might like to know that Wilkes and I have been hard at it
too. Janice Hudson confirms she was indeed tucked up in bed with
Kevin Fraser on Sunday morning. Alec Montgomery seems to be
innocent as a babe unborn – Polly says he's got no police record, not
even a speeding fine. Pete Fraser recently bought himself a bloody
brand new car. A BMW. And you and me are wanted down in Fridale
at the convent. Inspector Flight wants us with her when she interviews the Mother Superior. We should've been there ten minutes
ago.'

A police car already stood outside the convent when Douglas and
Venerables arrived. The young policeman behind the wheel looked

meaningfully at them as they approached. Then he rolled down the window.

'She's waiting for you. She's a bit irate. Doesn't like being kept waiting.' He was clearly relishing the spectacle of Douglas at the beck and call of a woman.

'We can't all come running whenever she crooks her little finger. She'll soon learn.'

'I hope so, sir. For all our sakes.'

Douglas went up to the gate and walked up to the small, Victorian red-brick house where the Sisters lived. An elderly nun let them in and showed them to the study where Sister Anne was talking earnestly to a tall fair-haired lady, and Father Paul. The stranger turned when they came in, and Douglas was confronted by a pair of sharp blue eyes as bright as a summer morning, and a smooth, immaculately made-up face, framed by sleek shoulder-length hair. The grey suit fitted her perfectly, and the small brooch on the lapel of her jacket winked at him. She looked – expensive.

'At last, Chief Inspector. We've had a job getting hold of you. I'm Felicity Flight. Arts and Antiques Squad, North East region.'

'Glad to meet you,' he said, taking hold of her hand and noting the firm grip. 'I can't think why you had a job finding me. My sergeant here knew my movements.'

'Then he was very reticent.'

Douglas sent up a silent prayer of thanks for Venerables' loyalty. He smiled a greeting at Father Paul and Sister Anne, and turned his attention back to Felicity Flight.

'I was interviewing a witness, Inspector Flight. So you've met my sergeant?'

'Spoken to him on the phone. Good to meet you, Sergeant.'

'And you, Inspector – you've introduced yourself to Father Paul and Sister Anne?'

'I was just going over the same ground I know you've already been over. But I like to hear things first-hand.'

'Carry on.'

'I intend to. I just wanted you to be here for my first visit – to hand over the reins, as it were. Then you can get on with your own business.'

Douglas fought back his irritation, conscious that Venerables was watching him with an amused expression on his face. Why, the woman was a *monster*. She might be a good looker, despite her height – he'd never liked tall women – but her cut-glass voice grated on his nerves. The sooner they could get away, the better.

Inspector Flight turned back to Sister Anne. 'So – about this safe. You found it securely locked, but the Gospel was missing. And no one was supposed to know the combination apart from you and Father Paul.'

'That's right, Inspector,' said Father Paul. 'I simply don't understand how anyone else could have stumbled upon it.'

'Are you sure, Sister Anne, that you kept the combination in a really safe place? One where no one would ever come across it, not even by accident? Somewhere special to you, and to you alone?'

Sister Anne looked at her sadly. 'The safest place on earth.'

'I'll take your word for it. Now, if you can take me over to the church and show me the safe, it would be of enormous help. I'm sure you have lots of work to do, Chief Inspector,' she said, turning to face Douglas: he felt his blood pressure rise alarmingly.

'A great deal of work, Inspector. And I would have been able to get on with it much faster if I hadn't been called out here on a fool's errand to hear you ask questions we've already had answered.'

Felicity Flight was unperturbed. 'I thought this was a good opportunity to meet you and your sergeant. It's always best to meet on site, so to speak. Anyway, let's meet again up at the Hall. There are lots of things I need to ask you. Meanwhile, perhaps Father Paul could go with me to the church.'

Nodding to Sister Anne and Father Paul, Douglas left the room, followed by a quietly chuckling Venerables. Outside, he exploded.

'By God, man, that woman's got a cheek! Of all the bossy, flint-faced . . .'

'She's attractive, sir. Not that I fancy her myself. A bit too severe for me. You could give her a try, though. What you see is what you get with her. Not like that Cameron woman.'

'Leave my private life out of this, Sergeant.'

'Oh, it's a "private life" now, is it? I thought Mary Cameron was a witness.'

'And so she is. Don't you go thinking otherwise.'

Chapter 8

Back at the Hall, Douglas sat down with Venerables. 'So, what's all the excitement about Pete Fraser? Why shouldn't he buy himself a new car?'

'He's a waiter, a part-time ghillie, sir. Where's he going to get that sort of money from? Take me, for instance; twelve years in the police and all I can afford is a bottom-of-the-range Ford Escort.'

'My heart bleeds for you. He might've got a windfall.'

'Aye, and pigs might fly. If he's won the lottery, then why haven't we all heard about it? And I don't reckon he's a gambling man. He's not the type.'

'Right, then we'll have him in.'

'Where? Berwick?'

'Don't be daft, Sergeant. You can't haul someone in for questioning if their only offence is buying a new car. No, we'll interview him here. Keep it informal, but let him know we mean business. We'll tape him if he agrees. Wilkes, go and fetch Mr Fraser.'

Douglas felt the old buzz of excitement surge through his veins. Nothing much to go on – just the hint of something not quite right – but they were off. Follow that scent. See where it led to. He glanced at Venerables. They were back in harness again: a team. Personal differences laid aside. He pushed the assertive Ms Felicity Flight right to the back of his mind.

Wilkes came in, followed by a wary-looking Pete Fraser.

'Sorry to disturb your afternoon's peace, sir,' said Douglas calmly, 'but we need to go back over a few points. You won't mind if we tape this meeting, sir? Just for our records. Makes our lives easier. Saves the sergeant here from taking notes; he's forgotten how to write, we spend so much time on computers these days.'

Pete visibly relaxed. 'So you're not arresting me?'

'Good God, man, what made you think that?'

'Because PC Wilkes here was so bloody officious. If that's how you treat innocent people, then heaven help the guilty.'

'I'm sorry you objected to the constable's attitude. He's new to the Force. Put it down to over-enthusiasm.'

Douglas looked at Wilkes with exasperation. *Damn these eager beavers*, he thought. *They have to learn that you can't get results quickly.* Patience, that was what was needed. Patience and perseverance; and lull the suspect into a false sense of security. Then sit back and wait.

'Now, shall we get back to you, sir? You see, we're still quite intrigued by this anomaly in your evidence. The fact that you stepped outside on Saturday night, about the time Ian McKenzie went to his dressing room. Now, you weren't going to tell us that, until Tom Emmerson mentioned it. People who have nothing to hide don't have to lie, do they? So what are you hiding?'

'I'm not hiding anything. I told you before – I didn't think it important. I was just putting some empties outside. It's what I'm paid to do.'

'But you see, Mr Fraser, we're pretty certain that someone signalled to the killers from inside the house when McKenzie went upstairs. Gave the go-ahead, as it were. It couldn't have been a coincidence that they knew exactly when to find Mr McKenzie alone.'

'And you think that I did that? Gave the signal? Then you're all barking mad. Why should I want Mr McKenzie dead? I keep telling you – he was good to us. One of the best.'

'And what about Mrs McKenzie, sir?'

'What about her?'

'You know what I mean. I happened to see you this morning, creeping along the corridor away from her room.'

'If you think that Pat and me have something going on between us, Chief Inspector, then you're making a big mistake. Yes, I did go to her room in the early hours of this morning. She sent for me. Gave me a ring down at the cottage. She was a bit distraught and couldn't sleep. I think she needed a bit of sympathy. We've always got on, me and her. She finds it easy to talk to me. So I said I'd pop up, make her a cup of tea, have a bit of a chat.'

Douglas thought of the beautiful, self-assured woman he'd seen that morning. She didn't look as if she'd had a bad night.

'Tea and sympathy? Hmm! Well, I'll have to believe you, though there's many who wouldn't. It'll be easy to check with Mrs McKenzie later on.'

'For God's sake, I'm allowed to bring my employer tea when she wants it! It doesn't mean that I'm screwing her. And even if I was, it's none of your bloody business.'

'I agree. Except it would give you a motive.'

'*A motive?*'

'For killing her husband. For all we know, the two of you could be crazy about each other. You could have set up the whole thing so that Pat could keep the estate without losing half of it in a divorce settlement.'

'You ought to be certified. It's not like that between Pat and me!'

'Then what is it like?'

'We're friends. I told you. She trusts me. She can ring for me any time of the night or day. But not for – personal services.'

'By all accounts, you reserved those for Mr McKenzie,' put in Venerables.

Pete whirled round to confront him. 'Who's been feeding you this pack of lies? It's Mr McKenzie wanting personal services now, is it? Don't be bloody ridiculous. The McKenzies are good employers – *were*, I should say – and that's all there is to it.'

'And in any case,' said Douglas evenly, 'you've got a perfectly good girlfriend if you want one, haven't you? Irene, the Bloodworthys' daughter. She certainly likes you.'

'She's OK.'

'Then why don't you cuddle up in bed with her? Like your brother Kevin does with Janice Hudson?'

'Kev? Why bring him into this? What's he supposed to have done?'

'Nothing at all. In fact he seems remarkably good at doing nothing. He likes to lie in bed for hours on Sunday mornings, he told us. He was tucked up in bed this Sunday when all hell had broken out up here and down in the village.'

For a second, Pete Fraser hesitated. 'Lucky for him. I didn't get the chance, not last Sunday. Too much going on here.'

'You can say that again. But let's talk about your job, sir. It's a good job? Pays well?'

'Could be better. Name somewhere that couldn't.'

'But when you go out on the shoots, people slip you the odd quid, I expect?'

77

'Some of them tip. Most don't. Mean buggers, for all they're so rich.'

'Did Mr McKenzie ever pay you any overtime? Or special bonuses?'

'No. I get my pay, and that's all. I'm happy enough.'

'Very commendable of you, I'm sure. And yet you earn enough money to buy yourself a brand new BMW! That takes a lot of doing.'

'I saved up for it,' said Pete quickly.

'Did you now? You must have a big piggy bank. Best part of twenty grand, I should say.'

'I saved hard. Always wanted a BMW. And I got a good deal. It's not one of the bigger ones, in any case.'

'My sergeant here envies you. He can only rise to a Ford Escort.'

'Then he should change his job.'

'I'm working on it,' growled Venerables.

'But you, sir. I'm still impressed that you could afford a BMW.'

'I economise. I live cheaply. Kev and me don't pay rent on the cottage. It's grace-and-favour, see. One of the perks of working for the McKenzies. And we get most of our meals at the Hall.'

'Then you've got it made. You and your brother. Right – end of interview, Sergeant. And stay around, Mr Fraser. We might have to speak to you again.'

'I can't think why. I've told you all I know.'

Pete walked over to the door. His body language was tense, even angry – but he didn't look guilty.

When the door closed behind him, Douglas glanced at Venerables.

'Come on, laddie – a drink's called for.' He looked at his watch. 'Five o'clock. We can get a pint at the Fridale Arms. It'll be open all day, that's for sure, what with the press piling in, and all the sightseers.'

'I could do with a pint too, sir,' said Wilkes plaintively.

'Bad luck, Constable. You stay here – get on with the paperwork. That should lessen some of your enthusiasm.'

They took their drinks into the garden at the back of the pub, where a family party was spending the last of an alcoholic afternoon. A large dog came over and sniffed Venerables' foot, then decided that Douglas was more to his liking. He stuffed his great shaggy head into Douglas's lap and looked appreciative when Douglas absent-mindedly patted him.

'I don't trust him, sir.'

'What the dog?'

'No – Pete Fraser.'

'Neither do I. But we can't bring him in yet. More evidence, that's what we need. So far, he's only actually lied to us once that we know of, about not going outside on Saturday night. He's worked out a good story for the car. You can check with the garage tomorrow, Venerables, but I'm sure it's all above board.'

'Oh, I'm sure the car's legit. It's where he got the money to buy it from that's the dicey part.'

'All in good time, laddie. But drink up. We've got one more visit to make before we go back and get on with our reports.'

'Janice Hudson?'

'Home in one. We're both on the same track.'

'Pete did look a bit anxious-like when you mentioned brother Kev tucked up in bed with Janice on Sunday morning. There's a nasty smell coming from the Fraser brothers; and it's getting stronger. And if you don't tell that dog to bugger off there'll be a nasty smell around you before much longer.'

Douglas impatiently pushed the dog away. 'Pete and Kevin Fraser,' said Douglas absently. 'Both connected to the McKenzie household in some way. Both not that keen on being questioned. Come on, laddie, let's follow our noses.'

Bedlam greeted them when they arrived at Janice's house – on the new estate in Fridale. Janice, a pretty, dark-haired girl, dressed in tight-fitting leggings and T-shirt, opened the door, glanced dismissively at their identity cards, and led them into the kitchen. Three women sat in one corner, smoking, while a half-dozen excited children chased each other round the kitchen table. One sat all by himself watching a video, which seemed to Douglas to be inappropriately violent for a child of his age. Plates of half-eaten sandwiches stood on the table, together with the remains of bowls of crisps; wrapping paper from chocolate bars was scattered everywhere, like so many exotic butterflies. A puppy sat in a corner savagely chewing someone's trainer. A child, wearing a paper hat and waving a plastic sword, attacked them as soon as they walked in.

'Brett, stop that!' screamed Janice, frantically trying to grab hold of him. 'He's a demon today. Comes of being a birthday boy.'

'That's all right,' said Douglas, dodging out of the way of the sword. 'We'd like a quick word with you, if we may. Perhaps we could go somewhere a bit quieter?'

'There's only the hall.'

'That's fine.'

'Not you, Brett. You stay here. Sylvia, could you sort him out?'

They went back into the tiny hall, while Sylvia slammed the door on Brett's vociferous objections.

'We're just checking, Mrs Hudson—'

'Call me Janice. Everyone does. And I'm no Mrs.'

'Janice, then. We want a bit of information on Kevin Fraser. Are you quite sure he was here with you on Sunday morning?'

'Why do you keep on about Kev? I've already had that bloody constable banging on about him. What's he done all of a sudden? Of course he was here. My mum had Brett, and we had a lie-in. Don't get much chance these days. It's like a madhouse here all week, or hadn't you noticed?'

'And what time did he leave?'

'He stayed here until around eleven. We got to bed late on Saturday night because of the disco, so we made up for it on Sunday morning.'

'Are you quite sure of this, Janice?' said Venerables.

Janice turned and treated him to a scornful smile. 'Of course I am. I'm not that stupid. I always know who's in my bed – and when they leave.'

'I'm glad to hear it,' said Douglas, intervening. 'Thank you very much for your time. We've heard all we need to know.'

'It must be something important, to make you come checking on me twice. You'll see yourself out, will you?'

They left the chaos behind them and walked down the path to the car. Suddenly, Douglas caught a glimpse of a twitching net curtain in the front window of the house next door. He looked at Venerables, who'd also noticed it. Nosy neighbours could be a godsend. Quickly, they walked past the car and into next-door's garden. Douglas rang the doorbell. A small, tight-lipped, middle-aged woman opened the door.

'Can we possibly have a word with you, ma'am?' said Douglas, turning on the charm and brandishing the ID.

She studied him doubtfully for a moment, then led them into a tidy sitting room. Douglas took in the velvet three-piece suite, a fitted shagpile carpet, the wall lights with pink frilly shades like little girls' party dresses. It was stiflingly hot.

'Are you friendly with Janice Hudson, Mrs . . . ?'

'Mrs Thoroughgood. I know her by sight, Chief Inspector. I couldn't say we are friends.' She looked disapproving.

'How about her boyfriend?'

'Kevin Fraser? He's a real tearaway. She ought to know better. She's got one fatherless brat – a right little horror – you'd think she'd have more sense than to get herself involved with a chap like Kevin. At least that Jock – him who owns the house – had decent manners.'

'Does Kevin stay there often?'

'He takes his turn.'

'Meaning . . .'

'When he's not there, there's usually a replacement. A lot goes on in that house after dark. She's not too fussy.'

'Do you know if Kevin stayed there last Sunday?'

She paused for a few moments, then smiled a tight little smile.

'Oh, yes, Chief Inspector. He stayed there all right. They didn't come in until the early hours and there was a fine old racket going on. The walls are very thin, you know.'

'Did you see him leave?'

'Can't say that I did. He usually stays around for a while on Sunday morning. They seem to loll around in bed till lunchtime, leave little Brett to his own devices. But this Sunday, funnily enough, they didn't.'

'How do you know that, Mrs Thoroughgood?'

'Well, come nine o'clock Janice was in the garden pegging out the washing, Sunday morning and all. Now, she'd not do that with Kev there. She was fully dressed too. So – no lie-in today, I thought.'

'Thank you, Mrs Thoroughgood. You've been most helpful.'

Back in the car, Venerables shook his head in disgust. 'Nosy old bitch. I can't abide women like her.'

'I love them, laddie. Eyes in the back of their heads.'

'I suppose you're right. But why did Janice Hudson lie? What's Kevin Fraser up to? This smell's become a stench, sir.'

'You can smell it a mile off. One more false statement from either of the Fraser brothers, and we'll have them in.'

'Can't we get them in now, sir?'

'Not yet, Sergeant. Patience. Wait till we've got it all stitched up tight. We'll get there – and soon. I have the feeling.'

'I hope Blackburn shares your sentiments.'

'To hell with Blackburn. He's stuck up in Berwick. He's no right to lord it over us.'

Back at the Hall, they made their way to the study. The door of the sitting room opened, and Mary Cameron emerged.

'Douglas! Still hard at work! How tired you must be.'

'It's my job, Mary.'

'Any – *leads* is the correct word, isn't it?'

'The plot thickens.'

'I hope you're not so busy that you can't take time off tomorrow to have dinner with me? All work and no play makes Chief Inspectors dull boys . . .'

Douglas turned away to avoid Venerables' knowing smile. But he couldn't repress the surge of joy that made his heart beat faster.

Chapter 9

He recognised the signs. If he kept on like this, Douglas thought, Blackburn wasn't likely to make old bones. Overweight, tense, he was sweating, although the room was cool at eight o'clock in the morning. Sitting behind his desk, fiddling endlessly with the pile of papers in front of him, continually rearranging a row of biros, he finally sighed deeply and stared irritably at Douglas.

'It's Tuesday, McBride,' he said. 'And still there are no proper leads. Suspects? Who are they? Where are they? As far as I can tell from the reports your team have filed, several people could have a motive for committing either of the murders, and robbing the nuns for good measure. Come on, man, for God's sake. I've got the press hounding me. They want a statement at twelve today, but what the hell am I going to say to them? "We've got everything under control;" "the police are pursuing several lines of enquiry;" "we'll be back to you when we've got something to report." The usual fudge.'

'It'll do for now. It's early days yet,' said Douglas philosophically.

'*It'll do*? Sometimes, McBride, I think we'd all be better off if you took early retirement. The Fairbrothers were on TV last night. They made a great impression. Mrs F in floods of tears, Mr F complaining that the police were doing nothing and that everyone seemed more interested in St Frida's Gospel than in the death of their son. The phone hasn't stopped ringing here. Everyone wants an arrest.'

'Then they'll have to wait. Better to wait until we're quite sure rather than arrest the wrong person and have hell to pay later. There'll be no quick arrest in this case. *Either* of these cases. The answer to McKenzie's death – let's call it murder number one – lies buried in his life at Reivers Hall. The solution to murder number two could be linked to murder number one; and the theft of the manuscript is linked to both. Probably. Possibly. We can't be sure at this stage. Anyway, Inspector Felicity Flight is sorting out the burglary. We can leave it in her capable hands.'

Blackburn snorted and glared at Douglas. 'Are you being sarcastic, Chief Inspector?'

'Not at all,' he said mildly. 'Inspector Flight is a very – positive lady. I'm sure she'll keep us all in order.'

'We're lucky to get her.'

'Anyone working for the Knocker Squad deserves our respect, sir.'

'*Knocker Squad?* By God, you've got a nerve, Inspector.'

'Knocker, as in knocking on people's doors, sir.'

'You don't have to explain police slang to me, McBride. But let me tell you that Felicity Flight's not one of your run-of-the-mill police officers. She's a high-flyer. You could take a leaf out of her book.'

Douglas decided it would be more tactful to backtrack. 'You mustn't let the media get to you, sir. They're just a pack of bloodhounds looking for someone to tear to pieces. You know it takes time and tact to get the right man. Wilkes is already rocking the boat with his gung-ho questioning. Put the pressure on and people clam up.'

'No need to teach your grandmother to suck eggs, McBride. Let me tell you, the days of leisurely enquiries over dinner are over. Today, people want to see justice done – preferably live on TV – and done speedily. Get the bastards who did it banged up behind bars.'

'You talk of justice, sir. What if we're not sure? What if – God forbid – we bang up the wrong people? That's not justice. That's giving in to mob rule. You know that's not the way. Tried and tested methods are uninspiring and slow and they're not telegenic. But we've always got there in the past. We've never made a mistake.'

Blackburn stared stonily across at Douglas, his breathing rapid, his face flushed with anger.

' "Uninspiring" and "slow" are two words which make my blood boil. Just don't say them to the pack of wolves outside. Now, if you please, man, give me a resumé of the Reivers Hall affair and make it anything but slow and uninspiring. Two minutes: that's all you're allowed. Start with the chief suspects.'

'Difficult to say at the moment, sir. The obvious ones are all squeaky-clean—'

'For God's sake, use your brain, McBride! Start with the wife. Did she want her old man out of the way?'

'I very much doubt it, sir. We don't know the contents of the will yet, but I'll bet that everything's above board. Why should she murder her husband? By all accounts he was only too happy for her to lead her own life.'

'Then who's this fellow who keeps turning up in the statements? Pete Fraser? Is he her lover?'

'Perhaps. But even if he is, Pat wouldn't have McKenzie murdered so that she and Pete Fraser could run off into the sunset together. That's not her style. It's not a grand passion between them. Love, lust, lucre; those are the motives for murder. And usually all three rolled into one.'

'And loonies,' said Blackburn sardonically. 'Don't forget them. The jokers in the pack.'

'No loonies here, sir. Just human wickedness. Original sin, if you like.'

'I don't like, McBride. Neither does that rat pack out there. The way they carry on, anyone would think we're the murderers. But let's get back to Fraser. There's an inconsistency in his statements, I see. All this nonsense about not thinking that putting out bottles counted as going outside. It sounds a load of rubbish to me.'

Douglas ventured a smile. 'That's quite witty, sir.'

'*Witty*? My God, McBride, anyone would think you're at a cocktail party rather than leading two bloody murder investigations! Watch those Fraser brothers. Something's not quite right there. Get to the bottom of it.'

'That's what we're trying to do, sir.'

'Keep hammering. Wear them down. Get them to spill the beans – if there are any to spill. Who else have we got?'

'In connection with murder number two, there's no one we're close to bringing in for questioning yet. Who'd want to kill Derek Fairbrother? There's no motive, no motive at all.'

'Unless, as has been suggested by Mr Alec Montgomery, someone wanted to create a diversion and run off with the manuscript. Who's this Irish chap? Sean O'Neill? I don't like the sound of him. What's he doing over here?'

'Sean O'Neill has every right to be here. We can't arrest him because he's an Irishman and likes old manuscripts.'

Blackburn got up and walked impatiently over to the window. Outside the police station, the road was blocked with cars, TV vans and journalists, all poised to go out live on the next broadcast.

'Damn them. They put us under unbearable pressure . . . What am I going to tell them, Douglas?'

Douglas felt a sudden, unexpected wave of sympathy for his superior. *He's lonely up there at the top*, he thought, *and he's fretting*.

'Tell them the truth. That we're doing all we can. Make them see that we can't risk charging the wrong man and that we're at an early stage of the enquiry. Say we're following up several leads and we'll be able to tell them something soon.'

'Make it very soon, for God's sake, McBride. Otherwise they'll have my guts for garters.'

'Be firm with them, sir. That's all that's required. And don't let them get you down. Now I must get back to the Hall, if that's all right by you. I can't be away from the incident room for too long.'

Blackburn turned round. 'Douglas – be careful. I've heard on the grapevine that you're getting your head turned by Mrs McKenzie's sister. Is that right?'

'Who's been gossiping, sir? Surely there's no harm in me talking to Mrs Cameron? She's a key witness, after all.'

'No harm at all. But, you silly old fool, she might turn out to be a suspect; and then where will you be? We know nothing about her. You mentioned motives; what's her motive? Why should she want to butter up one of my more mature Chief Inspectors?'

'Sir?' exclaimed Douglas, mortified.

'Oh, don't take on. I'm just being realistic. By all accounts she's rich and good-looking. She'll not be that desperate for company.'

'So that's it, is it? You're implying that a woman would have to be desperate to look twice at me?'

'Don't be childish, McBride. I'm only asking you to back off. Remember your position. You're leading two murder investigations; and I'm not happy about that, as you know. But I have no choice. You've got a lot on your plate. Just let go. Let Venerables deal with the Cameron woman. He's got a bit more experience than you when it comes to the lassies.'

I'll remember your advice, sir,' Douglas said stiffly. But he

86

refused to say he'd follow it. It was none of Blackburn's business, anyway.

Blackburn flicked down the text on his computer screen. 'Alec Montgomery. A good friend of McKenzie's – and keen on manuscripts. What've we got on him?'

'Not much so far. Polly Stride's working on him, but she seems to have drawn a blank.'

'Then take him by surprise. Ask him about his dealings with the McKenzie household. See what he says. Do anything you like – but lay off Mary Cameron. Or you'll live to regret it. And I don't want to lose you at this stage of the enquiry.'

Douglas left the police station by a side door and slipped over to where he'd parked his car: outside his house, which overlooked the ramparts down to the estuary of the River Tweed. The fine autumn weather was breaking up. Clouds were rolling in, and the sea looked troubled. He looked up at the solid, granite walls of his house, built to withstand the onslaught of time; strangely, they looked dull and inhospitable. For once, he felt no thrill of pride of ownership, no desire to stay. The pull was coming from the South, from Reivers Hall. He got in his car and headed towards the A1, glad to leave Berwick behind.

'Let's go for a wee stroll, laddie. There are too many ears listening in the incident room.'

'How was the Chief?' asked Venerables, as he fell into step beside Douglas. There was no sign of the fine weather breaking up here. The sun shone, the rowan trees were on fire with masses of scarlet berries, and the heather-covered slopes trembled with the onslaught of bees as the two men walked down the steep path towards the lake.

'He's getting edgy. Heading for a heart attack, if you ask me. The press are badgering him.'

'Same old story. Sometimes I feel sorry for journalists, mind. They've got pages to fill in their newspapers every day. No wonder they end up writing drivel most of the time.'

'Well, they've two juicy murders to get their teeth into at the moment.'

'*Very* juicy. Have you seen today's headlines?'

'I haven't seen a paper yet.'

'Drag Millionaire: Kinky Accident Ruled Out.'

'God, it makes me sick. What's Pat going to feel when she sees that? Besides, I don't think McKenzie was a millionaire.'

'He lived in a big house, and that's good enough for them.'

'Drag Millionaire. Why, Venerables? Why? Who'd want to do that to a corpse? Someone hated him, that's for sure. Now why do people hate one another, Sergeant? Who do you hate, Venerables?'

'No one, really. But I can imagine – anyone who cheated on me. Or stole Polly. I'd feel like killing them, right enough.'

'So – money, sex – that's it; and it's all up there in that house.'

'And who's at the centre of it, sir?'

'That's for us to find out . . . We ought to get back to the village. And God knows what was the motive for killing Derek Fairbrother. Money? Sex? Doesn't sound likely. Maybe it *was* a mistake.'

'Aye, it could be. And we've not got a clue as to who was the real target. Could've been anyone in that crowd. Good luck – and don't cross lines with Ms Flight. She'll not stand for that. Oh yes, while you were cruising along the A1 in that Volvo of yours, I've done some research on Fraser's car. Don't get excited. It was a straightfor-ward cash sale.'

'I don't like it, Venerables. Keep an eye on him. Shall we meet at twelve thirty? Fridale Arms?'

'Sounds good to me.'

They turned round and began to climb up towards the house. 'Oh – a letter for you, sir. From your lady friend.' Venerables took a letter out of his pocket and handed it to Douglas. 'Aren't you going to read it?'

'All in good time, laddie.'

'Sir – don't do anything I wouldn't do.' Venerables' face was kind.

'That gives me plenty of scope.'

'I mean it, sir. Sex and money, you said. Well, Mrs Cameron's got both. And you know nothing about her.'

'Enough of this!' Douglas snapped. 'You sound like Blackburn. Mary's a widow lady, devoted to her husband's memory, and she's on our side.'

'If you believe that, sir, then – I'll say no more.'

* * *

Mary's letter burned like a hot potato in Douglas's pocket, but he resisted the temptation to stop and open it. *Concentrate*, he told himself. *Finish the job. Get down to the square; go back to the scene of the crime, talk to Father Paul. Then, and then only, allow yourself the luxury, the pleasure, of reading the letter.*

He was surprised to see the police car parked outside the church. Sitting next to the driver was a smart woman with blonde hair, talking intently into her mobile. It was too late for Douglas to pretend he hadn't seen her. He parked his own car, and walked towards her as Felicity Flight finished her call and got out of the police car to wait for him.

'Hello, Chief Inspector. We meet again.'

'You'd better call me Douglas if we're going to see a lot of each other.' He was aware that he sounded churlish.

'And my name's Felicity.'

'Bit of a mouthful.'

She raised her eyebrows. 'It's the name I was born with. My friends call me Flick.' She didn't give any hint as to whether Douglas might fall into that category.

Douglas, remembering Venerables' previous remark, grinned despite himself. 'Flick suits you, lass. But I think I'd better stick to Felicity for the time being. So, are you always going to travel round in chauffeur-driven cars? We don't have that luxury.'

'Only today. Tomorrow I'll get round under my own steam.'

'Learned anything so far?'

'A long way to go yet, I'm afraid. The nuns are wonderful. So unworldly! I've had a chat with all eight of them.'

'I see. And no one knows anything about the safe combination, I suppose?'

She stared at him for a few seconds, then her eyes flickered with amusement.

'No one, Chief Inspector? Oh, I think that's a bit of an exaggeration. Not only do all the nuns know where Sister Anne keeps the code, but it wouldn't surprise me if the whole of Northumbria were in on the secret. Sister Anne kept the combination number in what to her, as she said, was the safest place of all. A holy place. Sacrosanct.'

'You don't mean to say she wrote it down on the fly-leaf of her Bible?'

'Almost. She wrote it on the inside cover of her prayer book – the one she takes to church for the Daily Office. It never leaves her side – so she says. But when I pressed her she admitted she sometimes leaves it in the church unattended.'

'I just can't believe this. How could she be so stupid, so careless—'

'Naive's the word. She never thought anyone would want to rob them of their precious manuscript. Why would they? Thieves and Gospels don't go together in her world.'

'Good God, woman, you've uncovered a right hornet's nest! What are you going to do next? Trace everyone who might've had access to Sister Anne's prayer book? It'll take you years.'

'I'd rather you called me "Flick" than "woman", Chief Inspector McBride. I don't like being patronised. And you can forget the "lass" as well. And pass the information on to your sergeant, if you please.'

'No need to take offence. Girls are always lassies up here.'

'OK. Then I shall call you "laddie". That's Northumbrian too. And yes – I do agree it's going to be a long haul. I shall have to rely a lot on her memory. Unfortunately, her memory's not her strong point.'

'Let me know if we can help.' Douglas felt conciliatory. 'Why not come and join my sergeant and myself for a bite to eat at the Fridale Arms? We usually meet up at this time.'

'Thanks, but I never eat lunch. I'll get back to Newcastle, see my colleagues, and then go for a jog.'

'Don't tell me you'd rather jog than eat a proper meal?'

She laughed, and her blue eyes lit up with mischief. 'Of course. Isn't that what all lady detectives do? You ought to take more exercise, Douglas. It clears the mind remarkably. You could come with me one day, if you like. But you'll need some trainers. Bye for now. I'll be around.'

Before he could answer, she got into the car, spoke to the driver who turned to grin knowingly at Douglas, and then they were away. He watched them drive off into the distance. Trainers? Jogging? He shuddered. *That'll be the day*, he thought.

Sister Anne looked out of her study window, and watched the police leave. Everyone was being so helpful! The lady detective had been especially nice. But so many questions – so many things they wanted her to remember. It was all so confusing. So difficult to think straight. But there was something she should have told the Inspector. Something that might be relevant. After all, she had been told that everything, however inconsequential it appeared, could be useful. It all helped to build up a picture, she knew. Then the bell sounded for midday service, and she pushed the thought to the back of her mind. She got up, picked up her prayer book, and walked across to the church.

Still reeling from his encounter with Felicity, Douglas took immediate refuge in the Fridale Arms. There was still several minutes to go before half past twelve. He bought himself a pint and took it across to a table in the corner. He looked quickly round to make sure he was unobserved. Then he took Mary's letter out of his pocket and began to read it. It was warm and loving, and Douglas felt his spirits lift. She wanted to see him tonight, for dinner, at a little restaurant tucked away on the edge of the Cheviots. Dunmoor Chase. She'd even drawn him a little map. *Well, why not?* he thought. He deserved a break . . .

'If it's not our Chief Inspector, drinking on duty,' said a voice from the next table. Douglas hastily stuffed Mary's letter in his pocket and glanced across at Tom Emmerson, part-time waiter at Reivers Hall. Pushing aside all thoughts of Mary Cameron, he beckoned him over.

'Come and join me. Same again?'

'Why, thanks.'

Douglas caught the barman's eye. 'You a regular customer?'

'Most days I drop in for a pint around this time. I'm back at Hunters now for the evenings, when I'm not wanted up at the Hall. And now Janice has pretty much shacked up with Kev I'm not too fond of working up there any more. Pete gets on my nerves too. What with buttering up Pat McKenzie and now floating around in his new car, he thinks he's way out of my class.'

'I thought you got on with Pete,' said Douglas, making signs to the barman to put Tom's drink on his bill.

'Cheers, Chief Inspector. I wish more coppers were like you,' said Tom, taking a swig out of the pint which the barman had brought over to the table. 'I used to, yeah. But he got a bit too big for his boots, see. I ended up doing more than my fair share of the work.'

'I suppose he had his own fish to fry?'

'You can say that again. The times I've had to cover for him . . .'

'Why, what was he up to?' said Douglas amiably.

'Oh, someone was always asking for him.'

'You mean when Mrs McKenzie sent for him?'

'Mr McKenzie, more likely.'

'And what exactly did Mr McKenzie want with him, now?' said Douglas, intently studying Tom's pale, shifty-looking face.

'I'm not telling. It's more than my life's worth.'

'Did Mr McKenzie ask for services of a personal nature? Come on, Tom lad – was McKenzie into fancy boys? You can tell me that, surely? You've told me as much before, up at the Hall. After all, he's dead. There's nothing to fear. Maybe that's where Pete's got his money from, eh?'

The insipid eyes flickered, then shifted over to the door as Venerables came in.

'Just in time, Sergeant,' said Douglas jovially. 'Meet Tom Emmerson. He was helping out up at the Hall the night Ian McKenzie died. Get yourself a drink, man, and come and join us. Stick it on my bill.'

'That's very generous of you, sir.' Venerables went over to the bar, got himself a pint, and slid up on the bench next to Douglas. The bar was filling up and Tom, helped by a couple of pints, was visibly beginning to relax.

'Now, about these fancy boys . . .'

Venerables choked on his beer. '*Fancy boys*, sir?'

'You could call them that, I suppose,' said Tom thoughtfully. 'Fancy boys, rent boys – it's one and the same thing.'

'And you were one of them?'

'Me? Never! I'm not like that. Besides, McKenzie never fancied me.' Tom looked wistful, perhaps imagining the BMW that could have been his had his personal charms been a little more enticing.

'But he liked Pete?'

'Oh, for sure. Not that Pete'd grant him his favours that often – he preferred girls. But he knew some who didn't.'

'And where would he find them, Tom? Surely not here in Fridale?'

'All over the place. I know he often went to Grimsby.'

'Grimsby?'

'Lots of young men out of work. The trawling industry's folded. When there's no jobs, people get money where they can.'

'So Pete procured young men for Mr McKenzie?'

'Procured? I'm not sure what that means. Pete introduced him to friends, that's all. Now sir, I must be off. I'm only supposed to take a half-hour break.'

'Tom, wait . . .'

It was too late; Tom had realised he'd already said more than enough. He dashed off, waving hurriedly to the landlord as he went out.

'You came on a bit strong there, sir,' said Venerables. 'Seem to have frightened him away.'

'He's a blabbermouth. And after only two pints of brown! We'll have another go at him later on, get him a bit more drunk. He could be very useful. But what's new up at the Hall?'

'Nothing much. Bloodworthy says Pete is seeing too much of our grieving widow, and shouts at him for parking his BMW next to the McKenzies' Rolls. But what about you, sir?'

'Detective Inspector Flight's on the warpath. It seems the world and his wife knew where Sister Anne kept the combination for the safe.'

'You've been chatting up Felicity Flight?'

'No need to look so surprised. She's a colleague, isn't she? Oh, by the way, she asked me to tell you that she doesn't like being called "lass".'

Venerables whistled. 'Every girl's a lass to me.'

'Not if they're feminists, they aren't. However, whatever she likes to call herself, she's found out that Sister Anne keeps the most important piece of information she's ever likely to handle in the inside cover of her prayer book – which, by the way, she occasionally leaves behind in the church.'

'Then dozens of people could have seen it. So – do you think this blue-eyed lass is capable of finding the Gospel?'

'Oh, she's capable all right. Likes to jog in her lunch-hour. Cast aspersions on my mental faculties. Mark my words, laddie, she'll end up Chief Constable – and soon, by the look of it.'

'No harm in having a bright lass on the job.'

'She seems to have made a favourable impression on you, Sergeant. And you were right – she likes her friends to call her Flick. With a "k".'

Venerables looked pained; the wind had clearly been taken out of his sails. 'Have you read your letter, sir?'

'That's my business, Sergeant.'

'It'll be Blackburn's business if you go out with that woman again.'

'Watch your mouth, Sergeant.'

'Seems like I ought to be watching yours. Anyway, time for a cheese toastie?'

'Aye, I'll join you.'

'On your bill, sir? Seeing as how you're in a generous mood.'

'I only pay for cheese toasties if they're in the line of duty. This one's on you.'

It was late when Douglas arrived at Dunmoor Chase, an exclusive small hotel noted for its fine cuisine. It was an hour's drive away from Reivers Hall, along narrow roads, up steep hills with precipitous summits. The hotel was tucked away in the centre of a pine forest and seemed specifically designed for romantic assignations.

Douglas, feeling excited and reckless, parked his car. This was living! This was what everyone else did. Maybe he was a bit long in the tooth and on the staid side, but there was always a first time for kicking over the traces. It was a dark night, the moon disappearing sporadically behind clouds which were building up from the North. A hunting owl swooped low over his head as he made his way to the front door. A fox coughed from a nearby thicket. And Douglas felt as if he were embarking on the biggest adventure of his life.

Inside the hotel it was warm, softly lit, sumptuously furnished. Mary was waiting for him in the lounge. Seeing her dressed in a clinging black dress with a plunging neckline, decorated with necklace and earrings that glittered in the soft light, Douglas was thankful that he'd found the time to change into a newly cleaned, light grey suit. He'd even dug out his one silk tie, given to him by his married sister last Christmas.

A fine malt whisky soothed his nerves. He found himself dishing out compliments, smiling affably at waiters. He felt like a different person. Mary guided him skilfully through the unfamiliar territory of a sophisticated menu and he tackled fresh oysters and wild boar with gusto. Over the port and Stilton he told her about himself: his upbringing in an Edinburgh manse; his regular church attendance;

94

and then his act of rebellion when he went into the police rather than follow his father into the Presbyterian ministry.

'My sister got away from Edinburgh as soon as she could,' he said, as the waiter removed the cheese.

'What happened to her?'

'Oh, she went off to Oxford. Read English, married a publisher. She lives in Surrey now. We keep in touch, sporadically. We exchange presents at Christmas, cards on birthdays – that sort of thing. I expect she'll come to my funeral.'

'Don't talk of funerals! You're still a young man.'

'I don't always feel like it. A lot of the time I feel like an old stick-in-the-mud lecturing my superintendent on the virtues of patience and perseverance in police work. A plodder, when I should be taking risks. I've never travelled in the fast lane, Mary.'

Mary leant towards him and put her hand over his. Douglas felt a sudden rush of desire that left him breathless. Would she smile like that, he thought, if he took her in his arms and kissed her? The idea sent his head into a whirl and he was appalled to find his body coming alive in parts which he'd hardly bothered to notice for years. He squirmed with embarrassment. Mary gave another of her soft, intimate laughs.

'But you must never take risks in police work, Douglas dear. In your personal life, yes, that's all risk; but you won't catch criminals that way.'

'Mary, I've never taken a risk in my life,' said Douglas, basking in the warmth of the endearment.

'Then it's time you started, Chief Inspector. And what's more, I've got a surprise for you . . .'

Chapter 10

The bed in Dunmoor Chase's bridal suite was a modern four-poster with soft clusters of peach-coloured net curtaining gathered together at each corner and tied with a satin ribbon. Underneath the canopy, folds of satin had been neatly arranged in tidy pleats, coming together in a central medallion like the underside of a giant mushroom. Someone had drawn the curtains; someone had turned on the bedside lights; someone had turned back the satin bedspread, revealing two soft and inviting pillows. Douglas took off his shoes. Through the connecting door he could see the bathroom softly lit from tiny lights in the ceiling; their reflection glinted like stars on the gold taps of the double-sized Jacuzzi bath.

Mary emerged from the bathroom, kicked off her shoes, and went across to Douglas. Gently, she removed his tie and laid it on a chair. Her eyes twinkled with mischief.

'Take your coat off, Douglas. Don't be shy.'

Gazing at her flushed and beautiful face, Douglas obliged. Smilingly she came into his arms. He breathed in her scent of honeysuckle and wine, buried his face in her soft curls. Never had he been so intoxicated; never had his body felt so alive. She slipped down the thin shoulder-straps of her dress and Douglas cupped his hands over her smooth, firm breasts. Lifting his head, he looked deeply into her eyes.

'Mary, my love, I have spent my whole life looking for you. Show me what I have to do.'

'Douglas, darling, just relax and enjoy me.'

Speechless with emotion, he bent down and kissed each breast in turn. He could feel her body respond to each caress; he knew that she wanted him. Together they fell on the bed, and with a quick, sinuous movement, Mary slipped out of her dress. Somewhere a window banged, the wind was rising, a dog barked. But it felt to Douglas as if the world belonged to them alone. No one else existed; nothing else mattered. He revelled in the warm smoothness of Mary's body; he found her lips and kissed her deeply. She tasted exquisitely of wine and warmth and desire. Hardly aware of her movements, he felt his shirt flutter to the floor. Then her hands began to caress his body and her mouth searched out the sensitive parts of his throat and chest. His body tingled with sensations he had never felt before, had never known existed.

'Oh, Mary, my beautiful love. I love you. Make it last for ever, my darling,' he heard himself say.

Then he felt her hands on the zip-fastener of his trousers. He reached up again and kissed each breast, hanging over his face like shining globes. His trousers followed his shirt and he took her in his arms once more, frantically kissing her face, her breasts, her firm belly. Her hands were everywhere, caressing his back, her fingers curling round the hairs on his chest, then stroking his penis which seemed to have a life of its own, something quite outside his control. She stroked and caressed him with her hands, her whole body, and he felt the world dissolve into one huge throb of desire. He pulled her to him, cradled her in his arms and rocked her like a child. She led him down to the secret place between her legs and he knew she was ready. Then the world exploded around him in a blaze of glory.

'My darling Mary,' he whispered as the tension mounted to an unbearable level, 'you are the most wonderful person I've ever known.'

They climaxed, gasping in each other's arms, and slowly, slowly, Douglas came down from cloud nine and his heartbeat steadied. He looked down into Mary's face. Her eyes were shut; there was a look of peace on her face. Douglas, having felt such intense pleasure, was grateful that she too had felt the same.

When he opened his eyes, daylight was already filtering in through the curtains. For a moment he had no idea where he was. Then he felt Mary next to him; her face on his pillow. Filled with a tremendous glow of satisfaction, he turned his head to look at her. How beautiful her face was in sleep, flushed, satiated, mouth slightly open, hair tousled. She looked like a picture he'd once seen in an art gallery in

Edinburgh of a saint in ecstasy. To Douglas, the image seemed wholly appropriate. She'd taken him to heaven last night; and what's more, he was hoping she'd take him there again.

A knock on the door brought him down to earth. 'Come in,' he managed to say. A waiter entered, carrying a breakfast tray. Douglas caught the aroma of coffee, and the welcome fragrance of bacon and eggs. He saw two tall glasses of fruit juice on the tray and a vase containing a half-opened scarlet rose. He glanced at his watch on the bedside table and sat up abruptly, waking Mary, who yawned and stretched like a contented cat. The waiter put the tray down on the table and went out without speaking. He clearly knew what was expected of him in the circumstances.

'Is it morning already?' she said sleepily.

'It's half past seven. Wake up, my love; it's breakfast in bed today.'

It was sheer bliss to eat breakfast with Mary sitting beside him. It was bliss to bath together in the huge whirlpool bath. It was misery to get dressed and think of the day ahead.

'Mary, I shall never forget last night and this morning. I shall never be able to thank you for everything you've done . . .'

'I've done nothing.'

'You booked this room, ordered dinner and breakfast – even down to the rose on the tray – and you've shown me how to . . .'

'You didn't need any showing. You were *wonderful*, Douglas.'

He felt such a surge of happiness that he wondered how he was going to get through the rest of the day without seeing her.

'When are we going to meet again, lass?'

'Soon. Let's just play it by ear.'

'Tonight?'

'Let things take their own course . . . What's on your agenda this morning, Douglas?' she asked as he started to get dressed.

'I want you to marry me, Mary.'

She laughed softly. She picked up her hairbrush and began to tidy her unruly curls. 'That's not what I meant, Douglas. I was asking what you were going to do today.'

'Marry me, Mary.'

'Marriage is a big word, Douglas.'

'Aye, so it is. But this is a big thing that's happened to me. I'll not be the same person from now on. Up to now, I've led a boring and utterly predictable existence. I've been alone. But you've changed all

99

that. You've shown me what's possible. I'm not a bad proposition, lass. I've got a house in Berwick, and a police pension waiting for me—'

'Don't let's be practical right now, love. Let's just enjoy the moment. We can work something out later.'

She put the hairbrush down and came over to kiss him. The bath-towel slipped off her shoulders and he saw again her beautiful breasts. His body responded and he felt his face flush; playfully she pushed him away.

'Chief Inspector! Control yourself. We have all the time in the world. Right now you've a murderer to catch, and I must get back to Pat before she thinks I've deserted her for good.'

'Aye, it's back to work for me, I'm afraid. But I'll be back, Mary. You may be sure of that.'

Reluctantly Douglas left her. He called at the hotel reception, only to discover that Mary had settled the bill in advance. So he drove off towards Fridale. He felt rejuvenated, brimming over with energy; a new man, on the brink of a new life. But his old life was still making urgent demands on him. He had a call to make – and old family friends were always a good source of information.

Still in a daze of happiness, Douglas drove off to Montgomery Hall. Alec, dressed in a blue silk dressing gown, opened the door.

'Not too early for you, sir? I only want a few minutes of your time.'

'Come in, Chief Inspector. You've got a job to do, and we all want to see Ian and Derek's killers behind lock and key. I seem to be much in demand lately. Your charming lady detective came to see me last night.'

Douglas gave a start. Flick wasn't letting the dust gather. He hoped she hadn't queered his pitch.

Smiling affably, Alec led the way into the kitchen, where he was obviously enjoying a leisurely breakfast.

'Any news yet?' he asked as he poured Douglas some coffee.

'Nothing definite. Early days,' said Douglas, gratefully sinking into platitudes. 'But the net tightens. Day by day suspects are elimi-nated, leads followed up. That's how it works.'

'And the finger of suspicion is pointing where, Chief Inspector?' Alec's voice was dispassionate, mildly amused.

'Too soon to talk about fingers of suspicion, sir. Most of our work at the moment is simply routine checking on people's stories.'

'Well, I must say you're a model for us all. I wish I could look so cheerful at nine o'clock in the morning! It takes me until midday to wake up properly. Mind you, Detective Inspector Flight looked as fresh as a daisy last night. A remarkable woman.'

'She wanted to know more about the manuscript, I suppose,' said Douglas, curious. 'She knows how cut up you are about its loss.'

'Yes, she was most sympathetic.'

'I'm glad to hear it. I know she'll do her best to get a result.' Douglas leaned back in his kitchen chair. 'I must say, I envy you this beautiful house. It's what most men only dream of. You must be very pleased you moved here, away from the London rat race.'

'Oh, I'd hardly call Chislehurst part of the London rat race. Admittedly, I used to commute to the City, but only after everyone else had started work. I was lucky enough to avoid the rush hour. And when I came back in the evening my mother always had a meal ready for me. She was devoted to my interests, I'm afraid. I suspect I was dreadfully spoilt.'

'It sounds to me as if you had it made, sir. Nice place, Chislehurst. I once met a friend at that pub on the Common – when I was on a course. Let me see, what was it called—'

'The Tiger's Head? That's a popular meeting place.'

'That's it! Did you live anywhere near there?'

'Just a short walk away. Prince Imperial Road. You might know it, Chief Inspector?'

'Can't say that I do. Did you always live there?'

'Oh, my mother liked it there. Nice neighbours. Do you take sugar, Chief Inspector? I'm sure you have a demanding day ahead of you, and sugar is good for energy . . .'

Douglas noted the abrupt change of subject, but decided to let it pass. He added two knobs of brown sugar to his coffee and absent-mindedly began to stir them in. He was finding it difficult to concentrate on what Alec was saying; more than anything he wanted to dwell on his thoughts of Mary, and what had happened last night. But years of self-discipline stood him in good stead and firmly he pushed Mary's image out of his mind.

'One good piece of news, Chief Inspector. I learnt from Inspector Flight last night that Durham's offered fifty thousand pounds to anyone who recovers the Frida Gospel. The thieves would never be able to sell it on the open market and fifty grand's a tempting offer.'

'I'm surprised Durham's got the money, if by Durham you mean the Cathedral Treasury.'

'The Goldberg Art Insurance firm have stepped in to fill the breach. They're very sound. Part of the old insurance company which I used to work for, in fact. It's in all our interests, of course, to have the Gospel back in safe-keeping.'

'Good news indeed. Unless the thieves have already got rid of the manuscript.'

'I sincerely hope not, Chief Inspector. I am trying very hard not to think of that possibility.' And Alec shuddered.

Douglas wanted to move away from the Gospel – that was Ms Flight's territory. 'Been up to the Hall recently, sir? Mrs McKenzie values your support, I know.'

'She's fine, considering what she's going through. I'm very fond of Pat.'

'I'm glad to hear it. Just one thing – as you are an old family friend, did Mr McKenzie ever discuss his will with you? It's just that we haven't yet been able to track it down. Mrs McKenzie has no idea where it might be. Presumably it's at Reivers Hall somewhere. We'll be able to check it out with her solicitors later, of course, as soon as it turns up, but it might save us a bit of time if you knew the main provisions. And if you could tell me the name of the family solicitors I'd be grateful. Mrs McKenzie was rather distressed when I last spoke to her – I didn't get as much information as I needed.' *And I was a bit preoccupied by her delightful sister*, Douglas added mentally, staving off pangs of guilt.

'I'm only too glad to be of help. They used Cameron, of course. Charles Cameron was both a relation by marriage and the family's legal adviser. His brother Bruce runs the firm now. It's still called Gordon Cameron and Sons, after the father, who founded the firm in Edinburgh. But under Ian's will Pat gets everything, of course. Ian told me that much. The house and the estate. Not that there will be a great deal of capital, I'm afraid. Ian was a big spender. Lived life to the full. Never bothered to provide for the proverbial rainy day.'

'I am surprised, sir. His lifestyle seemed to suggest an inexhaustible supply of funds.'

'His father left him a wealthy man. But Ian got through most of it. And the Hall costs a fortune to run. It's a bit of a millstone, really, but Ian would never consider opening it to the public, or turning it into a hotel, or making people pay for shooting parties. Oh, no. He was above all that. Then there were the foreign holidays, the villa in Provence . . .'

'They owned a place out there as well?'

'Yes, still do. Pat'll get it now. And the vineyard. It produces an excellent grape. That claret you doubtless drank last Saturday night, that came out of the McKenzie vineyard. I'm sure that when probate's out of the way Pat and Mary will be off to the South of France, and Reivers Hall will have to look after itself. And, who knows, I might just join them,' he said, placidly placing the last blob of marmalade carefully on the last piece of toast.

'You, sir?'

'Oh, yes. Pat will need someone out there to advise her. She hasn't a clue about money. A darling, but hopeless when it comes to practical matters. And let me say, Chief Inspector, but I have – expectations in that direction. Not yet, but . . . Soon Pat will be looking round for Ian's replacement. A woman like her won't remain single for long. And I think I've got a chance.'

'I didn't think you were the marrying type, sir.'

'That's only because I never found anyone who really attracted me. But Pat's different.'

'You'll be lord of the manor, sir. What with Montgomery Hall and Reivers and a vineyard in Provence, you'll be able to enjoy the life of Riley.'

'More likely I'll be taking on a cartload of debt. But I'm more realistic than Ian. I'd turn Reivers into a hotel. It wouldn't be a bad life.'

'Not bad at all. But I thought you said there was no money. Converting large stately homes into hotels costs a bomb.'

'That isn't a problem for me, Chief Inspector. My money – and the McKenzie name. It's what I've dreamed of.'

'I envy you, sir. And I hope it all works out for you. But you mentioned Mrs Cameron – she'll be accompanying her sister to the South of France, you say?' Douglas's mouth was dry.

'Mary? I'm sure she will,' said Alec, getting up and tidying away the cups and plates. 'She'll be off like a shot. She'll have no ties in England now Pat's free to leave. And there's a chateau waiting for her out there.'

'A *chateau?*' said Douglas, his heart turning a violent somersault.

'Oh, yes. There's a wealthy Frenchman waiting for her, out in

Provence. He's been pursuing her ever since Charles died. Funny thing, he's called Charles too: *Charles Le Duc*, that's what the sisters call him, although his real name is something d'Angoulême. Very aristocratic. Related to the French royal family, I believe, or what remains of them. He's not a bit like Charles Cameron, though. Le Duc is smooth-tongued and a handsome devil; the first Charles was on the rugged side in more ways that one. Le Duc owns acres of vineyards in Bordeaux. Mary's keeping him dangling – she tends to play hard to get. However, Pat's told me that she's finally decided to have him, so it'll be goodbye to plain old Mary Cameron, and welcome to the Duchess of Angoulême.'

Douglas put his coffee cup down carefully on the fragile saucer. His heart felt as if it were being attacked by a horde of demons armed with sharp knives. The pain was so intense that he almost gasped out loud. With difficulty, he managed to control himself.

'It seems to me, sir, that McKenzie's death did you all a good turn.'

Alec looked surprised. 'Oh, don't misunderstand me, Chief Inspector. We're all appalled by Ian's death. Such a tragic way to go. Shameful. But life must go on . . .'

'Aye, and you'll make sure it goes in your direction. Good luck with the grieving widow, sir.'

'Pat's not the grieving type. One door closes, another opens, where she's concerned. She's a survivor. But Ian was always a dear friend to me, Chief Inspector. I would never have betrayed him.'

'But now he's no longer around, you'll try your hand at a bit of courting?'

'Really, Inspector, you make it sound so blatant! I intend to be much more subtle.'

Douglas couldn't stop himself probing the wound, like a tongue exploring an abscessed tooth. 'Perhaps the sisters will have a double wedding.'

'I doubt it. Pat will have to wait for probate to clear, so her affairs can be set in order. Nothing like that to stop Mary, of course. She may feel that sooner would be preferable to later. The first Charles spent money like water – mostly on his yacht – and they had a big place in Oban, as well as the flat in Edinburgh. There was precious little left to her in his will. She had to sell the Oban house to pay off his creditors. But Le Duc will straighten her out. Meanwhile, a bit of old-fashioned wooing of the widow is called for. When she's ready.'

'She'll not be too hard on you, I think, sir. After all, she needs the money too, if what you say is true.'

'So you are a realist after all, Chief Inspector. I had you marked down as a bit of a romantic.'

'A romantic fool, most likely.' So had others apart from Venerables been observing his rapid slide into a hopeless love? His utter surrender to a woman who saw men as no more than cash cows? Had Venerables been right all along when he warned Douglas against Mary Cameron?

With his mind in turmoil, Douglas drove to Reivers Hall. Mary in love with a Frenchman with a bloody stupid name! It wasn't possible. Last night she'd told him she loved him. Hadn't she? At any rate, she'd shown that love in the most intimate way possible. She'd said she wanted to see him again. But he was assailed by doubts. She'd prevaricated when he'd suggested another meeting. He'd asked her to marry him; and she hadn't accepted. She'd shied away from any proper declaration of love between them. What had she really felt when he kissed her and stroked her body? Dear God, was it possible that she hadn't felt anything at all?

Arriving at the Hall, he sat in the car for a while, staring numbly out of the window. He no longer noticed the lake, the beautiful shrubs in their autumn blaze of glory. He saw only Mary's face as she lay beside him that morning. He saw her body as she slipped out of her dress. All this she'd done for him – not for some bloody Frenchman. Montgomery had got it all wrong. Perhaps Le Duc was a family joke between the sisters. Perhaps he was in reality a fat, old, garlic-eating roué who'd been chasing after Mary for years; someone she despised. He'd have to see her, ask her for the truth, clear up all his doubts and suspicions. Then another idea came to him. Perhaps Montgomery had been interested in Mary at one time and she'd given him the boot. *Hell hath no fury*, he thought. And now Montgomery wanted to blacken her name, ruin her chance of happiness, the real, true happiness which only he, Douglas, could give her. *Damn Alec Montgomery*, he thought with a surge of murderous rage. *He'll learn that he can't slander a beautiful woman and get away with it.*

A knock on the car window brought Douglas down to earth. Venerables was looking at him anxiously; he wound down the window.

'You all right, sir?'

'Of course I'm all right! Why shouldn't I be?'

'We were worried about you.'

'For God's sake, stop nannying me, Sergeant. I've been interviewing Montgomery.'

'You didn't tell me, sir, did you? We've got to know one another's movements, otherwise we get in a muddle.'

'Are you teaching me my job, Sergeant? I'm coming in to write up the report.'

'No time for that, sir. There's been a call from Berwick. Blackburn wants to see you. Now.'

Chapter 11

'I'll not beat about the bush, McBride. Do you deny that you spent last night with Mrs Mary Cameron?' said Superintendent Blackburn, at his most explosive.

'I'll not answer that, sir. It's my business, and no one else's.'

'Oh, yes it bloody well is. It's everyone's business at this stage of the investigation. I warned you about Mary Cameron. Until the case is closed she is out of bounds. We can't have senior police officers cavorting around with key witnesses. My God, McBride, I would never have expected this of you. Here you are, knocking on fifty, in the running for Superintendent if you crack this case – and you go and mess it all up over a bloody woman.'

'I've told you – Mrs Cameron and I are friends. There's no rule saying that I can't take a friend out to dinner.'

'But it didn't stop there, did it, McBride? Everyone up at Reivers Hall knows that you spent the night with Mary Cameron at Dunmoor Chase and that you didn't get back until this morning. Damn it, man, credit us with a bit of sense! Everyone knows that it doesn't take twelve hours to eat a meal. And I can't see you and Mrs Cameron playing Scrabble into the wee hours. So we must assume the worst. Now, what I am *really* interested in is, not your love life, but the reason why an attractive woman goes to all that trouble to soften up an officer who is leading the investigation into her brother-in-law's murder. There's only one answer, isn't there? And you're too besotted to see it.'

'She might just happen to like me, sir.'

'*Like* you? Don't be a bloody fool,' roared Blackburn, 'She's been buttering you up, that's what she's been doing, and looking at you now, sitting there with that smug, stubborn look on your face, she's damn well succeeded. She wants you off the scent, that's what she wants. She's hiding something, McBride, and you're too damn smitten to see it. She's got you just where she wants you.'

'And you're talking nonsense,' said Douglas recklessly, too hurt and angry to care what he said. 'Mary's a kind, wonderful person and I—'

'Don't give me that crap. I can't believe you'd risk your career for a few hours between the sheets.'

'It's not like that, sir,' said Douglas, incensed. 'It's far more than that to me. As a matter of fact, I've asked her to be my wife.'

'Then you must've gone right out of your mind. I suppose she turned you down?'

'She said she wanted time to think.'

'That's what they all say. It amounts to the same thing in the end. God, what a blithering idiot you are! I suppose you really believe that woman's fallen in love with you. I feel sorry for you, I really do. Everyone knows you've been taken for a ride.'

'Who's everyone, sir? My sergeant?'

'Venerables? He's the only one who's got a good word to say for you. No, Mary Cameron told her sister Pat, who reported it gleefully to one of the waiters, and round it went, until even the kitchen maid's laughing at you. Then Wilkes confirmed that you didn't come back to the Hall last night, so we are left in no doubt as to where you spent the night. It just won't do, McBride.'

Mentally cursing Wilkes and his keenness to do his duty, Douglas, deeply mortified, stared stonily at Blackburn. 'It was my free time, sir. No one expects us to work all night. I was back on duty by eight o'clock. I interviewed Alec Montgomery on my way to the Hall.'

'No one's got any free time on a murder hunt. All police leave's cancelled.'

'Everyone's got to sleep some time or other.'

'But not with witnesses, I'm afraid. I'm sorry, McBride, but there's only one course of action left to me. You're off the case. Chief Inspector Walter Willoughby's joining us from Durham CID. Get yourself as far away from Reivers Hall as possible. I'm sure you've got some leave due. And don't come back until we've closed the case. Get lost, Douglas, old chap. If you behave yourself, I'll see to it that you're reinstated. Willoughby will have taken over by now, so get into your Volvo and head off in any direction you like. As long as it's not West to Reivers Hall.'

'I've got to see Mary, sir,' said Douglas desperately.

'Oh, no, you haven't. I warn you – keep away from that place.'

'I must also see Venerables. Several things emerged from that Montgomery interview. I'm on the scent now, sir. It's not fair to take me off the case.'

'Let me be the judge of that, McBride. Write a report for Venerables to study. Now, be off with you.'

It was useless to argue; Douglas knew that. He'd seen several of his colleagues fall from grace in the past, he knew the form. But one thing he was certain of. Despite Blackburn's disapproval, he had to see Mary.

Douglas arrived at Reivers Hall just as Mary was climbing into her white sports Mercedes. He felt like a voyeur as she slid behind the wheel. She was dressed impeccably; her beige linen trouser suit and emerald-green silk blouse set off her copper-coloured hair to perfection. There was a golden quality about her that morning. He could almost smell her perfume. If he shut his eyes, he could feel the satin softness of her body—

He parked his car and walked over to her as she started the engine.

'Don't run away, Mary. I need to talk to you,' he said as she leant across to switch off the ignition.

'Not now, Douglas. Can't you see I'm going out?'

'You're not going anywhere until we've had a little talk.'

He took hold of her arm and gently but firmly pulled her out of the car. Then he steered her across to the stone balustrade which ran along the terrace in front of the house. He stared unseeingly at the terraced gardens dropping down precipitously to the river, which tumbled over waterfalls and rocks to the lake in the distance. On the horizon, the mighty summits of the Cheviots formed a dramatic backdrop to the human drama which Douglas was beginning to suspect was no more than commonplace.

'Last night, Mary, you and I went to bed together. We shared our bodies in the most intimate way two people can. Remember?'

'Of course I do. We had fun.'

'Is that all it was? Fun? Am I nothing more to you than a passing ship? Nothing permanent – just a wave of a hand and you're off? I realise that my talk of marriage was a bit premature – a silly romantic notion rising from the heat of the moment – but my feelings for you are genuine. I think you're the most beautiful person I've ever met, and I can't get over my luck at winning you. I might be old-fashioned, but in my scheme of things, when two people go to bed together that means there's something between them. Something a bit more serious than just – having fun. I thought you felt the same way. Mary, tell me straight. Did you feel anything at all for me last night? I must know.'

It was strange how clear-headed he felt at that moment. The anger was still there – the hurt, the embarrassment – but above all he had to know the truth. Only then could he take up the reins of his life again, however painful living with reality might be.

'As I said Douglas, marriage is a big word. I've got to have time to consider it.'

'But I imagine you didn't take long to consider the Duc d'Angoulême?'

'Who told you about him?'

He watched as her face flamed in anger and consternation. So he'd hit the nail on the head; Montgomery had been right.

'Never mind who told me. But it's true, lass, isn't it? I can see it in your face.'

'I'm fond of Charles, yes – and it would be to my advantage to marry him—'

'I'm sure of that. I understand he's got more than a house in Berwick and a police pension – but let that be. What I can't understand is why you bothered to bed a middle-aged policeman.'

'I like you, Douglas. You're kind and trustworthy. I thought we might have a good time together.'

'Is that so? And I also happen to be leading the murder investigation into Ian McKenzie's death. Now, which of those things persuaded you that I was worth bedding?'

'You've got it all wrong! If you think that I would stoop to sleep with you because I wanted to influence you in any way, you're mistaken.'

'I don't think so, Mary,' he said quietly. 'I think you knew exactly what you were doing. But things don't always go the way you want them to. You wanted to – butter me up, and you succeeded. But you also succeeded in getting me removed from the case. And now you're left with Chief Inspector Walter Willoughby. Are you going to try and butter him up too? If so, I ought to warn you that

Willoughby's a tougher proposition than me. To start with there's a Mrs Willoughby, who's the very devil when she thinks her Walter's up to something behind her back. She's not too keen on letting him off the leading rein. No sharing a Jacuzzi with our Walter, I'm afraid.'

'I'm sorry, Douglas. I never realised—'

'Oh, yes you did, lass. You just got yourself hoisted with your own petard, that's all. What was going on inside that pretty head of yours last night? Were you thinking, *soften up the old fool? Get him on our side?* Is that what this is all about? If it is, then I am going to find out if it kills me what's really going on. What is it you're trying to hide, Mary? You and your sister? We'll get there in the end, you know. Once the police start an investigation, they never give up. Whoever's in charge. Good luck with Willoughby. He'll be a difficult nut to crack.'

'I don't give a damn who's on the case! Very soon I'll be leaving the country—'

'And that's where you're wrong, lass. Take one step towards a port or an airport and you'll be arrested. You might think you've made a monkey out of me, but all you've really done is to draw attention to yourself. My superintendent's convinced that you must have something to hide if you went to all that trouble to seduce an old fool like me. You've done it now, lass. And until this case is wound up, you stay put. You'll have to sweat it out at Reivers Hall.'

'I've nothing to hide.'

'That's for Willoughby to find out. As for your Duke, I'd like to see the look on his face if anyone were to tell him where you spent last night.'

'You'd never tell him!'

'Don't worry – I'm not the kiss and tell type.'

'You wouldn't dare. As the lawyers say, it's a case of *quid pro quo*. You tell Charles, and I'll make a phone call to your superintendent.'

'Don't waste your breath, Mary. He knows the worst. It's all water under the bridge now. From now on I'm just Douglas McBride, not worth seducing.'

'I'm sorry I've blotted your copybook. Professionally speaking.'

'That doesn't matter one jot. What matters is what you've done to me. For a moment I really thought you were what I've been looking for all my adult life. A soulmate. I've never been good at relationships, but in you everything seemed to come together. It appears I was wrong. You took me for a ride, lass. An enjoyable one, I admit; pity we didn't agree on the destination first.'

'Don't upset yourself, Douglas. You're really very sweet; and not bad in bed. For an older man.'

'And you – for a mature woman – have a lot going for you. Good luck with French Charlie.'

He turned away before he said things he'd regret later. The truth stared him in the face. Mary had used him, and, though he knew thousands of people had suffered in the same way since man first walked the earth, it hurt.

He walked back to the Hall and into the incident room. He saw Venerables, and WPC Polly Stride, deep in conversation with Felicity Flight; Douglas gave a start when he saw her. She was really getting her feet under the table. Already he was beginning to feel superfluous, discarded like an old sock. He noticed Wilkes over by the window, staring at a computer, and behind his desk was a tall, well-built man with an exuberant outcrop of beard. Douglas, who knew Walter Willoughby by sight, nodded in his direction.

'McBride? Good day to you. I'm sorry to hear . . .'

'Oh, let it be, man. I'm sorry too. But it's time I had a change of scenery. A word with you, Sergeant,' he said to Venerables, who was looking at him mournfully.

'He reports to me now, McBride,' said Willoughby stiffly.

'Don't get irate – I'm not poaching on your patch. I just want a private word with Sergeant Venerables. And let me remind you that I may be off the case, but I'm still Chief Inspector McBride to you. I'm not defrocked yet.'

Venerables got up and they went out on to the front terrace. There was no sign of Mary, and the Mercedes had gone.

'God, sir, I'm right sorry all this has happened. I did warn you . . .'

'I know, I know. Don't rub it in. And take that hangdog expression off your face. It doesn't suit you. Listen – one or two things have cropped up. I might be a romantic old fool, but at least I've learnt something from my experience. Keep an eye on the ladies, Venerables. Mrs Cameron knows more than she's prepared to let on. I think it's possible she knows who wanted Ian McKenzie out of the way, and why. McKenzie and her husband, when he was alive, were buddies. Perhaps something went on between them.

'And watch Montgomery. He's got plenty to gain from McKenzie's death. You know the expression *cui bono* – who benefits? That's the key to this case. Montgomery admits he's got his eye on Mrs McKenzie and this place, and McKenzie's villa and vineyard in the South of France. He also knew Charles Cameron. The Triumvirate. That's what they were called. Three men. Two of them dead, one alive. And that one looks pretty pleased with himself.'

'Why don't we bring him in?'

'It's too soon. Physical evidence is what we need, and that's just what we haven't got.' Suddenly, he remembered his interview with Montgomery, when Montgomery'd quickly changed the subject at the mention of the road in Chislehurst where he'd lived, and he, Douglas had been too bemused over Mary Cameron to take him up on it. But now things were different ... 'Get Polly back on to that database. Tell her to contact all the local estate agents, and London ones, if she has to. She might have to refer to the Land Register. Tell her to find out the names of all the people who bought and sold houses in Prince Imperial Road, Chislehurst, over the last six years. Especially a single man selling an inheritance.'

'It's a crying shame you're off the case, sir. Walter Willoughby's a damn fool. He's already saying that he feels confident we'll be in a position to make an arrest by the end of the week.'

'I've heard he's an arrogant bastard. But he'll learn. All he'll do if he goes too fast is get the press excited and end up with egg all over his face. Watch the Fraser brothers, too, Sergeant. I've got a hunch they'll lead you in the right direction.'

'What about the manuscript, sir? What's happening on that front?'

Douglas shrugged. 'I'm sure Felicity's got it all under control.'

'Watch out. Here she comes.'

'I hope I'm not interrupting things, but – a word with you, Douglas. Before you leave for the Bahamas,' she said, as she walked over to join them. She looked cool and confident: Douglas felt even more like an old horse put out to graze.

'News travel fast,' he said, fighting back a bitter retort. 'I don't think the Bahamas is on the cards just yet, though. Something tells me that I'll be better off if I hang around this neck of the woods. But good luck to you all. Willoughby, Wilkes, Venerables and Flight. Sound like a good team to me.'

'We'll miss you, Douglas. And I mean that. I feel sure that you'll be back before long. We can't afford to have someone with your expertise and intuition off the case right now. And whatever anyone says, you've done us a good turn in – interviewing Mary Cameron.'

'Interview!' snorted Venerables.

Felicity raised one elegant eyebrow. 'Let's call it – an in-depth interview. You've helped us enormously. Mary Cameron is a suspect now. Why should she go to all that trouble to ensnare our Chief Inspector if she's innocent? Sorry, Douglas – no offence meant. She might just have wanted a good time; it's understandable. Douglas is a good catch. But it's much more likely that she wanted to distract his attention from someone or something.'

Was he hearing correctly? Was this woman, with her brittle self-assurance, actually paying him compliments? Or was she just drawing subtle attention to the fact that he was a fool and past it? He stared at her indignantly, but in those penetrating blue eyes, softened by kindness, he could see no malice.

'Many thanks for those kind words, Inspector Flight. You've helped me make up my mind. I think I will take that wee holiday – but North of the Border. Ardnamurchan Point, to be precise.'

'A wee spot of fishing'll do you good, Douglas,' she said, smiling sweetly. 'And please, do call me Flick. I know you're not used to dealing with women as equals, on a professional level at least, but let me tell you that on this case, being female is an advantage. Sister Anne talks to me freely – I doubt she'd do the same for you. It's easier for her to take me into her confidence, and something of interest has come up – Oh, hell, here comes the bearded one. Worried to death in case we're talking about him behind his back. Well I suppose he ought to hear this.'

Chief Inspector Walter Willoughby came out on to the terrace and walked purposefully over to them, his large face a mass of suspicion.

'What are you all up to out here? For God's sake, there's no time to waste gossiping. We've got work to do. You can say your good-byes to McBride later.'

'In fact, Chief Inspector, we were discussing the case. I was just saying,' said Felicity, evenly, 'that something has come up on my side of the investigation that might be of importance.'

'Then don't stand out here blethering away. Come inside.'

'I'd like Douglas to hear it. Before he leaves.'

'Oh, it's Douglas to you, is it? You're turning into a ladies' man, McBride. Don't forget you're off this case.'

'He's not going until he hears what I've got to say, Chief Inspector,' said Felicity firmly, taking control of the situation. 'Calm down, both of you, and listen to what I've got to say. I went back to talk to Sister Anne to follow up on my previous interview.' She turned to Willoughby. 'The problem of the safe combination not being secret after all – I expect you've read the notes? Anyway, when I arrived, I had the distinct impression that the old girl looked guilty. Like a naughty child. Well, we chatted away and suddenly she said she'd "just remembered something". She'd obviously realised she couldn't lie to me any longer. One day, about two weeks ago, she caught Sean O'Neill in her study. The safe was open, and he'd got the precious Gospel out. He was kneeling there, studying it. Can you believe it? He said he only wanted to take a look at it – after all, it's his passion, isn't it? That's what Sister Anne said, anyway. She told him to put it back. He did, immediately. He apologised profusely. Then she locked the safe and they left. She thought no more about it. She trusts O'Neill; still does. She won't hear a word against him.'

'Good God, what bloody fools these holy people are! They're not to be trusted with the week's shopping, let alone priceless manuscripts. This clinches it. Sean O'Neill. I knew it! I thought he sounded fishy. All that stuff in your notes, McBride, about being a teenager IRA firebrand. The Irish are all the same! Blow us all up, given half a chance. Let's get on to him, Sergeant,' he said, turning to Venerables, who was looking glumly at Douglas. 'I'm off to the Irish bastard's house, and I'll want you with me.'

'I don't think you should be too hasty, Walter,' said Douglas, seriously alarmed. 'And I suggest you keep your prejudices under wraps. O'Neill is a genuine lover of mediaeval manuscripts. He's an academic, an enthusiast. It's quite understandable that he should want to take a look at the Gospel by himself. And given that where Sister Anne keeps the combination number appears to be common knowledge, it's not surprising that he should seize his chance to take a wee peek at it.'

'When I want your advice, I'll ask for it, McBride. Don't talk to me about being hasty. At least I know where to draw the line between work and pleasure. Are you ready, Venerables?'

Venerables shrugged his shoulders in resignation, and set off after Willoughby.

'Good luck, sir,' he said, pausing by Douglas. 'We'll keep in contact, won't we?'

'Of course. Let's say I'll phone you each day as near to twelve thirty as possible, at the Fridale Arms.'

'Investigation by remote control, eh? I've never done that before. It's not going to be too easy, having two masters.'

'We must keep together. I'm damned if Willoughby's going to upset the apple cart at this stage.'

'Don't worry, Douglas,' said Felicity, intervening. 'I'll keep an eye on our Walter. He's not going to interview O'Neill unless I'm present for starters. We don't want that young man to take fright and disappear, not if he really does know something about the Gospel's disappearance. Enjoy your holiday, Douglas. Remember to send us a salmon.'

With a broad smile at Douglas and a cheery wave to Venerables, she was off. Venerables glanced at Douglas in appreciation. 'Now there's a girl . . . Are you really going up North, sir?'

'I'm thinking of it, yes.'

'Then take care. You've ruffled a few feathers round here, and you won't have me to look out for you.'

Chapter 12

It felt strange to Douglas to be back in the city where he'd spent most of his formative years. So much was familiar: the sturdy outline of St Giles's Cathedral; the tall granite buildings with their strange mediaeval turrets; the narrow wynds with their steeply descending steps and the maze of tiny passageways at the bottom. Douglas had driven all night from Reivers Hall and had arrived in Edinburgh in the early hours of Thursday morning. He'd booked into a small guesthouse halfway down one of the wynds in the old city, conveniently near the office of Gordon Cameron and Sons, Solicitors, where he'd arranged an appointment with Bruce Cameron at ten o'clock that morning.

It was all so familiar, yet he felt a stranger. Like feeling lonely in a crowd of friends. What had happened on Tuesday night with Mary had left its mark on him. He felt bruised, humiliated. But in a strange way he was also beginning to feel grateful for what had happened; he had tasted the food of the gods and survived.

Bruce Cameron was a dapper little man in his early forties. Neatly dressed in a dark suit with very shiny black shoes, his face smooth and unlined, he emanated brisk efficiency.

'Chief Inspector! What brings you up here?'

Knowing that he was going to have to lie through his teeth, Douglas took a deep breath. 'As I told you on the phone – we're in the middle of an investigation, sir, concerning the death of one of your clients. Mr Ian McKenzie. It's a bit like fitting together a jigsaw puzzle and it's just possible one of the pieces might be up here . . . This is a family firm, I understand?'

'I'll be very pleased to help if I can. Dreadful business. Yes, the firm was established by my father back in the twenties. My brother

Charles was head of the firm until his tragic death five years ago. Then I took over.'

'You must miss him. I've heard he was a fine man. I've met his widow – Patricia McKenzie's sister – and she told me a lot about him. She seems devoted to him still. No question of anyone taking his place. Funny business, him dying like that. Didn't it surprise you that such an experienced sailor would take the risk of going out single-handed in a Force Seven gale?'

'Force Seven's all right when you know what you're doing. But it can be lethal when you run into trouble. Large waves build up out in the Atlantic and come pounding in towards the rocky shore. There are plenty of wrecks along that coast to warn people what the sea can do.'

'And your brother's boat was well-founded, by all accounts?'

'Oh, yes. Charles loved that old tub of his. Took excellent care of it. But it's easy to be thrown off balance in a high sea and get tipped over the side.'

'No safety lines?'

'Charles never bothered with those.'

'Sounds a bit foolhardy.'

'He was the devil-may-care type. Couldn't be bothered with rules and regulations.'

'A bit on the arrogant side?'

'You could say that, yes. Always thought he was above ordinary mortals, that's for sure, at least where sailing was concerned. Never took a yachting exam in his life. Completely self-taught.'

'Must have caused Mrs Cameron a bit of worry.'

Bruce gave a short laugh as he rearranged the pile of papers in front of him. 'Mary? Oh, he didn't bother himself much with her.'

'What do you mean?'

'I suppose I shouldn't be telling you this . . . The fact is, that there wasn't a lot of love lost between Mary and Charles, whatever she might say. They pretty much led their own lives. Charles liked his yacht; Mary was mighty fond of some French Duke, a handsome devil by all accounts. He's loaded – she's been chasing him for years. The trouble with Mary is that she hasn't got any money – Charles spent it all, only left her his car – and she's getting a bit long in the tooth for the romantic stakes. I suspect the Duke may have found newer, more fertile pastures.'

Douglas did his best not to smile bitterly. 'And Mrs McKenzie?

I'd heard rumours that she might find a second husband in Alec Montgomery.'

'Alec? Well, that would be extraordinary. Now I come to think of it, he might think he'd nothing to lose if he married Pat McKenzie. He'd finally get his hands on Reivers Hall. And he's always got on well with Pat. Big responsibility, though – both house and woman.'

'You know Mr Montgomery, sir?'

'I wouldn't say "know". I've met him once or twice – he used to come up here with Patricia and Ian. It always seemed an odd friendship. Alec was always the City gent; Charles a bit on the wild side; and Ian the conventional squire. Alec was Ian's financial adviser; not that he ever took much notice of him. It might have been better for Ian if he had. There's not many McKenzie assets now apart from Reivers Hall and the estate in France. It'll be a millstone round Patricia's neck until she sells it – which she ought to do if she's got any sense.'

'Mr Montgomery thinks it will make a fine hotel.'

'Does he now? And I expect he wouldn't mind running it.'

'Does Mrs McKenzie inherit all her late husband's estate, I wonder? We haven't yet laid eyes on a will.'

'I can't answer that at this stage. I'm waiting for Patricia to find the will and send it to me. But, judging by Ian's past intentions – and he did consult me from time to time about his will – she'll probably inherit the lot, apart from a few minor bequests to friends.'

'Like Mr Montgomery?'

'Possibly. As I said, there wasn't a lot to leave; Ian McKenzie spent money like water. Anyway, money's not all that important to Alec. By all accounts he's a wealthy man.'

'If Charles, Ian and Alec were so different, how did their friendship develop?'

'Common interest, I suppose. Ian and Alec were great antique collectors. As I'm sure you know.'

'And Charles?'

'Not on quite the same scale. Whatever Charles bought, he bought on impulse and sold the following week at a loss. He was a pretty poor speculator. Never studied the market. Now, is there anything else you want to know?'

'You've been most helpful.' Douglas decided to risk it. 'I suppose the records of Charles Cameron's death will be at the Procurator Fiscal's?'

'Yes, you could take a look at them, although you won't learn much. Accidental death by drowning – a straightforward verdict—'

'I know they recovered the body.'

'The body came to them, in a manner of speaking. It was washed up on the north side of the Point, brought in by the tide. No signs of any violence on it except what the sea and the sand and the stones did to him. So you can quell your policemanlike suspicions.'

'And the yacht stays where it went down?'

'As far as I know.'

'No one attempted to raise it?'

'There was a lot of debate at the time, but the family didn't press for it. Apparently it went down in one of the deepest parts of the ocean off Ardnamurchan Point and it would have been impossible for regular marine divers to go down. They'd need saturation divers and special equipment for that depth, and as they'd recovered the body and there was no suspicion of foul play, the *Maid of Moidart* stays where it is.'

'*Maid of Moidart?* Sounds like Mr Cameron was a bit of a poet.'

Bruce roared with laughter. 'Charles a poet? Never. He bought the yacht off someone and wanted to change the name to something a bit more racy, but everyone told him it's unlucky to change the name on a yacht, so he didn't.'

'Might have been better if he had. The *Maid of Moidart* didn't bring him much luck, did it?'

Douglas stood up, shook hands with Bruce Cameron and made for the door.

'Come and see me any time you want, Chief Inspector,' said Bruce, smiling warmly. 'And where's your next port of call, may I ask?'

'The PF's office, of course. And then I'll take a wee trip to Oban. It's a long time since I've seen the Western Isles. Good day to you, Mr Cameron. I'll most certainly be in touch.'

'I look forward to it.'

Douglas left the office. Bruce Cameron listened to the lift creaking its way down to the ground floor. When he heard the door slam at the bottom, he picked up the phone and dialled a number. He waited, expressionless, until his call was answered.

'McBride's on his way to Oban now,' he said.

* * *

Douglas's visit to the PF's office confirmed what Bruce Cameron had already told him. Charles Cameron's death had been accidental: it was thought that he'd fallen off his boat in atrocious weather conditions and drowned. By the time he'd finished ploughing through the records, it was halfpast twelve. A call from a public telephone box to the Fridale Arms connected him to Sergeant Venerables with only a little delay.

'What's new, sir?'

'I'm going to Oban. Should get there this evening. What's it like down your way?'

'Our Walter's working himself into a lather. He's put everyone's back up. And guess what? O'Neill's scarpered. Flick was right. She said Willoughby was so heavy-handed she ended up feeling like O'Neill's solicitor.'

'You don't say. What's Walter going to do about it?'

'He's off on a man-hunt. He's in his element. It's time you were back here, sir. We need you.'

'Not long now, Sergeant. Give our Walter a long enough rope and he's sure to hang himself. How's pretty Polly?'

'She's a good lass.'

'And the formidable Flick?'

'Seething. She's really got it in for Willoughby.'

'Good on her.'

On his way out of Edinburgh, Douglas stopped at the cemetery. He bought a bunch of yellow roses from the stall-holder at the gate, and made his way to a secluded spot where there was a double grave, marked out in granite, its centre neatly filled in with stone chippings. Both graves nestled under a tall granite cross. He stood there for a few minutes reading the two inscriptions, one underneath the other:

'Reverend James McBride MA. Born 20th September 1925. Died 4th July 1987. The Lord is my shepherd.'
'Elizabeth Louise McBride. Born 10th May 1927. Died 8th July 1990. I shall not want.'

The vase in the middle of the grave was full of dead flowers; Douglas deposited them on a compost heap in a corner of the cemetery. Then he filled the vase with water, went back to the graves and put his roses in the vase. He stood there for a few moments, lost in memories of his father. He remembered now not his stern, uncompromising morality, nor the frequent chastisements for minor infringements of household rules, but his innate kindness and complete dependability. He had always been there when his son wanted him. He hadn't always agreed with what Douglas wanted to say, but at least he had listened.

Then he looked at his mother's inscription. She'd been a gentle, sweet-natured woman, always crippled with anxiety about her family. In an age of shifting moral values, of irresponsibility and uncertainties, these two undistinguished people seemed to him to be giants.

'I'm sorry,' he said, as he put the vase back in the centre of the granite chippings. 'Sorry that I didn't do what you wanted me to do. But I do understand now. After all these years, I finally understand. You wanted what you thought was best for me because you loved me. Well, I'm on your side; I am fighting the same battles that you fought. I am fighting the same enemy. You, father, called him the Devil; Nowadays we call it greed, lust, selfishness. I suppose it amounts to the same thing.'

Then he walked back to his car, got in, and headed off towards the West coast.

Arriving in Oban at six, he found a small guesthouse down near the quay. The owners, Donald and Eileen Adams, were pleased to put him up, as the season was rapidly drawing to a close. After a quick wash and brush-up he walked along the quay to the Highlander Bar, where hot meals were served. Whilst waiting for his steak and chips, he stood at the bar, relishing a Scotch and soda after his long drive. Then he noticed a man, perched on a stool further along the bar, giving him the once-over. Probably one of the local fishermen, Douglas thought; they were noted for their wariness of strangers. His face was the colour of old leather; his sea-washed eyes a startling blue; he was dressed in old trousers and a thick-knit sweater with leather patches on the elbows. After taking his time to size Douglas up, the man held out a hard, chapped hand.

'Hamish McIntosh.'

'Douglas McBride,' said Douglas, gripping the hand. 'Do you live around here?'

'Aye. Fishing when I can; tourist trips when I can't. Would you be wanting a boat ride tomorrow? It's best if you do – the weather's changing at the weekend. It's the season for gales, see. The autumn equinox. And there are hurricanes on the other side of the Atlantic and we always get the backwash. They'll hit us hard on Saturday night.'

Douglas didn't take long to make up his mind. Another bit of the jigsaw was sitting right next to him.

'Thanks for the offer. I'd like a wee trip up the Sound of Mull. What time do you go out?'

'Half past eight, if that's not too early for you. But if we leave at that time we can catch the tide on the way back.'

'That's fine by me. What's the name of your boat?'

'*Highland Lass*. A converted trawler. I've cleaned it up a bit for tourists. It'll cost you a tenner, mind.'

Next morning, after a huge Highland breakfast, Douglas walked down to the quay where Hamish was waiting for him. Even though he wasn't a nautical type, he could see that the weather was changing fast. It was still quite mild, but the sky looked ominous with banks of grey clouds shrouding the hills over on the island of Mull. The air was heavy and sticky, and Douglas felt he had lead weights on his feet as he climbed on board the *Highland Lass*. She was a small fishing boat, with seats arranged along the side of the low gunwales. She looked more like a pleasure boat than a serious fishing craft, but she seemed sturdy enough and the deep throb of the diesel engine sounded reassuringly healthy.

Douglas stood outside on the deck while Oban receded. Once into the Sound of Mull the breeze stiffened and he went to join Hamish in the wheelhouse.

'A bit short of punters today,' Douglas said companionably.

'Aye, well, the equinoctial gales keep the yachties in harbour and their owners in the clubhouse.'

'Get many yachties up here?'

'Aye. Bloody fools, most of them.'

'Did you know a yacht called *The Maid of Moidart*? I heard someone say it came to grief around these parts five years ago.'

'Charles Cameron's boat? I knew it well. And Cameron. Another bloody fool if ever there was one, but he had some good points. Generous. Buy anyone a pint and not think twice about it. But he was crazy to go out alone in gale-force winds. Not that it was all that bad that day; I've seen it worse many a time and lived to tell the tale. But these waters are treacherous, particularly where we're going now. There's a tidal race around the Point, and strong currents. If you're taken by surprise, the boat can stand on its head.'

'I thought Cameron knew what he was doing.'

'Most times; but not on that occasion. His body was washed up into one of those little coves you can see over there. Tide brings them in. He came in on the other side of the Point. We'll be there in a minute.'

'Can we see the actual spot?'

'If you've a mind to see it we'll see it. You've paid your money; you tell me where to go.'

They were out of the Sound now, and Ardnamurchan Point loomed ahead like a sleeping Behemoth. Once away from the shelter of the Sound, the boat began to roll around alarmingly and Douglas started to regret his over-indulgence in Eileen Adams's fry-up.

'What happened to the *Maid*, Hamish? Did they salvage her?'

'Man, you must be joking! The sea's mighty deep out here, and we're not even sure where she went down. In some places it's a mile deep, and there's no diver willing or able to risk such a dive, not unless he's related to the Loch Ness monster.'

'No one's reported picking it up on their ultra-sonic equipment?'

'Not a bleep. No, somewhere around here, the *Maid* went straight to the bottom, and it's as deep as hell down there. Nothing there but monsters, wallowing around in the dark and sometimes wandering off course into the lochs. Horrible place. We got old Charlie back and gave him a decent burial, so why bother about the *Maid*? The family didn't press for salvage, so she's down there with the monsters, and there she'll stay until she shifts.'

'Is that possible?'

'Aye, if there's a bad storm. All sorts of strange objects come up. This coast is littered with wrecks – some of them going back to the Spanish Armada. Now, sir, that's the place where old Charlie's body was washed ashore. Right there, on the starboard bow. Watch your step if you're going outside.'

They were off the Point now, and there was a clear view to the other side. Douglas struggled to open the door of the wheelhouse, and stepped outside. The wind hit him full on the face, and he had to grip hold of the side of the wheelhouse to steady himself. Suddenly aware that he wasn't wearing a life-jacket, he made a dash for the starboard side. The wind was cold and moist, and the grey, turbulent waves looked very close to the gunwales. The boat was wallowing around – Hamish had put it into neutral gear – and Douglas went down onto his knees so that he could hold onto the side of the boat and reduce the force of the wind on his face. He was beginning to feel dizzy and his stomach was lurching around horribly. Nevertheless, he somehow raised his head and stared across the sullen, heaving water towards the shore. He saw a small, sandy cove, nestling under the lowering cliffs of the Point.

Suddenly he was aware that Hamish was standing right behind him, almost touching him. Douglas, his instincts on full alert, jumped up, twisting his body sideways as he did so. He stared at Hamish in disbelief – but Hamish was looking fixedly towards the shore – seemingly unperturbed.

'Watch out, man! For God's sake – you nearly had me over the side.'

'I was going to hold on to you. The boat's lurching around like a drunken fisherman on a Saturday night, and you've got no life-jacket on.'

'You're the skipper, Hamish. You call the shots. I didn't see any life-jackets in the wheelhouse. Where the hell do you keep them? I haven't got X-ray eyes.'

'You didn't ask for one, sir. Some people don't like wearing life-jackets. If you'd asked me, I'd have given you one.'

'Oh, for God's sake, Hamish, let's get back inside. I'm freezing to death out here.'

'Take my arm and I'll give you a hand.'

But Douglas avoided Hamish's offer. He staggered unaided back into the warmth and comparative peace of the wheelhouse. Hamish followed him and went over to a locker in the corner, from where he extracted a life-jacket.

'Here you are, sir. If you want to go crawling round the deck, this is what you'll need.'

'I'll not be going outside again. Turn this boat around and let's get back to Oban.'

'Seen all you want, sir?'

'More than enough, Hamish.'

It was well after twelve when they got back to Oban. Douglas paid Hamish his tenner and went into the pub to put in his daily call to

Venerables. It was good to hear the familiar voice with its friendly Geordie overtones.

'Still alive, sir?'

'Only just. Someone wanted me out of his boat and into the sea about two hours ago.'

He heard Venerables whistle. 'Then you'd better come back here, sir. Sounds safer. Despite Mary Cameron.'

'Could be – but I'm hanging on here for a few more hours. I'll drive back overnight. And, Sergeant . . .'

'Sir?'

'See if you can fix me up somewhere to put my head down. Somewhere . . . private. I'll need to keep a low profile.'

'Problem already solved.' Venerables sounded smug.

'Really? You must be psychic.'

'The priest says he'll have you. Father Paul – he says he's got a spare bed. You'll be safe with him.'

'For a moment I thought you were going to say you'd fixed me up with the nuns!'

'It might come to that, sir. But given your recent record with the ladies, I think you'll be safer with the priest.'

'Careful, Sergeant!'

Venerables chuckled. 'It'll be good to have you back. And Walter's on the warpath. O'Neill doesn't stand a chance – no wonder he's scarpered. Montgomery's been spreading rumours, and Walter believes them.'

'Then the man's a blithering idiot.'

'I wouldn't argue with that. Now you, sir, keep out of deep water.'

'After today's experience, I fully intend to, Sergeant.'

After a substantial plateful of fish and chips at the pub, Douglas made his way to the coastguards' station. Robert Shaw, a bluff Glaswegian, was most hospitable.

'Yes, Chief Inspector, I remember Charlie Cameron very well. We had our eye on him – and so did Customs and Excise. But that's by the by now. The man's dead and his boat's at the bottom of the sea; and there the matter rests.'

'What was Charlie up to, Robert? Why did he go out that day? Hadn't he heard the weather forecast?'

'That didn't bother him. Our Charlie liked a bit of a blow. Not many other boats out there with him, see. No one watching him. Had the place to himself.'

'Surely he told you where he was going? His course, his ETA?'

'He never bothered us with those details. He liked to slip away on his own. A law unto himself. Until he came up against a law that was bigger than he was.'

'Couldn't you charge him?'

'What for? He's entitled to take risks. We did tip off Customs and Excise, but they never actually found anything on the *Maid of Moidart*. No, the least said about Charlie Cameron the better. You've seen the spot where his body was washed up, I take it? Hamish helped you out?'

'Aye – you could say that. Well, I'll be off now. Rough weather ahead, I've heard.'

'Storm-force winds tomorrow night. It's the hurricanes across the pond that cause the trouble – stirs us up good and proper. No pleasure trips for Hamish this weekend.'

'You'll let me know if you think of anything else? You can get in touch with me here.'

Douglas wrote down the telephone number of the incident room at Reivers Hall and gave it to the coastguard.

'You'll need to ask to speak to my Sergeant – Sergeant Venerables. He'll pass any messages on. And if the phone's answered by someone called Willoughby, hang up.'

Chapter 13

'It's good to see you, Chief Inspector,' said Father Paul, with a look of relief on his face. 'Come in quickly, out of the rain. You must've had a rotten journey.'

'A bit tricky, that's for sure. The wind's the main problem; it's getting up to gale force out there. I'm much obliged to you, Father,' Douglas said, as he took off his raincoat, and followed the priest into his study. 'I'm not welcome up at the Hall at the moment. Have to keep a low profile. I'm what they call a loose cannon.'

'Loose cannons have got to come to rest sometimes. Warm yourself whilst I make some tea. Or would you like something stronger?'

'Tea will do me fine. This is most kind of you.'

He crossed over to the fire and warmed his hands; autumn was drawing in quickly, he thought. As Father Paul made tea with the professional efficiency required of a parish priest, Douglas listened to the wind thundering in the chimney, puffing clouds of wood ash onto the hearthrug. He felt at home in this place. The furniture was old and worn, the armchairs solidly comfortable. He felt he belonged.

'Here, drink this, and then I'll take you up to your room. Could you manage a sandwich?'

'I'm fine, thanks, Father,' said Douglas, as he settled himself down in one of the armchairs. 'And incidentally, I'd be glad if you'd call me Douglas – I think it's time to drop formalities, especially as I'm not here in an official capacity.'

'Then Douglas it shall be. I was sorry to hear you'd been laid off the case. That new man's causing havoc around here at the moment. Wally – we all call him Wally, by the way, most disrespectful I know – has got it into his head that O'Neill's his prime suspect. He's hunting him over hill and dale. Of course there's no doubt that Sean's foolish to go off on his own at such a time, but that doesn't make him a potential thief and murderer.'

'Does, er, *Wally* really think that? What possible evidence has he?'

'None, except his own prejudices. He's convinced the place is crawling with terrorists. And Alec Montgomery isn't helping matters. He's siding with Wally and has been putting it around that not only did Sean know the safe's combination but that he shot young Derek by mistake. He alleges the gunman was really aiming at him.'

'That's bloody ridiculous. Why should O'Neill want to kill Montgomery?'

'Because Alec has always vigorously fought any suggestion of removing the Frida Gospel to Ireland.'

'But Sean O'Neill couldn't have shot either Montgomery or Derek during the procession. Several witnesses have confirmed that he stayed put in front of his house the whole time. He couldn't have shot them from that angle.'

'That's where Wally's terrorist theory fits in. He claims O'Neill was working with a professional hitman.'

'Then the man's barking mad. Sean O'Neill hire a hitman? Where the hell's he going to get the money from? Assassins don't come cheaply. Sean's an academic; he couldn't afford a hitman on his salary. Even if he wanted one. I've never heard of such lunacy.'

'Alec's spreading it around that he's part of some fanatical Republican organisation which wants to get Ireland's treasures returned to their homeland.'

'The whole thing's preposterous. Sean's interest in the Republican cause died a death years ago. I know an honest man when I see one, and Sean O'Neill's honest. He may have been a bit impulsive, naive even, in his youth,' Douglas said, thinking back to what O'Neill had had told him, 'but he's not a thief. Besides, he'd have too much respect for the manuscript to subject it to theft.'

'I agree, Douglas. And so does your sergeant. But Willoughby wants an arrest.'

'Aye, and Blackburn's under media pressure. It's a right kettle of fish we've got here.'

'Yes. So it's doubly good to have you back. Did you have a good holiday?'

'Holiday?' Douglas was momentarily confused. 'Oh, yes, very nice. Very nice indeed.'

'Good. Now you'll be fresh for the hunt. Let me show you up to your room. I'm afraid it's rather Spartan.'

Douglas put down his empty mug, stood up, and followed Father Paul upstairs. His room was at the end of the corridor; through the window he caught a glimpse of the church tower, black and sombre against the ragged clouds which parted to reveal a brilliant harvest moon. He looked round the room. The plain white-washed walls: the iron bedstead: the bare floorboards with a handmade rug by the side of his bed: all were familiar. Except for the plain wooden cross over the bed, he could have been back in his own bedroom in the Edinburgh manse of his childhood days.

Father Paul walked across to the window and drew the curtains. 'Your sergeant's coming tomorrow at eight, Douglas. I shan't be here as I have to say early Mass, but do make yourself at home. You'll find bread and cereal in the kitchen. Just help yourself. Make this house your second home. Your retreat, if you like.'

'Seems to be turning into a second incident room. Blackburn's not going to like this.'

'He'll like it well enough if we make a successful arrest.'

'*We?* Seems to me that you've taken on extra responsibilities as parish sleuth.'

'I *am* involved, Douglas. Of course I am. One of my parishioners has been killed; the Little Sisters, who are partly my responsibility, have been robbed; and one of the area's most prominent figures has been murdered in a most horrible way. And a young man I like and respect has fallen under terrible suspicion. I shall do all I can to assist you in finding the right man.'

He paused. Douglas looked at him curiously. He could see there was something troubling Father Paul; the priest looked worried, uncertain. Douglas dumped his overnight bag on the bed and turned to him.

'Come on, man, what is it? I can tell there's something on your mind.'

'It might be nothing at all, Douglas – but there is something. Sister Anne . . .'

'Sister Anne? What's her problem?'

'Only that – she's carrying a heavy burden. She was entrusted with the safe's combination number and she knows she's been

131

careless in looking after it. Your young lady detective seems to think that every Tom, Dick and Harry could have had access to it if they wanted to. The poor, innocent woman might as well have pinned the number to the front door of the church for all the world to see.'

How right he was, thought Douglas, remembering Sister Anne's discovery of Sean O'Neill with the manuscript two weeks ago. If Sean knew how to open the safe, then how many others did? Anyone else in Sister Anne's position would have had the combination changed after that incident, but it had clearly never occurred to her. Had she caught someone else in similar circumstances? *Just taking a look*, they would have said. *Of course I'll put it back* . . . Father Paul was right to be worried.

'Has she said anything to you, Father? Anything that might help us? If she has, you must tell us. It might be the one piece of information we are looking for. Something that could lead us to the thief, and maybe Derek's killer.'

Father Paul looked anguished. 'Sometimes she doesn't realise the implications of what she's telling me—'

'Then share it with me. For God's sake, man, you've just told me you want to help us.'

'I *can't* tell you. You see – she made her confession to me on Thursday. It was a formal confession; I was wearing my stole. So I simply cannot reveal what she said.'

Then Douglas understood: the classic dilemma. Standing in front of him was a person possessed of a vital piece of information, yet he couldn't tell what he knew. Father Paul, looking more and more agitated, bolted towards the door; Douglas made one last effort.

'Father, stop. If what Sister Anne's told you is relevant to the case you must tell us. A child is dead. Sean O'Neill could be found guilty of his murder.'

The priest looked close to tears. 'I can't break the seal of the confessional. If I did, how would I ever make my peace with God? I can't tell you what we talked about, but I'm extremely anxious about Sister Anne's safety.'

'Then she must have police protection, Father. This is a serious matter.'

'You can organise police protection for all you're worth, Douglas, but trying to get Sister Anne to accept it will be quite another thing.'

'You'll have to persuade her, Father.'

Father Paul smiled ruefully. 'As you should know by now, Sister Anne can be persuaded by only one authority, and that is the will of God. I can only pray that God tells her quickly to come to the police with what she knows. Now I'll leave you to your rest. God be with you tonight, and go with you tomorrow.'

'Are you thinking of taking holy orders, sir?' said Venerables with studied politeness as he walked into the kitchen the following morning. 'You look right at home here.'

'I'm not thinking of it yet, Sergeant. But it's a possibility for the future. I might need a change of career soon, mightn't I? Here, take a seat. Coffee?'

'Does Father Paul know you're helping yourself to his supplies?'

'He's been very generous. Now, let's get down to business. Good God, man, you look terrible,' Douglas said, suddenly realising that Venerables' drawn face belied the forced cheerfulness of his greeting. 'What's happened?'

'It's Flick, sir. She's been attacked. Last night, as she got out of her car here in Fridale.'

Douglas felt his heart sink. *Flick beaten up*? 'Is she hurt, for God's sake?'

'No, she's fine. It'd take more than a run-of-the-mill thug to put Flick out of action.'

'How did it happen, man? And when?'

'Last night, late. After midnight. She'd driven back from Newcastle, and was returning to the room she's renting here in the village. As she got out, the man – she thinks it was a man, he was pretty strong – seized hold of her round the neck, from behind. But the lass was on the alert. Seems she's expert in self-defence. Runs courses in Newcastle. She socked him one, and he ran off. She called up help, but as usual they were fast asleep at Operations, and help appeared when it was all over. So she made her statement, went to bed and by all accounts slept soundly. But the word's got round, of course. Wally Willoughby blames O'Neill. Says it's proof that he's got some pretty dodgy associates who're trying to derail our investigation. Everyone believes him, including Montgomery, of course. O'Neill's as good as dead, sir, when he puts in an appearance.'

'Then let's hope he stays out of the way. But I'm sorry about Flick. Are you sure she's all right?'

'Fit as a flea, sir. Back on the beat today. Nothing's going to put her off. She shares your opinion that this had nothing to do with O'Neill. But she admits that someone wants her out of the way. This was no random mugging. They were waiting for her. Muggers don't hang around in the small hours in places like this – it's not like the city.'

'Then she's in danger, Sergeant. She should have protection.' Both her and Sister Anne – Blackburn would have a heart attack when he saw the budget.

'She'll not have it. Says she must be free to do her work in her own way. At least she knows now what she's up against.'

'Let's hope she does. This alters things, Venerables. I made the mistake of treating Flick as an innocent abroad – a lassie who got involved with Arts and Antiques because she liked looking at pretty pictures – but it seems I'm wrong. After all, art thieves are just as ruthless as other criminals when it comes to saving their own skins, and Flick's too efficient for her own good. Looks like Art and Antiques isn't the soft option I always thought it was. But what else has happened? How, goes it up at the Hall?'

'Bad, I'm afraid. Bloodworthy can't abide Wally. Rose refuses to cook for him; Pete Fraser won't serve him. So Wally's got to fend for himself. Meanwhile he's called out the whole Force – Firearms, the lot – to find O'Neill. A witch-hunt's building up here in the village.'

'That's dangerous, Sergeant. Nothing's worse than mob rule.'

'That's what I keep telling him. But Wally wants an arrest.'

'And at any cost, it seems. And guilt doesn't enter the equation. But how are the other ladies? Keeping well?'

'Polly's fighting fit.'

'No, laddie. Mrs McKenzie and Mrs Cameron, I mean.' It was strange. Only twenty-four hours ago his whole body would have responded to the mention of Mary's name; but now, to his relief, he felt nothing. Almost nothing . . .

'The two harpies? Oh, right goings-on in that direction. Our Pat chucked Mr Montgomery out! He came courting her yesterday, and she gave him the boot good and proper. I saw him go off with a face like thunder. Pat and bloody Mary want to mickie off to France, but we've got instructions to hold on to them, so they're fuming. But how about you, sir? Got over your boat trip? You must be glad you're not going out to sea today. I heard it's Storm Force Ten off the Western Isles at the moment.'

'It was a useful little expedition. I wasn't wasting my time, laddie. We're getting there, but it's evidence we need. Not hearsay, not prejudice, not hunches – real evidence. Whatever Walter Willoughby says. So, how's Polly getting on with the Montgomery records?'

'Wally's taken her off that. Put her onto O'Neill instead. Surprise, surprise!'

'The fool! The interfering fool!'

'He's in charge now, sir. And O'Neill's his man. It's driving Polly up the wall, hunting through the Irish police files.'

'And finding nothing, I suppose?'

'Only that he went to school in County Cork and attended Trinity College, Dublin, got a first-class degree and went on to become a lecturer in Mediaeval History. Oh, and the Irish gardai have told him off good and proper – Willoughby, I mean. He did consort with a few questionable characters when he was a lad, but ever since he's been known to be dead against terrorism and violence. So he'd have the Irish police as witnesses for his defence if this goes to trial. Reckon Willoughby's days are numbered, sir.'

'Anyone can see the man's an idiot of the first order. Serves Blackburn right. Now, what are your plans for today, Sergeant?'

'Oh, I'm off to have a wee chat with our Janice. Nothing official, of course – don't want to frighten her.'

'Walter's orders?'

'Of course not. He's too busy setting his dogs on O'Neill. And while the cat's away . . . And you, sir? What will you do? Write the parish magazine?'

'I'll just try to be – inconspicuous.'

'You, sir? That'll be the day.'

Crouched in his tent, sheltered by a rock out on the Cheviots, Sean O'Neill watched the sun rise that Saturday morning, and thanked God he was out of the village of Fridale. He'd had enough of the snide remarks, the innuendoes, the downright hostility. Living in the centre of the village he was keenly aware of the hatred being whipped up towards him. And there was no reason for it. Any propensity he might have had towards criminal activity had been extinguished long ago. If there was anything in the world he really cared for, it was beautiful and priceless manuscripts. And one

135

manuscript in particular he cared for above everything else – the Frida Gospel. If it came to the crunch, he would prefer to see that manuscript safe and sound in an alien home than be a cause of conflict and misery. The manuscript was the important thing; not who owned it. The one thing that he dreaded, that kept him awake at night, was that the thieves might not respect it. That something so beautiful – something that had survived all those centuries, something that had been handed down to the present generation for safekeeping – should be damaged or destroyed by people who didn't appreciate its real worth, that was the real agony. How blind people were, he thought. How stupid. How could they think for one minute that he would have grabbed the Frida Gospel from the Little Sisters' safe and made off with it? He'd have died rather than subject it to such a violent act.

So, defeated by the atmosphere in the village, he'd come up here, to the grandeur of the Cheviots, to be alone with the birds. Last night he'd seen the capercaillies dance, had watched the golden eagles soar across the peaks of the mountains, had watched the wild geese gather in their formations to head South. He'd heard the wind get up, listened to the rain beating on the roof of his tent, and for a few hours he'd forgotten the hostility of bigots.

Suddenly he heard a sound that wasn't the call of a goose, or the raucous shriek of the cock pheasant. Motorbikes, way down below him. And cars. Unbelieving, he watched without moving as police, some armed, swarmed across the heather towards him. Rough hands gripped him. Rough hands dragged him away. He looked sorrowfully at the man in charge. Chief Inspector Walter Willoughby.

'In the name of God, what are you doing?'

'We're bringing you in for questioning. You Irish scum,' he said.

Sean stared at him bitterly. 'Let's hope British justice turns out to be all that it's cracked up to be. That it turns out to be on my side. Or will I be just another miscarriage of justice, locked up in a British prison because the police are too bigoted to examine the facts? You've got the wrong man, Chief Inspector. But you're too bloody ignorant to see it.'

Chapter 14

The news about Flick had upset Douglas more than he realised. It was always a heartfelt shock when a member of the Force was assaulted; especially when it was a woman. Not that Douglas didn't respect the work of women police officers. He appreciated their sensitivity in dealing with the public, their intuition when it came to investigation. But the fact remained that they were vulnerable. Douglas knew he was considered old-fashioned; he preferred to call it gallantry. He couldn't bear the thought that Flick was in danger. Someone wanted her off the enquiry. But who? And why? He'd have to have a talk with her soon and find out whether she had any suspicions as to who her attacker might be.

Meanwhile he wanted to see Montgomery, mainly to stop him spreading further rumours about O'Neill. No one was guilty until proved to be so by irrefutable evidence; if that weren't the case, then suspects would be at the mercy of mob rule. And that, in Douglas's eyes, would be the end of civilisation as he knew it. He knew this interview with Montgomery wasn't going to be easy.

As he drove out of Fridale towards Montgomery Hall he foresaw the problems ahead of him. He had no authority to conduct interviews; had no right to go snooping around private property. Blackburn would spin off to apopleptic heights if he knew, and as for Willoughby ... Not that he was prepared to take any notice of Willoughby. Neither did he give a damn about anyone else at that moment. He simply wanted to find out who had murdered an innocent teenager, robbed a group of nuns of a priceless manuscript. And he wanted to stop this persecution of Sean O'Neill. If the police weren't careful, they'd be getting sued for wrongful imprisonment.

He knew he'd have to tread carefully. He mustn't raise the alarm. Just keep sniffing around, and hope for that lucky break.

When he reached Montgomery Hall, Alec, appropriately dressed for the weather in raincoat and waterproof hat, was backing his car out of the garage. Douglas pulled up outside the main gate. As he walked up the gravel drive, Montgomery saw him in his mirror. He muttered something, got out of his car and came to meet him. There was something different about him today, Douglas noticed. He wasn't his usual expansive, urbane self. He seemed hesitant, on the defensive. Worry-lines marred his smooth face, and there were deep shadows under his eyes. Douglas had the distinct feeling that Montgomery wasn't pleased to see him.

'Good morning, Mr McBride,' said Montgomery, pleasantly enough; but there was no missing the emphasis on the 'Mr'. 'I didn't expect to see you here. I heard that you'd gone up North. A welcome break from your arduous duties.'

'I had a good trip, brief though it was. A shame I had to return so soon – I was very taken with the area. Nice boat ride along the coast. Very scenic; and Hamish McIntosh sends his regards.'

A long shot: but it went home. Montgomery looked startled.

'Hamish McIntosh? Am I expected to know him?'

'He seems to know you. He was a friend of Charles Cameron. He told me that you used to visit the Western Isles to see Charles. Along with Ian McKenzie. For the fresh air and the fishing.'

Douglas watched Montgomery intently as he regained control. The anxiety dispersed as if he'd spotted dry land ahead. 'Oh, yes, I remember Hamish! One of Charlie's Highland yokel friends. He had his own boat – some awfully naff name, *Highland Lass*, that was it. Very tripperish. His other boat was more like it, a good, fast motor-sailer with a reinforced steel hull. Excellent for foul-weather sailing. Not that I ever went out in it. Charlie did, of course.'

'*Highland Lass* was good enough for me,' said Douglas evenly. 'But it's odd he didn't mention his other boat to me. What did he call it?'

'*Eriskay*, if I remember correctly. A down-to-earth name for a no-nonsense boat. Kept it moored up in one of the lochs. Oban too expensive, I suppose. So are you thinking of continuing your little break in Scotland, Mr McBride?'

Douglas winced at Montgomery's patronising tone, but refused to be riled. He knew he was a nobody at the moment; and it suited him.

People thought he was harmless, an old bear with his claws cut. They'd never see him as a threat.

'Yes, I might well be going back there soon, when the weather calms down. I only called in to give you Hamish's regards.'

He turned to go, then paused as if he had just remembered something. 'Things have moved on while I've been away, I understand. Sean O'Neill seems to have run into a spot of trouble.'

'You could say that. But Willoughby's after him. He's a good chap, Willoughby. No waffling around fielding the ball. Hits sixes straight away.'

'Let's hope he doesn't get caught out,' Douglas said, grinning.

'I doubt that. O'Neill's consorted with terrorists back in Ireland – he admits that. He wheedles his way into our little community, chats up the parish priest, runs rings round the Little Sisters. He finds out the combination of the safe – Sister Anne stumbled upon him pawing through the Gospel, and he admitted to Willoughby he'd looked in her prayer book for the code. So he gets in touch with another of his terrorist friends and sets the whole thing up. Steals the Gospel from the church, either late on Saturday night or early on Sunday morning, and then gets his friend to take a pot-shot at me – all because I think the Gospel should stay in England, where it belongs. He would have killed two birds with one stone, only his rather inept comrade missed me. He would have shut me up for good and provided himself with a nice little alibi – oh, yes, we all saw him, smiling and watching the procession. And now I hear that one of his Irish cohorts have attacked your lady detective! Well, we all know the sort of regard they have for the British police force, so I suppose we shouldn't be surprised. Let's hope Willoughby pulls him in quickly, before he hurts anyone else.'

'Sounds as if you've got him well and truly buttoned up. It's easy, though, to arrange events with hindsight in order to prove a theory. I work the other way round – examine the events first, find the evidence, test it, then hit the six. That way the ball goes straight to the boundary. A good rule for cricket, I think.'

Montgomery looked sour. 'I'm sorry to hear you're off the case, Mr McBride. But we have to give the younger men a chance to prove themselves. Willoughby's a man of action, and that's what we need.'

'As long as we don't end up looking mighty foolish in court when our actions don't stand up to scrutiny.'

'We all know O'Neill's guilty as hell. If he isn't, then why has he bolted?'

'To escape from all the bad feeling, most likely. The man's only human.'

'He's a bloody fanatic. He'd stop at nothing to get what he wants.'

'And what about Ian McKenzie? What had Ian done to offend his Irish spirit?'

'Mr McBride, you've no right to ask me these questions. Get back to your holiday. I've nothing to say – except O'Neill's your man. It's obvious.'

'Nothing's obvious in this game, Mr Montgomery. But don't let me delay you any longer. Are you going anywhere special?' Douglas said, glancing at the car whose engine was still running.

'Durham. On business. I'll be back tonight. We're all still under curfew, remember?' Alec stared angrily at Douglas.

'Of course – I forgot. You're all to be tucked up in your burrows after dark. Still, with speedy Willoughby in charge, doubtless you'll soon be allowed out again.'

And Douglas, with a cheerful wave of his hand, walked back to his car and drove off. A couple of miles out of the village, he drew into a lay-by. He stopped, switched off the engine, and closed his eyes. Two murders, and a theft – gentle, scholarly Sean just wasn't capable of it. But he mustn't let his personal feelings for the man blind him to the evidence. It didn't look too good for Sean, he had to admit. He had links, albeit distant, with an IRA sympathiser. He had been found looking at the Gospel without permission. He had been present during the procession, albeit in the wrong place to do the shooting – though he could, of course, have been working with an accomplice. And then he had done a runner when things got a bit too hot to hold him. That was the most incriminating thing of all, as far as Douglas was concerned. But his instincts told him that Sean was innocent. They had to consider other options. Get away from Sean O'Neill. Consider the whole case. Work out how Ian McKenzie fitted into Willoughby's cosy little scenario. He opened his eyes as a particularly violent gust of wind buffetted the roof of his car. One thing he was sure of: the solution to the puzzle lay at Reivers Hall.

* * *

There was no doubt about it: Janice Hudson was giving him the glad eye. A few months ago Venerables would have responded, and once young Brett had been dumped on another accommodating mother he would gladly have mounted the stairs with her once the case was over. But not now. He'd spent the previous night with Polly and it had been good. He loved her; he knew that for certain. It was only a matter of time before he got hitched for the second time round. Still, Janice was clearly in the mood for a bit of male attention . . .

'That's a fine-looking lad you've got there,' he said, desperately feigning his admiration as he watched young Brett stuffing himself with Sugar Puffs, and the dog noisily hoovering up the droppings. 'Takes after his mother. You're not child-minding today, then?'

'It's Saturday. I don't child-mind on Saturdays – it's my day off. A shame the weather's so bad, otherwise I would have gone to the Gateshead Metro Centre. Never mind. I can always find plenty to do to keep out the cold.'

She looked archly at Venerables, smoothing out imaginary wrinkles in the front of her T-shirt. Venerables felt the usual tingle of excitement. He liked bold girls, girls who knew what was what, who were always ready for it. But then he thought of poor Polly stuck in front of her computer, trawling through Sean O'Neill's spotless and uneventful Irish past, and restrained himself.

'All on your own then, love?' said Venerables, playing her game.

'Just me and Brett, and the puppy,' she giggled. 'Of course, if you didn't have anything better to do . . .'

'No Kevin?'

'Kevin?'

He noticed the change in her. A sullen look replaced the provocative smile.

'I though you and Kevin were an item?'

'*Were*'s the right word. I haven't seen him for ages – at least a week. Not since he was here last Saturday night, after the disco. Even then he didn't turn up when he was meant to, to pick me up from the Hall. Said he had to work. I've heard that one before.'

'Still, I expect you were glad to see him when he did turn up. Gets a bit lonely on your own sometimes, I expect. And you're a very attractive girl. So you both had a nice lazy weekend, did you?' Venerables was praying that Janice's loyalty to Kevin had vanished along with her boyfriend himself. And he wasn't wrong.

Janice shook her head, looking piqued. 'Not really. He was up on Sunday at the crack of dawn. Seven thirty!'

Venerables knew that reminding her that she was contradicting her previous statement would only make her clam up. He kept going. 'That must have been a shame. It's nice to lie in on a Sunday morning, after you've been working hard all week.'

'We usually do – but he said he had to get away.' Now she looked downright indignant.

'Wild horses wouldn't drag me out of your bed, love. Where was he off to? Two-timing you, was he?'

'Not on your life! I'd not put up with that. No, he had work to do, he said.'

'That's bad luck. Anyone call round that morning? To keep you company?'

'No, no one. Oh – Pete Fraser phoned.'

'Pete? Now he's a good-looking lad. Why didn't you ask him to come round and console you?'

'You must be joking. He spreads himself around a bit too much for my liking. And he's not too particular who he bonks – if you see what I mean. No, I'm not interested in Pete Fraser. He only wanted to know where Kev was. When I said he wasn't with me, he rang off.'

'What time was that, love?'

'Can't remember. About half past eight, I suppose. Young Brett was shouting for his cereal – he's a greedy pig, and the pup had peed on my new carpet and I had to get the washing machine going. He could have been trying to call Kevin for hours, for all I know, 'cos when I was dusting round I noticed that Brett had been playing with the phone and left it off the hook. Must've done it on Saturday evening, before he went off to his gran's. He's a right little bugger sometimes. You need eyes in the back of your head, honestly.'

Venerables played it cool. 'You're doing a grand job, lass. Well – it's been really nice having a chat with you. You've been ever so helpful. Any chance of popping down the station to go over what you've told me – just to make it all official, like?'

Janice froze. 'But . . . look, I might have got it wrong. P'raps it was Saturday morning when Kev went out, not Sunday. I get confused, what with Brett pestering me all the time. Now I think about it, I reckon I've just got muddled. I'm sorry to waste your time.'

Venerables sighed inwardly. He knew as well as Janice did that she hadn't got it wrong. But clearly she was too wedded to Kevin's cause, or too frightened of him and Pete, to commit herself – yet. He'd give her time. He didn't want to push things and end up with a key witness who backtracked on everything she'd said in court. He'd wait until Janice was good and ready before he forced the issue.

'That's OK. I know how it is, when you're rushed off your feet. Don't worry about it – it's been nice chatting to you anyway. I'm going to love you and leave you now, Janice. If you think of anything else, let me know.'

With difficulty Venerables extricated himself from Brett's sticky clutches and managed to avoid kicking the puppy on the way to the door. *Win some, lose some,* he thought. But at least they now had a pretty good idea that Kevin was lying.

Venerables drove straight to the Fridale Arms. The bar was crowded that Saturday morning; recent events were bringing in the curious, and Ben Knowles, the landlord, was making the most of it. Venerables spotted Tom Emmerson perching on a stool at the bar; he nodded in his direction in a matey fashion. Douglas had managed to grab a table in the far corner of the room, and had even managed to hold on to a chair for Venerables, despite numerous attempts from fellow drinkers to claim it for themselves.

Douglas moved up to let Venerables in. 'How's Flick, Sergeant? No delayed shock?'

'I've not seen her since I saw you, but I'm sure she's fine. Don't worry too much about her, sir. She'll be all right. Tough as old boots.'

'Janice let her hair down?'

'You could say that. Our Kev *was* with her late last Saturday night, Sunday morning. But he left early. And Pete phoned to ask for him and found him not there. Unfortunately she's not prepared to change her original statement yet, but I think she'll come round.'

Douglas whistled. 'So the nosy-parker next door was right! I wonder what Pete said to Janice? Told her to keep stumm, I expect.'

'Whatever he said, she's forgotten it now.' Venerables looked concerned. 'You, sir – are you all right? Not grieving over that Cameron woman?'

'Grieving, no. Angry, yes. But I've learnt my lesson. Romance isn't for me.' Douglas looked wistful.

Venerables was moved. 'You mustn't give up, sir. Someone else will come along – and she'll straighten you out. A nice lady Detective Inspector, now, expert in Arts and Antiques. That's what you need.'

Douglas tried to look stern. 'You seem to have a one-track mind, Sergeant. Just keep it on the job. Get onto Pete Fraser and see what he has to say now that Janice has spilled the beans.'

'And you're forgetting Tom Emmerson. He hates Pete and Kev because they get all the lassies. He'd do anything to see them locked up. He could lead us to that last piece in the puzzle.'

'Fix him, Venerables. And listen – Sister Anne must have protection. Get cracking on that; and never mind Wally,' said Douglas, seeing the look of misgiving on Venerables' face. 'This is our case, remember. Whatever Blackburn cooks up, we're in this together.'

'I feel I'm riding two horses, sir.'

'A good trick to learn, Sergeant.'

Just then the bar door crashed open, and the wind caught it and dashed it back on its hinges. As if blown in by the gale, a boy, about fifteen with cropped hair and two studs in his nose, fell into the room.

'Dad – they've got O'Neill! And old man Fairbrother's gone and set fire to Weavers! Petrol everywhere. The lot's going up.'

Douglas and Venerables leapt to their feet. 'Weavers,' said Douglas. 'Number five, Weavers Cottages – that's Sean's house. That bloody fool Walter Willoughby's started something here. Let's get down there and stop him from doing any more damage.'

Chapter 15

By the time they'd got to the scene, the fire had taken hold not only of number five, Weavers Cottages, but also of the house on the other side. Fanned by the gale-force wind, massive tongues of scarlet flame leapt up towards the black cloud-covered sky, and a pall of acrid smoke, lifted by the wind, drifted up Church Lane, where it hung over the squat Norman church tower like a dirty bridal veil. The intense heat shimmered over the square; sparks from the window-frames and doors fell on the gathering crowd like grape-shot, causing the horrified onlookers to shriek and curse like demons in hell. And almost unnoticed, comforted by a firefighter, an old woman wept for the destruction of her life's possessions.

Douglas, deeply shocked, looked at Venerables. 'By God, Willoughby's got a lot to answer for! See what happens when you blacken a man's reputation?'

'You're so right, Douglas,' said a voice behind him. He turned and saw Flick, her face white, her eyes soft with compassion. 'You've got to be bloody certain you know what you're doing when you start putting labels on people. This lot's out for blood. They want an eye for an eye; and Sean fits the bill perfectly. Never mind about evidence; never mind about establishing the truth; take someone, preferably an outsider, charge him, destroy his life, kick the bastard while he's down. And what happens? The innocent suffer. And a good man, Derek Fairbrother's father, faces the possibility of a prison sentence for trying to avenge the death of his child in the only way he can.'

'My sentiments exactly,' Douglas said. 'This is a bad day for Fridale. Let's hope they keep the mob away from O'Neill. They won't be able to hold on to him for long without just cause, and unless more evidence comes to light, he'll be back in the village. And then the trouble'll start. People want a scapegoat. They'll not calm down until we clear up this mess. Who torched the house?'

'It was definitely Derek's father. They caught him with the empty petrol can in his car,' said Flick. 'And he's not denying it.'

'Damn Willoughby and his blundering incompetence!'

Douglas turned and walked away. There was nothing anyone could do. The professionals were there to put out the flames, to counsel, to restore order. But no one could put back the clock. He turned back to Venerables.

'We'll get the bastard responsible for all of this. We'll find him and bang him away for life. To hell with the Willoughbys of this world! We'll get him, even if it destroys us both.'

'I'm with you, sir. All the way. And Flick.'

'Of course I am. I thought I'd been brought here to investigate the theft of a manuscript. But try as I might, I can't separate the robbery from the homicides. And I know O'Neill's not guilty. Now I'll get back to the Hall. Polly and I are onto something. But it could take us a long while.'

'Anything I should know about?'

'Not yet, Douglas. I don't want to raise your hopes. It's just a hunch. No real evidence yet – and evidence is the only justification for bringing people in. Otherwise we end up with chaos.' And she waved a hand despairingly towards the blazing cottages, her face pale and tense.

'I'll come with you,' said Venerables. 'Want a lift?'

'No, thanks. I'm independent now. But thanks all the same.'

And she walked off towards a white Mazda MX5 parked on the far side of the square. Venerables whistled.

'She's a bit of a goer, sir, underneath that icy exterior.'

Douglas nodded slowly. Yes, there were certainly unexplored depths to Felicity Flight.

Up at the Hall, Venerables immediately went in search of Pete Fraser. He found him in the cellar, sorting through racks of wine.

'You're wanted upstairs, Mr Fraser,' said Venerables grimly. 'In the incident room, if you please. I've got some questions to ask. On the record.'

Pete Fraser's dark, brooding face took on a defiant expression.

'What the hell's all this about? Are you acting on Willoughby's orders?'

'Willoughby's my superior officer, yes.' Venerables felt that was a neat way round the question. 'Now, upstairs.'

In the incident room, Venerables nodded to Wilkes, who turned on the tape recorder. He trotted out the usual formalities.

'Now, Mr Fraser – back to last Sunday morning. I want to know if you made any phone calls.'

'For God's sake, man, be reasonable! My employer had been murdered. We were all rushing around like blue-arsed flies. I can't remember what I did.'

'Then I suggest you try a bit harder. Did you phone your brother, for instance?'

'Kev? Of course not. Why would I phone him? I knew he wouldn't be home anyway – he'd told me.'

'You know his girlfriend, Janice Hudson?'

Pete looked wary. 'Janice? Yes, I know her.'

'She says you telephoned her at home that Sunday morning about half past eight.' Venerables crossed his fingers, hoping Pete wouldn't ask whether she'd made a statement to that effect. 'You wanted to speak to Kevin. He wasn't there, as it happens – yet he says he was. We want you to tell us what you said to Janice that morning.'

Pete dropped his eyes. 'I can't remember. For Christ's sake, we were all under pressure up here! Anyway, I think she's got it wrong. I'm pretty sure I never phoned Janice. I wouldn't have had reason to.'

'You're quite sure of this, Mr Fraser? Remember – this is a taped interview. Think carefully before you answer.'

'Yes I'm sure. I never phoned Janice last Sunday.'

'Thank you, Mr Fraser. We can check on your statement, of course. BT put a trace on all calls from this house from the early hours of last Sunday. But we wanted to hear what you had to say first. Thank you, Wilkes. I think this interview has just about concluded.'

'He said he didn't phone Janice, sir,' said Venerables when he joined Douglas in his Volvo. 'But he's lying.'

'Trace that call, Sergeant. If he's lying, then he wants to shield his brother. We know Pete himself can't have been up to anything – he was under our watchful eye pretty much all of Sunday. He wasn't allowed out of the Hall. Now why should he lie for Kevin?'

'Can't we haul them both in?'

'Not yet. We don't want to do a Willoughby. Leave the Fraser brothers to stew in their own juice for a bit.'

Venerables' mobile rang – a call put through from the incident room. Venerables took it, and turned to Douglas. 'Message for you, sir. From a Robert Shaw – Oban coastguard. Hurricane-force winds last night and this morning. He says the yacht's shifted. They're going to try to get divers down tomorrow and he wants you to be there.'

'Tell him I'm on my way, Sergeant.'

Chapter 16

Robert Shaw was in high spirits. The sound of the gale-force winds lashing at the plate-glass windows of the Oban coastguard station, and the thunder of the sea crashing against the rocks below, was music to his ears.

'The *Maid*'s come up!' he shouted to Douglas. 'Out of the depths she's come. The incoming tide and the strong current have brought her into Craggy Cove like a dream. A fisherman out looking for crabs spotted her. The water in that cove shelves to a hundred and fifty feet, so they're going down tomorrow – with any luck. It'll have to be in the afternoon because it's too risky to go sooner. The sea's in a bit of a state at the moment, but give it twelve hours or so and it'll be different altogether. You're coming out with us, of course, Chief Inspector? After all, it was your idea to send divers down. I still think it's a bit unnecessary.'

Douglas, pleased at the unofficial reinstatement of his rank, nodded in agreement. Despite his recent experience of rough seas on Hamish's boat, he wouldn't miss this for worlds.

'You're keeping an eye on Hamish, Robert?'

'Hamish? Why, what's he done?'

'Maybe nothing at all. But I reckon he'll be interested in the *Maid*'s shifted position. You could try to find out where he and his boat were on the night Charles Cameron died.'

'Aye; but it was five years ago. I remember afterwards he was here with us in Oban, waiting to see if Cameron's body came up.'

'And his yacht? Not *Highland Lass* – his proper boat, *Eriskay*. Do you remember if it was tied up here in the marina?'

'Probably not. He's got a mooring up in Moidart. But I can have a look and see if it was in our marina that night.'

149

He turned to one of the many computers and scrawled through the data.

'No, there's no record of it being here. *Highland Lass* was here, of course – but then it always is. Not *Eriskay*. He doesn't bring it down South much, I know – he likes to sail further afield. Over to the Hebrides, up to Stornaway, even over to Ireland. It's a deep-water boat, see, with a good reinforced hull on her.'

'Then maybe we ought to have a wee chat with Mr McIntosh. See if he can recall where he was on that September night – I reckon he'll remember well enough if he wants to.'

'I'm glad you're back with us, Chief Inspector,' said Robert, thumping Douglas's back in jovial fashion. 'You've got a good head on your shoulders. Glasgow'll be sending up their scuba team tomorrow, and then we'll have a better idea what happened to the *Maid of Moidart* five years ago.'

That Saturday night, Mary Cameron was restless. The wind was shrieking round Reivers Hall, sometimes rising to a high-pitched howl which grated on her nerves. After a couple of hours she couldn't endure it any longer. Just as she had done when she was a child, up in the cottage on Skye, she went along to her sister's room. She knew Patricia would also be awake.

'Come and join me,' Pat said when she saw Mary standing in the doorway like a ghost. 'It's too wild a night to sleep. Here – get in.' She pushed back the duvet to let Mary climb into bed. 'Let's snuggle up together like we used to. Do you remember how mother always used to find us in the same bed when she came in to wake us up in the mornings for school?'

'I remember how bloody cold it always was,' said Mary, slipping into bed next to Patricia and pulling the duvet up round her chin. 'We'd have frozen if we hadn't slept together. Those were the days. No warm bed like this; no carpets; no hot water, unless mother stoked up the boiler.'

'Because father was too drunk to bother,' said Patricia, putting an arm protectively round Mary. 'But we were McDonalds, weren't we? McDonalds of Skye!'

'And a branch that the other McDonalds ignored. And who could blame them? Father disgraced us and mother was too ill most of the time with all those kids to care.'

'We had our pride, though.'

'Fat lot of good that did us. We were the lucky ones – the only two to get away. It was our brains and our bodies that were our chief assets, not our bloody name.'

'But it helped us all the same. Went down well with that American. Americans are suckers for ancestry. Do you remember him? What was his name?'

'Grant Oppenheim. How could I ever forget him? Those were the days, Pat. Remember that villa in Florida . . .'

'The ranch in Texas. The apartment in Manhattan.'

'Which one of us do you think he loved most?'

'You were the youngest, Mary.'

'I think he loved us both. We certainly gave him a run for his money.'

'Pity about his wife.'

They stopped talking for a moment, each lost in her own private reverie. Then Mary giggled.

'Yes, the old bitch got the lot! But we nabbed the jewellery. Helped ourselves just in time, before the old guy pegged out.'

'And diamonds are certainly a girl's best friend.'

'We deserved them, big sister. Payment for services rendered.'

'You can say that again. The things I did for that old sod. I would-n't go through that again.'

'We could make a new start. Now that you're a respectable widow.'

'We could. But we're getting distinctly long in the tooth to attract the millionaires, don't you think?'

'Oh I don't know. What about old Alec? He'd have you like a shot.'

'It's the Hall he wants, not me. Besides, I've already told him to get lost. Hovering around like a bloody vulture.'

Mary turned over to put an arm round her sister. 'Remember – we want him on our side.'

'I can't stand that creep near me.'

'He's rich. And he knows everything. It would be one way of—'

'I won't have him in my bed. No, Mary, there are limits. I know you don't mind using your wicked wiles whenever it suits, but I do. Just look at what you did to poor old Douglas.'

Mary looked nettled. 'I thought young waiters were your special-ity.'

'Better than middle-aged coppers.'

'We wanted him off the case, remember?'

'No need to make his life a misery.'

Patricia turned over with her back to her sister. After a pause, Mary put an arm round her and held her close. Two of them, deaf to the wind, safe in the warmth and security of a shared bed.

'Old farts like that shouldn't be in the police force,' said Mary drowsily.

'Perhaps not. But we've been lumbered with a bigger creep now. Wally Willoughby.'

'He's not got the brains he was born with. Douglas was different. He was asking too many questions, sniffing round just a bit too enthusiastically for peace of mind.'

'Still, you ruined his career. Don't you feel any remorse?'

'Oh, I don't know. It was a nice way to go. He enjoyed it, anyway.'

'I'm sure you gave him something to think about. When's French Charlie going to put in an appearance?'

Mary didn't answer.

'Mary,' Pat said, cautiously, 'he's not brushed you off, has he? He couldn't. Not after all these years.'

'I've not heard from him for ages.'

'He'll write soon. I know he will. When he finds out Ian's dead and you're free to come to France. Anyway, there's plenty more fish in the sea.'

'Not many with sixty acres of prime-quality vineyards to swim around in.'

The wind continued to rattle the doors and windows, to bellow down the chimney. Mary, curled up against her sister's back, suddenly shivered.

'It's all going wrong, Pat, isn't it?' she whispered.

'Don't worry, love. We've still got the Hall. And the name. McKenzie's just as good as McDonald as far as society's concerned. We just need to get organised, that's all.'

'We need a good solid injection of capital. You should really think seriously about Alec, Pat. At least he'd make the Hall a going concern.'

'I can't do it, Mary. Ian was good to me. I can't just—'

'You don't have to *love* him to marry him! You didn't even *fancy* Ian, and yet you were happy enough. Marry Alec and lead your own life. After all, that's what happened with Ian. Same for me and

Charles. There was never any trouble, because we all knew the rules. You let Ian indulge in his little pleasures; I ignored Charlie's goings-on. And he ignored me. You could say we had the perfect marriage. Pity it all had to end.'

'Maybe you could start a new career, Mary. Marriage guidance.'

They both laughed, but Mary still couldn't banish that uneasy feeling. The wind was unsettling, and her imagination was conjuring up too many unpleasant memories.

'I'm glad we had no children, Pat,' she murmured.

'Except for the one that got away.'

'Surely you don't have any regrets over that little episode? It would have been bloody inconvenient to have had Grant's child at that time. It would have been the end of your life.'

'Some life, Mary. Just look at us. Two ageing harpies, living in a huge mausoleum we can't afford. No cash – not much, anyway. Ian was practically on his uppers. No prospects. If I'd kept the child, at least I'd have had something to show for it all.'

'And Ian would never have married you, that's for sure. He hated children for one thing, and he'd never have agreed to bring up some-one else's child.'

'Perhaps it would have been better for me if I'd never met Ian.'

'Good God, Pat. How can you say that? At least you've got this place. And the villa in France. If you'd kept the child you would have been on the scrapheap.'

In the dark, Pat smiled grimly. 'It seems to me, Mary, that all I did by marrying Ian was delay the inevitable.'

In the early hours of Sunday morning, Pat woke up with a start. The wind was still blowing strongly but it had passed its peak, and had dropped down to a bad-tempered grumble. She lay there in the dark, listening. Something had woken her. She recognised the feeling of her body being on red alert. The accelerating heart-beat; the dry mouth; the tension across her shoulders. She waited, but nothing happened. No sound of footsteps padding along the corridor, no sound of glass breaking. No doors creaking open. Eventually she drifted back into an uneasy sleep, only to be woken up at half past seven by an urgent knocking on the bedroom door.

She got out of bed, leaving Mary still asleep. She reached for her dressing gown, put it on, and opened the door.

Arthur Bloodworthy stood there, his usually florid face deathly pale, his body shaking.

'Madam, we've been robbed. The cabinet. It's all gone. Mr McKenzie's Chinese porcelain's been stolen!'

Chapter 17

The police launch skimmed along the coast towards Ardnamurchan Point. On the starboard side, Douglas caught sight of the inlet which locals called Craggy Cove, because of the high cliffs which towered above it, making it inaccessible for all but abseilers from the path above. Already the news had got around that a yacht had shifted its position and the clifftop was fringed with a sprinkling of curious spectators, hoping for a slice of Sunday afternoon drama.

The launch turned towards the shore and the swell propelled them into the cove, straight towards the cliffs. It was necessary to hold the boat firm with two anchors. The police scuba divers, looking sinister in their black rubber suits and masks, their canisters of oxygen strapped to their backs, flopped over the side and disappeared beneath the choppy waves. Those left on board could only settle down to wait.

Douglas stared down into the water, trying to distinguish the outline of the yacht. But saw nothing in the cloudy water. The storm had not only brought in the *Maid of Moidart* but also all the flotsam of the sea. Pieces of wood, washed as white as bones by the salt water, bound together by plastic bags. Giant fronds of bladderwrack seaweed, swirling backwards and forwards around the launch like newly washed curtains. Innumerable yoghurt pots and crisp packets. A wooden crate. Orange peel. A water-logged teddy bear. Everything, it seemed, had been sucked into that cove.

Except for the chatter of the police radio, it was peaceful. Douglas sat quite still, both hands gripping the gunwales as the launch lurched around on the swell. A black-backed gull dived low over his head to retrieve a half-eaten sandwich from the debris; another

155

joined in and, shrieking and cursing, the two huge birds tugged and fought over the bread as if it were their last meal.

Minutes passed and there was still no sign of the divers. Each canister of air gave the diver one hour under water, so there was plenty of time for the divers to carry out a thorough inspection of the wreck. The boat rolled around on its anchors and Douglas, feeling the effects of the long drive and the lack of food and sleep, found himself nodding off.

Suddenly there was a splash and the boat rocked violently, jerking him awake. The first diver had reappeared, followed quickly by the second. They were hauled on board and stood there recovering, shaking the water off their face-masks.

'She's there, all right,' said Andy, a solid Glaswegian. 'On her side, with her name for all to see. Mast's gone – and sails, of course. But there's also a bloody great hole in her bow, just below the waterline. It wasn't a wave which tipped her over, sir. She was rammed.'

Douglas set off for Fridale that Sunday afternoon, arriving late at the vicarage. Father Paul looked at him sympathetically.

'You're certainly clocking up the miles, Douglas. This must be costing you a small fortune in petrol. Come on in – your sergeant's waiting for you.'

They went into the study, where a fire was burning. Douglas, chilled from his drive, moved towards it gratefully.

Venerables' dispassionate face registered a glimmer of something resembling pleasure when he saw Douglas. 'Good to see you again, sir,' he said.

'And you. So what's new on your patch?' Douglas went on.

'Fairbrother's been arrested for arson. The family's in one hell of a state. All Willoughby's fault, of course. McKenzie's will's turned up – his solicitor's got it now. And Pete Fraser *was* lying when he said that he didn't phone Janice Hudson's house last Sunday morning. We've confirmed that the call was made from Reivers Hall. And to cap it all I've just heard from Tom Emmerson – a good little snout he's turning out to be – that there's been a robbery up at the Hall. A whole cabinet of Chinese porcelain's been nicked. And no one's reported it. That's a bit odd, to say the least, isn't it? Usually the 999 call follows immediately after the break-in. For insurance purposes, if nothing else. It's all go in Fridale, sir. But what happened North of the Border?'

'The *Maid*'s been located. Divers found she'd been holed in the bow. There's no doubt about it – rocks wouldn't have made such a clean cut. She must have gone down like a stiff with weights on his legs.'

'Got any idea who did it?'

'The police are interviewing a Mr Hamish McIntosh. He owns the right sort of yacht for a ramming job. The question is why he'd want to do away with Charles Cameron. Did someone pay him to do it? Or hire his boat that evening? The trouble is it's five years since Cameron died, and Hamish will have squared up his alibi right enough after all this time. It'll be the devil of a job to prove anything.'

'Did they find anything inside the yacht, sir?'

'They'll be lifting her this week, and then they'll take a good look inside her. We'll soon know if Cameron was up to anything.'

'What's his widow going to say when she hears her deceased husband was deliberately dispatched to the bottom of the sea and not tipped out of his boat by a freak wave?'

'I doubt if she'll be all that bothered. She seems to take most things in her stride. It's a rum set-up, Sergeant. Two sisters. One of them finds her husband strung up in his dressing room wearing one of her skirts; the other's husband is rammed at sea and sent to a watery grave. But neither of them seem that interested in finding out the truth. I get the impression they just don't want us asking questions. Don't want us digging below the surface. One thing's for sure – both those husbands had something to hide. And their wives aren't naive. They'll have known that they were getting into when they married them. Where's Willoughby, by the way?'

'Up in Berwick, with Sean O'Neill. But they're both coming home tomorrow. I saved the best news till last. They've dropped charges. There's not a shred of evidence against O'Neill and the gardai told Berwick in no uncertain terms that they were making a very big mistake. Willoughby's been rapped over the knuckles for pursuing a suspect with insufficient cause, and Sean's a free man.'

'With everyone looking at him sideways, thinking he might just be guilty. What a bloody cock-up. Where's the poor fellow going to live? If I were him, I'd be champing at the bit to get back to Ireland.'

'He's staying here with us, Douglas,' said Father Paul quietly.

'I've got an attic room which he can use. He's determined to stay right here in Fridale until the manuscript's recovered and Derek Fairbrother's murderer is caught. He's a stubborn man. Brave. And angry.'

'He's every reason to be. My God, how I feel for him. How he must hate the police now. Let's hope Willoughby's got the decency to resign after this. Just look at his record over the last few days. One man arrested on the flimsiest of evidence – if you can call it that: he's Irish and took a peek at a manuscript without asking first; another man arrested for a crime he'd never have committed if Willoughby hadn't started spreading rumours. That's why we must go carefully, Sergeant. We'll get there, whether I'm on the case or off it; but gently does it. Tighten the net; watch the fish trying to wriggle free, then haul it in. And take care of Tom Emmerson. He's valuable. Just what we need – an informant with inside knowledge and no moral scruples whatsoever.'

'He's costing me a bit, sir. Likes his beer.'

'Give him whatever he bloody well wants. Keep him happy.'

'And now,' said Father Paul calmly, 'before I say Compline, I am sure you could do with a cup of tea.'

Patricia McKenzie lit her twenty-first cigarette of the day and stared incredulously at Arthur Bloodworthy.

'I don't believe this. Are you quite certain? Not insured? My husband *didn't insure* his collection of porcelain?'

'That's right, madam. Mr McKenzie never insured the contents of that particular cabinet. I remember him saying that he could never afford the premium.'

Patricia looked sceptical. 'So we've lost the lot?'

'It seems so. Of course, we must check with his broker tomorrow. He appears to be away this weekend. I am sorry, madam.'

Pat glanced angrily at her sister, who was drinking neat scotch and gazing out of the window. 'Did you know about this, Mary?'

'Me?' she said, turning to face Pat. 'Of course not. I never enjoyed Ian's confidence. You should have insisted he insure the porcelain. I can't believe the premium was that vast.'

Pat shrugged hopelessly. 'Ian never discussed business with me. Not that I encouraged him to – I just expected him to take care of it. Let's not cry over spilt milk. The bloody china's gone; and good riddance,

I say. I could never see why Ian was so crazy about it. What does interest me is who could have opened that cabinet without breaking the glass. Someone used a key. None of us heard a thing last night.'

'That's right, madam,' said Arthur indignantly, 'that cabinet was locked. The key's kept in the key cupboard in the pantry and it's still there.'

Patricia looked thoughtful. 'Then it sounds like an inside job. We'll have to check on the staff.'

'That's not going to be easy, madam. Everyone feels under suspicion after what happened last Saturday. They're not likely to be very co-operative.'

'Then I'll have their living quarters searched. And your cottage, while I'm at it.'

'Mine, madam?' Arthur's face turned a deep purple. 'You don't think that I'd rob you?' he spluttered. 'I hope you'll withdraw that remark, madam, and present me with an apology.'

'Oh, stop fussing, Arthur. I don't think for one minute that you've turned to thieving at this stage of your career. But someone might have thought he'd plant a few bits of china on you to keep us all busy while he mickies off with the rest of it.'

'I didn't think . . .' said Arthur, mollified.

'I don't employ you to think. Just do what you're told. Now run off and have a rummage through everyone's living quarters. If they refuse, that'll look suspicious in itself. Oh, and Arthur – no need to tell the police. They've got enough on their plates as it is.'

'Madam, I don't know that we can keep something like this quiet for long. I expect the police have already been informed. Not by me, of course – that goes without saying – I'd never act without consulting you, but there are other people working here, and news travels fast. However, I'll start searching. Maybe we'll find something.'

'You'll be lucky,' said Mary sardonically after Arthur had left the room. 'That stuff went off this estate last night like greased lightning. Pity the wind kicked up such a racket. No one heard anything, not even a car starting up. The thief had it made. But is it wise, sister dear, not to report this to the police? They're going to be mighty furious when they do find out.'

'I know. And you're right – I don't really have any option. But I'm uneasy. You see, Mary, Ian never did tell me where he acquired that stuff. And as far as I know he never went shopping in China . . .'

* * *

Late that night, Pete Fraser was summoned to Pat's room. When he went in, she was sitting at her dressing table, dressed in a silk negligé, brushing out her copper-coloured hair. She swung round to face him. He looked decidedly attractive, she thought regretfully, savouring his moody, dark face, his curly hair, the slim body and the muscular legs emphasised by tight jeans. His dark eyes, though, were not smouldering with desire as they usually did. In fact, he looked positively resentful.

'What do you want, Pat? I thought you said I was to keep away while the police are here.'

'It's not your body I want this time, Pete. I want to talk to you – that's all. Think you can remember how to do that? Why don't you have a drink? You know where the whisky is. Help yourself, and pour one for me too.'

Her voice was conciliatory, but her body was tense. She looked like a sleek jungle cat, he thought, as he went over to pour out two stiff measures of whisky in the Stuart crystal tumblers set out on the little table by the side of her bed. He knew her moods; she was often like this. She'd let him stroke her, then she'd pounce. He'd learnt that the hard way. But she still turned him on, however sharp her claws.

She took the drink he offered her and looked him up and down.

'Nothing seems to bother you, does it, Pete? Ian's death; last night's robbery – it's all grist to the mill to you, isn't it? What it is to be young and resilient. I envy you. You look after number one and sod the rest.' She licked her lips, mesmerising him. 'You could have opened that cabinet last night, couldn't you?' she whispered. 'You knew where the key was kept. It'd be child's play for the likes of you. Come on – own up. You came in last night, didn't you, when we were all asleep? The row the wind was making would have covered any noise you made. You chose your moment well. You took the china, didn't you? It's just the sort of thing you would do. You'd rob your own grandmother if she had anything of value to steal.'

Pete took a large gulp of whisky. She had her claws out now, right enough. She liked to show them off now and then, just as a warning. He shivered. She had teeth too; sharp, white teeth. And she drew blood. Claws and teeth – scratch and bite – that was our Pat. Whereas Ian, he'd always been a gentleman.

'Don't be a fool, Pat. What would I do with a load of china?'

'I'm not suggesting that you wanted to put it on your mantelpiece. You'd sell it, Pete, that's what you'd do. You sell anything, even yourself, if the money's right. But I don't think you'd have the brains to dispose of it all on your own. Come on, Pete – who are you working for? Who's paying you?'

He finished his whisky with one gulp and came over to her. He looked down and caught a glimpse of the curve of her breast which her silk negligé had fallen open to reveal. He felt himself becoming aroused.

'I work for myself. That's how I like it. I didn't steal that china – and I don't know who did. You've searched my cottage, and that hole you call my bedroom here in the Hall. I like to keep my nose clean and enjoy myself. And at this moment, I know exactly how to do that.'

He reached out and casually pulled down the front of her negligé, revealing both breasts. They gleamed silkily in the soft light of the lamp on the dressing table.

Putting down his glass, he knelt down in front of her and kissed her neck and shoulders. He felt her shiver, but her fingers were in his hair. He remembered the jungle cat. Slowly, and methodically, he began to lick each breast in turn. He knew exactly how to subdue her.

Then, suddenly, he ripped the flimsy material of her dressing gown apart and buried his head in the soft flesh of her belly. He felt the fingers tighten their grip.

'Tell me you didn't do it, Pete. You wouldn't rob me, would you? You'd never hurt me?'

'Of course not. You know how I feel about you . . .'

His head was now between her legs; he heard her sigh, felt her body squirm with pleasure. Slowly, she slipped off the stool onto the floor. Thoroughly aroused, he fell on top of her. He felt her nails dig into his back, felt the raking pain. But he knew how to silence her.

He heard her gasp with pleasure, and felt the claws withdraw into their sheaths. He'd tame her again, just as he always did. He could always tame them: Pat, and Ian. Especially Ian. But not that other bastard.

Chapter 18

Early on Monday morning, Douglas was woken by a call from Venerables.

'Berwick's been on the phone, sir. Blackburn wants to see you.'

'Does he, now? Then he'll have to wait. I've not had breakfast yet.' Douglas knew he didn't have to rush. He'd won that particular battle of wills.

By ten o'clock, Douglas was confronting a morose Superintendent Blackburn. The man seemed to have shrunk since he'd last seen him; the blustering self-confidence had vanished. Instead he looked hunted, and his once-fleshy face was furrowed and worn.

'Morning, sir. You wanted to see me?' said Douglas calmly.

'Sit down, sit down, Douglas,' said Blackburn with a false attempt at bonhomie. 'Been up North, I hear? To the West coast? Bit rough, I expect. There've been gales down here, and it's always much worse the further North you go. Still, you've had a rest, and that's what counts. Nice hotel? Good food? I hear the mussels are excellent in Oban—'

'I didn't have much time to enjoy the high life, sir. There was a lot going on up there. But I did manage the odd boat trip.'

'Yes, so I, er – so I hear. Beautiful part of the coast. Now, Douglas, I won't beat about the bush. We've had a few problems while you've been away.'

'Really? I thought Walter Willoughby was a very capable man. Very conscientious. Very – decisive.'

'I wouldn't say that. He's in too much of a hurry for my liking. In fact, to be honest, Douglas, he's fouled things up good and proper.

163

Not to mince matters, he jumped the gun and landed us all in the shit.'

'Oh dear. I *am* sorry to hear that. Too much haste, not enough speed, I suppose. Still, it's better to have someone on the case who keeps things moving. You don't want old plodders like me.'

Blackburn looked extremely sheepish. 'Look, Douglas, I – I think there's room for every sort of policing style in today's Force. And you and Venerables make a good combination. Your thoroughness and, er, experience; Venerables' youthful vision. Willoughby's all very well when it's simply a matter of sending a ferret down a hole to kill a rat, but this is a complicated case. Two murders, a major theft – I don't think he quite grasped the delicate nature of the investigation.'

Douglas tried to look impassive. It wouldn't do to gloat. 'Well, sir, slow and steady wins the race, as the proverb goes. And we did have a particularly volatile situation in Fridale. The death of a young lad – it's bound to cause anger. And when people see someone being driven off in a police car they're bound to jump to conclusions. Lucky for us that O'Neill doesn't seem the litigious type.'

Blackburn sat down heavily. He looked crumpled, defeated, like a fat candle melting in its own wax.

'Don't rub it in, man. I know we rushed in with hobnailed boots on, but we're under pressure. Willoughby's still certain that O'Neill's guilty but he'll never be able to prove it. And we've lost time. The manuscript'll be long gone by now.'

'Sir, I'm certain O'Neill wasn't your thief. We haven't even explored the other possibilities. By all accounts everyone knew where Sister Anne kept the combination number. She's simply not sure exactly who might've been able to take a wee peek at it. Either that, or she won't tell us.'

'You've obviously been talking to Inspector Flight, McBride. She's convinced that nun's hiding something. Douglas . . . we want you back on the case. I'm sorry about what happened with that Cameron woman, but you did step out of line. I don't think you'd disagree there. But we need you to get on and clear up this mess.'

Douglas, studying the mournful face of his superior, felt his heart soften. He knew that was the closest Blackburn ever came to an apology. But there were things to get straight before he could accept the challenge. 'You can't just ignore what Willoughby's done, sir. I

164

won't go back on the case with him trying to arrest every Irishman in sight.'

'I've sent him back to Durham. He'll be out of the way. And you've got Felicity to help you. We need to handle this one with a bit of tact and diplomacy. Look before we leap. Don't start a panic. People are very jittery at the moment.'

'You don't have to tell me that, sir. The whole case will collapse around our ears if we jump to the wrong conclusions.'

'All right, all right, I admit it. Willoughby was an incompetent fool, and I made a mistake in appointing him. But I was desperate. I needed a quick result, and he had a reputation as an officer with a high clear-up rate. You don't understand the pressure I'm under. You know what the press are like. If we don't pull someone in, I'll be pilloried. I'll be the laughing stock of the media. They're the ones who call the shots today, McBride.'

'Then you have to stand up to them, sir. Stop that lot hanging around the station for a start. Tell them that they're causing an obstruction.'

Blackburn shook his head sorrowfully. 'No, no. We must keep them on our side. It doesn't do to antagonise them. Just think what some papers would say if they decide to make an issue of O'Neill being brought in for questioning because the police officer in charge, namely Walter Willoughby, happens to have it in for the Irish! My God, Douglas, they'll have our guts for garters. Our press officers will have a devil of a job getting our nose clean again. We've simply got to make some progress soon, otherwise it won't be just Inspector Flight seconded from another force. Next it'll be the Yard up here, snapping at our heels.'

'I agree, sir. Mustn't let the grass grow under our feet. So where does all this leave me?'

'I want you back in harness, Douglas. Get moving. Catch the bastards and restore people's confidence in the Northumbrian police.'

'What's happened to Derek Fairbrother's father, sir?'

'He's out on bail. We've charged him with arson.'

Douglas sighed. In this whole sorry mess, the only person they'd actually managed to arrest was simply trying to enforce his own sort of rough justice on the person he believed had murdered his son.

'I just hope he won't be treated too harshly, sir. He was strongly provoked. Mostly by us, I'm afraid to say.'

Blackburn winced. 'Yes, Douglas. I know. And I'm sure no jury is going to treat him with too great a severity. After all, what parent bereaved in similar fashion wouldn't be tempted to do the same, given the chance? Anyway, you can leave the recriminations to the Chief Constable. He's seeing me in an hour's time. Something for me to look forward to, eh? Oh, and Chief Inspector . . . good luck.'

Feeling as if he were leaving a lonely Crusader in charge of a beleaguered citadel, Douglas left headquarters and drove South to Fridale. There was no time to lose. Any more foul-ups and the Force would be disgraced once and for all. Not that he cared about Blackburn; he'd been a fool and deserved all that was coming to him. Not that he gave a hoot about Willoughby. But he did care about Sean O'Neill. And the Fairbrother family. They hadn't done anything to deserve these tragedies. They were the innocent victims, and out there somewhere was the person or persons who had brought this evil upon them. But not for long, he thought; not for long. And, as he drove down the A1, he allowed himself to indulge in a small glow of satisfaction. It was good to be in charge again. Officially, anyway.

First of all, he had to have another chat with Alec Montgomery. He might be able to shed more light on the relationship between the McKenzies and the Camerons. The Highland connection.

At half past twelve he arrived at Montgomery Hall. The place looked deserted, but a curtain was drawn in an upstairs window, suggesting that someone was at home. Still in bed? he wondered. Was Alec ill? Or just lazy?

He rang the doorbell and waited. Nothing happened. He rang again, and looked up at the curtained window. No sign of life. He walked round to the side of the house. All was as it should be. A cock pheasant called his mate, followed by a scuffling in the shrubbery; a rabbit bolted across the lawn.

He walked round the back of the house to the kitchen door, which was locked. Montgomery had obviously gone out for the day. As he walked round to the far side of the house, he spotted another door: a small wooden affair with an old-fashioned latch lock. He lifted the latch and pushed it open. Stairs led down to a cellar. He went cautiously down the stairs, aware that he hadn't a search warrant; he would get into serious trouble if he was reported. He found himself in what appeared to be a junk room. Another door led into the servants' area, with its stone floors, store cupboards, and oil-fired boiler.

Then along a passage and into the kitchen. As expected, all was neat and tidy, but the kettle was cold, and there were no indications that anyone had recently eaten breakfast.

Taking a huge risk, he went into the sitting room, the dining room, and the study in turn. Nothing. He hesitated. The curtained window bothered him. Should he go upstairs? He didn't want to be suspended all over again. But, he reasoned, by entering the house in the first place he'd already committed himself. He climbed the stairs.

Quietly he opened the door of the first room he came to. There was Alec Montgomery, sitting up in bed dressed in silk pyjamas. As Douglas went in, Montgomery turned his head and Douglas recoiled. The man's face was a nightmare. Even in the pale light of the curtained room, Douglas could see the deep bruises covering his plump cheeks. His lower lip was torn and swollen. His nose was grotesque: a shapeless mass of purple flesh. One eye was closed; the other deeply bruised.

'Good God, sir. What's been going on? You look terrible.'

'Douglas McBride, you've no right to come creeping round my house! I'll report you for this. But as you are here, and since you ask, let me tell you: I had a fall. A bad one. I was out on the moors taking a stroll, and fell down into a gully. This eye was the result of a particularly unpleasant rowan bush which stopped my fall; the rest is due to my face coming into sharp contact with a rock.'

'You need a doctor, sir. That lip needs stitches. Looks like a hospital job to me.'

'McBride, please leave me to see to my own affairs! How dare you come prowling round my house?' Alec was angry now. 'I take it you haven't a search warrant? If that's the case, then please get out of my house before I phone your superiors. You've no right to be here. You're off the investigation. You're no more than a private citizen.'

Douglas smiled. 'Don't get distressed, sir. It won't do you any good, not in your state. And you can call me Chief Inspector again. I'm back in harness; and I have every right to be here. When I checked on your house, I found a back door open. Now, given what's gone on around here recently, it seemed to me unwise to leave your house unsecured. When I didn't get a reply to the front door, it occurred to me that a burglar may already have entered the premises. So, in fact, sir, you should thank me. At considerable risk to myself, I

167

was endeavouring to protect your property. And now it's my duty to persuade you to seek medical assistance.'

'Just leave me alone, will you? I'll be all right. My housekeeper can always come in if I need help. She's Mrs Knowles – you know Ben Knowles, the landlord of the Fridale Arms? She's his wife. Anyway, I thought you were on holiday . . . Chief Inspector,' he said, after a pause.

'I was. Just a wee trip back North. Oh, and guess what happened while I was there? They salvaged Charlie Cameron's yacht. The storms brought it to the surface. The bow had a bloody great hole in it, so it looks like the Glasgow police will be reopening the case.'

'This will be upsetting news for Mary,' said Montgomery, his battered face registering concern.

'I expect it will be,' said Douglas equably. 'And she may have other shocks in store. They're lifting the yacht later this week, so we may have a better idea of what Charlie Cameron's nautical activities really entailed.'

Alec frowned. 'Did you see Hamish again?'

'Hamish? Oh, he was otherwise engaged. He's being questioned by the police at this very moment. Now, let me give you a hand, sir. You'll be needing some food, and that face seeing to. I'm on my way to the Fridale Arms now, so I'll tell Mrs Knowles to come and take care of you. It's not good for you to be all alone in the dark.'

'He's been beaten up, Sergeant,' said Douglas, forking up a chip. They were in the Fridale Arms; he'd been a bit later than usual, but Venerables had waited for him. 'And what's more, he hasn't reported it. And he doesn't seem to want a doctor to look at him. Told me some cock-and-bull story about falling over on the moors – as if he'd be going for a stroll up there, with the weather we've been having! So who's got it in for Alec Montgomery, I wonder?'

'Well, there's O'Neill, for one,' said Venerables, shaking the bottle of tomato ketchup over his plate of chips. 'Montgomery's got a lot to answer for there. But it's queer how folk in these parts don't like reporting things. The Hall gets burgled, and we only hear about it through staff gossip. Very strange.'

'Why don't people report things, Venerables?'

'They've got something to hide. Don't want questions asked.'

Douglas took a mouthful of beer. It was good to be with Venerables again, mulling over events. Two minds were always better than one.

'And too many people around here have violent and bitter ene-
mies, Venerables. McKenzie gets strung up, then a boy gets shot – by
mistake, we can only assume – and now we find out that Charlie
Cameron's death wasn't accidental. On top of all this, Alec
Montgomery gets beaten up. Then there's the theft from Reivers
Hall, which no one wants us to know about. What's the link?'

'They were all pals, weren't they? And by all accounts,
Montgomery was sweet on Pat McKenzie. And still is: even though
she's given him the boot. I got that bit of news from Tom Emmerson
who said Montgomery was at the Hall on Saturday night, and stayed
for quite a long time.' Venerables took out a notebook and opened it.
'An hour and a half, to be exact. From eight o'clock to nine thirty.'

'Emmerson's earning his keep, then?'

'He keeps a weather eye on things.'

'What's his attitude towards the Reivers Hall set-up?'

'Hates Pete Fraser like poison. Jealous because Pete's got a way
with the girls. And Tom's only got a low-powered motorbike and
Pete buys himself a bloody great BMW. I have to say that Tom's also
got a mind like a sewer. He lives in a pretty lurid fantasy world.'

'What do you mean?'

'You have to take what he says with a pinch of salt. For instance,
according to Tom, Pete was bonking Pat McKenzie at the same time
as he was bonking her husband. And each knew what the other was
up to. I find that a bit hard to believe, don't you, sir?'

Venerables' attitude to this subject seemed unnecessarily prudish
to Douglas. 'When it comes to – bonking, as you call it, Sergeant – I
keep an open mind.' For who'd have thought he – Douglas – would
ever have bedded a witness during a murder investigation?

'And Charlie Cameron? Did he enjoy Pete's favours too?'

'Can't say. Tom never met him. His wife's always played around,
though. But not with Pete Fraser.'

Douglas winced. Would he ever escape from Mary Cameron? He
forced himself to concentrate on what Venerables had said. 'There
could have been a sexual motive behind the attack on Montgomery,
of course. People don't usually want to own up to their sexual pecca-
dilloes. That's probably why he didn't report it.'

'Or maybe it's just something more straightforward – like
Montgomery not paying his debts. Better not get too fanciful, sir.'

'Human beings are never straightforward, Sergeant. Surely I don't
have to tell you that. We never know what goes on behind the net

curtains. And whatever trouble Montgomery was in, I doubt it was financial. He's not short of a bob or two. When are you seeing Emmerson again?'

'This evening. Around opening time. I meet him on a daily basis.'

'Good.' Douglas glanced at his watch. 'Come on, lad – eat up. There's plenty to do. And we're partners in crime again.'

'What's next on the agenda?'

'Let's go and find Kevin Fraser. Get to the bottom of this Sunday-morning business.'

'And after that?'

'Back to Reivers. I want to have a wee chat with Mary Cameron.'

Venerables looked alarmed. 'I shouldn't do that if I were you, sir. You don't want to get caught with your trousers down again.'

'Relax, Sergeant. I'm quite capable of controlling myself. I think she might be rather interested to learn that her husband's death wasn't accidental.'

'Don't be too sure of that, sir. She might not want us poking around in the ashes of a case she thought was closed.'

'That remains to be seen. I also want to see Mrs McKenzie. She might like to have a shoulder to cry on now, seeing as how her husband's valuable collection of Chinese porcelain's been stolen.'

'Don't be too sure of that either, sir.'

'Sergeant, do I detect a growing note of cynicism in your comments? You used to tell me that people aren't as bad as they seem.'

'No, they're worse,' said Venerables, stolidly eating his last chip.

Douglas laughed. 'How's Polly getting on with her research, Sergeant?'

'Flick's giving her a hand, when she's not dashing off to Newcastle to consult her database there. Apparently, it's more comprehensive than ours.'

Douglas nodded, satisfied. 'She knows what she's doing. And it keeps her out of harm's way.'

'I'm not so certain about that, sir. We still don't know who was behind the mugging. She says she's got a hunch; but being a conscientious detective she's not saying anything until she's got a bit more to go on. She's good, is that girl. Keeps plugging away and waits patiently for the breakthrough.'

'Well, good luck to her.'

Chapter 19

The deep-throated baying of the Frasers' Rottweiler greeted them as they drove up to Lake Cottage. The dog had been locked up in the outhouse and, as they left the car and walked up to the cottage, they could hear a frenzied scratching at the woodwork and loud snorts coming from underneath the door.

'Thank God he's locked up,' muttered Venerables. 'He'd make mincemeat of us both.'

The gales of the previous week had blown themselves out and the sun was shining on the surface of the lake. A light breeze rustled the reed-beds which fringed the edge of the water. Kevin didn't appear to be at home, but Douglas wanted to make sure. As he walked round the side of the cottage, he spotted a man standing thigh-deep in the water, cutting reeds and tying them up into bundles with one deft turn of his arm. Piles of these bundles were stacked on the grass. Douglas beckoned to Venerables, and together they walked down to the lakeside. As they approached, the man stopped work and stared at them.

He was old; perhaps he looked older than he was, for his back was bent through years of hard manual work. He wore an ancient battered hat which covered most of his face, but his brilliant blue eyes flashed across at them like twin beams from a lighthouse.

'You're police, aren't you?' he said. 'I'd recognise you anywhere. Come after Kevin? What's that little devil been up to?'

Douglas and Venerables sauntered over to him. 'And who might you be?' asked Douglas amicably.

'Folk call me Tinker; but my real name's Fuller. Jo Fuller.'

'And what are you doing here?'

'What does it look as if I'm doing? I'm cutting reeds, that's what

171

I'm doing. Thatchers need reeds, and I provide them. There's a shortage of reeds at the moment – all them posh City folk as come up here and buy up old cottages find when they've moved in that the roof's falling to pieces. So they want new roofs – and that's where I come in. Mr McKenzie, God bless him, a real tragedy he died, let me cut into these beds. It does no harm to thin the reeds out at this time of the year. I asked Mrs McKenzie and she told me to carry on as before. So here I am.'

'You know Kevin Fraser, Tinker?' said Douglas.

'Everyone knows Kevin. Just as everyone knows me. And what's more I ain't going to tell you nothing about him. Not without his permission, anyway. I can't say as he's a pal of mine, because he ain't, but he's done me a few good turns so I keep mum about what he does. Not that he does much,' he added hastily, 'just picks up the odd pheasant or two. Nearly always slips a brace to me. Mr McKenzie used to turn a blind eye, because his shoot's well stocked and he never missed one or two. We don't have to look far when we feel like a pheasant for dinner. Nothing wrong in that, is there? Either we get them or the crows do.'

'We'll not go into Kevin's poaching activities just now. Leave that to the gamekeepers. But maybe you know where he is right now? Where can we find him?'

'That's easy. He's got a job on up at Holloway's. Holloway's the Builders, just along the Alnwick road.'

'Thank you, sir,' said Douglas feelingly. 'We'll be off now and leave you in peace. Thanks for your help.'

'Don't mention it. Are you going to see Kevin now?'

'That's the general idea.'

'Then tell him that Janice Hudson's been looking for him.'

'Did she say what she wanted?'

'No, but by the look of her I wouldn't like to be in young Kevin's shoes.' Tinker pointed significantly at his middle.

'Got a bun in the oven, has she?' said Venerables coolly.

'Looks like it to me. I might not be much of a ladies' man, but I do know how lassies carry on when a bairn's on the way. She looked a bit angry-like, so I expect Kevin's been giving her the slip. She'll not catch him like that. It's the oldest trick in the world. It'll need a clever lass to fix Kevin Fraser.'

* * *

They found Kevin stacking bags of cement in Holloway's yard. His swarthy, handsome face darkened when he saw the two policemen.

'A word with you, sir. Anywhere private we can go?'

'There's only the shed. That'll have to do.'

'Sounds ideal. We won't take up much of your time.'

Kevin led the way to a rickety shed in one corner of the yard. Inside there was a battered wooden table, covered with dirty mugs; the air was thick with stale tobacco smoke.

'What's all this about then?' he asked nervously as they went in and he closed the door.

'We're investigating the murder of Derek Fairbrother which took place last Sunday. The fifteenth of September, to be exact. We've been looking through our files, and we've come across an inconsistency in your story. You told us that on the night of September the fourteenth, you and Janice Hudson . . .'

'I can't remember that far back.'

'It's only a week ago. And it wasn't an ordinary night. Ian McKenzie, your brother's employer, was murdered; and the following morning Derek was shot in the village. Now let me remind you what you told us before. You said you went to a disco with Janice Hudson and then came back to her place at about three in the morning. You stayed there till the following day.'

'That sounds about right. What's wrong with that?'

'Nothing at all. But you didn't stay long, did you, sir? Not as long as you told us. The next door neighbour saw Janice hanging out her washing at nine o'clock on Sunday morning, so you can't have had much of a lie-in, can you? Janice originally told us you both had a lie-in that Sunday morning, but now we find that's not true. And we know now that your brother Pete tried to phone you at Janice's house early on Sunday, but you weren't there. He denied making that call, but we know he's lying. Calls can be traced. And Janice admits she wasn't telling us the truth either when she said you were there till late on Sunday morning.' Douglas didn't mention that she'd refused point-blank to make a statement to that effect. 'So what's going on? What are you trying to hide? Either you were there, or you weren't. And if you weren't, then where the hell were you? Come on, sir, try a bit harder. What the devil were you up to on Sunday the fifteenth of September after half past seven in the morning?'

Kevin looked fixedly at Douglas as if he were trying to make up

173

his mind. He wasn't such a smooth customer as his brother. Finally he shrugged his shoulders.

'All right. It makes no difference. You'll find out anyway. Yes, I did leave Janice's house early.'

Douglas sighed. 'Thank you, sir. Perhaps you could have told us that in the first place. So where did you go?'

Kevin looked shifty. 'Poaching, of course.'

'Poaching?'

'On the McKenzie shoot. He'd had a shooting party the day before; you were there, so you know I'm not lying. Sometimes the dogs don't always pick up everything that's shot, and as I needed some pheasants, I went out early, before anyone else did. I was lucky. I picked up about four brace.'

'Did you take a gun with you?'

'A gun? Of course not. You only need your eyes to spot a winged pheasant. And a bloody good stick if you find any that need putting out of their misery.'

'Can anyone support your story, sir?' said Douglas. Kevin's story sounded plausible enough, he thought; estate workers often went after the pickings when there'd been a shoot the previous day. 'Who did you sell the pheasants to?'

'I sell them anywhere I can. Everyone in these parts knows Kevin Fraser's pheasants. They're cheaper than anyone else's; and fresher.'

'Just give me a couple of names.'

'Knowles at the Fridale Arms always has as many as I can provide. His deep freeze is packed with them. Useful to have a supply of cheap game when you run a pub.'

'And you're quite sure you don't own a gun?'

'I've told you. No. My brother's got a shotgun, of course, but he's a ghillie. He's got a licence. I just pick them up off the ground. That's all.'

'Janice knows you do a spot of poaching?'

'Janice? Of course. She's partial to a bit of game herself.'

'Then she will confirm that you went off early last Sunday morning in order to bring home the dinner?'

'You'll have to ask her.'

'We intend to. As a matter of fact, she's been looking for you this morning, sir. Tinker told us to pass on a message. I wonder what she wanted?' Douglas's voice was deceptively innocent. He knew his words might rouse Kevin to anger, and he wasn't wrong.

174

'Then she can take a running jump! I'm fed up with the stupid bitch. They're all the same, girls. They let you fuck them and then they think they own you. The stupid bitch has got herself knocked up – she says it's mine. But I'm not having that. It could be anyone's. She's got one bastard already and I'm damned if I'm going to take on another one. If it is mine, then she's planned it, that's for sure. Girls these days don't get knocked up unless they want to. So tell Tinker that if she comes looking for me again, I don't want to see her. What's more, if she keeps pestering me, I'll sock her one.'

'I wouldn't do that, sir, if I were you. It'll only land you in our lock-up on an assault charge.'

They drove off in thoughtful silence. Finally Douglas broke into their reverie. 'Check on those pheasants, Sergeant. I don't trust Kevin Fraser, and I don't like his alibi. All my instincts are telling me he's a crook.'

'And where would we be without our instincts, sir?' said Venerables enigmatically.

'Nowhere at all, that's for sure. Don't worry – I'm not about to do a Willoughby. Instinct backed up by hard evidence; that's the way.'

'And a fair dollop of imagination.'

'No place for imagination. Just trust your instinct, and then take a hard, critical look at what it's telling you. I'll drop you off at the pub and you can ask Knowles if he's bought any pheasants recently.'

'And you, sir? Where are you going?'

'Me? To the Hall, of course. Where else?'

Chapter 20

It was amazing how casual the rich could be about their possessions, thought Flick, as she waited for Pat McKenzie in the dining room. The alarm system at Reivers Hall was at least twenty years out of date, and yet the house was crammed with treasures. Any security expert worth his salt would have advised Ian McKenzie to update the whole system, install security cameras, and make sure that really valuable items were separately protected. And if Flick had been in Ian McKenzie's shoes, she would have thought seriously about getting a big, loud, guard-dog. As it stood, Reivers Hall was a burglar's dream. Anyone with a bit of know-how could walk in, pick up a few valuables and walk straight out again. And by all accounts that was exactly what had happened in the early hours of Sunday morning. Someone had entered the house, walked up the stairs, opened the cabinet in which the porcelain was housed, using his own key, removed every last piece of china, and marched off with it. Really, people like the McKenzies deserved all they got.

The door opened and Pat came in. Flick noticed that, for once, she looked tired; consequently she looked her age. She sat down on the heavy Victorian carver chair at the head of the table.

'Have you found anything yet, Detective Inspector?' she said hesitantly.

'I'm afraid not, Mrs McKenzie. But I'm sure you can see our difficulties. It would have helped if we'd been told about the theft as soon as it happened.'

'That was our fault, I'm afraid. There was a stupid misunderstanding. In all the panic, I thought Bloodworthy was going to call you – and he thought I was. We only realised that neither of us had done so

177

when, by yesterday evening, you hadn't arrived. So rather than call you out so late, we waited until today.'

'Thieves have a habit of hiding their haul until the dust has settled,' said Flick. 'Then they look for a customer. We can't search every barn, cellar, cave and attic in the country. We have to go through the usual procedure of trying to find out who might have a particular interest in this collection, who was in the neighbourhood at the time when it was stolen, who might have seen or heard anything on Saturday night. Tedious and slow, I'm afraid, but there's no alternative.'

'Well, in answer to the first of those questions, everyone we knew – including all the guests who were present a week ago at our ill-fated dinner party – admired Ian's Chinese collection.'

Flick nodded. 'We're working through the list. Most lived some distance away and most of them have alibis for that night. Can you think of anyone else?'

'I hope you're not insinuating that it was one of our family friends who robbed us, Inspector Flight. If you are, then I think you're quite mistaken.'

Flick sighed; it was always the same. No one ever believed their friends could do the dirty on them, yet in ninety-nine per cent of the cases she'd dealt with over the last five years, it was someone well known to the family who'd tipped off the thieves. Ordinary burglars didn't tend to rob country houses. In the first place, they were inaccessible; they usually had excellent security arrangements; and their spoils were eminently traceable.

'I'm sure you're right, Mrs McKenzie. But your thief definitely had some knowledge of this house. They went straight to the cabinet – they didn't so much as move anything else. They had keys to the house and the cabinet. They knew how to switch off your burglar alarm – which, I have to tell you, isn't exactly a difficult feat. They—'

'Professional thieves are up to all sorts of tricks, aren't they?'

'That's true. But how did they know exactly where to look? Have you considered that? By the way, has your insurance company checked out your security system? They usually have very stringent requirements where the protection of valuables is concerned.'

For a moment, Pat looked uncomfortable. Then she collected herself and looked defiantly at Flick. 'Ian didn't insure the porcelain. In actual fact, no one would cover it. Not at a premium we could afford.'

Flick was speechless for a moment. 'I find that astonishing. There are insurance companies which specialise in *objets d'art*. You could have insured it for part of its value at least.'

'Ian didn't think it was necessary. And now, if you've no news for me, I must get on with sorting out Ian's affairs. The police keep pestering me with questions about the will and I can't give them the answers they want. Ian's study's been turned into an incident room and the whole house is at sixes and sevens. Would you please excuse me?'

'Of course, Mrs McKenzie. I'm sorry for all the upheaval, but I'm sure you appreciate that it's unavoidable. One day soon you'll be left in peace.'

Pat walked stiffly out of the room. Flick strolled over to the window and stood there, lost in thought. Then she gave a start. A car was coming up the main drive: Douglas's Volvo. And it was really good to see him back.

Douglas had driven up to Rcivers Hall through the late autumn sunshine. Never had the estate looked more beautiful than it did today, he thought, admiring the rowan trees blazing with scarlet and the heather-covered banks of the stream alive with bees contentedly going about their business. Ahead of him was the house, its sandstone walls mellow in the strong sunlight, the Virginia creeper – already turned blood-red – winding over the Gothic-arched front door and edging its way towards the first-floor mullioned windows. A fine house, he thought. Built with McKenzie money, and McKenzie energy. And two fine women inside, enjoying the comforts which McKenzie men had provided.

Yet, as he slowed down to look at the artificial waterfall that cascaded down from an artificial miniature cliff, never had it seemed more corrupt. A man had died here in mysterious circumstances and the ripples of that death had somehow reached the surrounding area, creating an overwhelming atmosphere of hate and suspicion. Yes, he thought, Reivers Hall was undeniably beautiful, but it reminded him of the glittering beauty of a poisonous reptile. Admire it, but keep your distance: it could strike at any moment.

He parked his car by the front door and rang the bell. Arthur

Bloodworthy opened the door, and peered furtively out. When he saw Douglas, he opened it with a visible sigh of relief.

'Glad to see you, sir. You're back with us again, I hear.'

'It seems so. I'd like to speak to Mrs Cameron and Mrs McKenzie. One at a time, if it's convenient.'

'They'll be glad to see you. What with Mr McKenzie's terrible death, and now this burglary, they're in a bad way. It'll be a relief when it's all over – the killer found and locked up – and then they can get on with their own lives. Let me take you to Mrs Cameron's morning room. It'll be quiet there – the rest of the place is still swarming with your men, taking fingerprints and moving all the furniture around. It's too late, of course. No use locking the stable door when the horse has already bolted.'

Bloodworthy led Douglas to a small room at the front of the house, a room he'd never seen before. Somehow it reminded him of Mary: the jewel-coloured carpet; the softly glowing watercolours; the long, elegant windows looking out onto the park; the rich brocade curtains.

While he waited for Mary to arrive, he walked over to the fireplace and studied the watercolour on the wall above it. It depicted two girls in Victorian dresses sprawling on the grass, their heads close together. One was making a daisy chain; the other blowing at a dandelion clock. A picture of idyllic childhood. Was this the sort of childhood Mary had enjoyed, he wondered? Safe, secure, happy? If so, what had turned her into the manipulative, ruthless woman she was now? Beautiful, certainly – but callous, devoid of any compassion.

Then Mary walked in. And Douglas found he could look at her now without his heart turning somersaults. His eyes could meet hers without wavering. *So*, he thought ruefully, *this is what happens when the flames of passion are stamped out*. Was it really only a week ago that he had stood like a schoolboy, tongue-tied in her presence?

It was Mary who lowered her eyes first. Then, 'How are you, Douglas?' she said, in that soft Highland voice of hers which had once melted his heart. Suddenly, he had a mental picture of her as she had been in that hotel; caressing him with soft words, eagerly helping him to undress, flattering him until he'd been reduced to putty in her hands. It hadn't turned out quite as she'd expected, however. She'd made sure that he was removed from the investigation – but never would she have expected him to be reinstated. And now the ball was in his court. No longer was he dazzled by her loveliness. She'd met her match; and Douglas knew he was going to win the game.

'I'm fine, thank you, Mrs Cameron. I won't keep you long. I know you've had more trouble here. A shame about your sister's porcelain.'

Mary shrugged her shoulders dismissively. 'Oh, that's Pat's business. I always disliked that Chinese collection, personally. I could never understand what Ian saw in it.'

He found himself studying her intently as she spoke to him. She looked less composed than when he'd last seen her. There were shadows under her eyes, and her hair, still a glorious autumn colour, seemed less glossy, more brittle. Douglas found himself wondering whether she dyed it.

'You've been away up North, I hear,' she went on, getting into her social stride. 'We've all missed you. Chief Inspector Willoughby was a walking disaster.'

'I'm glad to know I was missed. Yes, I took a trip to Scotland – to your neck of the woods, as it happens. I went to Edinburgh first, and had a wee chat with your brother-in-law.'

'With *Bruce*? Whatever for?' she exclaimed as Bloodworthy came in with a tray of tea.

'The family's solicitor is an important person when there's been a death. He spoke of his brother. He told me a lot about Charles's tragic yachting accident.'

As she poured out the tea, she seemed more at ease, despite the mention of Charles's name. He wondered whether this was due to the fact that she was performing a familiar ritual. Or was it due to something else? Maybe the conversation had moved into what she saw as safer channels. Whatever it was, somehow or other he had to puncture her composure.

'Yes, he was devastated by his death. Just as we were,' she said, as she handed Douglas his tea.

He had to admire her. She might be the archetypal hypocrite, but she knew how to put on a good performance. She had poured the tea with a steady hand and handed it to him with a demure look. There was no hint of embarrassment. It was if a curtain had come down in her brain, shutting off the memory of past events. He felt a ripple of irritation. How could she be so calm? How could she carry on as if nothing had happened between them?

'It was so stupid of Charles to put out in that gale,' she went on, prattling effortlessly. 'Single-handed sailing is always risky. But there it is. He was always a dare-devil. I suppose that's what attracted me to him in the first place. I could never stop him from pushing himself to the limit.'

'Mrs Cameron,' said Douglas decisively, carefully returning the delicate cup to its saucer, 'Charles Cameron's death was not an accident. The Oban coastguards have located his yacht. It now appears that he was murdered.'

At last he had shaken her. 'Murdered? But – that's impossible. Charles's death was an accident! The yacht capsized during a storm, and went down in one of the deepest parts of the sea. There was never any mention of *murder* . . . Good heavens, Chief Inspector, we went over the evidence again and again at the inquest. It was clearly a case of misadventure. We also reached the conclusion that there was no possibility of salvaging the wreck, so how—'

'The storms of the last few days were much worse up North. The sea was so churned up that the yacht shifted, and she was brought into shallower waters – a coastal inlet where it was possible to send down divers. That's what I was doing when I went to Scotland, Mrs Cameron.'

'Do you know this for a fact, Chief Inspector? Or is it just supposition?'

'Mrs Cameron, I'm a police officer; I don't deal in suppositions. I watched the divers go down. They found a large hole in the bow of your husband's yacht. She'd been deliberately rammed. She must have gone down like a stone – your husband wouldn't have stood a chance.'

Now he'd totally shattered that polite façade. She was visibly moved. She slumped back against the cushions on the sofa and looked anxiously at Douglas. There was something else in her expression too. What was it? Fear? Yes, that was it. Mary Cameron was afraid.

'Now, who'd want to ram your husband's boat, Mrs Cameron? By all accounts he was well-liked. Local people spoke well of him to me. Hamish McIntosh—'

'Hamish?' she said quietly. 'Did you meet Hamish?'

'Of course. Everyone who goes to Oban meets Hamish, I imagine. He's one of the fixtures. He took me to the place where your husband's body came ashore. He's a great character. Not badly off, either. Owns two boats: a fishing boat turned pleasure craft, and an ocean-going yacht which he keeps in Moidart. Lucky man.'

He watched the thoughts drift across her face like clouds across the sun. He waited. Suddenly he had all the time in the world.

'My husband liked Hamish,' she said. 'Didn't trust him, of course; Hamish would do anything for money. And I mean anything. He was supposed to sell fish, and crabs and lobsters, but we knew he wasn't too particular what else he sold, if you get my meaning. Just before the accident, my husband came across Hamish on one of the islands, selling drugs to a couple of American tourists. He had big quantities of the stuff on board his yacht, he must have been supplying dealers. Charles didn't report him – Hamish was a friend. And you don't shop friends, do you? Charles warned him, of course. Said he'd have to report him if he went on selling drugs. Now I see what must have happened. Hamish got alarmed, he saw a way of silencing Charles for good. It's obvious, isn't it, Chief Inspector? Hamish McIntosh murdered my husband! He waited until Charles went out on his own in bad weather, then he followed him, rammed his yacht, and sent him to the bottom.'

She'd jumped to her feet in her agitation and was staring at Douglas, her eyes wild.

'Mrs Cameron, what you've just told me is very interesting. Why didn't you tell the police at the time? It would have helped them enormously.'

'We had no reason to think Charles's death was anything other than accidental. The coroner thought so too. I never gave Hamish so much as a thought. But now things have changed . . . Are you going to arrest the weasel?'

'That's not up to me. Glasgow police are reopening the investigation. I know they've got Hamish in for questioning, and they've extended the time for which they can hold him until the yacht's been raised. And when they raise it they'll be able to give it a thorough going-over.'

His phone bleeped. 'Excuse me – I must answer this.'

It was Robert Shaw at Oban. 'We're raising Cameron's yacht tomorrow. Any chance of you being here?'

'I'm a bit tied up right now. You'll keep me informed, won't you, Robert?'

'I will indeed, Douglas. And good luck with your investigation. The plot thickens, I expect?'

'It certainly does. In fact we've got one hell of a stew on our hands.'

He turned to tell Mary Cameron the news just as Pat McKenzie came in. She, too, looked somehow different. Her face was pale, almost grey, and there were shadows under her eyes. There was a new wariness about her, he noticed. The two women were on the defensive.

'I'm at the end of my tether with police questioning,' Pat said wearily. 'Your lady detective's been giving me the once-over about our porcelain, but I managed to escape. I thought I'd come and keep Mary company. And then I find you here!'

'I'm sorry you've been bothered. But I'm glad you've joined us. As it happens, I was going to send for you anyway. We were talking about Charles Cameron. It seems his death wasn't an accident after all. He was murdered.'

Pat's face turned even whiter as she looked at her sister, her shock apparent. 'Is this true, Mary? What's happened?'

'Charles's yacht was deliberately holed, apparently. Hamish McIntosh is being questioned.'

He couldn't be sure, but Douglas had the distinct feeling that the two sisters exchanged a quick, conspiratorial glance. He was going to have to deal with two minds now. Two minds running along the same track.

'Hamish? That sounds about right. I always thought he was a shifty so-and-so.'

'It seems you were right. Do you remember that time when Charles told us that he'd come across Hamish selling drugs on one of the islands?'

Again the sisters glanced at each other. 'Yes, of course I do. It all fits in. Hamish obviously wanted to silence Charles. So what's going to happen now, Chief Inspector?'

'It's not up to me, Mrs McKenzie. It's up to the Glasgow police. But I've just heard from the coastguards that they're raising the yacht tomorrow. Then we'll know a bit more.'

Again the look: these sisters worked as a team, it seemed. And they knew more than they let on. But gently, gently . . .

'It seems to me, Chief Inspector,' said Pat bitterly, 'that you seem more interested in a murder which took place five years ago than finding who murdered my husband last Saturday week.'

'Have patience – we'll get there in both instances. I've got no reason to be worried about the way things are going.'

'Are you anticipating making an arrest soon?'

'When we've got evidence.'

'When will that be?'

'As soon as we're ready. Now, I think I'll leave you two ladies in peace. I ought to have a word with Inspector Flight.'

'She's waiting for you, Chief Inspector. In what was once our study.'

'And you'll get it back again, madam. Very soon.'

When he'd gone, Pat looked at her sister. 'He's onto something, isn't he? I can tell. Time's running out for the McDonald sisters. I heard from Bruce today. The will's turned up. He didn't go into details, but it looks like my bastard of a husband's left me nothing except this place. Without any sort of income I simply can't afford to live here much longer.'

'There's always the vineyard.'

'That's heavily mortgaged. And we've never made any money from it. Damn Ian! He spent money like water, buying every treasure he clapped eyes on with money he didn't have. And of course, he never asked too many questions about the provenance of the things he bought, so he could never sell them on the open market. No, Mary, it's all up to you now. You marry your French Charlie and I'll come along and camp in your spare bedroom. We could have some fun. It won't be a bad life.'

Mary got up and went over to her desk. She picked up a letter and smiled at Pat sadly.

'French Charlie's dropped out, Pat. I suspect he thought I was a bit too hot to handle. And he wants heirs. Mind you, he says his *aux revoirs* very elegantly.'

'That's too bad, Mary. I was relying on the Duc.'

'We're on our own now, Pat.' She moved close to her sister, gave her a hug. 'We've got each other. It'll be just like the old days.'

'Hello, Douglas,' said Flick, looking up from the computer in the incident room. 'Any news?'

'We're getting there. But why don't you and I have a wee stroll on

185

the terrace? Take advantage of our congenial surroundings. Any progress on the robbery front?' he said, as she got up and followed him outside.

'I doubt whether we'll ever retrieve that porcelain,' she said, as they stood facing the sun, enjoying the view and each other's company. She'd proved herself to be a reliable and caring colleague; and she certainly knew her job. Pleasant to look at, too. Knew how to dress. He approved of her grey pleated skirt and low-heeled shoes, and the brilliant blue blouse made of some silky material which made her look feminine but not predatory.

'There are one or two things about this case which I find strange,' she went on. 'Ian McKenzie owns a whole lot of priceless china, and never insured it. Now, in my experience, that means one of two things: either the person simply couldn't afford the premiums – which may well be true in McKenzie's case – or they know there's simply no point in insuring stolen property because they'll never be able to make a claim. And another thing: Mrs McKenzie only called us the day after the china had been taken. She claims a mix-up, but it seems mighty peculiar to me. Not to mention that the security alarm system they've got at Reivers is like something out of the Ark. Mrs McKenzie told me that Ian had been meaning to replace it for years – mind you, getting a place the size of Reivers Hall properly fitted out as regards security would cost a king's ransom. His wife doesn't seem particularly upset about the theft of her husband's collection of porcelain. In fact, I find her attitude almost hostile; she seems to resent us being here at all.'

'There's a lot going on where those two sisters are concerned, Flick. But how are you? No ill effects from the attack?'

She shrugged her shoulders dismissively. 'Don't worry about me. I'm trained in self-defence. Got a black belt years ago when I took up judo at college. And thank God I did!'

'You certainly fought back effectively. Any idea who was responsible?'

She didn't answer immediately, and when he looked at her enquiringly she remained thoughtful. 'I've got my suspicions. I was involved in a case in London eight years ago, before I went to work for the regional squad in Newcastle. A theft from an art gallery. And I think whoever was behind it knows I've come up here and is taking the opportunity to try and settle old scores. But I'm not sure. Not yet.'

'You must take care, Flick.'

'Douglas, don't be an old woman. I can take care of myself. I've proved I know how to disarm an attacker – pity I wasn't so good at holding on to him. But I always hit where it hurts.'

'My God, lass, I'll have to keep on the right side of you.'

'You, Douglas? You'd be a walkover.'

Ben Knowles was fast asleep when Venerables arrived at the Fridale Arms. His wife had gone off to tend to Alec Montgomery, and he'd taken the opportunity to put his feet up. It took a lot of effort on Venerables' part to wake him after his usual five-pint lunch. Eventually he stumbled to the door.

'What d'yer want?' he asked blearily.

'Pheasants, Ben,' said Venerables. 'Where d'you get your pheasants from?'

'Hell's teeth, man! You wake me up to blether on about pheasants . . . I get them from all over the place. Buy them from anyone who comes into my bar wanting to sell them. This time of the year the place is lifting with them. Come and have a look, if you must.'

He led Venerables into the kitchen at the back of the pub. Pots of curry and stew were sitting on the cooker ready for that evening's customers; piles of unwashed plates and cutlery were stacked on the wooden table. A cat was sitting in the middle of them, contentedly washing its whiskers. Obviously Mrs Knowles had left her husband to clear up. She was in for a shock when she came home. Venerables decided never to eat at the Fridale Arms again. He glanced at the large freezer cabinet under the window.

'In there?'

'Aye.'

Venerables opened the lid. The freezer was bursting with mournful-looking birds of every shape and size, stuffed into polythene bags.

'Are these pheasants?'

Knowles peered down into the freezer and prodded a frozen carcass in a desultory way.

'If you say so. I leave all this to my wife.'

'It looks as if she stocked up quite recently?'

'As it happens I can answer that one. She bought a few brace off young Kevin Fraser last week. They'd had a shoot up at the Hall, and he always goes off afterwards to pick up the ones the dogs leave behind.'

Venerables heart sank. 'Can you remember exactly when she bought them?'

'Sunday week it was. He arrived late in the afternoon with them. I remember because the place was full up with all the gawpers coming to see where the boy was shot, and his timing wasn't that good – seeing how the birds were really Ian McKenzie's property. He was a bit of a nuisance, getting in the way – everyone wanted drinks, seems crime-spotting's thirsty work – and I told him to push off. But the wife needed the birds, and so she dealt with him.'

'Is he one of your regular suppliers?'

'You could say that. Now, can I go back to sleep? I've got to open up soon.'

'Yes, off you go,' said Venerables, disgruntled, as he left the pub and walked to his car. Bloody pheasants! *Get them from all over the place.* And especially from Kevin Fraser. Still, it didn't mean that Kevin was out of the picture. He would have had plenty of time to pick a few pheasants up between half past seven or thereabouts, when he left Janice Hudson, and half past nine, when young Derek Fairbrother's life came to its premature end.

Chapter 21

It was late when Douglas arrived at the vicarage. Father Paul opened the door and welcomed him inside.

'Is O'Neill with you?' asked Douglas, as he followed the priest into the hall.

'Sean's been here ever since he got back from Berwick, Douglas. He's no intention of going anywhere until things are sorted out once and for all.'

Father Paul looked shattered. His face was creased with worry; his eyes were bloodshot. Also – much to Douglas's surprise – he could smell whisky on the young priest's breath.

They went into the sitting room. Sean O'Neill was slumped on the sofa. On the table in front of him was a nearly empty bottle of Irish whiskey and two glasses. He looked up blearily.

'Come in, Chief Inspector,' he said sarcastically. 'Come and join the party. Tell us the news. Arrested any more suspects? Any more houses gone up in smoke? Oh, what a joy it must be to be a policeman! The power you have! Come and celebrate my release from your custody! Another glass, Father. The Chief Inspector must be thirsty after all his exertions.'

Father Paul was sufficiently sober to look severely at the Irishman.

'Pull yourself together, Sean,' he admonished. 'This is Douglas McBride, not Walter Willoughby. Douglas is a just man, a conscientious police officer—'

'And he's more than just to the ladies, so I've been led to believe,' said O'Neill, staggering to his feet. 'We all know why he was suspended. Tucked up between the sheets with one of the grief-stricken sisters up at the Hall. And I don't blame him. Who'd want to bother with a holy Gospel or a couple of murders when there's two ladies begging for it? Police? Don't you talk to me about the police. I'm fed up to the back teeth with the lot of them. They're enough to make the saints turn in their graves. Tell me, Chief Inspector, why the hell doesn't Scotland Yard step in and sort out this mess? You're behaving like a pack of demented bloodhounds running round in circles after they've lost the scent; and there's no one to bring you to heel.'

Douglas, dazed by tiredness, reeled back from O'Neill's onslaught. He hadn't expected this abuse – not from Sean. He was grateful when Father Paul came to his rescue.

'Stop this, Sean! Shouting won't get you anywhere. We all sympathise with your feelings, but give Douglas a chance. Give him a drink and let him get to bed.'

'I'll pass on the drink, if you don't mind. But I'll say yes to my bed. I'm sorry, Mr O'Neill. You've been through a terrible ordeal, and Willoughby treated you shamefully. I hate to say this of a fellow officer, but he had no right to bring you in for questioning. He sparked off a witch-hunt. The only consolation – and I know it can never right the injustice done to you – is that Willoughby's been reprimanded. Sent back to Durham. I'm sorry, man. I really am.'

Suddenly, the young man crumpled. He collapsed back on the sofa and stared blankly into space.

'It's shameful,' he mumbled. He repeated the word several times. Douglas waited for him to speak.

'Holy Mary, Chief Inspector, it's a wonder that I haven't gone out of my mind with all these accusations! I've lost my reputation, my home . . . All because Montgomery thinks I was out to get him that Sunday morning because he's always been against me lobbying for the Gospel to be taken to where it rightly belongs. Even though I was standing outside my front gate, and couldn't have shot either him or Derek if I tried. But that's not good enough for him. He suggested I was working with some IRA hitman who did my dirty work for me. The idea'd be amusing if it weren't so offensive. It's been a terrible time, and the only one who's given me any support is the blessed Father here.'

Douglas felt intensely sorry for the young man, and fiercely angry at the prejudice and hate that had reduced him to his miserable state. He sat down on the armchair facing the sofa and leant towards him.

'Mr O'Neill, if it's any comfort, I believe you are entirely innocent. And I will do all that's humanly possible to find the real killer.

We've got our suspicions – but we can't afford to make the same mistake twice. I know it's difficult, but please be patient. We've got to keep our heads clear if we're going to make an arrest.'

'An arrest at this stage, Douglas?' Father Paul was looking at him intently.

'We're well over a week into the investigation now. We ought to be fairly certain that we're working along the right lines.'

'Then I shall pray that your intuition is supported by real evidence this time round. Come on, Sean, let's get to bed. I've drunk more than I've ever drunk in my life, and I hate to think what I'll feel like tomorrow.'

Sean sighed, leant back and shut his eyes. Father Paul went over to an oak chest and took out a tartan rug. Then he paused, as if he wanted to speak but couldn't find the right words. Douglas decided to prompt him.

'Father, do you have something to tell me now? About Sister Anne? I know you were worried about her safety – that's why we put a policeman on guard outside the Little Sisters' community. Are you able yet to tell me what it was she said to you?'

Father Paul clutched the rug to his chest, as if for comfort.

'My position hasn't changed, Douglas. I can't reveal the secrets of the confessional. It simply isn't possible. But this coming Thursday I shall see Sister Anne again. And I will try to persuade her to come and see you. It's all I can do. The confessional is sacred, Douglas. There are no exceptions to the rule. If there were, then people would lose confidence in our blessed sacrament of penance. But I will certainly talk to her again.'

Douglas sighed. He recognised defeat when it stared him in the face.

'I'd be grateful if you could do your best, Father. We need all the information we can get. Meanwhile, we'll keep guard over Sister Anne until we're sure she's safe.'

'Thank God for that.'

A gentle snoring indicated that Sean had finally succumbed to exhaustion and alcohol. Father Paul carefully placed the rug over his sleeping body and picked up the glasses.

'A terrible pity,' he said, looking sorrowfully at Sean's recumbent body. 'He's been a victim of so much hate. Let's hope he sleeps well and long.'

'His head'll be feeling mighty sore tomorrow morning, that's for sure. Now I'm off to my bed, otherwise I'll not be able to climb the stairs. And it's not because I've been drinking.'

That Monday night, Sister Anne found sleep eluding her. There was nothing new in this; as she grew older she seemed to need less sleep, but it still annoyed her intensely. Her mind clicked away relentlessly, sorting out the day's accumulated impressions. It wouldn't shut down. She'd spent thirty years of her life in Fridale as the head of the Community of Little Sisters, and she'd devoted herself to serving them, with the help of the blessed St Frida. They had all been so proud to be the custodians of the magnificent Gospel which the saint had brought with so much trouble to this part of Northumbria, to be kept safe from the ravages of the Norsemen. And she had let the saint down! It was all her fault. Everyone had told her that the safest place for the Gospel was in Durham Cathedral Treasury: or the British Museum, or the library of Trinity Hall, Dublin. But she had obstinately insisted on keeping it here, in their own church. And now she had betrayed their patron saint, and she would never forgive herself.

As she lay there, staring up at the ceiling, she began to explore her motives for wanting to keep the manuscript, against the advice of all the authorities. And the more she thought about it, the more certain she became that her motive for wanting to keep the Gospel here was not so much because she wanted to serve St Frida, but a selfish desire to keep the manuscript as an ornament to their community. It was pride, she thought. Pride had been her downfall. And now she was being punished. The blessed St Frida had deserted her. In an agony of remorse, she called out to her beloved friend, and received no answer. So this was to be her punishment: alienation from the love of St Frida, who had never before deserted her.

She thought wistfully of the manuscript: its beautiful marginal illuminations; the brilliant colours of the pigments which those seventh-century monks had used; the soft vellum cover with its engraving of a great eagle, the emblem of St John. Shapes, colours, danced in front of her in a kaleidoscopic medley. Oh, if only the police could find it! Never again would she be so stubborn, so arrogant as to think that she and her little community could look after it safely.

'Forgive me, forgive me, blessed Frida,' she whispered. 'I see now that I'm old and proud. I should have taken other people's advice, but in my sinful pride I thought we could manage. But I was wrong.

192

I shall never again be able to rest until I feel that you have forgiven me.'

There was no reply. Feeling utterly desolate, she got up and walked across to the window. Dawn was just breaking. The birds were beginning the first verse of the dawn chorus and she could just make out the figure of the policeman standing in front of the main gate of the convent. She still had qualms of guilt every time she saw that policeman. They'd wanted her to allow a couple of officers to stay on the premises – even keep watch outside her room – but she couldn't allow the sanctity of a holy place to be destroyed in such a manner. The other nuns would have been most distressed to have their privacy invaded – and in any case, they were all in God's hands. He alone would protect them. As a compromise, Sister Anne had been forced to accept a single officer, but she'd insisted he stay outside the boundaries of their house.

Another day had started. Another restless, guilt-ridden day. She picked up the book of the Daily Office and tried to comfort herself by reading the service of Morning Prayer prescribed for Tuesday.

'The night has passed and the day lies open before us,' she read. Gradually the beauty of the words cast their spell and she began to feel less agitated. On Tuesdays, it was Sister Agnes's turn to ring the Angelus which summoned the other Sisters over to the church to say the Morning Office. But Sister Anne was wide awake and it was nearly time to rouse the others, so she would do Sister Agnes a good turn and ring the bell for her. Perhaps that would encourage St Frida to forgive her.

Dressing quickly, she went down to the side entrance of the house, unlocked the door, and made her way across the graveyard to the church. In the dim, white light of the dawn, she could just distinguish the shapes of the tombstones. She thought of her predecessors lying there, holy women all, devoted to the blessed saint. Oh why had she been the one to let St Frida down?

Unlocking the tiny North door which the Sisters always used when they went into the church for their services, she walked quietly into the dark interior. It was very cold, and she shivered as she made her way to the crossing under the tower where the bell-rope was looped back against a pillar. Although the dawn light had not yet penetrated the church, she knew her way round blindfold. There was no need to turn on any lights. She genuflected towards the high altar where the small red eye of the sanctuary light glowed in the darkness. It was comforting to know that there was the blessed sacrament announcing the presence of Christ.

Then she thought she heard a sound behind her. A creak of the door. Probably Sister Agnes. She reached for the bell-rope. She was old and frail and the bell was heavy; she should have left it for Sister Agnes, but she had felt so strongly that she must do something positive to reinstate herself in the saint's good books. Summoning all her strength, she pulled the rope. Dong! Dong! Dong! Three times. Three, the number of the Trinity. Dong! Dong! Dong! Three more. Three lots of three. And, as she'd been trained to do, she thought of the Incarnation. Christ, who was God, who died for all. She felt a gleam of comfort as she gathered her strength for the last three pulls on the rope. Dong! . . . And then the rope dropped out of her hand.

Someone had crept up behind her. Someone had raised a heavy iron bar and brought it down on her skull with a sickening crunch. Sister Anne fell forward onto the stone floor. And a pool of blood began to spread around her like a crimson carpet.

Silently her attacker left the church, walked swiftly across the graveyard, climbed over the wall, and disappeared into the surrounding woods towards the main road.

Sister Agnes awoke to the sound of the bell. She tut-tutted with annoyance when she realised that Sister Anne must have beaten her to it. She crossed herself and, as was customary, thought of the Incarnation. She counted the three chimes, as she always did. Then, alarmed, she jumped out of bed. Sister Anne hadn't finished the Angelus! What could she be thinking of? Dressing swiftly, she ran to the church.

Chapter 22

'Wake up, Douglas. Wake up, for God's sake! Something terrible's happened!'

Douglas opened one eye and saw the frantic face of Father Paul close to his own. He sat up immediately.

'What is it? What's happened?'

'Sister Anne's been murdered – in the church of all places – while she was ringing the Angelus. It's what I've been dreading for days!'

Douglas flung on his clothes, and they rushed over to the church. On the stone floor under the tower Douglas saw the tiny body of the nun, lying in a crimson pool of her own blood, her head smashed open. Never before had he felt so appalled, so angry. He turned to the priest, whose face registered his own feelings of sorrow and remorse.

'You knew this might happen! And yet you refused to give us the information which might have saved her.'

His words seemed to pull the priest together. 'It makes no difference. Even her death makes no difference. I can't tell you what I was told in the confessional. Only God knows what passed between us that day. But I pray for you, Douglas – you and all your team – pray that you find the evil person who committed this terrible crime. That you find him quickly, before he strikes again.'

'Don't worry – we'll get the bastard, that's for sure. This is the Devil's work, and we've always been a match for him.'

He spoke rapidly into his mobile phone, asking for a police surgeon, a Scene-of-Crime team, an ambulance and reinforcements.

'Seal off the village,' he said sharply to the young constable who'd just joined them. 'Were you on duty at the gate?'

The constable looked deeply shocked. 'I was there all night. I saw nothing. I heard nothing, not until the bell rang.'

'Get help and start searching. The usual thing – tracks, tyre marks, murder weapon. It looks as if the bastard hit her with a bloody great crowbar. He'd not get far carrying that thing, so he probably chucked it away. I want this bastard caught.'

They found the tracks leading through the woods at the back of the nuns' house to the main road. And they found the murder weapon – a heavy crowbar, designed to force open wooden crates. It had been wiped clean of fingerprints, but it didn't need Forensic to tell them whose blood and hair it was on the tip of the bar.

Whilst the SOCOs set about their work, Venerables joined Douglas in the church. Flick was with him.

'A dreadful thing to happen, sir,' he said soberly. 'What sort of person would do this?'

'Someone who was frightened she might shop him,' said Flick tersely. Douglas looked at her.

'What are you doing here, lass? This is no place for you.'

'I've every right to be here, Douglas. This lady was murdered because she knew who stole the manuscript. This is as much my province as yours. Let's not quarrel about who does what. We're all in this together.'

'You're right there, Flick. Someone knew she was possessed of a vital piece of information. Something that could finish them for good. The priest knows, but wild horses won't drag it out of him. The seal of the confessional – it's enough to make you weep.'

Venerables glanced at the priest, who was now kneeling beside the corpse. 'No, he'll not tell, that's for sure. He never will.'

'Surely you don't approve, Sergeant?' said Douglas in amazement.

'Approve? It's not up to me to approve or disapprove, sir. It's up to God. It has to be, otherwise no one would confess anything.'

'There must be exceptional circumstances, surely?'

'No exceptions, sir.'

'Have you ever *made* a confession, Sergeant?' asked Douglas scathingly. He was taken aback by this revelation that Venerables had a spiritual side to his nature.

'Me?' said Venerables, looking inscrutable. 'I suppose I must have done. A long time ago, when I was at school. Made up most of it, I expect.'

PC Wilkes came over to speak to them; he'd been sent over from the incident room up at the Hall.

'They've found tyre marks, sir. Vehicle parked in the lay-by where the path comes out of the woods. A motorbike. Marks led away from Fridale, but we lost them when the surface of the road got a bit rough.'

'Who owns a motorbike around here, Sergeant?' said Douglas.

'Only two people I know of, sir. Sean O'Neill – and Kevin Fraser.'

'*Sean*?' said Father Paul, who'd come across to join them. 'You can't suspect . . .'

'Did you go in and check that he was still asleep this morning?' said Douglas severely.

The priest looked bewildered. 'No. I came straight over here as soon as I got the message.'

Suddenly the church door opened wide, as Sean pushed his way past the policeman on duty. When he saw the body on the floor, he stopped and cried out in horror.

'God help us! Why her? What's she done, Chief Inspector?'

'Done? She's done nothing. It's what she knew that mattered. Now, sir, one question – and I do need an answer,' he said firmly, as the young man began to look defiant. 'Your motorbike? Where is it?'

'Have you gone raving mad, Chief Inspector? My motorbike's a heap of charred metal. It went up in smoke, that's what happened to it. It was parked in the entrance lobby of my cottage. I lost it, along with the rest of my possessions.'

Suddenly the penny dropped. 'You bastard,' he shouted, 'you don't think *I* had anything to do with this?'

'Calm down, sir. We've found some tyre tracks. We have to ask everyone who owns a motorbike round here.'

But Sean wouldn't be placated. 'Yes, and you start with me! Who's prejudiced now, I wonder? You're no different from the Willoughbys of this world. You're a policeman, just the same as him. Well go on – arrest me. Never mind that I was sleeping off a skinful of whiskey early this morning. I must have done it – because I'm Irish, aren't I?'

'I'm sorry to have upset you, sir,' said Douglas evenly. 'I'm only doing what I have to do. Thank you for helping us.' But he knew Sean O'Neill would never trust a British police officer again.

They left the rest of the team to continue their routine procedures on and around Sister Anne's frail body. Once outside, Douglas turned to Venerables and Flick. 'Let's get over to Lake Cottage. I wonder where Kevin is this fine and sunny morning? Are you coming with us, Flick?'

'No – you catch the murderer. I'll stay with the victim, and have a go at the priest.'

'You'll be wasting your time, Flick,' said Venerables. 'He'll never tell. Leave it to us to find the killer. That's the only way.'

'I can be very persuasive, Sergeant.'

'So I've heard, Detective Inspector. So I've heard.'

Kevin Fraser was in the kitchen making himself a mug of tea when Douglas and Venerables arrived at Lake Cottage. He looked up in surprise as they marched in without knocking.

'Not you again?' he sneered. 'Got nothing better to do than harass innocent citizens?'

'Cut the backchat, son – just answer our questions,' said Douglas tersely. 'Where were you early this morning? About an hour ago, to be exact?'

Kevin laughed in astonishment. 'An hour ago? In my bed, of course! And now I'm off to work. If I'm allowed to, that is.'

'And how do you intend to get there, sir?'

'On my bike, of course . . . What the hell's all this about?'

Douglas refused to be drawn. 'Just tell me a bit more about your movements last night, if you don't mind.'

'As a matter of fact, I do mind, but I've no option, have I? I wasn't out after pheasants, if that's what you're thinking. I drank a few drams at the Fridale Arms – you can check on that – and had a row with Janice. So I came back here to sleep. And now I'm running late because of your bloody stupid questions.'

Certainly Kevin had a crumpled look, as if he had indeed just got out of bed. His motorcycle gear hung on the peg by the door: the boots – scuffed, but showing no signs of fresh mud – stood on the floor nearby. Douglas nodded significantly to Venerables, who left the room. Soon they could hear his footsteps tramping over-head.

'Bed's still warm,' he said when he reappeared; Kevin gave him a withering stare.

'Let's take a look at this motorbike of yours, sir. And shut that damned dog of yours up, for Pete's sake.'

'He's a guard-dog, and he's doing what a guard-dog should do. Telling me that there's two fools snooping around disturbing my peace.'

'Just get on with it, and cut the cackle,' said Venerables impatiently.

Keeping up a continuous grumble, Kevin slipped on a pair of battered trainers and led the way out to the shed, where fierce scratching sounds and frenzied barking indicated that the dog was getting more and more irate. But when Kevin spoke softly to it through the door, the noise stopped immediately. When he opened the door, the dog began to wag its tail.

'He seems to like you,' said Venerables, keeping his distance.

'I feed it, what's why,' said Kevin, going into the shed. 'Now what the hell's happened *here*?'

He looked frantically round the dim interior. Douglas caught sight of a lawnmower and boxes of garden implements – but there was no signs of a motorbike.

'It *was* here, Chief Inspector!' said Kevin desperately. 'I always put it there.' He indicated a spot by the wall. Oil stains on the ground testified to the truth of this statement.

'Last night I put it away when I came back from Janice. I swear to it! Someone's stolen my motorbike!'

'That's very unfortunate, sir. Someone gets murdered in the early hours of this morning, the attacker gets away on a motorbike – and yours is missing. I wonder where it's hiding, sir? I think you'd better give work a miss this morning, and come along with us.'

'And I think you're a pair of bloody incompetent morons. Someone's stolen my bike! My property. So why are you treating me like the guilty party? I'll come if I must, but you've made a mistake if you think I had anything to do with your murder. I don't even know what you're talking about.'

'You'll know soon enough, sir.'

* * *

That afternoon, Douglas and Venerables left Berwick, where they'd been interviewing Kevin Fraser, and drove quickly along the A1 to Fridale in Douglas's Volvo.

'Another dead end,' Douglas said bitterly. 'When are we going to get a proper break?'

'Are you quite certain he had nothing to do with it, sir? Those tyre marks did come from a Yamaha bike, and that's what he's got.'

'Thousands of Yamahas around, all with identical tyres. We can't get him on that. Janice Hudson's confirmed that he was with her till late last night. His bed was still warm this morning. His biker's gear looked unused. The bastard who killed Sister Anne ran off through woods, Sergeant – woods muddy after recent rain. He'd just bashed a crowbar down on an old lady's head, so his clothes must have been in a bit of a mess. But there were no traces of blood or mud on Fraser's cycle gear.'

'He could have changed into another set and hidden the first lot.'

'In that case we would have found them by now. The men searched that wood very thoroughly, and I doubt he'd have had time to hide them further afield. No, I'm pretty certain Kevin's not Sister Anne's killer. He didn't react like a guilty man. His surprise when he saw us was genuine.'

They drove on in silence. 'Funny,' said Venerables suddenly, 'that dog didn't wake him up barking when the thief broke into the shed and took his bike. Not much use having a guard-dog if it doesn't wake up the owner of the house. And it barked at us right enough.'

'Maybe Fraser's a heavy sleeper. And he'd be used to the dog's barking. Maybe he thought it was a fox on the prowl. They've got a habit of coming to people's houses at night, scavenging round the dustbins.'

Douglas accelerated impatiently, pleased to find that the old Volvo, like its owner, could still put up a good performance. 'Let's meet this informant of yours, Sergeant. Tom Emmerson. Why don't you call him up on your mobile? We'll meet him in the pub. See if he's got any other little titbits for us. We might have to step up his fee, of course.'

'That's not a bad idea,' said Venerables, picking up his phone.

The pub was already packed when they arrived. Emmerson was there, in his usual place, perched on a stool up at the bar; Douglas felt the now-familiar twinge of dislike when he saw him. No one, he knew, liked snouts; but he liked to think that he was above the common prejudice. Informants were, after all, doing the public a favour. But all the same, he couldn't take to them. They were essentially furtive creatures, crawling out from under stones, earning money by eavesdropping, snooping, ears always pinned back to pick up salacious gossip. Yet where would they be without them? If anyone was going to give them the vital lead in this investigation, Douglas suspected it might be this pale, skinny youth, with his petty jealousies.

Venerables seemed untroubled by such qualms. He pushed his way eagerly over to the bar. Seeing Emmerson's glass was empty, he called for a round, at once – they were served quickly; Ben Knowles knew that it was more than his job was worth to keep the law waiting, especially since they'd seen the contents of his freezer.

Collecting their pints, they made their way over to the far corner of the bar, by the window, where it was relatively quiet. Conscious of curious stares, Douglas realised that the time of Tom Emmerson's usefulness was running out. If he, Douglas, disliked an informant, even more did the general public dislike someone who habitually drank with police officers.

He nodded to Venerables, and made a quick visit to the Gents. When he returned, he noticed a faint grin on Emmerson's sallow face. *Good*, he thought; *Venerables has upped the stakes. Now, perhaps, Emmerson will come up with the goods.*

'All's well with you, sir?' said Douglas, deliberately hearty.

'Aye, not too bad. Hunters are taking me on full-time next week.'

'So you'll not be needing us then?'

'Oh, I wouldn't say that.' He looked towards Venerables greedily.

'I bet you won't be sorry to leave Reivers Hall. Funny old place.'

'And it gets funnier.'

'Meaning?'

'Montgomery's been snooping round Pat, as usual. He keeps coming back for more. He was there Saturday, and again last night. He looks terrible, by the way – face like a boxer's after he's lost the big fight. He didn't stay long. But I must say he's persistent. And he'll take anyone on. He was just leaving yesterday when along comes Pete Fraser and they had a wee blether.'

'What time was that?'

'Couldn't say. Must've been getting on. It was almost dark.'

'And what were you doing when this was going on?'

'I was, er – talking . . . well, sort of getting to know Irene. You know – Bloodworthy's daughter. She helps out at the Hall in the evenings – clears up the kitchen, that sort of thing. I thought I might stand a chance with her now.'

'And did you?'

'Could do. Early days yet. She was giving me the come-on.'

Douglas winced. The thought of anyone cuddling up with Tom Emmerson made him feel queasy.

'I thought she'd a thing going with Pete Fraser?'

'Apparently Pete's gone off her. He's like that. Love 'em and leave 'em, that's his motto. He's been buttering up Pat McKenzie and hanging round Montgomery, so she got fed up. She's looking around for someone else. And that's where I came in.'

'The best of luck to you. You hang on to young Irene. She's a very valuable property. Pete still got his car?'

'You bet. Swanks around in it like he's lord of the manor.'

'Does he ever ride a motorbike?'

'Not our Pete. Why should he? He's moved on to better things. His brother's got one, mind.'

'Did you hear what Montgomery and Pete were arguing about, Tom?' said Venerables casually, balancing his glass on the window-sill.

'I couldn't hear much. I was behind the bushes with Irene. I was trying to concentrate on her.'

'I've got the picture.' Venerables sniggered; Douglas tried not to shudder. 'But you might have overheard something. Was it a friendly chat? Or a bit of an argy-bargy? Come on – you know what I mean.'

'They weren't talking much, put it that way. I took a look in their direction at one stage and saw Montgomery'd got hold of Pete by his shoulders and was shaking him like a rat. Pete looked as if he was going to sock him one, but he caught sight of me and stalked off. Montgomery looked a state – all shaking and stomping around. Then he got into his car and drove off like a maniac. Then Arthur Bloodworthy came out and found us and there was a row, and he told me to bugger off, and I did. But I'll be back tonight. I don't give up all that easily, and I know Irene fancies me. And now I've got the job at Hunters I've got prospects.'

'That's the spirit. Lassies like a bit of ambition,' said Venerables sarcastically.

Suddenly, Douglas caught a glimpse of PC Wilkes's head rising above the crowd round the bar. Wilkes beckoned to them; leaving Emmerson to finish his beer, they pushed their way over to him.

'Call for you today, sir, from Oban, at eighteen hundred hours. Confidential. Here's the number.'

'Thank you, Constable,' said Douglas, thankful for once for Wilkes's officiousness. 'My car's outside. Wait here for me, Sergeant.'

He walked over to his car, got in and dialled the number. Robert Shaw answered.

'We've lifted Cameron's yacht, sir. Something under her cabin floor which might interest you. A bloody great box of coins – gold ones. With a Roman emperor's head on them.'

'Coins? Where the hell did they come from?'

'Stolen some time ago from Hexham Museum. Curator said they were found buried somewhere along Hadrian's Wall, dated around the four hundreds when the Legions were pulling out. Apparently the haul would have represented a whole year's pay for the soldiers. The hoard was buried, or so I was told, to keep it out of the hands of the invading Picts, whoever they were, who were attacking the garrisons at that time. Probably the chap who was detailed off to bury the coins was hit over the head with an axe and no one knew where he'd buried them until the archaeologists came along this century and found them. And Charlie Cameron stole them. Or so it seems. I've learnt a lot of history today, sir. My head's still spinning.'

Douglas whistled. 'And where was he going with the soldiers' pay, do you suppose?'

'Oh, somewhere across the pond. Good buyers over there. No questions asked.'

'And someone stopped him pretty abruptly, it seems. This is good news, Robert. Excellent news. Just what we've been waiting for.'

'Glad to be of use. You coming up to see us?'

'I'll be coming up tomorrow; but not to see you. I think I ought to pay a quick visit to Edinburgh.'

Venerables emerged from the pub to join him. 'Good news, sir?'

'Could be. Another bit of the puzzle. A significant bit. Seems we've got a lot of thieves North of the Border, Sergeant. As bad as the reivers of times past. They steal manuscripts, Chinese porcelain, and hoards of Roman coins. And they stop at nothing; they'll even hit old ladies over the head if they get in the way. Get the thieves and we'll get Sister Anne's murderer. And Derek Fairbrother's, I shouldn't be surprised. Now let's put down the ferrets, and sit back and wait for the rats to bolt. We've got a right pack of crooks here – fences, hitmen, the lot. I'm off to Edinburgh tomorrow – just a quick trip. You get Pete Fraser in for questioning, and hold on to him. We'll want to know everything about his activities last night and in the early hours of this morning. Don't let him off the hook. Turn the screws if you have to.'

'Pity you didn't live in the past, sir. The Inquisition would have given you a job like a shot.'

Chapter 23

'I can only spare a few minutes, Chief Inspector,' said Bruce Cameron, looking distinctly nettled as he ushered Douglas into his office. 'My first client's due soon.'

'I won't be longer than I have to, sir,' said Douglas firmly. He had driven through the early hours of Wednesday morning and was not prepared to let Cameron tell him what to do.

'I can't see what possible help I can be in your enquiries. I've already spoken to you at some length.'

'Oh, I think you can help us. It's for your own good if you co-operate.'

'Are you threatening me?' said Cameron angrily, sitting down heavily in the leather armchair behind his desk.

'Whatever gave you that idea? But first, allow me to give you an update on your late brother's yacht. It's been recovered. She shifted into shallow waters during last week's storms, and they were able to salvage her yesterday.'

'Yes, yes,' said Cameron impatiently. 'Obviously the coastguard called me, as I was Charles's next of kin.'

'Then I expect you've already heard that there's a large hole in her bow. Someone, it seems, wanted to sink the *Maid of Moidart*.'

Cameron looked uneasy. 'Oh surely not, Chief Inspector. Let's not over-dramatise. I expect she struck a rock. The West coast of Scotland is pretty lethal. The chart for that area's covered with marks indicating rocks, some of them drying out at low water, some of them only just concealed. Very treacherous.'

'Mr Cameron, the place where your brother went down had no rocks near the surface. The water was far too deep for that. I think we must assume that your brother had enemies.'

'That's a preposterous suggestion. Who on earth would want to harm Charlie? He was one of the most highly respected men in the Highlands.'

'It seems pretty obvious to us that this was murder, Mr Cameron. And as to being respected – well, what if I were to tell you Charles had stolen property on board? A hoard of Roman coins, in pristine condition. A year's pay for the Roman soldiers stationed on the Wall. Stolen from the museum at Hexham.'

Now he was getting somewhere; Cameron was clearly taken aback. 'You do surprise me,' he managed to say at last. 'He was never the slightest bit interested in coins. Even if he were, he'd never steal. My brother wasn't a thief, Chief Inspector.'

'I didn't say he was. But I do think that he knew a good thing when he saw it. In other words, Mr Cameron, I think your brother was a high-class fence. He was, we think, off on a trip to the States to sell this particular hoard. It's a reasonable supposition because he had the right sort of boat to take him there, and he wouldn't have been able to sell the stolen coins in this country so easily. But someone decided to put an end to his little expedition. Who would do that, Mr Cameron?'

'What are you getting at, Chief Inspector?' shouted Cameron, jumping to his feet. 'If you are insinuating that I aided and abetted my brother's criminal activities, then be careful—'

'Calm down, sir. I'm not suggesting that you had anything to do with your brother's business ventures. But you might know the names of those who did. Think about it. Take your time. Maybe you'll remember them later. Are you interested in art yourself, sir? Was that something you and your brother had in common?'

'I like antiques. Most people do, don't they? That doesn't mean I go round breaking into museums. I resent this line of questioning. I go to sales, like thousands of other people do. I buy on the legitimate market.'

'Do you go alone, sir?'

'I don't need an adviser, if that's what you mean. I buy what takes my fancy, but I err on the side of caution.'

'How about Charles?'

'As I told you, Charles could be a poor judge at times. That makes me think that this hoard of Roman coins may well have been sold to him as legitimate. He was so reckless, he'd never have thought to check its provenance.'

'Then why did he have it on his boat?'

'Perhaps he was buying on behalf of someone else. I know nothing about it. I was not my brother's keeper. Now I'm sure my client has arrived, and I must get on with some work. Why don't you ask Mary Cameron? She'd know who her husband's friends and associates were. Charles used to see a lot of the McKenzies, too. They were as thick as thieves.'

As soon as the words were out, Bruce looked as if he wanted to kick himself. Douglas couldn't resist saying, 'Metaphorically speaking, I hope, sir.'

'Chief Inspector, I have to tell you that I find your whole attitude pretty offensive.'

'No offence meant, sir. But don't let's keep that client of yours waiting too long. Just a couple more questions, then I'll be through. Hamish McIntosh, now. He was one of Charles's acquaintances up in Oban. Awkward character. Nearly tipped me out of the boat last time I went out with him.'

'How extraordinary! Hamish is a fine sailor – one of the best. You must have made a mistake. Hamish knew my brother quite well. There's a strong camaraderie in the sailing community.'

'Maybe I was a bit hasty in judging him. However, Mary Cameron seems absolutely convinced that he murdered her husband. He's talking to the Glasgow police at this very moment.'

Bruce Cameron looked startled. 'Hamish? Talking to the police? You mean, you've arrested him?'

'Oh no, sir. He's just being held for questioning. At this stage, anyway. Now just one more thing, sir, and then I'll be on my way. Ian McKenzie's will. Any news on that?'

'This is highly irregular, but if it'll be of any help, hold on while I get the McKenzie file,' said Bruce Cameron, obviously relieved at getting off the subject of his brother and onto safer matters.

Cameron left the room, returning minutes later carrying a legal document. He flipped nervously through the stiff pages for a few minutes, then finally looked up at Douglas.

'I thought I knew of Ian's intentions,' said Bruce Cameron. 'We often talked about matters relating to his estate. But it seems there is a new will, made just before his death. Here it is.'

Cameron took out a long, brown envelope. 'Actually, one of your men found it on Ian's desk in the study – I gather you're using it as a makeshift office, and it got put into a file containing other personal papers of Ian's. The envelope is addressed to me, but obviously he didn't have time to post it before he died. It's an interesting document.'

He'd been right to come here, Douglas thought; right to leave the main line of investigation to Venerables, even if that meant being hauled over the coals later on by Blackburn. Cameron looked a worried man. Douglas knew that look and found it satisfying.

'There's no doubt that the will is legitimate,' Cameron went on. 'It's dated and signed by two witnesses, neither of whom are beneficiaries – in this case Peter Fraser and Tom Emmerson, two of Ian's employees. As I said, it's interesting. You see, the main beneficiary – apart from Patricia, of course, who gets Reivers Hall and the estate in France, which I understand is heavily mortgaged – is a man I've never heard of. Someone called Duncan Hughes. There are three other beneficiaries – the three members of the Bloodworthy family, who are rewarded for their loyal service by bequests of five hundred pounds each. But Duncan Hughes gets the rest.'

'Where does Mr Hughes live?'

'Twenty-six Stocker Road, Grimsby, apparently. I must admit that, had I known what Ian was planning to do, I would have advised him very strongly against it. Not that Ian had a great deal of capital to leave; over the last few years he's spent rather too extravagantly on his collection. But Reivers Hall is extremely expensive to maintain, and I'm afraid that Ian has left poor Patricia virtually penniless. Apart from the income from the vineyards, which has always been negligible, she has nothing.'

'And you have absolutely no idea who Duncan Hughes might be? Mr McKenzie gave no reason for the bequest?'

'He didn't, no. But then, it isn't that uncommon for unknown individuals – unknown to the family, that is – to turn up as beneficiaries in wills. Often people feel they would like to reward someone who has done them a good turn in the past for no reward. Mr Hughes could be an old school friend, an ex-colleague – I really have no idea. Whoever he is, Ian clearly thought a great deal of him.'

'Does he know he's a beneficiary?'

'I'll notify him in due course – I can't tell him exactly how much until probate has cleared, but I wouldn't want to get his hopes up. It won't be more than a few thousand pounds or so, I shouldn't imagine. Now, is there anything else you want to know? I'm keeping a client waiting.'

'That's plenty to go on for now. Thank you, sir,' he said briskly, 'you've been most helpful.'

Leaving a visibly anxious Bruce Cameron to deal with his first client, Douglas hurried out to his car. Before he drove South, he called Berwick.

'Douglas McBride here. I want a trace put on all calls to and from the office of Bruce Cameron.'

He arrived at Berwick Police Station just as Venerables and his colleagues were thinking about lunch.

'Good God, sir, you do get around,' said Venerables cheerfully.

'You're not joking. And I thought I'd come off the beat years ago!'

'Is all this gallivanting wise? You look as if you could do with some sleep.'

'Oh, stop nannying me, Sergeant. Plenty of time for sleep when this is over. What's been happening here?'

'Pete Fraser claims he was tucked up in bed the night before last, just like his brother. But I'm not satisfied, sir. He doesn't look like a man with a clear conscience. Won't look me in the eye, for one thing.'

'You've still whittling away at Kevin?'

'You bet. We've got an extension for him, so we can hold him a bit longer for questioning. But we need more evidence, sir. Witnesses. We need someone to surface so we can bust their alibi.'

'It'll happen, Sergeant. Just keep them talking for as long as you can. I'm going back to Reivers now. And then on to Grimsby.'

'Grimsby? Another fishing trip?'

'You could call it that, Sergeant. Leave this lot when you can, and join me later in Fridale. I'll be needing your help.'

'Blackburn's been looking for you,' Venerables said gleefully.

'Has he, now? Tell him to hold his horses. Time's at a premium for me. Oh, yes – do a chaser on Polly, Sergeant.'

'Polly?'

'She's doing a search for me.'

'But there's nothing to write home about on the Fraser brothers. Minor traffic offences, that's all.'

'I'm not talking about the Fraser brothers.'

'I know she and Flick have been busy trawling through the database. Flick's acting a bit strange. Like she's got something up her sleeve. All in good time, she keeps saying; and she's getting on our nerves. Time is what we haven't got.'

'I'll have to speak to the lass.'

'She'll be up at the Hall, sir, if you're thinking of calling there. She's got the bit between her teeth, all right. Seems she thinks she knows why someone attacked her the other night. Someone she thinks she recognised might also have recognised her.'

'Sounds a bit Byzantine, Sergeant.'

'Come again, sir?'

'Look it up, man. Yes, she hinted as much to me. I'll go and see what the beautiful Flick's up to.'

The fine collection of rare and exotic shrubs, lovingly collected by previous McKenzies, glowed in the autumn sunshine. It was unnaturally warm, Douglas thought, as he clambered out of his car. The air was clammy, oppressive in its dampness, like a Turkish bath. There was no wind, and the tall heads of the Michaelmas daisies drooped languidly in the still air like a row of exhausted guards on sentry duty. Even the birds were silent. The unsettled equinoctial weather was going to erupt into a thunderstorm, and nature was bracing itself.

Then he saw Mary, sitting on a wooden seat under the great cedar at the side of the house. A book lay open on her lap, but it was obvious she'd no intention of reading it. He walked quietly over to her; it was not until he was a few feet away that she noticed him. She gave a start and jumped up, letting the book fall on the grass. She stared at him nervously, just as Bruce Cameron had done. They were all wary now, he thought. Rats sensing the onslaught of the ferrets.

'I'm sorry to disturb you, Mrs Cameron,' he said evenly. 'This won't take long.'

'Chief Inspector, we're quite used to being disturbed by now.'

'You've been very patient, Mrs Cameron. I'm afraid I'm going to ask you something that you might find distressing. How much did you know about your husband's activities?' he said. He picked up her book and sat down on the seat; she perched uneasily next to him.

'Charles?' She looked confused. 'Not much, really. He was a solicitor in the family firm – all rather dull. I was never the slightest bit interested in the details. I do know his business never brought him much joy. He spent what money he earned as soon as he had it. As you know there was precious little left when he died. Really Charles wasn't cut out to be a solicitor.'

'And what about his – sidelines? I understand he was keen on art and antiques?'

'He was a collector, for sure. Like Ian, and Alec. He was always going off to auctions and sales, hunting around for interesting *objets d'arts*.'

'And what did he do with these – *objets d'arts*?' said Douglas, hesitating over the unfamiliar vocabulary. 'Put it this way, did he buy and sell on behalf of other collectors?'

'Oh, Charles was strictly an amateur. He loved beautiful things; and he wanted them for himself. Unfortunately he made some disastrous buys along the way. He didn't have Alec's instincts.'

'And when he died, what happened to his collection?'

'It was all sold, along with the house, to pay off his debts. Ironic, isn't it? He spent his life building up a collection which he couldn't afford, only to have his executors sell it after his death to pay off the debts he incurred in buying it in the first place.'

'And – did coins form part of that collection? You see, when they lifted his yacht, they found a box of Roman coins on board.'

She stared at him uncomprehendingly. 'How extraordinary. Are you sure you're not mistaken? What would he be doing with a box of Roman coins?'

'I thought you might know the answer to that. Customs and Excise are very interested in this find. So is the curator of the museum at Hexham from where they were stolen. We are assuming that Charles Cameron received this hoard and was taking them out of the country to deliver to an overseas buyer. In fact, Mrs Cameron, we are coming to the conclusion that your husband was a high-class fence. Now, a fence needs a supplier, and he in turn needs men to do the jobs for him. He needs a gang to back him up. The chances are that some of those gang members are still around, still carrying on their illegal activities, and we're interested in finding them. So let's take a look at some of the people who associated with your husband. Your deceased brother-in-law, for instance. Ian McKenzie. Do you think he was involved in your husband's activities? No – please don't get up.'

'I don't know anything about my husband's – little hobbies. All I know is that he wasn't up to much as a businessman. I hope he was a better crook than he was a solicitor. Now, I've got a lot to do, and there's a storm coming on, so . . .'

She was lying; he could sense that. And she was frightened. Frightened of what? That her comfortable world was going to be exposed? That people would know that her husband had been nothing but a common criminal? Soon her reputation would be lying in tatters around her. And without that protective armour of respectability, she would be finished.

'A few more questions, Mrs Cameron—'

'You've got no right to come here, Douglas McBride, delving into my past,' she said, taking refuge in anger. 'I'm quite sure that what my husband might or might not have done five years ago is of no relevance to your present investigation. What a lousy policeman you are! Almost as rotten as you are as a lover. God, when I remember how hard I had to work on you . . .'

Douglas winced. That had hit home. But he managed to stop from launching into acrimonious recriminations. Mary Cameron was scared, and she was going to attack with every weapon in her armoury, keeping the Exocet missile till last.

'What went on between us a week ago is also not relevant to the present investigations. Let's draw a veil over that. I'm sorry these questions upset you, but I've got a job to do, and if you won't help us, we'll still get there in the end. Don't underestimate us. And just think, when everything comes out in the open, how will you feel then? If you refused to assist us? Sister Anne was killed because she had a pretty good idea who, besides herself and Sean O'Neill, had access to the safe in the church. That person might be someone you know too. Someone who might have had dealings with your husband, who is still actively involved in the illegal buying and selling of works of art. And you won't help us because you're worried about your good name.

'Reivers Hall,' he said bitterly, looking up at the proud façade of the house. `God knows what goes on here. But behind the dinner jackets and the expensive dresses, the arrogance of the men and the beauty of the women, evil lurks. The old Border reivers robbed each other, murdered, took the law into their own hands; and the modern reivers are no different. They steal one another's possessions: they kill anyone who gets in their way. They carry the same names – McKenzies, Camerons. And they are all tarred with the same brush.'

'Oh, stop preaching, Douglas. You sound like a sanctimonious Presbyterian minister. You call us reivers. We're survivors, that's all.

212

We don't fold up when the going gets rough. We don't admit defeat. We fight on till the end.'

'Aye, Mary, and it's bumbling old fools like me who have to clear up the wreckage left behind on the battlefield. Let's put an end to this conversation. It's getting us nowhere, and as you say a storm's coming.' He decided to catch her off guard. 'Have you ever heard of a man called Duncan Hughes?'

She looked at him stonily. 'Never. Why?'

'Just wondered . . . Oh, yes, I do have one piece of information which might come as a surprise to you and your sister. We've brought Pete Fraser in for questioning.'

'Then you really are a fool. Pete Fraser? Pete's just a self-serving opportunist.'

'That sounds about right. We haven't charged him yet, but I have high hopes.'

Mary watched him walk away, a tall, dignified figure. For a moment she felt a tiny pang of remorse. She'd lost someone who could have been a good friend, had things been different. But not now. From now on, survival was the name of the game.

She found Pat in the study, writing a letter. 'Pete's been taken in for questioning,' she said, without any preamble. Pat turned round, and Mary saw by the look on her face that this wasn't news to her. 'It's not an arrest, Pat,' she went on.

'Not yet. But I don't trust Pete. He'd say anything to save his own skin. I told Ian he should never have made an enemy of Pete. He ought to have treated him properly. Pete's got a grudge against us. First Ian played him up, and now he's fallen out with Alec. I don't like men with a grudge, Mary. They're dangerous.'

'I wouldn't worry about Pete. He's smitten with you. He'd never say anything to upset you.'

Pat gave a hard laugh. 'That's a joke, sister. He knew I couldn't resist his charms. He'd shop his own mother if he thought it would get him off the hook.'

'They're onto Hughes, you know,' said Mary suddenly. 'Don't start fainting on me,' she said hastily, as she saw the colour drain away from Pat's face. 'It's all due to that bloody McBride. I don't know how they tumbled it. Someone gave him Hughes's name. If they pick him up and Hughes starts blabbing, we're done for.'

213

'I told you, Mary, to hold onto McBride! You could have got him off the scent. He was all set for a mega-infatuation, and you blew it. Now he'll be out for revenge.'

'What're we going to do?'

'They won't be able to prove anything against us. We'll ride out the storm, that's what we'll do.'

'Where will we live?'

'Why here, of course. I'll have to sell the French estate – it's riddled with debts. Someone will buy it. Someone richer than us. And we'll turn Reivers Hall into a hotel. Set someone in to manage it for us. If the worst comes to the worst, we could always work as chambermaids.'

Douglas needed a drink and a sandwich, and he needed to talk to Venerables. But first, he had to see Flick. He went into the study and saw the two girls staring fixedly at their monitors, red-eyed with tiredness. He felt his heart warm to both of them.

They glanced up as he approached. 'Any news?' he said to Polly.

'The Fraser brothers have kept me busy, but nothing's turned up of consequence. Flick's drawn a blank, too.'

'No record on Montgomery?' he said, turning to Flick.

'No, damn it! All's above board. But what bothers me is that there's no record of a Mr Montgomery selling a house in Prince Imperial Road in Chislehurst over the last six years.'

'Then check out all the buyers who have sold houses there during that time. Particularly the single men. Check other roads too, just in case he lied. Though if he lied about it being Chislehurst, we're finished.'

'That's what I'm doing. But there's a surprising lot of them. It's a slow business.'

'Well, keep at it, lass. Sorry,' he said, as she turned to glare at him. 'Old habits die hard. Ease up, you two. We can't have you both having heart attacks; not at your age.'

'We'll all be in intensive care, sir, if we don't clinch this case soon. As it is, me and Flick'll both need glasses,' said Polly acidly.

The Fridale Arms was just opening when he got there, and he found Venerables deep in conversation with Tom Emmerson. Judging by the row of empty glasses in front of their informant, Tom was already pretty well-oiled. Venerables looked up from his solitary glass. 'Evening, sir. Still doing the rounds? Allow me.' He got up and ordered two pints from the bar.

'Add a cheese sandwich to the order, Sergeant. On second thoughts, better make it two. So – how's our friend Tom?'

Tom didn't respond; his eyes were glazed. Venerables chuckled. 'Getting a bit tired and emotional.'

'Then tell him to sober up. Come on, lad – wake up. What's my sergeant been saying to you?'

'He's my friend. Nothing wrong with Sergeant Venerables,' said Tom, drunkenly truculent.

'I didn't say there was. Now, before they chuck you out, one more question. Then we'll let you sleep it off. Does the name Duncan Hughes mean anything to you?'

'Duncan?' mumbled Emmerson. 'Sure – everyone knows Duncan.'

'Really? What can you tell us about him?'

'Lives in Grimsby. Was a trawlerman but the fishing packed up and he decided on a career change . . .' he said, dissolving into ribald laughter. 'More money in that than looking for herrings,' he went on, when he'd got control of himself. 'He's got a lot going for him, has Duncan. Very busy boy.'

He eyed Douglas's sandwiches longingly; Douglas ignored the look. 'Did McKenzie ever take Duncan up to the Hall?'

Tom Emmerson's look grew more pointed and Douglas relented. 'All right – get the boy another pint and a sandwich. He's a growing lad. And I can't eat with him staring at me.'

Venerables got up to give the order while Douglas tackled his own sandwiches with famished single-mindedness.

'What was the question again, sir?' said Emmerson blearily.

'Did Hughes get taken up to the Hall?'

Emmerson snorted. 'No! Course not. Pat would've gone spare. If you're going to have affairs, then don't bring them home, I always say. Besides, Pete would have torn him to pieces.'

Venerables dumped the sandwich down in front of Emmerson, who attacked it voraciously.

'Ta. Not good to drink on an empty belly. Well, as I was saying, all hell broke loose up at the Hall when Duncan became number one in Ian's affections. Reckon Pete thought his overtime'd soon be a thing of the past.'

'Did Mrs McKenzie know what was going on?'

'Pete said she did. He also said that McKenzie told her she had to put up with it if she wanted to stay married to him. After all, she had the house and the use of his plastic. That's what he said.'

Just then, the door opened, and a girl came in. She was pretty in a fragile sort of way, her long hair tied back with a piece of ribbon. Her tight yellow T-shirt and pencil skirt showed off her curvaceous figure, but her face was white and pinched. She stared anxiously around the room, and visibly brightened when she saw Venerables.

'Hello, Janice,' he said. 'Come and join us, love.'

She made her way warily to where they were sitting. Venerables got up and pulled up another chair. 'Here – sit down, lass. You look all in.'

She sat down heavily, and glanced at Douglas and Tom. 'I want to tell you something. But not in front of him,' she said, staring at Tom with her large, blue-ringed eyes. He'd finished his sandwich and had shut his eyes. He was starting to look distinctly green around the gills.

'That's no problem,' said Venerables, grasping hold of Tom and dragging him to his feet. 'Where's your cooler?' he shouted to Ben Knowles, who was replenishing the bottles behind the bar.

'Outside,' he said, indicating the door with a wave of his hand. 'Take him into the garden. There's going to be a storm any moment now – the rain'll wake him up.'

Venerables dragged Tom outside and hoisted him onto a wooden garden seat at the back of the pub. Then he went inside and resumed his seat next to Janice, now quietly sipping a tonic water.

'What's up, love?' said Venerables sympathetically. 'What's Kevin been up to now? I did warn you, didn't I? Kevin wasn't the right one for you. You want someone reliable like me. I would have made you a grand boyfriend.'

Douglas looked scathingly at Venerables, but said nothing. This was Venerables' scene. Better if he kept out of it.

'Kevin? That bastard . . . He said he loved me. And I believed him, didn't I? I'm carrying his kid, you see. Well, now he knows I'm pregnant, he doesn't want to know me any more. Said I was a little tart – horrible things, he said. I couldn't bear it. He said he hated Brett, kept on at him. Once I found him thumping him on his back. Could've hurt him badly if I hadn't come in just then. But I still loved him, that is until he told me to get rid of this kid, even though it's his.' She began to cry, hopelessly. 'He's walked out on me, and I haven't a clue where he is. I don't trust him any more. I'd like to see him punished. Why should he always expect me to tell lies for him? He won't do anything for me. He deserves all he gets.'

Venerables moved closer, putting an arm round her thin shoulders. 'That man doesn't deserve you. A fine lass like you – you're well rid of him.'

'That's what I think,' she said, brightening. 'I'm fed up with the Fraser brothers. Take last Sunday – not the Sunday just gone, the one before – he was tossing and turning all night, muttering to himself. He was out of bed while it was practically still dark. I got up too – couldn't sleep with him crashing about. I'd done all my housework and a load of washing by nine o'clock. On a bloody Sunday!'

Douglas said a silent prayer of thanks for Mrs Thoroughgood, and all nosy neighbours.

'Anyway, he put on his gear – his biker's gear, that is. Big padded jacket. And his black woolly hat – he wears it in cold weather, when he goes after pheasants. He put this hat on, and off he goes, and I didn't see him again until later on. He told me he'd gone out poaching, and not to tell anyone. Honestly, it's not that big a deal, is it? The birds rot in the fields if no one picks them up.'

'And what time did he leave you, lass?' said Venerables quietly.

'Quite early. About half past seven. I thought it was a bit odd, but I assumed he wanted to go poaching. Thought that was why he told me to keep quiet about it – maybe he'd had a bit of a run-in with a farmer. Then Pete phones and asks me where Kevin is, and when I told him he'd gone out, Pete tells me to keep mum. But why the hell should I? They don't care what happens to me.'

'You've been very useful, lass. A great help. Now drink up your tonic water and get off home. You did right, coming to see us. We'll need another quick word soon – just to get all this on tape.'

'All right. It doesn't matter now. You'll come and see me some time, Sergeant?' she said pitifully.

'Of course I will! Just you try and stop me. You forget all about Kevin Fraser. We'll take care of him.'

They got up to go, and she carried her drink across to the bar, where she began to chat happily to Ben Knowles just as if nothing had happened. Once outside, Venerables looked quizzically at Douglas.

'Seems our friend Kevin's got a lot to answer for, doesn't it?

Now all we need is someone to come forward and bust Pete Fraser's alibi. And we're home and dry. But now where're we off to, sir?'

'Grimsby, of course. And I'll need your help. But first I have to call Berwick and tell them to keep hammering away at the Fraser brothers. And then I have to see a priest.'

Chapter 24

St Frida's Church was packed out that evening. Locals, tourists, religious contingents from Durham and Newcastle – all had come to join in the night-long vigil, to share in the collective grief of a community shattered by tragedy.

Douglas and Venerables stood at the back of the church, which was engulfed in autumn flowers and lit by hundreds of tiny candles. It was almost silent. Douglas was thinking of his father. He hadn't wanted his son to join the police force. He'd made no attempt to hide his displeasure when he'd heard of Douglas's decision. He'd always wanted him to follow in his footsteps, and his grandfather's, and enter the church. But this evening, he was more certain than ever he'd made the right decision; had his father been alive, Douglas knew he would have approved. These people depended on him, and Sergeant Venerables, and the rest of the police force – just as people had depended, for a different sort of guidance, on his father and grandfather and the Father Pauls of this world.

Suddenly, he forgot his tiredness and the prospect of another long night ahead. He vowed that he wouldn't let these people down. He'd not rest until he'd hunted down the evil monsters who had shattered the peace of this beautiful village. He turned to look at the place where he'd last seen the body of Sister Anne. Now it was covered with a great heap of white lilies, which filled the church with their sweet fragrance, exorcising the horror of that memory. But for Douglas, that memory would never be dispelled.

He became aware of someone standing close to him. It was Father Paul, dressed in a plain white alb, his face pale and haggard with sadness.

'It's good to see you here, Douglas,' he whispered. 'And Sergeant

Venerables. We decided to hold this vigil tonight to pray for our shattered community and to ask God to forgive the perpetrator of all these crimes.'

'We have to catch him first,' said Douglas practically. 'After that we'll think about forgiveness.'

'He's a human being, just like us. Weak and fallible. Who knows what pressures he's under?'

'I reckon only God knows that.' Douglas hesitated. 'May we have a quick word with you, Father?'

'Come over to the vicarage. There's no one there at the moment; Sean's sitting with the Little Sisters, down there in the front pews. The Bishop's going to send us some professional counsellors tomorrow, but Sean's doing a great job comforting them. That young man has great strength. Perhaps that's because he's suffered himself.'

He led the way out of the church. 'I do hope my appeal about Sister Anne's killer has done some good, Douglas,' said Father Paul earnestly, as he unlocked the front door of the vicarage and led them into the study. 'It went out on national and local TV, and on the radio. Let's hope someone comes forward to help you with your enquiries. Someone might have seen a man on a motorbike that morning. Are you any nearer to a conclusion of this terrible business?'

'We're still short of proof,' said Douglas cautiously. 'But your appeal may have jogged someone's memory. People often forget they've seen something unusual until they're actively prompted into remembering.'

Father Paul's face lit up. 'Like that sketch map you asked me to draw after Derek was murdered. I'd never have remembered where everyone was in the square in so much detail if you hadn't made me put it down on paper. After you took the original map away I did actually have another go at redrawing it – just to see if I could remember anything else. But I'm afraid I drew a blank – if you'll forgive the pun.'

He went over to his desk and drew a sheet of paper from one of the drawers. 'There – everyone marked in position. All the houses; the pub; the church; the place where the gunman stood. I even gave him a symbol this time. His woolly hat.'

Douglas's heart leapt. 'That's most useful,' he said, studying the diagram and passing it over to Venerables. 'Could I hold on to this for the time being?'

Father Paul looked surprised. 'Of course. I'm glad it's of some help.'

'It's more than that. It confirms our suspicions. Father, you might ask that congregation of yours to say a prayer for us. We're going to need all the help we can get.'

'We've been praying for you all along. And now let me add my blessing. God keep you and your sergeant safe.'

'We can't go wrong now, sir,' said Venerables laconically, as they walked to the car. 'Not with all those people praying for us.'

'Let's hope not. I'm not taking any chances. Come on, Sergeant – we'll need a fast car. And you'll be driving it.'

Venerables looked pleased. 'But sir – aren't you supposed to be the boss?'

'I shall be taking a wee nap, Venerables. I know we've got God on our side, but even He rested on the seventh day.'

It had turned midnight when they reached the outskirts of Grimsby. Twenty-six Stocker Road turned out to be a small terraced house down by the port, where a line of trawlers were tied to the quay like a row of used cars waiting for auction.

An elderly man, dressed in a shirt and pyjama trousers, opened the door when they rang the bell. His eyes were bleary with sleep and he reeked of stale whisky.

'Duncan Hughes?' said Douglas, producing his ID card.

'Not here. I'm his dad.'

'Where is he? Do you know?'

'Most likely down at Dandy's. That's where his sort hang out. Anyhow, what's he been up to? I always warned him that one of these days he'd fall foul of the law.'

'We only want to have a few words with him, that's all. He's done nothing wrong, as far as we know. Now, sir, point us in the direction of Dandy's, if you don't mind.'

The room was hot and cloudy with tobacco smoke. Through the gloom they could see men dancing together to a strong electronic beat. Most of the men were stripped to the waist; the atmosphere in

221

the place was stiflingly hot, almost as hot as the air outside which hung lethargically over the port, waiting breathlessly for the storm to break.

Douglas and Venerables pushed their way through the zombie-like couples to the bar. The barman glanced at their cards nonchalantly and continued to serve customers.

'What do you lot want?' he said, curtly. 'We're all above board here.'

'I don't doubt you for a moment. We want to speak to a Mr Duncan Hughes, that's all. Is he here tonight?'

The man paused for a second, then shrugged and nodded towards a young man who was gyrating in the far corner of the room. He was good-looking, Douglas noted; medium height and muscular build, with a head of curly dark hair. He was bare-chested except for a silver chain at the base of his neck. He looked as if he was no stranger to the game. His black leather trousers were impossibly tight. The sweat gleamed on his smooth arms and chest, as if he'd been polished with oil. He stopped dancing when Douglas and Venerables came over and looked at them enquiringly.

'Mr Hughes? A word with you, please,' shouted Douglas above the heavy thud of the music. 'Can we go somewhere quiet? We can't hear ourselves think with all this racket going on.'

Hughes glanced at the barman, and then led them sullenly towards one of the EXIT signs.

'Out here. It's the only place there is.'

They went out into a corridor, which was lined on each side by a row of silent men, eying each other speculatively. They vanished like mist as soon as they saw Douglas and Venerables. At the end of the corridor, the Gents sign glowed like a red eye.

'What's all this about?' said Hughes belligerently. 'You're spoiling my evening.'

'Sorry about that, sir. We'll not take long. Were you acquainted with an Ian McKenzie?'

Hughes stared at Douglas in astonishment, then burst out laughing. 'Acquainted with . . . You could say that, yes. Old Ian and I were very good friends. I was sorry to hear he came to a grisly end – Christ, you don't think that *I* had anything to do with it?'

'We're not thinking anything at the moment, sir. Just answer our questions quickly and you'll soon be back with your friends. Where did you meet McKenzie?'

'A guy called Pete Fraser brought him here. He introduced us.'

'And so you had what might be called a regular arrangement?' Duncan nodded. 'How often did you meet?'

'Once, twice a month. Sometimes more. Towards the end, he got a bit possessive-like. He began to come over all monogamous. Wanted me to go and live with him somewhere – out in the country. Can you beat it?'

'And you didn't fancy that? Where did you go, Mr Hughes, when you wanted to be alone with Mr McKenzie?'

'I didn't take him home, if that's what you're getting at. I took him on *Gladys*.'

'Gladys?'

'My dad's trawler, but he lets me use it. I've done it up now that there's no fishing. Put in a new engine, and a shower. It's very comfortable. Great for parties.'

'Where is it moored?'

'Down on the quay, opposite the Trawlerman. That's the pub, in case you were wondering.'

'Did Mr McKenzie ever invite any of his friends down? For a party on *Gladys*, I mean?'

'Once or twice. Ian liked to party. But then, when things got a bit heavy, and he liked to keep me for himself, he began to resent the others coming along.'

'What happened?'

'Oh, you know . . . People started to get jealous. It all started with a bit of fun, and then the old green-eyed monster came stalking along and before you knew where you were, the knives were out.'

'Anyone in particular cause trouble?'

'Only when I made a mistake and the two of them turned up at the same time! Then the fur flew. Funny thing – the older and richer the client, the more they carry on.'

'Did you meet him here, the second man, sir?'

'No – at one of Ian's parties. He was rich, but a right pain in the ass, if you'll excuse my French. He hated Ian – really hated him. Ian and I had been together for a while, and we had something a bit special. Then he came along and expected special treatment. Made me a bit nervous. He couldn't stand the thought of Ian having me.'

'What's his name?' said Venerables suddenly.

'You'll not know him. He's very discreet. Keeps himself to himself—'

'*What's his name?*'

'We've got him, sir,' said Venerables triumphantly, as they dashed back to the car.

'Wait, Sergeant. What do we charge him with? OK, he likes to meet up with male prostitutes. But whatever they get up to, they do it in private. We can't arrest him. Not yet. Back to Berwick. Let's have another go at the Fraser brothers.'

'It's one o'clock in the morning, sir.'

'So what? We'll wake 'em up.'

'Which one'll you take, sir? The big fish or the little one?'

'The big one, of course. Who else?'

In the main interview room of Berwick Police Station, Douglas confronted a hostile and unhelpful Pete Fraser. Things were going badly. *It's always the same*, thought Douglas irritably. *Just when you think everything's tied up, the chummie turns all awkward and recalcitrant. You can't get blood out of a stone.*

'Come on, Fraser. We all know you were involved in McKenzie's murder. You gave the signal to the murderers, didn't you? Why did you do it? For money? Who's paying you, Fraser?'

'I had nothing to do with McKenzie's murder! I've told you all this before. I went outside to put out the bloody crate of empty bottles! That's all. Does that make me into a criminal?'

'It could make you an accomplice to murder. Let's take a look at your more recent activities in the McKenzie household. Nice little earner you've got there, eh?'

Pete looked sullen. 'It's nothing special.'

'Oh, come on. Driving round in a BMW – everyone's green with envy, a young chap like you.'

'I told you – I saved up.' But Pete looked unconvinced by this explanation.

'Don't waste your breath, laddie. We've spoken to Tom Emmerson – he knows all about your little scam. And Duncan Hughes has confirmed his story. McKenzie paid you for sex and for procuring him boys, didn't he? Nice little sideline for you, if you're not fussy.'

'OK, I admit it – he sometimes paid me a bit extra if I did him a good turn. If he wanted to give me a thousand quid every so often, I wasn't complaining.'

'I bet you weren't. You bled him dry, didn't you? It wasn't just the spending on his collection and the upkeep on the Hall that emptied his bank account – it was your greed.'

But Pete was unrepentant. 'If he wanted to give me money, that was his business. I wouldn't be daft enough to stop him, would I?'

Douglas decided to try a different tack. 'Well, there won't be any more where that came from. Except if Mrs McKenzie decided to oblige. You're keen on her, aren't you?'

'Everyone is. She's a good-looking woman. And her and me've always got on.'

'Reckon you might become her toy boy.' Pete looked cocky, refusing to repudiate Douglas's suggestion. 'That is, if Alec Montgomery doesn't get there first.'

'That bastard? Pat wouldn't look twice at him!'

'I didn't realise you felt like that about him. I always thought you were in cahoots.'

'Me and Montgomery? You must be joking. I hate his guts. He's a bloody cheat and a liar. And if I find him sneaking round Pat again, I'll give him something he'll not forget in a hurry. Bloody creep! He couldn't satisfy Pat. He's not capable of it. He doesn't get his kicks from women.'

'Really? And how did you find that out?'

Pete Fraser shrugged his shoulders dismissively. 'Pat told me. She knew Ian and Montgomery liked the rent boys.'

'So how did Mr Montgomery cheat you, sir?'

'The trouble with Montgomery is that he's bloody mean. Promises one thing, and then doesn't deliver. Expected me to do his dirty work for nothing.'

'It's bad news when people do the dirty on you, isn't it, sir? Why not demand payment in advance? To be on the safe side?'

'No good. He wants results before he pays up.'

'Results? What did he ask you to do? Burgle Reivers Hall? Beat up Inspector Flight? Bash an old lady over the head while she's saying her prayers? Yes, that gave you a turn, didn't it?' he said, as Pete Fraser jumped to his feet and glared furiously at Douglas. PC Billings, standing by the door of the interview room, moved forward; Douglas waved him back.

'Sit down, Mr Fraser. You didn't like to be reminded of that, did you? An old lady who'd never harmed anyone in her life, left lying there in a pool of her own blood. How can you sleep when you think of that? Why did you kill her, Fraser? Because Montgomery told you to? Because she'd seen him leafing through her prayer book, looking for the combination of the safe, and he thought she might tell someone? He must have paid you well. You took your brother's motorbike, drove to the church. Montgomery had got you a key to the North door – he'd visited the Little Sisters often enough to take impressions of the necessary keys. You went in, locked the door behind you, and waited. You were going to wait for her after the service because she always stayed on after the other nuns had gone. You didn't know your luck that morning, because she got up early to ring the bell for morning service. You killed her, didn't you? And then you drove off on your brother's motorbike—'

There was a knock on the door; Douglas interrupted the interview. A police constable came in and spoke to Billings, who handed Douglas a slip of paper.

'Glasgow police want a word with you, sir. Will you make the call?'

'Aye, give it to me,' said Douglas, taking the phone and dialling the number. 'Is that you, McCloud?' he said to Glasgow's Head of CID.

'McBride? Hamish McIntosh has made a confession. We've been keeping him out of his bed, and he's had enough. He admits he rammed Cameron's yacht five years ago. Hated Cameron, it seems. Apparently, Cameron threatened to shop him for drug-running, and he took his chance to get even. It wasn't just drugs he dealt in, though. He was a fence. Shipped art and antiques to overseas buyers.'

'Who did he work for?'

'Still works for him. The same man apparently suggested he might want to bump off Cameron to keep him quiet, and paid him well for doing it. Apparently, this man and Cameron had been partners, but Cameron, ever the maverick, was becoming a bit untrustworthy. Taking too many chances. Customs and Excise even got close to him once – that's when he threatened to bust Hamish for drug-running, in an attempt to keep them off his own back. So Cameron had become a bit of a loose cannon and it suited everyone to get him out of the way. When we told Hamish he might get a few years off his sentence if he started naming names, he didn't hesitate. Shopped Bruce

Cameron as well – we got your call saying that his line was being monitored, and we overheard one to the man Hamish named. Mr Cameron was giving an update on your little visit. We're bringing Cameron in. So it's over to you now. And the best of luck, man.'

'His name, for God's sake, McCleod?'

'Here, calm down – I'm just coming to that . . .'

Douglas turned to look at Fraser triumphantly. 'Come on, Fraser – you might as well own up. You worked for Alec Montgomery, you've admitted that. You did his dirty work for him. But you didn't expect it to turn sour, did you? What went wrong? He didn't pay you enough? He tried to wheedle his way round Pat McKenzie? You beat him up, didn't you? But you didn't do it properly. He still had a hold on you. And you didn't know he'd want you to commit a brutal murder. Why waste time protecting him any more? We know he's behind all this. It's only a matter of time before we arrest him. So do the sensible thing and tell us the truth.'

Just then PC Billings came back into the room. 'Detective Inspector Flight's here, sir. Wants to see you urgently. She's with Blackburn.'

Douglas looked at Pete Fraser in contempt. 'Watch this man, Billings. The tape's running. Call me instantly he wants to make a statement.'

Flick looked tired, but excited. 'We've got him, Douglas!' she said. 'Pete Fraser – we've got a witness. Arthur Bloodworthy's made a statement. Seems he saw Father Paul on *News at Ten* and it triggered something in his memory. He saw Pete Fraser coming home in the early hours of Tuesday morning, dressed oddly. He was wearing the waterproof trousers which people wear when they drive motorbikes. Now this struck Bloodworthy as strange, because Pete hasn't ridden a motorbike for a while, not since he got his BMW. However, Bloodworthy thought nothing of it, until he saw Father Paul on TV. Then he remembered. They've found the motorbike, by the way, and the rest of the gear. It was hidden in one of the outbuildings in the Hall. Forensic's analysing the bloodstains on the jacket. Any minute we'll hear if they match Sister Anne's blood group.'

Blackburn was puffed up with pride. 'You see, McBride? Good

job we got the specialist squad involved, isn't it? They've solved one of your murders for you.'

'That's not all I've found out,' said Flick, looking apologetically at Douglas. 'Polly and I have been checking the database, sussing out our main suspect. We came up with a total blank where Montgomery was concerned. And no house in Prince Imperial Road, Chislehurst was sold under that name. But we did find an Alex Potter who sold a house which he'd inherited from a Mrs Ivy Potter six years ago. Interesting man, Mr Potter. Back in the seventies, he served time in Ford Open Prison for fraud. Then he went on to bigger things. He must have learnt a thing or two in prison, because then he served time in the Scrubs for breaking and entering with a bit of violence thrown in. Then he went up in the world. Took up art collecting. Now it's at that point that I came into contact with him, in the late eighties, down in London. He was the brains behind one of the art thefts I was investigating. When I came up here and met him, he recognised me before I recognised him. He's put on a lot of weight since I last saw him. That's when he tried to get rid of me. Or got one of his thugs to have a go. After that prison sentence, he kept a low profile. He changed his name, and bought Montgomery Hall. Invented a whole new identity for himself.'

'Go and get the bastard!' said Blackburn with unusual animation. 'She's cracked it! You're a wonder, Felicity, love.'

'Hold on, sir. We don't know that Montgomery's behind our present spate of murders. All that Flick's ascertained is that Montgomery's done time for past offences.'

'But he's an art thief. He would have wanted to get his hands on that Gospel. Not like Sean, who only wanted the Gospel kept in a safe place, preferably back in the country where St Frida came from. No, Montgomery would have sold it. Sold it to the highest bidder. Why are you waiting?'

'Evidence, sir. Watertight evidence. He's clever, and he's rich. We don't want him wriggling around on a badly baited hook. Someone's been doing his dirty work for him, and we know who it is. But he won't go the final furlong.'

The phone rang: the desk sergeant, wanting Douglas. 'Calls are coming in thick and fast after that priest's broadcast. This one's called Tinker, believe it or not. Wants to speak to you.'

'*Tinker?* Who the hell's Tinker?'

'Other name's Jo Fuller. But he says you'll know him as "Tinker".'

Then it clicked: Tinker, the old man they'd met cutting reeds at the edge of the lake by the Fraser brothers' cottage.

'Let me speak to him . . . Tinker, it's Douglas McBride speaking. What is it, man?'

He listened. Then he looked at Flick. 'We've got Pete Fraser now, good and proper. That old man Tinker starts work early at this time of the year. He saw Pete Fraser leave the cottage in biker's gear early on Tuesday morning. The bastard went into the barn. The dog, of course, didn't bark because he knew him, so Kevin wasn't woken. He wheeled out his brother's motorbike – and drove off. Where's Venerables? I think – at last – we're ready to make an arrest.'

'He's next door to you, McBride,' said Blackburn, 'interviewing the brother. With any luck we can kill two birds with one stone.'

Back in the interview room, Douglas took up his position in front of a defiant Pete Fraser.

'It's all up, Fraser. We've got two witnesses. One saw you leave the cottage and ride away on your brother's motorbike on Tuesday morning: the other one saw you walking back to the Hall afterwards. We've found the bike, and the gear. We've got the murder weapon. We're matching blood found on your clothes with Sister Anne's. Your criminal career's over. I'm going to charge you with robbery, murder and accessory to murder. That's going to get you locked up for a very long time.'

'Damn you, McBride! Don't you see I was only following orders? Same as my brother. It's Montgomery you want. And McKenzie, if he wasn't already dead. They were as bad as each other.'

'I'm not arguing with that. But if you fill us in now on exactly what happened, it'll be better for you in court. And I have to tell you, we know your brother's in this up to his neck as well, and his girl-friend's not exactly been reticent. We've got Kevin next door as we speak. So why not tell your side of the story so we can get the facts right?'

Pete looked down at his lap; his hands were balled into fists. When he looked up again, he seemed somehow smaller, defeated.

'Right. So where do you want me to start?'

'How about on the night of the big party at Reivers Hall? The night when Ian McKenzie died.'

'One thing you should know is that Montgomery and McKenzie hated each other's guts. They used to be hand in glove, but they didn't trust each other any more. Montgomery'd got hold of all those Chinese bowls and stuff for McKenzie – it was all bent gear, of course – but McKenzie had never paid him for it. Montgomery liked his debts paid. And then they were both in love with the same bloke, see. Duncan Hughes – well, you know all about him. Bloody bastard. I was the apple of McKenzie's eye till he came along. And when McKenzie called me in to witness his will – well, I knew that witnesses can't benefit from wills, so I knew McKenzie hadn't remembered me. I guessed he'd changed his will because he wanted to leave Duncan something – why else would he do it? I went ballistic, I can tell you. After all I'd done for McKenzie! So when Montgomery asked me to help him give McKenzie something he'd remember, I didn't hesitate. Mind, I didn't know they were going to murder him. I reckoned they just wanted to rough him up a bit, give him a fright so he'd pay Montgomery the money and leave Duncan Hughes alone.

'All Montgomery wanted me to do was stand at the back door and wave a torch about when McKenzie was in his room having a snooze. He always did that after a big dinner, regular as clockwork – then he'd come back and join in the dancing. That was what I did when I put the dead men out. I saw Montgomery with a couple of other blokes come out of the shadows and run, sort of crouching-like, towards the house. Then I buggered off – I didn't want to get involved. Went back to the kitchen and helped out. Then you came rushing in and said that none of the staff could leave the Hall because McKenzie had been murdered.

'I tell you, I was shit-scared. And there was worse. See, McKenzie had asked me to help him get revenge on Montgomery. I said no – I wasn't going to do him any favours any more. But I knew he'd pay well, so I told him to get in touch with Kev. Blood being thicker than water, and all that. Then Kev told me that it was all arranged, that McKenzie had given him a pistol – I knew he had one, he kept it in his study, but I don't think anyone else did – and that he was going to shoot Montgomery during the religious parade. Well, soon as I knew McKenzie was dead, I panicked. I didn't want my brother risking arrest for nothing, not if he wasn't going to get paid. So I kept sneaking off to phone Janice's house – I knew Kev'd be going back there after the disco. But the bloody phone must've been off the hook or something. I couldn't leave the Hall to tell him in person 'cos of the cops swarming all over. I didn't get through to him until half past eight the next morning and by then he'd already left for Fridale. It was too late. I told that silly cow Janice to keep her mouth shut about where Kev had been that morning, but I should have known not to trust a bloody woman.

'I'm not surprised Kev missed. He always was a crap shot – not like me. And I don't think he'd ever fired a pistol before in his life. He doesn't even own a shotgun – he always borrows mine if he needs it. So, after all that, he ended up winging the wrong bloke. Funny, really.'

Douglas didn't feel a bit like laughing. He turned as the door opened and Venerables appeared. Douglas looked at him enquiringly. 'Good timing, Sergeant. Any progress your end?'

'Kevin Fraser's made his confession. Once Kevin knew Janice'd shopped him he admitted McKenzie had asked him to shoot Montgomery. He wouldn't admit he was a lousy shot, of course – said Montgomery dodged out of the way at the last minute. And poor little Fairbrother got caught in the middle of someone else's feud.'

Douglas shook his head sadly. 'What a pair you are, you Fraser boys. How well you served your masters! You provided them with everything they could possibly want, didn't you? You'd even kill for them, such was your loyalty. And you didn't care if others took the blame. You didn't give a damn about Sean O'Neill, hunted down like a dog for something he didn't do. You never thought of Derek Fairbrother, little more than a child, an innocent – or his father, desperate for some sort of revenge. My stomach turns at the sight of you.'

'We were under orders.'

'And that's what the guards at the concentration camps said at Nuremberg. You had a choice, Fraser. We all have choices. Now, I've got another choice for you. You can either tell me the rest of the story, so at least the judge will know you've co-operated fully, or you can exercise your right to remain silent. What'll it be?'

* * *

'After the dust had settled, I went to Montgomery. Told him I wanted payment. But he started making difficulties. Told me he wasn't finished with me yet, and I'd have to work a bit harder before I got any money out of him. I was furious. I did him over.' Pete's voice was tinged with pride. 'But he's a right stubborn bastard, he wouldn't give in. He said if I broke into Reivers Hall that night and nicked McKenzie's china collection, he'd sell it overseas and give me half the proceeds. He said even dead men should pay their debts and he was entitled to it. Well, I had a pretty good idea what that little lot must be worth, and there didn't seem much risk to me. I'm a member of staff, I've got a key to the back door – if anyone caught me on the premises I could always say I'd come to see Pat. She'd vouch for me. She's glad to see me any time. And I knew the code to turn the burglar alarm off – to be honest, that alarm system's so ancient a child could stop it from working. And I knew where the key to the cabinet was kept. So I went in there with a packing crate and did it. No hassle. Took it back to Montgomery. Only then the bastard tried to cheat me again! I saw him at the Hall a couple of nights later and he said someone was onto him. That old nun – he said she knew that him and me had stolen the manuscript. I said, no bloody way, mate, that had nothing to do with me – he'd told me he'd done it alone. But he said if I didn't help him he'd shop me for my part in McKenzie's death if he was arrested, so it was in my interests as well as his to stop the nun grassing on him. And I wouldn't get paid. I wasn't happy – I was bloody *un*happy – but I had to do what he said. He gave me a set of keys to the convent and the church. And the rest you know.'

In the end Pete Fraser told Douglas everything, including the names of the two heavies who had dressed McKenzie in drag and strung him up while Montgomery stood by and watched – one of whom turned out to be the same man who had attacked Felicity Flight. And at the end of Fraser's detailed statement, Douglas felt like a very old, very weary man.

Flick was waiting for them when they left the interview room. 'Are you going to get him?' she said.

 'Straight away.'

232

'I'm coming with you.'

'No, Flick. You stay here. Potter could be dangerous when cornered. The sight of you will really make his blood boil.'

'He'll know where the Gospel is, Douglas. He might even have it with him. He must have crept into the church before the Sisters went over for the service on the day of the procession, opened the safe, and taken out the Gospel. He must have put it somewhere until the procession was over – somewhere in the church, most likely. There are plenty of cupboards – the cleaning ladies have one, for instance, where he could have put it while he went out to watch the procession. Easy to recover it later on, before he told Sister Anne to check the safe. I was brought here to find the Gospel. I clinched this case, Douglas. And I'm bloody sure that I'm going to be in at the kill. You owe it to me. You can't stop me, anyway – I've got my own car outside.'

'That little toy? You'll not get far in that.'

'It got me here, Douglas; it'll get me back again.'

'She's got a point, sir. She's entitled to be there. But why don't you come with us? The Merc's the fastest car we've got, Flick. And we have to get a move on. Once Montgomery knows we've arrested the Fraser brothers, he'll want to get out of the country as soon as possible.'

'OK, I'll come with you, Sergeant. But I can't promise I'll come quietly.'

'He's gone, sir,' said Venerables; he'd taken a call on his mobile as they drove up to Montgomery Hall.

'*Gone*? Who the hell let him go? Someone was supposed to be watching his house!'

'Constable on duty said he was there at ten. Lights went on in his bedroom and stayed on. But he must have slipped away. Gone out through the back and up to Reivers Hall. Pete Fraser's BMW's missing – he must have taken that.'

'God damn these incompetent constables. Didn't they learn at police college that lights on doesn't mean someone's there? The oldest trick in the book! Put out a general alert for the BMW, Sergeant. I wonder how much start he's had. What's the time?'

'Four o'clock, sir. Sun rises in an hour – not that it will be much use to us. This storm's just about to break and we'll not get much daylight until it's blown itself out.'

'Then we'll have to do without the sun. Get on to Berwick. We'll need the whole caboodle – a naval patrol boat, that's the fastest boat there is, and a handful of Marines. We can't take any chances,' he said, as he turned the car round.

'Where are we going, sir?'

'I've had enough of stupid policemen for one day. Where do you think we're going? Grimsby, of course.'

They arrived at the quay in Grimsby just as the storm broke. A coast-guard cutter was waiting for them and they climbed on board in torrential rain that drenched them to the skin. Douglas glanced out to sea and saw with dread the grey expanse of heaving water, the waves dashing against the harbour wall, the cloud of spray tossed up into the air like a fountain as each wave broke. They were in for a rough morning.

The skipper of the cutter was a man called John Downey, a dour ex-trawlerman. 'It's a bit choppy out there,' he told them stoically. 'The *Gladys* is on course for Rotterdam. He'll not get there. Choppers trailing him. Three men on board – Hughes and his father, and your man.'

With a roar of the powerful engines, they were off, out of the harbour. Suddenly they were flung violently into the air as they hit the cross-currents of the Humber estuary. Douglas, caught off balance, went down on one knee on the deck, desperately trying to keep control of his stomach which, despite being completely empty, still seemed to want to disgrace him. He glanced at Flick. Dressed in one of the coastguard's waterproof jackets, her face glowing with excitement, she was standing up in the bow of the cutter next to Venerables. So she was a good sailor, as well as everything else.

'Hang on, sir,' said Venerables, who was anxiously scanning the sea ahead of them. 'There she is! Damn,' he exclaimed, as another crash of thunder coincided with another huge wave. 'There they are! Look.'

Hanging on to the side of the boat for dear life, Douglas looked out to sea. Eerie flashes of sheet lightning lit up the scene ahead. He saw a trawler bouncing along on a south-easterly course. A helicopter was swooping down towards it; a naval patrol boat was rapidly closing in.

'They're shouting for Hughes to stop, sir,' said Venerables, seeing

234

that Douglas was in no state to make sense of events. 'He's taking no notice. We're catching up. Come on, come on!'

Douglas leant over the side and retched agonisingly. For all he cared, the *Gladys* could go to hell. The sooner they got back on *terra firma*, the better.

Venerables and Flick, however, were in their element. Despite waves hitting them head-on, the water pouring over them, they stood there together with Venerables gleefully shouting out his commentary, until Douglas could bear it no longer. He hauled himself to his feet and, hanging on to any fixture that came to hand, eased his way slowly along the deck until he stood next to them.

'Feeling better? Don't be sick over me, sir. I don't mind sea water but I do mind . . .'

His words were lost in another crash of thunder. The cutter was catching up. Suddenly, Douglas forgot his discomfort as the spectacle taking place in front of them was illuminated in all its Wagnerian splendour by another flash of lightning. The helicopter was now hovering over the *Gladys* and a man was leaning out, shouting to the skipper of the trawler, who in turn was shouting to the other men on board. The naval boat was coming up alongside the trawler. And the coastguard cutter was closing in.

Then the trawler cut its engines. Tossing around like a wild beast caught by the hunters, it came up into the wind. Douglas cheered and threw up his hands in triumph. They'd got him! Caught him redhanded, trying to escape with God only knew what on board.

'Get down, sir,' said Flick, suddenly hurling herself at Douglas and toppling him to the deck. A rifle shot rang out. When they raised their heads, they saw Alec Montgomery, gun in hand, standing on the deck of the *Gladys*. He raised the gun once more. And then another rifle shot rang out, this time from the direction of the naval patrol vessel. The Marine made no mistake. Montgomery fell.

'Good shot,' said John Downey casually. 'Now, let's see what they've got on board.'

They drove back in silence to Reivers Hall. The storm had blown itself out, and had taken their enthusiasm with it. Like soldiers, when the battle was over, they were exhausted.

'You can drop me off here, sir,' said Venerables. 'You'll want to tell Father Paul the news yourself, I expect.'

'Aye. He'll be glad to know that his prayers have been answered. Sean will be delighted – and relieved. And the Sisters will be glad to know their Gospel's been recovered. Along with a rather nice collection of Chinese porcelain – but I doubt they'll care about that.'

'Tell them we're holding on to the Gospel until we put it where it'll be safe,' said Flick wearily.

'At least it didn't end up in Rotterdam . . . Seems our friend Duncan's been shipping stuff over there for Montgomery in that trawler of his for some time now. Must be well on his way to becoming a millionaire, what with all those rich clients and a thriving export business. Not to mention his little inheritance.'

'He'll not need much money in prison,' said Venerables grimly.

'Pity Montgomery won't be going to join him. I've seldom come across a man with fewer moral qualms. And he was the ultimate opportunist, wasn't he? Even when a young boy had been murdered in front of his very eyes he saw his chance. Thought he could set O'Neill up as a suspect for the theft of the Gospel and ensure that we never even considered any other possibility. And then he gets Pete Fraser to break into the Hall so he can repossess McKenzie's china collection! I suppose he figured that McKenzie wouldn't be wanting it any more . . .'

They reached the gate of the Hall. 'Out you get, Sergeant. Tell the Sisters the news. It's been a long night. Don't forget to tell them that Flick here saved my life.'

'Think nothing of it, Douglas,' said Flick. 'I couldn't have you killed. Not just when I was getting to know you.'

'You know, it's a funny thing,' Venerables said philosophically. 'I used to respect people like Montgomery. People who'd made a success of their lives. But they're worse than everyone else, aren't they? Take the Fraser brothers now: I can understand them. They're just crooks on the make, with everything to win. But the McKenzies and Montgomerys of this world have everything to lose. Big house, money, reputation – and they go and chuck away the lot. I wonder why they do it?'

'Don't ask me, Venerables.'

'Maybe it's love they need. Speaking of which . . . Looks like Polly and me might be getting hitched this Christmas.' Venerables looked bashful. 'I, er . . . take it you'll both come?'

'Just you try and stop us, Sergeant.'